The
Talk
of
Pram
Town

Also by Joanna Nadin

The Queen of Bloody Everything

The
Talk
of
Pram
Town

JOANNA NADIN

MANTLE

First published 2021 by Mantle
an imprint of Pan Macmillan
The Smithson, 6 Briset Street, London EC1M 5NR
EU representative: Macmillan Publishers Ireland Limited,
Mallard Lodge, Lansdowne Village, Dublin 4
Associated companies throughout the world
www.panmacmillan.com

ISBN 978-1-5290-2462-3

1 3 5 7 9 8 6 4 2

A CIP catalogue record for this book is available from the British Library.

Typeset by Palimpsest Book Production Ltd, Falkirk, Stirlingshire
Printed and bound by CPI Group (UK) Ltd, Croydon, CR0 4YY

Visit **www.panmacmillan.com** to read more about all our books
and to buy them. You will also find features, author interviews and
news of any author events, and you can sign up for e-newsletters
so that you're always first to hear about our new releases.

For Ryan, and in memory of The Square.

Some who read these pages at this time may feel almost as if they have wandered into fairyland, that it is too good to be true, that such things can have no relation to the present bleak and troubled times.

Sir Ernest Gowers, foreword to the
Harlow New Town Plan, 1947

To think when I was a kid I planned to conquer the world and if anyone saw me now they'd say, 'She's had a rough night, poor cow'.

Nell Dunn, *Poor Cow*

Connie

London, April 1970

She could have used the last of the money to get rid of it. Michelle had said her cousin knew a bloke who knew a woman in Stepney who'd do the deed if she didn't want to deal with doctors. She didn't. But she didn't want to see a woman in a backstreet in Stepney either, it turned out, despite all her Nell Dunn dreams. And, besides, it was too late now.

'You sure you don't want anyone, love?' The midwife, thickset and florid, offers her a damp flannel. 'Your mum? Everyone needs their mum.'

Connie, pale and sweating, shakes her head to both. 'Not me. Jesus Christ.' She groans as another contraction grips her, quick and vicious.

'Nearly there, love.'

Nearly there. She hears him grunt the words into the wet shell of her ear. 'Nearly there,' he tells her, as if he knows she's hoping. She sees him too. Sees the whites of his eyes tinged liverish. Sees the pores of his nose where a single hair pokes through. Sees his thing, fattened and angry and jabbing at her. Worse, she can smell him sometimes. His too-close

1

breath bitter with coffee and sickly with Polo mints. His still-buttoned shirt Omo-white and rotary-line fresh. How quickly the thrill of being wanted had faded. How had she ever thought him handsome? A catch?

The rest of it is blurred, faded at the edges by time and distance and sheer determination. Did she say 'no'? Maybe not. And if she said 'stop' it was weak, or in her head. And she'd flirted with him, hadn't she? Led him on like her mother said she always did, so it was no more than her just deserts.

This was no more than her just deserts.

'Bloody fuck!'

The midwife doesn't flinch – heard it all before, perhaps. But the mother in her head tuts and ticks her off. And you can bugger off as well, she thinks.

And yet, fifteen minutes later, as the baby crowns, threatens to stretch and snap her wide open, it's her mother she calls for, red-eyed and desperate.

Months later, broke and alone, she goes home. Baby in a borrowed pushchair, all her world in two carpet bags, back to Pram Town she slips, only to find the car gone, the curtains drawn, the front door double locked.

They've actually bloody gone away! To the Lakes, she presumes. Same as every year. As if nothing has happened. As if she – they – don't even exist.

Perhaps they don't. It's not like she's been in touch. And their names don't even match now. The Earnshaw chopped off and replaced with Holiday; half of Constance rubbed out and tweaked for effect. She's a different person now. Not that girl – their girl – anymore.

The baby gurgles, the chips of mirror in Connie's skirt twinkling in a bright slice of sunlight.

She smiles. 'Well bugger them, Sadie,' she says aloud. 'Or bugger her, anyway.' And she pushes the buggy down the side return, roots around under a stone cherubim, and lets them in with her father's secret spare key.

She doesn't take much: her diary, two dresses, five pounds from the Pinnacle Biscuits tin in her father's study. Just enough to get them to their next stop, wherever that might be. Wherever there's a cheap bed and bar work and an open mic. She eats two digestives, takes a belligerent piss in the downstairs lavatory and deliberately omits to flush. Then, baby on board, she's out and down the road before anyone can catch them. Before her parents get back from their tedious road trip and ask what she's done. Before Martha gets back from tedious school and asks where she's been. Before Mr Collins gets back from tedious work or tedious choir and asks why she did it and where the devil is his money?

'Thief,' he barks after her for that night in '69.

'Thief,' her mother shrieks for today and for ever.

But, fingers in her ears, 'Tralalala, I can't hear you,' she replies, and she's off like a rocket, little Connie Holiday, sweet Connie Holiday, the singing gymslip mum.

The bus is almost empty, a fact she cannot fathom. Why would anyone stay in Harlow when London is on the doorstep? A vast dance floor waiting to be waltzed through. A diamond, waiting to be plucked. She picks up the baby, grizzling for milk now, pulls up her top, not bothering to wonder if the two other passengers might glimpse and glower and grumble. It's only skin, after all. Nothing to be ashamed of, whatever she's been told.

Sadie sucks, satisfied, her eyes wide, and green enough for cricket. Despite them, Connie can't see him in her at all, thank God. There's her father's freckles, her mother's moue of irritation, and her own hair, a surly brunette, though hers is dyed now, platinum as sand, only the roots revealing her inheritance. It was Michelle's idea, and bathroom handiwork. 'You can't be a star if you don't stand out,' she'd said.

Turns out it takes more than a bottle of bleach to turn Connie Holiday into Marilyn Monroe or Marianne Faithful. But she won't be deterred. She is dogged, if not really qualified. Bloody-minded, her father would say. And she daren't think what words her mother might come up with. But so what if she never got her A levels? So what if she never even finished school? It's not like she's stupid. She could have shone if they'd let her try. If she could have been bothered. But she didn't need to. She bets Mick Jagger never passed a single exam, after all. Or, if he did, it would have been art. She'll be fine, she tells herself. More than. Has to be. Because it's not like she can ask Sadie's father for anything. Not like she wants to.

She kisses the sweet fust of the baby's head. 'This time next year, I'll be on top of the world,' she promises.

'I'll be a star, Sadie. You'll see. A star.'

Sadie

Leeds, July 1981

'Mam?' She knocks twice, but soft, so as not to alarm. 'It's nearly ten!'

But the bed don't give and the floorboards don't creak and the door stays shut against the morning.

Sadie, eleven, sighs, long and important. 'Well, don't moan to me when you miss the best bits.' She sticks her hands on her hips, oblivious to the lack of audience. 'That's all I'm saying.'

She clatters down the stairs to sit in the kitchen, her sandals slap-slapping, meant to mither, but still her mam's room stays stoppered like a bottle. 'Wedding of the century, and she's in bed,' she adds to no one in particular. 'I ask you.'

She opens the fridge, thinking she'll snaffle a cocktail sausage from under the cling film – street party's not till three and they won't miss one chipolata. But the paper plate's gone, its wrapping snatched off and abandoned, and Sadie remembers last night's commotion – 1.13, according to the digital watch Elvis Jenkins gave her last Christmas; 1.17 if she'd asked the speaking clock, which her version always lagged behind. Though she weren't supposed to check it anymore; couldn't anyway, not since the phone got cut off.

There'd been singing too, until gone half past – 'Son of a Preacher' and 'The Windmills of Your Mind' – and the gurgle and churn of a hot bath running. Must've been a good night. A big crowd down the Legion. Tips and drinks and her mam the glitter in the middle of it all, tipsy though she probably were. Better that than the one that came off shift every day at Morrisons, sore and maudlin. Or the one that got angry with Elvis for this or for that, or with herself for nothing at all.

A month ago Sadie'd caught her in the mirror, hauling her face around like it were biscuit dough.

'I'm ancient,' she'd wailed. 'Thirty.'

'You're twenty-nine and a bit,' said Sadie, and she weren't wrong.

'Close enough,' her mam had snapped back and Sadie had kept her gob shut after that.

Truthfully, Sadie did think she were a bit old. Thirty seemed an impossible number of years. Though her mam didn't look ancient exactly, not like Cheryl Pendleton's, who was thirty-one and had a double chin and a bit of a moustache in the wrong light. Maybe it happened overnight. Maybe you went to bed twenty-nine and smiling and woke up thirty with a face as creased as a pleated skirt and dark bits under your eyes that you had to cover with Rimmel.

'I was supposed to be on telly by now,' her mam had carried on. 'Have records to my name. Christ, I spend all day ringing up sliced white in an overall, and my nights in a miniskirt so I can get jeered at by the likes of Norris

Godfrey. I don't even own the telly, let alone get on it. It's rented. Rented! What sort of mother am I?'

'Mine,' Sadie had said, no more than a whisper, and clung to her back briefly, a monkey child, the shrunken spit of her. Though, her mam's hair is dyed as light as Lady Diana's now and nearly as short, where Sadie's still hangs in dark curtains, only her fringe trimmed neat so it skims just below her eyebrows. 'Open your face right up,' Donna-Next-Door had said as she snipped away, and she weren't wrong.

Sadie pictures next door then: the front room with its fourteen-inch colour set and a cerise rug with shagpile so deep you can stand a Wotsit up in it and it still won't reach the top of the tufts, and she knows that 'cause her and Deborah have tried enough times. She checks her watch again: 10.11. So 10.15 in real time and only just over an hour to go and she don't want to miss all the arrivals. Donna says that's the best bit – judging what everyone else is wearing – and Deborah agrees, and she's got seven months on Sadie so she's not to be argued with.

Besides, the tick-tock waiting is too boring and her want too enormous. 'I'm going,' she shouts up the stairs. 'See you in a bit.'

And this time she don't even wait for an answer, just slips out the back into the ginnel, and straight through the gate of Number 9.

Donna-Next-Door can't fathom it. 'She'll be sorry,' she says from the settee, pointing her cigarette as if to emphasize the point, the curls of smoke adding a certain glamour to the front room, curtains shut against the sun. She sits back, taps ash into a commemorative saucer. 'She's all right though, love?'

Sadie – her and Deborah already side by side on their stomachs on the rug, separated by a bowl of Twiglets and two Panda Pops, cherry – nods. 'Aye,' she replies. 'She's fine.'

Better than – least yesterday. Bright and shining with something and not even out of a bottle. A secret, she thinks. Maybe they're going to Skeggy, after all.

'Royal wedding effect,' says Deborah, knowledgeably. 'I read about it in *Women's Realm*. It's like an epileptic. Everyone's catching it. Tons of women are getting engaged. Maybe Elvis is going to—' She stops, gasps, Twiglet suspended mid-sentence. 'I bet he already did.' She gapes, as if caught out by her own brilliance.

Sadie bristles, though only because she's the one who's read every Nancy Drew and she didn't see it coming. 'I think she'd have told us, wouldn't she?'

'Unless she's biding her time,' suggests Deborah. 'So as not to spoil it for Diana. Steal her thunder, like.'

'Aye,' says a doubtful Donna, buffing her own burgundy do. 'That'll be it.'

Deborah nudges Sadie's foot with a pink flip-flop. 'You'd have a new dad.'

Sadie shrugs and stuffs a handful of Twiglets in her mouth so she can't answer even if she wants to. A new dad might be nice, she supposes. Any dad, really. And Elvis is okay, even if he is a drinker and Welsh and wears a catsuit on stage so tight you can practically see his thingy.

'I'll knock for her in a minute,' says Donna. 'When this bit's done.'

This bit is the coach and horses – things Sadie's only read about before, then wished for herself. Prayed a potato might suddenly puff up, pumpkin-like, and turn to burnished wood and wagon wheels; that the ants in the back alley might be good as mice. But you need a fairy godmother for that sort of thing, she supposes, and not even Donna with her mobile salon can come up with that kind of transformation.

'There's a lot of dress in there,' says Deborah, echoing the telly.

'Like Cinderella,' says Sadie, but quiet, because fairytales aren't for girls about to go up to big school.

'Shame to have her hair so short,' adds Donna, know-ledgeable.

'You said you liked it!' Deborah protests, her own Lady Di bowl re-trimmed only last Tuesday.

'Aye but you're eleven, not twenty-whatever, and you're not getting wed.'

Deborah sniffs. 'I'm going to marry Buck's Fizz,' she says.

'All of them?' asks Donna, lighting another cigarette.

'Ha ha,' replies Deborah, snide.

It'll be Bobby G. She and Sadie have already agreed that, as Deborah's older and got the better legs, she gets first dibs, so Sadie's left with the other one – Mike, he's called – but she don't mind really. They look practically the same. Same white teeth, same long hair, same highlights. And you can't tell the difference when you kiss the *Smash Hits* poster anyway. Maybe it's the same with actual men.

'That bridesmaid's a right cow,' Deborah adds.

Sadie turns her attention back to the telly. 'Which one?'

'The one that looks like a cow, duh.'

Sadie flinches, but she won't show it. 'She's all right. She looks a bit like Julie Newman,' she adds. Julie Newman is thirteen and wears a 32C bra and once let Stephen Butterworth touch the straps, according to Deborah.

'Does not,' says Deborah.

'Does too,' says Sadie.

'Sadie's right,' says Donna, so that Sadie, briefly, brims with satisfaction. 'She does have the look of a Newman about her. It's the teeth. Like a horse. Oh, hang on—' She sits up, her cigarette a baton or wand. 'Here she comes! Here comes the bride!'

Sadie turns to Deborah, lets her mouth drop, deliberate, 'cause it deserves a gawp. All that fabric, shining like beaten egg whites, and stitched with crystals, thousands of them, probably by elves.

'Ivory silk taffeta,' Deborah says, repeating the commentary.

'Yards of it,' adds Donna.

'Better than Deirdre Langton, in't it.'

'Barlow now,' says Sadie. 'She's Ken's.'

'It's Ken I feel sorry for,' adds Donna, and they both nod, knowing.

'I like the tiara best,' Sadie says. And she does, glimmering pink as it is in the sun. She wishes she were the kind of girl who could get away with a tiara, with any kind of diamonds. Though it's probably only princesses get them.

And they don't tend to wear striped vests and dungaree shorts, not even ones from Tammy Girl. Though she'll be in lemon yellow later, for the street party, her and Deborah both.

'Look at her laughing,' notes Donna. 'She won't be smiling like that tonight. Not with old Charlie boy,' she adds. 'State of him.'

'Mum!' protests Deborah.

Sadie sticks pretend fingers in her ears, though she's heard it all before and more besides. Her mam up late with Donna in the kitchen, giggling about Elvis and Donna's man, John, who works on the building sites, is out on one now, down Kent way. And it's worse since Donna started using their house for salon business, on account of the drains at Number 9 – round at all hours, talking dirty and smirking.

Sadie sniffs, but all she can make out is cigarettes and Twiglets and the too-much Tweed that Deborah's sprayed on herself for the occasion.

'Them pageboys look like right fancy nancys,' says Deborah, changing the subject.

For once, Sadie agrees. Their coats are a bit tin soldier and their trousers are a daring, dangerous kind of white – the kind you can't drink Cup-a-Soup or eat ketchup in. Elvis found that out. He spilled some on his catsuit once, the day before a gig, then shouted at Mam to fix them. Which she didn't. She told him to fix them himself, 'cause last time she looked, having a penis didn't prevent him being able to walk to the launderette or operate a washing machine. Sadie wishes she'd had fingers in her ears then and all. And after, when the payback came.

'Can't believe yer mum's missing this,' says Donna then, as if she can see right into Sadie's brain.

'I said she'd be sorry,' Sadie says.

'Though getting wed in the morning's a bit odd, if you ask me,' Donna continues. 'You want an afternoon do, then a finger buffet, then the dancing – band and a DJ. If you start now, where's it all going to end up? Head down the toilet, that's where.'

'Oh my God!' shrieks Deborah, piercing the vision. 'She got her words wrong.'

'She did and all,' adds Sadie, nodding at Donna. 'She said Philip first.'

'Philip Charles,' Deborah confirms.

'Right, that's it.' Donna stands, ash scattering from the lap of her denim skirt into the deep cover of the rug, where it's swiftly trodden into oblivion by three-inch wedge heels. 'I'm fetching yer mum. She'll not want to miss the rest of this. They'll be back down the aisle soon. Divorced, if she don't get a shimmy on.'

Sadie looks up. 'Shall I come?'

'No, love. You enjoy it. Tell us what we've missed. I'll only be a moment.' Then she's out the back door, hollering 'Connie!' at the top of her voice, not mithering if thin-lipped Mrs Higgins can hear her. Not today.

Sadie squidges in next to Deborah, picks up another Twiglet. 'That one next to Prince Charles was all right,' she says, ingratiating. 'I bet he'd like you.'

'Aye,' agrees Deborah. 'Maybe Diana should've gone for

him instead. Only then she wouldn't get to live in the palace, would she? I'd do owt for that.'

'Even marry Prince Charles?' Sadie's sucked on her Twiglet until the Marmite's gone and it's claggy as a cat biscuit. And she should know.

'Marry any old prince,' confirms Deborah. 'Still, she can always divorce him and they'd have to split it. The palace, I mean. And the horses and dogs and that. My mum and John might do that one day. If he don't stop the building thing. Only she says he'll not get the house or any of her porcelain dogs. Only over her dead body.'

Sadie swallows, says nowt. 'Cause it's not the first time she's heard it. The same words have been whispered in their kitchen twice in the last two weeks alone, once when Janice Batty was in earshot, albeit head under the dryer. But Deborah's waiting, poised for acknowledgement. 'It's not that bad,' she offers eventually. 'Not having a dad.'

Deborah makes a noise that Sadie knows to be scorn. 'Like you'd know any different,' she says, and gets up and turns the volume knob so the buzz and hum of the crowd is a bee in Sadie's ear.

Sadie don't rise to it. Donna'll be back any time now anyway, and her own mam and all, and they'll have something to say about going deaf, and square-eyed too, she doesn't wonder.

But when Donna comes back, less than two minutes gone, it's alone, and with a face as pale as that taffeta. 'Sadie, I . . .' she begins, but the rest of the words won't come out.

'What?' asks Deborah. 'What's gone on?' Then, eyes

goggle-wide and wanting, 'Has there been a burglary? Dad said we were to be careful 'cause it were a thieves' paradise with everyone at street parties or round each other's, glued to the box.'

'No, love,' her mam tells her. 'No burglary.' But it's Sadie she's looking at all the while, like she's willing her to understand whatever it is without saying, maybe.

But what else can it be? 'Is it the chipolatas?' Sadie tries. ''Cause she were just starving when she got in I think, and she said she didn't know why she were even bothering with them 'cause Peggy Megson'll probably do eight hundred any road as it's all she can cook.'

'No, love. Not that.' Something in Donna seems to snap then, her back straightens and she flies to the sideboard to pick up the phone.

But it's already taken, the party line ringing with Mrs Higgins's many opinions. 'Oh, for Christ's sake, Mary,' Donna spits into the receiver. 'It's an emergency!' Then, to the girls, 'Who calls up in the royal wedding?'

Deborah shrugs. At the word 'emergency' Sadie thinks first of fire alarms, and then of the *Towering Inferno*, and the *Poseidon Adventure*; pictures her mam trapped underwater, with only Gene Hackman to save her. But her mam can hold her breath. Her and Sadie had practised after that, just in case – could do more than a minute.

'Mary, I'm not one to swear—' Donna continues.

'She is,' hisses Deborah.

'Mary, will you get off the frigging phone?'

Sadie sounds the word in her head. She's heard her mam

say worse but she don't mimic. Knows better than that. Unlike Deborah, who whispers 'frigging' with a grin that even Sadie, confused as she is, feels is misplaced.

Apparently swayed by swearing, Mrs Higgins must have put down her receiver, because Donna starts to dial, Sadie clocking as each number spins.

Nine.

Nine. Bloody Nora.

Nine.

Her stomach plummets.

The other end takes seventeen seconds to answer, probably watching the box themselves. 'Thank God. Ambulance,' Donna says eventually. 'Seven Adelphi Terrace.'

The emergency person asks something else, and Donna looks at Sadie.

'It's my neighbour,' Donna says. 'I think she's . . . Well . . . I think she's . . .'

'Mum!' Deborah yells. 'She's what? What is she?'

Sadie waits, her chest tightening, her insides slip-sliding with the imminence of it, whatever it is.

Donna shakes her head, burgundy hair catching in the back-door light. 'Christ on a bike, I shouldn't be saying this. It's not right.' But she says it anyway, and she looks straight at Sadie as she does. 'Her name's Connie Holiday. She's twenty-nine. And I think she's . . . Well, I think she's dead.'

Jean

Essex, July 1981

Sixteen minutes past five and Jean Earnshaw – fifty-three, stiff and prim – slips the Pinnacle Biscuits' paper into the Smith Corona, spins the carriage and begins:

July 28th 1981, she types, the black and white imprint quick as a blink. But then her fingers, a moment ago a flicker, sit rigid, unable, it seems, to press return, or press anything at all. For she is mesmerized, momentarily, by that date.

Twenty-eighth.

Eight days gone – or, to be precise, twelve years and eight days. The same night they put a man on the moon, so she can hardly forget, not properly. But it gets . . . less vivid, easier with each change of calendar. No, in fact, she barely thought about it at all this year. Bernard has long stopped mentioning her, thank heavens, and aside from him there's only the Collinses to bring it up and they are far better bred than that. She'd probably not be thinking about it at all if it wasn't for Shelley Pledger.

She's one of the office girls – the new one with the awful earrings and, if you get too close, a bit of a squint. She'd asked Jean, three days ago, if she'd 'got any'. 'Any what?'

16

Jean had replied, as if it might be biscuits or cigarettes or sweets, all of which were entirely unlikely. 'Kids,' Shelley had said. Jean had been startled then, had to steady herself, to swallow. 'No,' she'd replied. 'And I don't have ten cats either, if that's what you're thinking.'

Shelley had pulled a face at that, probably reported it back in sniggers in the staff kitchen. 'Frigid Bridget' they call her behind her back. Though obviously not behind enough. Not that she cares. Perhaps they think Bernard is made-up. A figment of her imagination. If she had any imagination, it would hardly be Bernard she'd conjure, she wanted to say. But, no, that was unfair. He was dependable. He meant well. And wasn't that all you could ask, really?

Anyway, better she is Frigid Bridget, plain as a stair-rail, than the other way. She'd once worn wide, defiant trousers, painted her lips sticky with crimson. But look where that had got her. So it was water off a duck's back, the names and the whispers. Really, she pitied them with their obvious clothes and desperate hairdos and godless souls. Pitied that they lacked both manners and ambition. Pitied that they were content with Friday nights at the Painted Lady or, worse, the Birdcage, and some swaggering braggart from the factory floor.

If she were their age, had their opportunities, she would be off to college, to university. Or at least listening to Jan Leeming on the six o'clock news and practising vowels. Every time Hayley Harris spelled her name out loud with a 'haitch' she wanted to scream. Not that she would, ever, of course. A shudder sufficed. But still, it was irritating.

It had taken her only weeks, after all. Watching from the office of the Finsbury School for Girls. Learning to talk properly: to pronounce her 't's and drop her *love*s and *darlin's*; learning to walk tall, as if the Bible were balanced on her head – not that they'd ever used that, but *Vanity Fair*, hard-backed and heavy and a choice not lost on her, veritable Becky Sharp that she was, or that the headmistress declared her, anyway.

She bats the thought away, refocuses her ire on Hayley and Shelley and the rest of them, gaudy as parakeets and about as useful. If she'd had their chances, well, she wouldn't be sitting in Pinnacle Biscuits at fifty-something, typing out the kind of invoices a monkey could manage.

'You're still here.'

Jean comes to, musters a smile, contained, proper, at Maurice – or Mr Collins, rather, while she's at work, at least in front of the girls – 'Yes, I . . . I'm just finishing the month-end business. Because of the public holiday.'

'Jean.' His voice is a warning but well meant. 'You know the others were all off at four.'

'They'll only have to catch up on Thursday.'

'Always the last one standing,' he says then, the laugh that accompanies it obvious, but appreciative she thinks.

'I can give you a lift,' he offers. 'The bicycle will fit in the boot.'

'I've got the car,' she replies. 'Now Bernard doesn't need it for work.'

'Of course. Of course.' He pushes back his hair – still thick, if grey at the edges. 'You'll be watching,' he says, not a question. 'Tomorrow. The wedding,' he adds, as if, for some inexplicable reason, it might be anything else.

She hesitates, thinks for a minute of saying no, just to see what he makes of her audacity. But what would be the point in that? 'Of course.'

He makes a coughing noise. 'I think Barbara's hoping to get some tips.'

She takes a moment to work out what he means, then remembers: the vellum envelope, the printed invitation that she slipped quickly into a drawer before Bernard saw and said something she didn't want to think about. Because Martha – Maurice and Barbara's mouse of a daughter – has finally found herself a husband. A dullard of a man from what little she's seen of him – once at Sunday service, once at tea – but it was something, she supposed.

'But it's all already planned, isn't it?' she says. 'At the golf club? And surely she has the dress.'

He shrugs. 'All a mystery to me,' he says. 'Five bridesmaids,' he adds. 'Five.' As if it's several too many. Though they both know it's one short, his face turning red with it as he realizes. 'Well, I'll see you after, anyway. Barbara says you're in charge of sausage rolls.'

It's vol-au-vents, actually, mushroom and chicken, but she cannot see the gain in correcting him, so she just says, 'Yes.'

'Well, tomorrow then.'

She nods. 'Tomorrow.'

'Well, I think she's a picture.' Bernard is still reading the paper – *The Sunday Times*, eking it out for the week now he's retired – but peering over now and again when the commentary warrants it. 'Isn't she?'

For all his socialist ideals, his one mildly drunk suggestion that ushering in a republic might have its advantages, he's still a royalist when it comes down to it. Still went out to watch the fireworks at the Town Park last night, the beacon being lit. He gets that from his mother.

Jean has no such left-wing pretensions but there's something about this wedding that galls, even appals her. The dress is the nub of it. Like a toilet-roll holder, if you think about it, one of those knitted things she'd once aspired to – before Barbara corrected her, told her they were as common as nets. That's it, she thinks: the dress is common. Vulgar, all that extravagant fabric when it's only going to be worn once. She'd made do with a suit, hadn't she? Not even new. Not that she was comparing twenty minutes at Islington Town Hall followed by meat pie of undetermined origin at the Rose and Crown with this, but even the Queen hadn't gone quite this far to town.

The cameras are outside now, panning the Mall. Half a million thick, that crowd, or so the commentator told them. Though how he'd counted she had no idea. But there they were, all packed like sardines into – into what? Stands? She felt herself flinch at it, at the urgency of it all, the possible surge of them, the horrible proximity. All sweating and desperate, though for what exactly she is unsure. 'How do they even go to the toilet?' she wonders, aloud this time. 'And where?'

'Portaloos,' Bernard says. 'It's in the paper.' He shakes it, as if she might be confused.

She ignores him, transfixed, against all her wishes, by the television. She is scanning the sea of believers, cannot help it. A habit that, unlike cigarettes, drink, she has struggled to check. It's less pressing now than a decade ago, but still, when the chance arises, she finds herself scouring crowds, picking through pink-pixelled faces and matchstick bodies at Greenham, on protests and picket lines, or, once, at its worst, a Jimmy Connors match. As if Constance had ever been the tennis type.

But it had become her addiction, her sole vice, as impossible as it was. Like trying to find a needle in a haystack, a watch dropped in the forest. And what would she have done if she'd spotted her? She could hardly have stormed down there and hauled her home, protesting. Though perhaps that wasn't the point – getting her back, subjecting her to some kind of retribution. Perhaps she just wanted proof of her ongoing existence. Proof of life.

This, though, is worse than Wimbledon. The very last place she might turn up. She had abhorred the royals, after all. Declared them 'parasites', 'leeches on society'. She'd called the public – her mother assumedly included – worse though: 'duped', 'stupid' and, once, 'pathetic lemmings'. Borrowed words, Jean was sure of it, but from whom?

'Weather's a blessing,' Bernard says then.

She looks up, caught in the act. 'Pardon?'

'It's a blessing,' he repeats. 'The weather. Are you quite all right? You look peaky.'

'I'm perfectly fine,' she says – snaps almost, but is then needled with guilt. 'Sorry. Perhaps the heat is a bit much.'

'I'll open the back door, shall I?'

She feels herself twitch at this, at his utter lack of ability to just *do* something without question. It's kindness, she knows. But she hardly deserves it, not that he realizes that. And somehow it feels awful and clawing and she wishes he would stop. It's only worse now he's home all day as well. Though at least she has her own work. Bernard says she can stop, God knows they don't need the money. As if it's that easy. Because then what would she do? Moon about over weddings, and watch more television? How squalid.

'Well, that's that.' She stands and snaps the telly off, an action she realizes too late must appear almost triumphant. 'Street party,' she qualifies. 'Food won't make itself.'

'Right,' says Bernard. 'Shall I help you?'

'Honestly, Bernard, it's forty-eight vol-au-vents to heat up, not Christmas dinner. I can manage.'

Bernard looks hurt. 'Right you are.'

She shouldn't have snapped. Again. 'I'm sorry,' she says, briskly, a dab of cotton wool on the wound.

Really, though, he's too much at times.

All of it is too much.

Or not enough.

The party is bearable, the vol-au-vents remarked on for their lightness and flavour. Though Barbara says perhaps the chicken was a mistake – sitting around in all that afternoon heat – and she hopes no one gets sick. They'll not be having chicken at Martha's wedding, of course, or rice, for that very reason.

Jean ignores her, clears the plates from the trestle tables, says perfunctory goodbyes, puts away the china platters.

'Thank goodness that's over,' she says.

'Yes,' says Bernard, not really agreeing. 'Quite.'

But it's not his fault that he can't understand. Can't see how these things aggrieve her. These grand occasions, these moments when life might brim up and spill over the edges, taking her with it. She is the one at fault, it was her poor choice that led to this – this precariousness. Not Bernard. Never Bernard. Bernard is honest, solid, and, aside from the weight gain and the loss of some hair, the very same Bernard he was thirty years ago when they married. But she – she has chosen this life. She has chosen this self, this woman wound tight as a bobbin of cotton, forever checking the end of her thread is tucked in for fear it might catch and she unspool somehow.

It had almost happened once – that night in 1969. Not an accident, the end not snagged or trapped, but deliberately pulled, or so she chose to see it. But Jean had ravelled it back, righted herself, carried on if not regardless then at least stoically, given the circumstances. And tomorrow will be twelve years and ten days clocked off. And it will be easier still. And so the days will be ticked off until one morning, perhaps, her penance will end.

That's what she's thinking as she wills herself to sleep in the thick heat of the July night and the confines of the twin bed. That's what she's thinking when she wakes to the seven o'clock alarm, washes, dresses sensibly for the wretched weather.

That's what she's thinking when, before she walks out the door, the phone rings, shrill and insistent at far too early an hour.

'I'll get it,' she calls to Bernard, who's still at the table, head buried in the Special Edition. It'll only be Maurice, she thinks. Offering a lift. He never listens.

But it's not Maurice. It's not anyone she knows.

It's a woman called Donna, who says something ridiculous. And with it, her end catches, is yanked, and she spills metres of beige thread over the hallway floor.

Sadie

Leeds, July 1981

In the wake of those words, several things happen.

The first thing: Sadie promptly vomits up half a packet of Twiglets and a cherry Panda Pop into cerise shagpile, while the crowd on the Mall applauds and Deborah, incredulous, pulls a face like a gargoyle.

'Sorry,' says Sadie, staring at the grim pinkness.

Donna shakes her head. 'Don't matter, love. It'll wash off.'

Sadie don't think it will; there's still a Quality Street stuck to the rug from Christmas. But try as she might to think about sick, she knows she's got to acknowledge the other thing. 'What happens now?' she asks. 'Will I go home?'

Donna, appalled, shakes her head. 'Christ, no, love. You stay here with Deborah.' She glances at the carpet again. 'Or maybe in the bedroom. For now.'

And so that's where she's sat – surrounded by Deborah's elaborate menagerie of Barbies and Sindys and whatnot on mauve candlewick and focusing on a poster of The Nolans, wondering which one she might be (probably Coleen, because Deborah's bagsied Linda) – when the ambulance arrives. Thing number two.

At that, something in Sadie lifts. Because, if they're taking her to hospital, maybe she's not totally dead. Because when someone's totally dead, like Mr Bannerjee at Number 17 was last August, because of being ninety-six, a different thing – a private ambulance – comes. Though it's odd it's called an ambulance when it's more of a van. Not much different to the one Elvis Jenkins drives round off season. Though his has got his name on the side and a picture of the King, which wouldn't look right on an ambulance, she supposes, cheering though it might be. And also ambulances don't go round picking up stuff off the back of a lorry like Elvis does, or so her mam says.

'What do you suppose they're up to in there?' she asks Deborah, in deference to her seven months' extra experience and infinite insight gleaned from magazines.

'One of them'll be doing mouth to mouth,' she answers. 'The tall one, I expect. The other one probably isn't allowed because of his moustache.'

Sadie nods, the door of hope opening a chink and an inch of light filtering in.

'But it will be in vain,' Deborah continues, slamming it shut again. 'Because she were already dead for ages probably. So the tall one'll do a cross on his chest, because of your mum being Catholic, and the other one will say stuff about them doing everything they could.'

'But my mam's not Catholic,' says Sadie quickly. 'She's not anything. She says . . . She says God's a load of cobblers.'

Deborah raises her eyebrows, a miniature Donna. 'I wouldn't want to be in her shoes now then.'

Sadie tries to think of something to say to that, but words won't come, and in any case there's a kerfuffle outside, so they kneel up at the windowsill to watch.

There's Mrs Higgins, hands on her hips, her lips probably thin as a lemon slice. There's Mrs Hepworth next to her with Billy, Mivvi in his gob and his six-year-old eyes a-goggle. There's the Mehtas, seven of them, little ones behind bigger ones, behind Mr Mehta in a brown suit. Even he's had the day off and they open at Christmas, which Mrs Higgins says is heresy and Mam says is bloody useful, thank you very much.

And there's the ambulance men, green as the Hulk but not half as magic, because behind them, in a black plasticky sack on a trolley, rolls a body. And behind it, Donna, sobbing, and smoking a fag.

'Blimey,' says Deborah.

Sadie says nothing. You can't be a bit alive in a black plastic bag, she supposes.

She feels weird then. Not sad, exactly, just strange. Like time has slowed down till it's thick as treacle and everything's a bit blurred. She should be sad, she knows. That's what happens on telly. Someone dies and everyone's wailing. She cried when Bambi's mam died. And when Petra off *Blue Peter* went. And Deborah's cried twice today already. Though one of the times she were looking at herself in the mirror when she did it, which Sadie's not sure counts.

Time still drips as the ambulance pulls off but the crowd stays milling – getting their two pence worth, Mam would have said – bothering Donna. But Donna, usually Queen of

Chinese Whispers, isn't playing today. Instead, she scuttles back in, slams the front door and goes straight into the kitchen.

When the girls find her, she's pouring herself a Martini into a half-pint glass borrowed from the Black Horse.

'What happened?' begs Deborah. 'Was she proper dead, then?'

Donna downs the drink in two. 'God, will you just put a sock in it for a moment.' She looks at Sadie. 'I'm so sorry, love. They tried their best but there were nothing they could do.'

'Told you!' says Deborah, triumphant.

Sadie's not sure what she's supposed to say or do still, so she says nothing, keeps her mouth clamped tight as a pickle lid.

Donna frowns. 'You're not going to be sick again, are you?' she asks. 'Because you'd be best off in the yard if you are.'

Sadie shakes her head.

'Where've they taken her?' Deborah's gob's not stoppered up. Ever.

Donna's watching Sadie, mind on the lino maybe. 'There'll be a post-mortem.'

'What's . . . What's one of them?' she manages.

'They have to cut her open,' says Deborah. 'To check what happened.'

'Aye.' Donna's frowning now.

'Don't they know?' asks Sadie.

'They think . . . Christ, maybe it's best not to say.'

But Sadie finds even she wants to hear it. 'What?' she asks.

Donna takes a breath. 'They think she might have choked.'

'On what?' Deborah's big on detail.

'Doesn't matter,' says Donna.

'On them cocktail sausages,' Sadie finds herself saying. 'She took the whole plate.'

'Maybe,' says Donna.

'She choked on a sausage?' Deborah is incredulous again. 'I wouldn't want to go like that. At least murder's interesting—'

At that Donna smacks Deborah on the leg, a red welt against white skin and a royal-blue ra-ra.

'What?' Deborah demands, eyes brimming now, though Sadie's pretty sure it's only her pride that's stinging.

''S'all right,' says Sadie. 'I don't mind.'

She does a bit though. Not about what Deborah said, about murder, but how it happened: the sausage. Why didn't Mam bite it properly? Or perhaps she tried to swallow it in one. Though she told Elvis off when he were showing Sadie how to catch peanuts in her mouth, in case one went down the wrong hole and got stuck, so you'd have thought she'd have known better.

'Will they tell you when they've worked it out?' she asks, quiet.

'I . . . No, love. I'm not next of kin.'

'Sadie is,' says Deborah, cat not keeping her tongue for long.

'Aye,' agrees Donna. 'But she's a minor.'

'A miner? No she's not.'

29

'Not that kind— Christ,' Donna shakes her head. 'A child. She's a child. They need a grown-up to talk to.'

'Like Elvis Jenkins,' Deborah suggests.

At his name, something in Sadie burgeons. Elvis can come back from Skegness and fix this. That's what he's good at. Washing machines and fridges and, once, the gas fire, though that didn't work out that well for his quiff. But still, he got it working again.

But Donna don't agree. 'Love, they're not married.'

'Like who then?'

'Well, like other relatives.'

Deborah looks at Sadie, impatient.

But Sadie can't help. 'We don't have any. Not to talk to.'

'Not to talk to, perhaps,' Donna says. 'Not before. But that don't matter now.'

'D'you mean like an uncle or something? 'Cause I don't think I have one of them.'

'She means your dad.' Deborah is breathless with potential.

Sadie shrugs. 'I don't have one of those either.'

'I didn't mean your dad, love.' Donna glares at Deborah. 'Christ, she won't even tell *me* who that is. Wouldn't,' she corrects herself. Then blurts out a sorry with the sob and the snot. 'Sorry,' she says again. 'I meant . . . I meant her own mum. That's next of kin.'

'My nan, you mean.'

Donna nods. 'Aye. What's her name?'

But Sadie's pockets are empty again. 'I don't know,' she says. 'Mrs Holiday?'

Donna coughs out a swear. 'You know that's not your real surname.'

'What?' Sadie is stunned for the second time that day, the rug pulled out from under her, still covered in sick. 'What is, then?'

'God, I don't even know.'

That's thing number three. The hunting.

The house is terrible empty. She can feel it the minute they walk in. Though she were skinny as an imp and barely taller than Sadie, her mam took up so much space with her singing and her spangles that, without her, the air's fallen slack, like a balloon that's sagged or a slow-punctured tyre.

'Where'd she keep her papers?'

Sadie makes herself concentrate. 'Like what?'

'Bills and the like,' Donna says. 'Official stuff.'

'Love letters.'

'Deborah!' snaps Donna, but Sadie's eyes widen at the possibility.

'Top drawer.' She nods at the one to the right of the sink.

Donna hauls at it and out spills a life: brown paper envelopes and pieces of card, and other stuff too. String and Sellotape and a thing Sadie knows to be called a tampon, but what it's for and where it goes she don't like to think about.

Donna picks it up quick, pushes it into her pocket. 'You two go on upstairs. Get your things, love,' she says to Sadie. 'You can sleep with our Deborah tonight.'

'Brill!'

Sadie's not sure 'brill' is the word but she nods all the same. 'Come on,' Deborah says, then is up the stairs, clattering, rabbit-quick.

Sadie's slower, finds her legs are a jelly, her sandals stuck on the treads like it's quicksand or slurry. She fetches up at Deborah in the end, though: akimbo on the landing outside her mam's canary-painted door.

'Should we go in, do you think?' Deborah asks.

Sadie slackens, swirls inside. 'For what?'

'I don't know. Check for mess?'

Sadie thinks about it, dismisses it quick. 'What if there's . . . What if there's blood?' she worries. 'Or . . . or something else?'

'Like what?'

She thinks about the little religion that's been doled out at school. 'Like . . . a soul.'

Deborah pulls a face again. 'What do they even look like?'

'I don't know,' Sadie admits. 'Maybe a bit like a ghost?'

The thought of her mam all see-through and sheet-clad sends Sadie sweating, but Deborah's face lights up as if she's won a prize.

'That'd be something. Better than murder. Ricky Osgood'd go mad with jealousy.'

'Aye,' says Sadie. 'But can we not – you know – go in.'

Deborah sighs. 'Suit yourself.' And she trudges along the landing to Sadie's room, Sadie two steps behind. Always.

There's a hiss of release as Deborah opens the door and Sadie sees her things all laid out as she left them: lined up on the mildewed windowsill and along the mantel.

This is what she packs:

* one nightie: Scooby-Doo
* her yellow dress
* two pairs of knickers: Thursday and Friday, just in
  case
* her elasticated snake belt, red and white
* three I-Spy books: *Number Plates*, *Garden Wildlife* and
  Sea Creatures
* her Whimsey goat
* a pine cone, still rattling with seeds
* the commemorative wedding coin she'd queued
  behind Deborah for, only to be told it weren't real
  silver, just painted that way
* a dictaphone: tape inside but batteries missing.

Necessities and treasure. Just in case.

The dictaphone had been a present from Elvis. For her
birthday. Instead of the cassette player he'd promised, but
she didn't mind, not much. Her mam weren't so keen on
hers, though.

'What am I meant to do with that?' she'd asked.

'Shopping lists?'

'Who do you think I am? Vera bloody Duckworth?'

'I don't know. Songs, then.'

But she'd not bothered with the songs or the dictaphone
and who knows where hers has gone. Top of her wardrobe
probably, along with the rest of her rubbish.

The hamster'd been Elvis's idea and all.

'Can she bring Dave?' Deborah yells down the stairs.

'Who the heck's Dave?' Donna yells up them.

'The hamster!' As if she's stupid. 'Can she?'

'Aye,' Donna replies. 'But hurry up, will you.'

They do hurry, Sadie with her gingham gym bag on her back, Deborah carrying the cage out front like it's a glass slipper on a cushion, along the landing, past the still-slammed-shut door holding in the soul, and down the wood of the stairs into the kitchen, where Donna's waiting, in her hand an inky blue book she's holding like it's a winning ticket.

'I got it,' she says. 'Blimey, you won't believe it.'

'What?' says Deborah, Dave and his cage tipping and teetering.

But, 'Here.' She hands the thing to hands-free Sadie, page open at the back.

'Let me see.' Deborah's over her shoulder, Sadie shrugging her off for once, wanting this pip, whatever it is, for herself for a minute.

She reads. In small print, blue ink, neat type: *In case of emergencies.* Then, in black italic capitals, the names she didn't even know she'd been waiting for:

JEAN & BERNARD EARNSHAW

Below them, their home:

3, THE GREEN

OLD HARLOW

ESSEX

And a number: *22319*

It's Sadie's turn to tilt and spin and she drops the book and has to grip her fingers tight in her fists to keep herself still and ticking. Because of those names. Because all that time she had a family, hidden in the kitchen drawer with the bills and the string and the tampon. And she wonders for a minute who else might be squidged in. A long-lost brother? Her dad, perhaps? No, not him. Not likely. At least a cousin, though, like Donna's one, Brady, with the shaved head and the Rubik's Cube he breaks apart to finish.

'Your nan and grandpa,' Donna confirms.

'Blimey.' Deborah's got the book now. 'Look at that.'

Sadie comes to, snatches it back. 'Leave it.'

'All right. I were only saying.'

'Pair of you,' Donna says then. 'Come on.'

'Come on, what?' demands Deborah.

'What do you mean, what? We've to call them, haven't we.' Not a question. A definite.

'What about the cat?' Deborah asks then.

'What about it?'

'We can't just leave it here. Not with—'

'Leave it some biscuits,' Donna interrupts. 'Now get a bend on.'

Deborah's still smells of sick 'cause there hasn't been time to clean the rug, but Donna just shuts the door on it, says she'll deal with it later. Probably pick it off, by then.

'Dining room,' she says, and off they troop, Dave and all, to the back – not a dining room at all, really – to find the phone.

Mrs Higgins is still busy gassing out front, so there's no one to shout at, just numbers to dial and a tinny ring in the distance – at 3, The Green – and Sadie's breath held so her throat hurts and her legs jiggle with need at this link that strings from Leeds to there, this place she's never heard of and people she's never known.

But three times the phone goes, then four, then five and still no one picks up.

'Why aren't they answering?' Deborah's indignant.

Donna clatters down the receiver. Snips Sadie's string. 'Street party, I expect. Same as everyone.'

'Or dead,' says Deborah. 'What? They might be!'

Donna ignores her. Says she'll try again later. And she does and all. Five times, each time Sadie asking for just one more, just in case. But then Donna says she's got John to get hold of now, and that sick won't mop itself up, so just drop it and they'll do it in the morning. Maybe best not to spoil the day.

'Maybe,' says Sadie, her day spoiled rotten already.

Her and Deborah lie top to tail, too hot for the candlewick but they've strung it up like a canopy anyway, from the ceiling light, though Sadie said it were dangerous but Deborah don't care.

'Are you sad?' she asks her.

'Aye,' says Sadie, and it's not a lie, but it's still not exactly sadness that's in her but something else. A sort of gap, like back at the house. As if something's gone and needs to be pumped up or plugged.

'You can cry if you want,' says Deborah.

And Sadie tries, makes a kind of whining sound. Then pinches herself to see if that helps but it don't.

'Sorry,' she says.

''S'all right. You'll be in shock,' says Deborah. 'I saw it on *Corrie*. It'll hit tomorrow, probably. You won't be able to stop bawling then. It'll be awful.'

'Aye,' says Sadie. 'Probably will.'

But tomorrow's not so awful. Because when they go down in the morning the sick's been cleaned and Dave's been fed and Donna's already waiting by the phone with a fag.

And this time when it rings, the strings don't sever or snap, the link stays tight as you like, then there's a click and a cough – Donna – and a distant 'Hello?'

It's a woman. *The* woman. And her voice is muffled 'cause it's into Donna's ear she's going, but still, it's real, and posh as sandwiches with the crusts cut off.

'Harlow double two three one nine,' she repeats.

And Sadie sings with it.

Because it's Jean Earnshaw.

It's a nan.

And it's hers.

Connie

Leeds, January 1981

New Year's Resolutions 1981

1. *Sort out LIFE! To wit:*
2. *Eat better.*
3. *Vitamins!*
4. *Drink less.*
5. *London bookers – call!*
6. *Doctor – make appointment?*
7. *Elvis – deal with him.*

The second and third are for Sadie's sake really. Crisps aren't a food group; she's not stupid. But it's hard between shifts and gigs to muster up meat and two veg and she's not sure mushy peas really count. The fourth, well, that's an annual entry but this time she definitely means it. Last night is the last time she's letting Elvis get her into this state. Letting herself. She's going to be thirty this year – flaming ancient in circuit terms – and if she wants to be taken seriously, if she wants the London lot to take her at all, then she's got to sort herself out, sober up, buckle down.

Besides, she felt it again in the Legion last night – that sudden quickening in her chest; the mouse-soft pattering turning into a frantic stampede, and then the swift sinking into black. Only for a few seconds – seconds she told everyone – Elvis, Billy Rigby, Thick Jimmy King – were down to one too many vodka and Cokes. But they weren't, can't be, because it's happened when she's stone cold sober as well, straight as they come: mid-shift at Morrisons in the biscuit aisle; on the bus back from Roundhay, sunburned and sung out and grinning; sitting on the front wall with a cup of tea and a ciggie watching Sadie and Deborah skate precariously along the pave—

She pauses to let the roil of nausea complete its belligerent spin, and the biro – one of Elvis's, 'borrowed' from the bookie's – slips from her fingers, drops to the floor and rolls, inconveniently, under the fridge, coming to a rest, no doubt, amongst the jetsam of dead ants, desiccated peas and wayward Frosties. 'Christ,' she intones. Why's life so difficult? So spiteful? 'Like walking through meat in high heels,' Donna once said, and at the time she'd snorted at the image, ridiculous as it seemed. But now, as she leans down from the plastic chair and pushes her fingers into the sticky filth under the Electrolux, she feels it: everything is treacle-slow or stupidly quick or just that bit out of bloody reach.

'What're you up to?'

Elvis.

Empty-handed, but with a patina of chip fat and crumbs and cat hair clinging to her skin, Connie sits up quick, letting the pages of her notebook flap shut so all he can see from over her shoulder is the gloss-red of the cover and the looped italics spelling 'Silvine'.

'Nothing. Just . . . a shopping list.'

He leans over so she can smell the stale Carling on him, the curry he had after, the sweat from bed, pushes one hand down her shirt – his, really; a faded grey from a T-Rex tour – and grasps her left breast, the nipple hardening against her will and want.

'Stiff as a peanut,' he says, a note of triumph in his tone, then kisses her neck wetly.

She shrugs him off, pulls her bare legs up and the T-shirt down over them. 'I'm just cold,' she explains.

'I know a cure for that,' he says, his hand slipping down again.

'Not showering?' she asks.

'Later. Where's Sadie?' He pulls at her tit again, rolls the nipple in his fingers and then squeezes so she has to cover a gasp.

'Deborah's.'

'Staying over?'

'For tea. She'll be back by seven.'

'It's only six. Don't need more than an hour, do we?' His hand pushes further down, into her knickers – yesterday's, but clean enough – and he feels for her with his middle finger, his palm against her pubic hair. 'You're wet already, dirty mare.'

'Elvis,' she tries to warn. But her resolve is weakening. She's tired; too tired for a fight anyway. And she is wet, can't deny it. Never had any trouble getting that far, even if it is just a Pavlov's dog reaction to his persistent groping.

'Come on,' he urges. 'I'm gagging.' And he takes her hand and presses it against the rigid outline of his dick, springing as it is against sagging cotton.

Her hand held there, she thinks to protest, but in the end lets her defiance deflate. Who doesn't want to be wanted, after all? 'All right,' she agrees. 'But upstairs.'

And so she rises, trails him up the narrow treads, her wrist in his hand, ready to get it over with.

'Bloody thing.' He snaps off the condom and, still propped against the pillow where he'd spent the entirety of proceedings, flings it in the bin, where it lands, flaccid, on top of a mass of fag ends and panstick-stained cotton wool. 'Goal for Jenkins!' he yells, then nods at imagined applause, before lighting up an Embassy.

Connie, under the covers now, sighs silently, but takes the fag when he hands it to her.

'We could always give them up,' he suggests.

She breathes out a plume ceiling-ward. 'What? Ciggies?'

He laughs. 'Rubbers, love.'

She frowns. 'You know the pill doesn't agree with me.' Or with anyone around her, sending her 'mental', as some had had it.

'I meant give everything up. You know.'

'Know what?'

'Con . . . Come on.'

Jesus fuck. 'A baby?' She hadn't meant to sound quite so alarmed, but alarming it was. Unthinkable, even.

'Well, you don't have to be so enthusiastic.'

'I . . . I just—'

'Not like you're getting any younger. Thirty,' he adds, rubbing in salt.

'Thanks for reminding me.' She hands back the fag.

He takes it, takes a drag. 'Older you are, harder it'll be. Look at my mam.'

Dead at forty squeezing out her second, and doesn't Connie know it; had it slapped into her once, lest she forget. 'I just . . .' have plans. The London bookers. The last chance.

'Is it last night?'

'Last night?'

'The fainting.'

'God, no. It's not—'

'What, then? I'd be a cracking dad, wouldn't I? Sadie loves me, doesn't she?'

That she can't deny. 'I know, but—'

'Come on, Con?' He's rolled over now, fag burning away in an ashtray Sadie made in art class, hands on her again, hoping for seconds.

She twists aside, swaps it for a consolation prize. 'I'll think about it,' she concedes.

She won't, though. Or only to list the reasons – on page two of her diary – why it's a bad idea, terrible, the timing only the opening gambit. For what would she do now with a baby? Defenceless as a fledgling and just as needy. Who's going to look after that while she's stuck on the till at Morrisons? And Sadie's one thing – old enough and clever enough to be left or sent round Deborah's – but a baby's different, and she can hardly cart a newborn round the pubs and clubs. Perhaps she'll have to go back on the pill after all; suck up the anger, the anxiety, the mithering, as Donna would call it. Maybe she can ask the doctor when she sees him about the other thing.

If she sees him.

Because she's all right right now, isn't she? Maybe she's worrying over nothing. Maybe she just needs to eat better and drink less and get some oranges down her. It was only palpitations, after all. Only a bit of fainting, and who hasn't fainted at least once in their life?

'Mam!'

Shit. Connie snaps to as the back door slams, heralding Sadie's entrance with its disregard for etiquette or tricky hinges. 'Coming,' she calls, then reaches over Elvis, snatches up the smouldering cigarette and takes the last drag of nicotine before stubbing it out on the pink-glazed clay. 'Pass me my knickers, will you?'

'Hey,' he says, holding up a hand. 'I'll go.'

'You don't have to.'

'Watch,' he says, swinging out of bed and pulling on his Y-fronts and the Eagles shirt. 'Cracking dad. Just you see.'

And before she can tell him that a pair of trousers wouldn't go amiss he's off down the stairs to Sadie, and she's left in bed with the sobering thought that, never mind the drink and the vitamins, she's to tackle Elvis, and soon, before his feet are so far under the table he'll take it for his own.

Jean

Essex, August 1981

It's Bernard who organizes it all. Talks to the hospital, the coroner, that woman – Mrs Maltby; 'Call-Me-Donna,' she'd said. Well, no thank you very much, though Bernard obliges. Bernard obliges with all of it. Says he'd rather be busy, says if he sits still he'll only dwell.

So the dwelling is left to her, rigid in the sitting room while all about her Bernard busies himself and the world spins in a nauseating whirl, her serried life, so well regimented, so neat and tidy and tucked in, turned upside down twice over by a single phone call. So that she can feel her tight-spooled self sprawling and straggling, threatening to fray, to become unkempt as a rag rug, as her mother.

When she first found out, when that woman had told her the necessary details, and some unnecessary besides, she had hung up, shut herself in the lavatory, and crouched on the floor while her breakfast flumed into the green porcelain, then, after it, a torrent of tears took with them the scant dab of mascara she had allowed herself, the dusting of powder. Ten minutes later she'd emerged, blinking as a newborn, and, thrown for that moment, she had let Bernard hold her, given him a long-forgotten form of comfort, let him comfort her. But the proximity, the clinging limbs, were all too much; she couldn't breathe, couldn't function, and so she had reminded herself – reminds herself now – of that hard pearl of truth: that the girl – the woman – their daughter – was already dead. Or good as.

When had they last heard from her, after all? Or of her, even? That summer, perhaps. They'd been on holiday, her and Bernard – a week in the Lakes, wet and wordless, but they couldn't not go, she'd told him. No, it was business as usual, or what would everyone think? What would the Collinses think? But when they'd got back, late on the Sunday, the house was altered. The back door gaped, a key still dangling from the lock. Bernard told her to wait where she was, did a cursory search for items, but found the windows intact, the television in place, her pearls undisturbed, still nestled in velvet. Only the tin money was missing. Nevertheless, Bernard wondered if they'd been burgled, but she'd known who it was even before she noticed the toast crumbs, the smear of margarine on the work surface, the knife abandoned in the sink. For only Constance ate without a plate, prefer-ring to chew as she leant against the fridge or wandered bored and boneless as a cat, a habit Jean had found both impolite and increasingly infuriating, and told her so, which is no doubt why she did it. But it wasn't just the missing money and the mess; there was also something tighter about everything, as if the rooms were holding their breath, as if they were keeping a secret or awaiting a scene.

There would have been one, without doubt. After what

she'd done. And why had she come back anyway? To gloat? To beg?

To stay?

Jean had doubted the last, but, clutching at this one small straw, forced herself to walk the few roads over from the old town to the new estate, to Mark Hall Moor to ask that Michelle Spencer what she knew.

'She needed some money,' the girl had told her, kohl-rimmed eyes black as a panda, a hank of limp hair twisting in her fingers. 'But I didn't have nothing.'

Anything, Jean had thought automatically, but had, at least, not said it. Not this time. Instead she'd mustered, 'Well, where did she go?'

But Michelle had just shrugged, ever the exasperating child, unable to express herself other than 'wow' and 'I suppose'. Jean had turned to go then, resigned to silence, but Michelle had mumbled something, then coughed, as if the words were caught in the back of her throat.

'Pardon?' she'd asked, spinning on a sensible heel.

'She had . . . She had . . .'

Jean bristled with impatience. 'She had what?' Said sorry? Hardly. The word wasn't even in her lexicon. Nor, for that matter, was lexicon, despite Jean's best efforts. 'Well, do come on, spit it out—'

'A baby,' the girl blurted, her raw dough skin pinking quickly. 'A girl. Sadie Marie. She, you know—'

That was the last slice of the knife; the icing on the terrible cake of it. 'I know what it means,' she'd interrupted. 'Thank you very much.'

A baby.

And in a swift instant, then, as now, she is back on the ward. Dettol-smelling, feet in stirrups as if she's straddling a horse, not heaving out a child. It had taken hours, thirty-seven to be precise, not aided, the midwife told her, by her seeming unwillingness to dilate. 'Come along,' she'd called, pinch-faced and brisk, as if hollering at a dog. 'Another inch or so. Anyone would think you wanted to keep it in.'

Jean had said nothing, just offered another prayer that, when it did come out – because she'd known it must, however much she had willed it otherwise – it would look . . . right. 'Your husband here?' the midwife had asked then.

'I don't know,' she'd lied.

Because of course he was there. Faithful as a hound and just as persistent, Bernard had insisted on coming. 'Where else would I be?' he'd asked, after she'd mopped up her waters, sobbed swiftly and efficiently, then come downstairs and told him it was time, though more than a month too early, if they were going by the wedding. 'It's the future,' he'd added, his hand on her bump.

Always the future. As if his gilded vision were solid, a yellow-brick road stretching inexorable towards some unnameable brighter tomorrow. The folly was she'd believed him. Believed childbirth was her penance and Constance her salvation. Believed that, after the ordeal, God would have forgiven her and Bernard wouldn't even know and the future really would be as perfect as he painted it.

Her salvation. She almost laughs.

Because, seventeen years later, look what Constance had

done. And then, cock of the walk, had come swaggering back with a baby of her own, as if it were the prize, the cherry on the cake. Sadie Marie – even the name chosen to taunt her. So common. Almost French, for heaven's sake. And what was she supposed to do with that information anyway? She could hardly have fetched the girl home – she didn't even know where she was. And besides, Connie was no prodigal daughter. No, the whole thing was an embarrassment, a mess sent to test her. Well, she was as stoic as Abraham, quite able to strap this Isaac to the altar if that's what it took.

And so she had, parcelling up that piece of information along with her disappointment and her shame and putting it away on the shelves in the shed along with the single box of belongings and Bernard's winter pickles. To be stored indefinitely. And though it beat still, like an organ under the floorboards – Poe's terrible telltale heart – time had dulled the thud, lessened the dread. Once or twice Bernard had nodded towards it, asked her: 'Do you want to . . . ?' But she'd shake her head. 'No, thank you. Not at the moment.' Never at the moment. Until he'd stopped asking altogether and now . . . Well, now it was moot, wasn't it. Nothing to be done, she told herself. Had to tell herself.

Except for the Child.

'Surely there's some kind of . . . man who can have her?' she'd suggested, after Bernard had come off the phone to Call-Me-Donna, with her endless sniffing and awful vowels.

But Bernard had shaken his head. 'Just a boyfriend and he's away working. Caravan park, apparently. They've left a message. But he's not . . . He's not the father.'

'And so we're . . . we're just expected to . . . to . . .'

'We're family,' Bernard had told her.

He'd said that before, after her father had died and he'd suggested her mother move in with them.

'No!' she'd snapped, flinching at her own outburst, the door-slamming finality of it. 'She'd hate it,' she clarified. 'Besides, Gerry's round the corner.'

'Still, wouldn't it be nice to offer?'

But she hadn't let him then.

This time, though, his were the last words on the matter.

'For how long?' she said at last.

'Until, well, I don't know,' he admitted. 'Let's see, shall we?'

See what? she thinks. If they can bear her? If she can them? And what about her job? Is she supposed to give that up now? It's not about the money, of course; they have sufficient from Bernard's pension and her own clever savings. No, it . . . it gives shape to her days. And more than that, Mr Collins – Maurice – needs her. She's the 'pin in Pinnacle Biscuits', isn't that what he said?

Besides, she's too old to raise a child. And Bernard may be at home and willing, but he's got twelve years on her. He can hardly be off to the park or out on a bicycle at his age. And what about later, when the Child is older, when she wants to go out and meet boys? Well, if Bernard thinks she's going through that again, he's got another think coming.

So, yes, she will 'see', but only for Bernard's sake. And with clear vision, a hard heart, and her head above everything.

*

She tries to keep that in mind on the drive, tries to focus on the task at hand, but something is awry. The swill of her she puts down to travel sickness, the pangs to the fact she's not eaten since breakfast and it's nearing – what? – six hours on the road? And every second of them taut as tripwire and hung with things unsaid. But the sudden wash of it when they drop down into Leeds – the laundry strung from fence to fence, dirty smalls aired in public; the infants in the mill of it, scab-kneed and snot-nosed, and swearing, she suspects – the utter vulgarity of it all: that surge of something is memory. This is miles from Finsbury, from Farringdon, and decades too, but the picture is as vivid in its mimicry as its disappointment, for this, this . . . horrible squalor is the pressing, oppressing kind she had worked so determinedly to escape. But then Constance was always drawn to the tawdry.

'It's too late to fetch her,' she says. 'She'll be ready for bed.'

'She's eleven,' Bernard reminds her kindly, 'not four. And better to meet her now than in the morning, surely? When she'll be in the back of the car for hours.'

She is fully aware of the exact age of the girl and all its implications, but still she tries. 'She doesn't even know us. She won't want to stay in a hotel with strangers.'

'We're not . . .' But he trails off, knowing he cannot win on that point, tries a new tack. 'She's about to live with strangers. She's sharing a bed now, as it is. At least in the hotel she'll have her own.'

He is uncharacteristically unmovable in all of this. Guilt, she thinks. Though entirely misplaced, given he – they – did nothing wrong. 'Very well,' she says. 'But can I at least freshen up first?'

'Of course,' he concedes. 'Of course.'

In the hotel room – tired but functional, three single beds – she attends to her suitcase with as much precision as she packed it, taking time to unfold and hang, to place and stack. 'It's only one night,' Bernard had said that morning, as if she'd forgotten, as if she wasn't deliberately stretching out tasks to fill such elastic time. 'Will you be long?' he asks now, as she stands in the strip-lit bathroom, white-knuckled hands gripping the rim of a pink sink.

'Coming,' she says to herself, trying to find a brightness she knows she could once muster but seems to have lost the knack. Then repeats it out loud, as if saying will make it so, will make it easier. It doesn't. It takes a minute more for her to prise her fingers from the porcelain, to dab her eyes with toilet roll, to unlock the door.

'We could always have stayed at . . . at the house. Perhaps,' Bernard tries.

The thought is mortifying. 'No we couldn't.'

She knows it was nothing sinister. Not suicide. And not, thank heaven, the sausage Call-Me-Donna had suggested. It was her heart, apparently. Long-standing. As if she should have known. As if . . . At that she feels the thread catch again, has to find her end and tuck it in. 'Well, come along then. Best get this over with.'

The street is everything she dreaded and all she imagined, terraces in red rather than pale London stock, but the same

51

sense of grim inevitability about them. A sort of giving in to life. She can hardly countenance that this is where Constance chose to settle. It must have been temporary, surely? A stopgap. Or perhaps she chose it out of pure defiance. It would hardly surprise her. The one time they took her to Islington she revelled in it, begged to stay behind, to live on pink wafers. 'Dog biscuits,' she'd wanted to say to her. 'That's what I had for my tea once. That's what you'll get if you stay back with her.' But instead she'd snatched her hand and hauled her squalling to the car while Bernard apologized. Again.

Well, she got her wish. In the end.

The house itself is like a shut eye – curtains drawn, as if in mourning – and she shuts her own to it as well, keeps her blinkered vision on Number 9, where they're to press the bell for Call-Me-Donna, who's been minding the Child. 'Sadie,' Bernard insists on reminding her, but she cannot admit it to herself, let alone say it out loud.

Perhaps they are doing the right thing, she lets herself think then. Rescuing her. Because this isn't suitable at all: this woman with her absent husband – oh, she's heard all about that from Bernard – and this house with its scattered plastic toys on the doorstep, its stickers on the windows, its nets – dreadful things. No, this won't do at all.

It is a feeling that is only amplified when Bernard rings the doorbell, which tinkles out a tinny 'Dixie'. Horrid. The woman that answers is alarming – her hair the desperate red of an ageing actress or a diffident hippy. Not even the courtesy to be coy about its falsity.

'Mrs Earnshaw?' she says and promptly bursts into tears.

Jean recoils and Bernard touches her on the shoulder, fleeting but firm, and she is grateful, this once, for his acknowledgement. She is not a demonstrative woman. Public emotion has always struck her as vulgar, reminded her of her father, drunk and stumbling, or her mother, goggle-eyed and tongue flapping, passing on gossip with a dollop of false horror on the side. She doesn't know what to do with it now but pretend it isn't happening.

'So, will you bring her out?' she asks. 'The Child.'

The woman wipes her nose on her wrist, leaving a snail trail of stringy mucus. 'Sorry, love,' she says, ushering them inside instead, into a narrow hallway carpeted in swirling orange, and the stench of trodden-in tobacco and cheap meat. 'Come through. They're watching the box.'

There follows a fresh round of sobbing and Bernard wrestling with the kitchen roll and eventually she takes matters into her own hands. Like pulling off a plaster, she reasons. Best to just get it over with. And she braces herself and walks into what can only be described as a front room.

At first she is thrown, for there are two of them, sitting cross-legged on a pleather settee (she cannot call this thing a sofa, however much it pains her otherwise), and her stomach drops at the possibility of a mistake, at the absurd notion that she is expected to take on not just one child but twins – one Sadie, one Marie. But on closer inspection the one on the left clearly belongs to Mrs Maltby – her hair its original colour, thank heaven, but far too elaborate for a child. The other one, though, the other one has a face as pale as whey and hair the colour of a hardened conker, waist-length and poker-straight, with an untrimmed fringe she can barely peer out from.

'Blimey,' says the other one, and, sharp-elbowed, nudges the Child, as if she might not have seen, might not already be staring, mouth catching flies like an imbecile.

Well, they'll put a stop to that sort of gawping soon enough, she tells herself, and steps forward onto a hideous pink rug, catching the faint taint of vomit as she does so. She steadies herself imperceptibly, holds out a hand. 'You must be –' she takes another breath – 'Sadie,' she says. 'I'm Mrs Earnshaw.'

The Child nods, struck dumb it seems.

The other one, though, is nothing but words and all of them awful. 'Blimey,' she repeats. 'Blimey, Sade. It's yer nan.'

Sadie

Leeds, August 1981

'If you died, who'd have me?' Sadie'd said one day.
    'Why?' replied her mam. 'What are you plotting?'
    'Nothing . . . just . . .' She couldn't put her finger on it, still less say it, but the worry lurked, squatted inside her, a small thing, but grim all the same.
    'Well I'm not going to die, so it doesn't matter,' her mam had said, and put on some Dusty, then danced her round the front room so she was dizzy enough to be sick.
    Only she had, hadn't she? She'd gone and died without deciding.
    And so she don't have a choice.

Sadie's not taken with them as much as mesmerized, this Nanna and Grandad – though she's not to call her that, got to call her Grandma, the lady said. There're a lot of other things she's not supposed to say either, but she's forgot them already so strange is this day. This week, even. Though even 'strange' don't quite cover it. It's almost like she's watching herself from outside in. Like she's in a TV show or out on stage like Mam. Only without the swank and the sparkle and the songs. So that this girl, sitting here in the hotel dining room at the white-clothed table on the wine-coloured banquette, with the silver salt shaker and the no ketchup, don't seem entirely right, entirely Sadie.

'Don't you like your chicken?'

She starts, stares up at the lady then back at her plate, at the chunks of pale meat and pool of congealing cream sauce flecked with . . . something. 'It's got bits,' she says.

The lady takes in a breath sharp and hissy as a spit, but the man touches her arm and she snaps her trap shut.

Sadie wonders what were going to come out.

'You're probably not that hungry, are you?' says the man. The Grandpa.

She shakes her head, glad of the back-up. Though rightly it's a lie. She could murder a Wagon Wheel or a bag of crisps. Prawn cocktail, preferably.

'Perhaps you'll feel better at breakfast.'

'It's included in the room,' says the Grandma.

'Breakfast is in the bedroom?' she checks, 'cause that sounds better. How she and Mam liked it, when Elvis were away, which were half the time. Propped up in her bed, Mam with her tea and cigarette, and her with her Frosties.

But the man shakes his head. 'Free, she means,' he says. 'There's everything, as well. Eggs and bacon and sausage—'

'Bernard!'

The man's face goes pink and sickly. 'Oh, gosh . . . I mean . . . I'm sorry. Here.'

He hands her his napkin, and Sadie takes it 'cause what else is she supposed to do? Only she don't need it. Not as

56

if she's likely to cry at a word. Or at owt really. She's still not sobbed, not proper. Welled up a bit. But if she clamps her teeth tight and her fingers in her fists it bobs off soon enough.

'It must . . . It must all be a shock,' says the lady. 'A horrible shock.'

Sadie nods. 'Aye,' she says, for politeness as much as anything, because the Grandma is right la-di-dah, as Deborah would say. Had said, in fact, when they'd gone upstairs to fetch her bag.

'She don't look like she's yer mum's mum,' she'd added, voice fat with practised suspicion, eyes widening for effect. 'What if she's not?'

'Not what?' asked Sadie.

'Not yer grandma, duh. What if they're strangers going to kidnap you for yer money?'

'I an't got any money,' Sadie'd said then. 'Only two pound seventy left from my birthday. Do you think they'd want that?'

'Probably not.'

Deborah's right though. She don't look like Mam. She don't look like a grandma at all, still less a nanna. Nannas are fat and happy and permed, and this one don't even have grey hair. It's pale and pleated and pulled so tight she don't look like she can smile. Her voice though – the la-di-dah – she can just about hear Mam in it. The way she says 'bath' like it's suddenly got itself an 'r' in the middle. 'Pass' and all, as in salt and pepper. Sadie tries it out for herself then. Says 'barth' under her breath.

'Pardon?' says the lady.

Sadie snaps up. 'Nothing,' she says. 'I were just . . . the bath.' She says it right this time. Normal.

'Barth,' says the Grandma again. 'You can have one when we get back to Harlow. It's bedtime now.'

Sadie checks Elvis's watch. 'It's only just gone seven,' she says. 'I don't go until half eight earliest, not in the holidays.'

'Well, we've got a long journey tomorrow,' says the Grandpa. 'Several hours. More if we stop.'

'Aye,' says Sadie.

'Yes,' says the lady.

Sadie frowns. 'Yes?' she repeats.

'Exactly.'

Sadie's not sure what that's all about, but before she can question anything, like the possibility of pudding, her plate's been taken and her chair yanked back and then she's off along the claret carpet, scampering to keep up with the Grandma.

It's only nine o'clock, the sound of the town and the staying-up sunlight sneaking in through a chink in the curtain making it impossible to sleep. Her face is tingling and all from where the Grandma was at it with a damp flannel, so hard she thought her skin might slough off and leave her skull bare for all the world. Perhaps she thought there was something stuck on there. Perhaps she thought the freckles were dirt or worse. 'Ow,' she'd said in the end, and the woman had stopped at that, and Sadie had stood on tiptoe and looked at herself in the mirror, seen her face pink and glistening.

'Clean as a pin,' said Sadie. Because that's what her mam always said. Well, not always; just when she remembered to do things like wash faces. Then she'd smiled, because smiles were catching, according to her teacher Mr Wilkinson, who smelled of aftershave and dog and always asked after her mam.

But maybe the Grandma was immune, because she dropped the flannel in the sink and disappeared back into the bedroom, and by the time Sadie had had her wee and flushed and washed her hands and flipped the light off and on and off again, just to see how long it took, and got back into the bedroom, she was under the covers in the furthest away bed, with orange foam in her ears and her eyes shut.

She'd crept along to her corner after that, taken out her treasure – her elasticated snake belt, red and white; her three I-Spy books: *Number Plates* and *Garden Wildlife* and *Sea Creatures*; her Whimsey goat; her pine cone, still rattling with seeds; her commemorative wedding coin she'd queued behind Deborah for; her dictaphone, batteries missing – lined them all up on the bedside table, and counted them. Then she'd got into bed as well and burrowed under the covers so only her face peeked out. Ten seconds later, the light had flipped off and she heard the Grandpa murmur. 'Night night,' he'd said. 'Sleep tight.'

'Make sure the bugs don't bite,' she'd replied without thinking.

She thought she saw him smile at that, caught off her, after all, so he can pass it on to the Grandma, one bed over. But maybe it was just in her head. Wishful thinking.

'Grandma.' She says the word then, whispers it, rolls it round on her tongue to test it, taste it, see how it feels. It feels weird. Like saying a swear almost, like there's magic in it, and power. She wonders then that she never heard it on her mam's lips. Though perhaps her mam never had a grandma. Though Sadie hadn't thought her mam had a mam either and look what had turned up.

Her stomach yawns noisily, unfed since a ham sandwich at lunch and a Mivvi on the wall while they watched the bigger Mehta boys play cricket. She wishes she'd taken the biscuits Donna had tried to press onto her, but the Grandma had hauled her off before she could snatch them. Still, there's breakfast. 'Comes with the room,' she says to herself. Then she squeezes her eyes so tight there's only blackness, pulls the sheet over her ears to block out the sound and smell of them. And she tries to sleep.

What little she gets is fitful, adrift as she is on foreign waters. Her head awash with dinner-with-bits, with the rasp of the flannel, with the snores of the man, so uncanny she feels seasick, as if what little chicken she did get down might decide to make its way back up her gullet at any minute. But she can't have that, so at 4.14 her hand has to grab at the Whimsey and cling to it, to the ceramic goat that's both raft and rudder to steer her back to safe harbour. When she wakes, it's still gripped in her fingers, and slippery, so she wipes it on her nightie before she packs it away with the rest of the treasure and gets herself dressed for the breakfast that comes with the room.

In the end she manages a slice of toast (brown not white, because the Grandma said it were better) but she don't know what to make of the grapefruit, grilled like a kipper, and ignores the orange juice and all, filled as it is with more bits. But it's all spit-spot quick and then she's being told to 'try for the lavatory' before she's strapped in the car, her bag in the back.

'Are we to fetch the rest of it?' she asks the Grandpa, as he fiddles with the ignition – a word she's learned from Elvis along with 'gasket' and 'crankshaft' and 'Christ-on-a-bike'.

'The rest of what?' says the Grandma.

'Our stuff,' she says, matter-of-factly, thinking of her Puffin books lined up on the shelf, the shampoo and toothpaste, the dresses crammed into the cupboard on the landing that Mam said she'd inherit when she'd grown a bit and got boobs.

'I don't—'

'Of course,' the Grandpa butts in. 'We'll stop off on the way.'

'Good heavens. Whose is that?'

They're in the kitchen, staring at the hair that's furred on the lino in dandelion clocks.

'Donna's, I s'pose,' says Sadie. She'd not even noticed it before, so used to it was she. 'Well, not Donna's. Mrs Fazackerley's, I reckon. But Donna did it. She's a mobile hairdresser.' She says it carefully, trying to dust it with glamour and ambition like Deborah does.

The Grandma don't see the coating. 'But why is it here?'

Sadie grimaces. 'The van's broke and her drains have gone.'

And the Grandma don't have an answer for that, so they get on with the business at hand – picking and packing – but not too much.

The Grandpa does most of it – only he goes in Mam's room and comes out with no more than a box, tops it up with the bits and bobbins from the drawer where he'd lived himself, hidden inside a passport, till just days ago.

Something in Sadie slips. 'Is that it?' she says. 'Cause it don't seem right that that's all her mam amounts to. Not when she spilled over the edges of life like hot milk: messy and sticky and visible. Where're her dresses – peacock-bright and cut low so the tops of her boobs show 'just enough'? Where're her shoes – stacked and stilettoed, patent leather as polished as glass, so bright so you could see your knickers in them, she'd said, though Sadie had never quite managed it? Where's the bittersweet smell of her? The smell of cigarettes and Impulse and the metallic tang of a licked penny? That last were the smell of the supermarket, she'd said, the smell of real life bringing her down. But she washed it off of an evening, sprayed on her glitter and shine and went out to dazzle all the same. Where's all of that?

Then she sees it, gleaming in the dimness of this situation like a diamond that's rolled off a ring: it'll be 'cause it's only for the moment. 'Cause Elvis'll be fetching her, bringing her back here, and then it'll all carry on like it did before. Well, not exactly the same. She's not stupid. But still recognizable, with a rhythm: she'll go to school – secondary now, walk there with Deborah – and after she'll make the tea – fish fingers and chips or, if they're feeling fancy, a Crispy Pancake and vegetables – and she'll wait for Elvis to come in with a box of something that's been hawked down the Mitre: desk fans or foot spas or even a dog. Yes, that's what'll happen, she's sure of it. Can feel it in her waters, like Mrs Fazackerley always says. And glowing with it, she picks up her suitcase and the cat along with it.

'I don't think so,' says the Grandma, face like she's chewing lemon pith.

'But it's Not Even Our Cat,' says Sadie.

'Well, if it's not even your cat, then it's certainly not coming.'

'It's a he not an it and he's ours now. Well, mine,' she corrects herself. 'He just come in one day off the street, bold as you like, and sat on the mantel. Then Elvis come in and said, "You got a new friend, Sadie? What's he called?" and I said, "He's not even our cat," and Mam said, "That's a bobby dazzler of a name," and so there you are.' She can see the Grandma doesn't agree. 'I've got a hamster too. Want to see?'

'Not really.'

'He don't bite.'

'Doesn't.'

'Exactly.'

The Grandma sighs. 'What's that called then? Not Even Our Hamster?'

'Don't be daft. It's Dave.'

The Grandpa laughs, a short snorting sound that makes the Grandma twitch and stiffen.

Sadie shrugs an apology, though she's not entirely sure what's she's said or done. 'It were that or Jesus, and Mam said she didn't want the flaming saviour in the house, not even if all he did were spin on the wheel.'

'Lord help us.' The Grandma pats her forehead with a hankie. Perhaps she's ill. 'Cause the Grandpa puts his hand on her shoulder then.

'I don't think we can manage the cat,' he says. 'But a hamster wouldn't be too much trouble.'

Sadie thinks about it, weighs it up. A cat for a hamster, a hamster for a cat. One out of two's not bad and Donna'll feed him, till Elvis comes back. Till Sadie comes home. 'He's at Deborah's,' she says finally. 'Shall I fetch him?'

The Grandpa nods, and off she bobs, out the back door and into the ginnel, to fetch her pet and beg a favour.

The Grandma's still not happy though. Says he'll have to travel in the boot.

'What if he can't breathe?' says Sadie. 'What if he gets scared?'

'It's a hamster, not a human,' says the Grandma. 'And it's not even awake.'

'He. But what if he wakes up and it's dark?'

'Then he'll think it's night-time,' says the Grandpa, leaning over her to buckle her in.

Sadie smiles back at him. 'Or a power cut, perhaps?'

'Exactly,' he says.

'Bernard!' snaps the Grandma.

'Coming, dear,' he says, and settles into his own seat,

slams the door with a clank, sealing them in with the smell of tacky plastic and air as thick and hot as soup.

Sadie's not happy at being strapped down, truth be told. She don't normally have to be, not in the back, any road. Elvis's van she's up front, high and mighty and queen of the road, he tells her.

'How long till Elvis gets me?' she says then. Best to check, after all.

But no one answers. Perhaps they've not heard her.

'Elvis Jenkins,' she carries on. 'He's Mam's boyfriend and he's the North of England's foremost Elvis impersonator. His real name's not Elvis, it's Daffyd, but he says no one wants to see a King of Rock and Roll called Daffyd, so he's kept it for always.'

She can't see the Grandma's face from here, but her voice is scrinched. 'Mrs Maltby said she hadn't got hold of him yet.'

Mrs Maltby is Donna, she knows that much. But why's he not answering?

The Grandpa catches her eye in the rearview mirror, his all wrinkled, hers squished in a frown. 'A caravan park's no place to stay,' he says. 'Not at your age. Not . . . given what's happened.'

Something fractures. She frowns. 'Elvis said it's got a shower with a toilet in it. Like actually *in* the shower. And there's a swimming pool.'

'Still,' says the Grandpa.

The Grandma says nowt. Not even a 'We'll see', which is her answer to everything else, and Sadie feels a pip ping into her gullet, hard and sore and stuck. She swallows once, then again, but still it won't budge. So she tells herself something good instead. That Grandpa don't mean for good. Just till Elvis is done at the caravans. Till the holiday's over and the season is finished and everyone has to go back to real houses and real lives. Normal things. Then he'll get her. Even Deborah said so, when they'd said goodbye. They'd not hugged – though Donna'd kissed her forehead so she'd had to wipe off the scarlet and the spit. But Deborah'd given her a packet of pink Hubba Bubba and her rippled hairband, the latter just for lending, she'd said, 'Till you get back.' So there you were.

The Grandpa starts the engine, not coughing and barking like Elvis's van but low and rumbling – the fat purr when you press your head to a cat.

'Wagons roll,' he says, almost a shout.

The Grandma jumps. 'For heaven's sake, Bernard!'

But Sadie catches his eye again, and this time he winks. And a wink is a kiss and a secret and a promise and all. Her mam told her that.

And she takes that promise and pops it in her pocket along with the pine cone and a photo of Mam she's nicked from the fridge. Then she watches, nose pressed to the window, as Leeds – as her life – marches past in a steady cavalcade: Mr Mehta's on the corner with its Royal Wedding window and display of buckets and spades that Elvis said were mental and Mam said were at least 'optimistic'; the gates of her primary school, padlocked for summer, though she can see in the field some boys with a ball – the

Hendersons, she reckons, Kevin and Dane, one taller, one wider, but both annoying; the Morrisons where her mam sat and rang up packets of ham, Battenburg cake, a slice of pie in aspic. Until the redbrick terraces, the ginnels and snickets, the mica-flecked tarmac that Mam said was diamonds, are small as toys, then nowt but pictures, flickering in her mind's eye.

Then, puff! They're gone.

Connie

Leeds, January 1981

They're eating tea – Bird's Eye fish fingers, peas (frozen, not tinned, some still determinedly hard) and disappointingly flaccid carrots – when Elvis comes in, a box on his shoulder that promises the world but will deliver, she suspects, substantially less. Though Sadie's not so cynical.

'What've you got?' she calls, mouth gaping so Connie can see that a wodge of masticated fish sits unswallowed on the pink of her tongue.

'Sadie, please don't talk with your mouth full,' she tries.

'Sorry,' says her daughter, who swallows, then turns back to Elvis. 'But what is it?'

'Here.' Elvis plonks the box on the table, sending cutlery clattering and the salt cellar – 'borrowed' from Frank's Cafe on Roundhay Road – skittering off and onto the lino, where it spins like a top for a moment before coming to a clunking stop against the cat, who howls and shoots into the front room.

'Really?' Connie picks it up and slams it back down.

'What's got yer mam's goat?' says Elvis, in mock horror.

'Peas,' says Sadie knowledgeably. 'They don't cook as quick as tinned.'

'Peas,' repeats Elvis. 'Well, you won't be wanting peas when you see this.' And he opens the box, dips in his hands and, like a conjuror with a white rabbit, pulls out a tall white plastic thing, with a sort of slot in the front.

'What's that when it's at home?' asks Sadie.

'SodaStream,' he says, like he's announcing the FA Cup draw.

'What's one of them?' asks Sadie.

'Makes fizzy drinks,' he says, like it's flaming obvious. 'You fill the bottle with water and flavoured syrup, slot it in, and then the button adds the bubbles.'

'How does it do that?' Connie peers at it, unconvinced.

'How the hell should I know? It just does. Got a dozen more in the van and another hundred where they came from if we want them. Jimmy reckons we'll make a fortune.'

'It doesn't even say SodaStream.' Connie is still inspecting the gadget, handling it like it might go off at any moment. 'It says "Fountain O'Fun".'

'Well, we'd not make anything flogging off the real thing, would we?'

'So it's knock-off.'

'Identical copy.'

'Knock-off.'

'I don't mind what it is,' Sadie interjects. 'Can we use it? Does it work? Can I fetch Deborah? She'll go mental when she sees it.'

'Go on then,' he tells her, and she's off like a rocket, never mind her plate's still half full.

'Elvis,' she begins, but he's already sat down, shovelling in Sadie's leftovers.

'See they've charged the Ripper,' he says, mouth as packed as Sadie's was.

She looks away. 'I know.'

Donna had come over earlier, said they should open a bottle, celebrate being safe again, celebrate Deborah and Sadie being able to play out till all hours, blessed relief that would be come summer. But she'd said she couldn't, was off the drink for a bit.

'You had five Bacardis last night!' Donna had squawked.

'Cutting down, then,' she'd replied. 'And anyway, it's not even four yet.'

'Never stopped you before.'

'I know.'

'Oh, wait. You're not . . . ?' She'd winked then, her crisp claret-coloured hair tilting with it.

'Not what?'

'Up the duff!' Donna had yelled.

'God, no.'

Not a chance. Not even with Elvis begging. She'd stuck to her guns with the condoms and had got a chart in the back of her diary as well, days when she might be ovulating marked out in red so she knew to have a headache, just in case the thing slipped off, or had had a pin stuck in it. She knew a woman that'd happened to in Wales: Scary Leslie. Got a kid with a spastic boot nine months later and the husband had left her anyway in the end. Be easier if Elvis just left now, did the dirty for her. Not that she's not got reason. But telling him . . . What if he flies off the handle? Flies at her? She can't have Sadie seeing or hearing that.

God, she's already knocked her thighs on furniture enough times, walked into enough doors that Sadie suggested padding things with the roll of insulation foam Elvis had brought back from the Mitre's refit and which is now propped up against the stairs.

'Stranger danger.'

'What?' She comes to.

'You want to be drumming that into Sadie: steer clear of dodgy men.'

'But he's in prison.'

'In general, I mean. There'll be others. That's why it's good I'm around. Man of the house, and all that. Keep the weirdos out.'

Then, swift as a hit and just as stinging, she slips back to another house, another man, his breath mint-tinged, his clothes fresh-laundered. 'Not always strangers,' she says. 'The danger.'

'What's that meant to mean?'

Back again, she looks over at him, Bird's Eye's finest poised at his lips like a cigar. 'Not you,' she says, quick.

'I should bloody hope not.'

No, Elvis wasn't a Ripper, wasn't bad as that. He had his black moments, his slapping. But he wasn't downright dangerous.

Was he? No.

But nor was he the knight in shining armour she'd fallen for two years ago.

He'd promised so much up on stage at the Adelphi – rhinestones and glitter and trousers so tight you could see the shape of him, the heft. But like most things round here, that was only for show. The reality is an occasional day job in long-haul and a more frequent but even less reliable one selling tat off the back of lorries with Jimmy King. The back room's already piled high with it: calendars with a month double-printed, jigsaws with pieces missing, foot spas that don't heat up or else boil your toes. 'We'll make our fortune, babe,' he always said, like some downmarket Dick Whittington, seeing pavements paved with gold where others saw dogshit and ringpulls. But that was on the good days. On the bad he'd rail against the forces that kept him back: his dead parents, the government, and her, most of all, with her class, her inheritance.

'I haven't got one,' she'd tell him.

'But you're posh,' he'd slur, her chin in his hand, her back to the wall. 'Listen to yourself. You don't come from nothing with a voice like that.'

She didn't bother telling him he wasn't the first to be busy with his hands, that the accent was practically slapped into her, that Harlow was no different from Leeds or Llandudno, just a bit newer.

She thinks of it now – the houses, compact and concise; the parks, expansive and bland; the dreadful cement. So much cement. Or is it concrete? Is there a difference? Christ, why is she wondering about concrete? Though perhaps concrete was the point. The great leveller, her father had called it. You could build palaces out of it, he'd claimed. Not that they'd managed a palace. Everything was so small and self-conscious; even the skyscraper – The Lawn – had been eclipsed in a matter of months. Gibberd's ambition tempered in the end by the constraints of the council, the small minds of locals and the pay packets of London's slumpoor. No wonder her mother had hated it – like saving up for a lifetime for a ballgown only to be able to afford a pair of beige slacks from Marks.

The thought of the woman plucks at her, a band of elastic snapping round her aorta so she is rendered breathless and faint.

Again.

She'll make that appointment in the morning. Has been meaning to all week. And then that'll be another ticked off her list, along with the cutting down on the booze, and the better food and the vitamin C – the glass bottle of orange discs sitting smug on the Formica; one a day for all of them, not including Elvis. Though he'd taken three anyway, claiming he was bigger and needed more, making Sadie spit out her own in laughter then claim another one as that had got cat hair on it from the stray that hadn't shipped out yet.

The back door bursts open then, Deborah leading the way (as always), no matter it's not even her home, her dad, her machine to be tested. 'Show it us!' she demands. 'Can I go first? Have you got Coke?'

'Hold your horses,' Elvis says, though he's doing no such thing. He's up already, rummaging in the box for the accessories, pulling out two packets. 'Lemonade,' he reads, 'or Irn-Bru.'

'What's iron brew?' asks Sadie.

'Disgusting is what,' says Deborah, ever the expert. 'We'll have lemonade.'

Connie watches as he faffs with the packets, sets up bottles, sends water fizzing all over the kitchen and the girls, squealing only half in surprise, the other in sheer delight at the attention. Not even caring when the final result tastes more like medicine than lemon, when it's about as sparkling as week-old tonic.

Fortune, eh? she thinks, but doesn't say, not this time.

No, he's not terrible. But still, something's to be done.

Doctor tomorrow, and then, next, Elvis.

Another two ticks off the list for her, almost as satisfying in the thinking as the deed.

Jean

Leeds, August 1981

The hum and rumble of the Vauxhall Viva threaten to lull Jean into slumber and she pinches her thigh to snap herself out of it. Sleeping in a car is on a par with eating in the street or passing wind in public (or, frankly, at all). No matter how little one has managed to snatch in the night. No wonder her head is skittering from this to that, then to now, her heart with it, tip-tapping far too up-tempo.

It's not grief. Can't be. Grief, she thinks, is all-consuming, debilitating, and she has no time for that, hasn't the stamina, has chased it away after that initial blip. No, it's the oddity of it all. This thing in the middle of them. The Child in the back of the car, the stranger in bed in their room last night.

She'd not slept with a child in the room since Constance turned six months, when, on the advice of both Barbara Collins and Dr Spock, her cot was moved to the back bedroom, yellow-painted, and away from the road, though not, sadly, from the Nesbits' wretched dog, barking at the moon and the sun besides, sending Constance into a frequent and appalling caterwaul. This child was quiet at least. So quiet that at one point she found herself checking for her breath above Bernard's awful snore. But then the Child had rolled over, muttered something about dust, and, irritated at her own worry, Jean had turned to face the wall and listed kings and queens instead. Fat lot of good that did.

Perhaps she had managed an hour, but then, some time around seven, Bernard had coughed, ending with that infernal goose-honk, and of course the Child had woken and after a wee and a glass of water the endless questions had begun their steady stream.

'How old are you?'

'How tall are you?'

'What's that thing on your cheek?'

By heaven, she was brazen. When Jean had let her hair down, the Child had admired it. 'You should wear it like that,' she'd said. 'It sets off your face right nice. Some people say old ladies shouldn't have long hair but I say do what you fancy.' Bernard had laughed at that, while she'd shut herself in the bathroom to finish off her business.

But in the car there was no escape from it.

'But why isn't there a funeral?'

'Not everyone has a funeral.'

'Even my hamster – not Dave, the one before that, Elsie, she were ginger – even she had a funeral.'

'Was ginger.'

'Was ginger. And Julie Newman at Number Four, her uncle Malcolm died and she missed a whole week of school to go to Florida for it. Deborah says, anyway.'

'Well, this is different.'

'How is it different?'

She'd clammed up at that, waited for Bernard to step in. Which, reliable, dependable man, he did.

'Maybe later we'll have a memorial. Of sorts.'

'Will we?' The Child spoke for her, words that hammered at her mouth, but she could not let out.

'Maybe,' Bernard confirmed.

'When? When Elvis is back? He could sing at the service. Julie Newman said her uncle Malcolm had a male-voice choir at his. They sung "My Way" and "Bread of Heaven" and "Bohemian Rhapsody". It were quite the send-off . . . *was* quite the send-off.'

Say something, Jean wills him, her fingers gripping the rim of her seat.

'Well, perhaps not "Bohemian Rhapsody",' he obliges, touches her thigh, stiff and stockinged. 'How about we talk about it another time?'

But even that isn't an end to it. The Child really is tireless.

'When we've got the ashes back?'

'Maybe then.'

'When will that be?'

'A couple of weeks or so.'

'Can I come?'

'I don't think so.'

'But what if they give you the wrong ones?'

'They won't.'

'Deborah – she's the girl next door. She said her mam Donna's friend's cousin got given the wrong baby at the hospital and they never knew for four years. Four years!'

That is it. 'Bernard, can we please stop at the next services? I think we could all do with . . . stretching our legs.'

'Aye. I'm bursting for a wee as well.'

She counts to three, breathes, smiles. '"Need the lavatory" would have sufficed.'

They stand, side by side at the filthy sinks, Jean's face fixed in the mirror, the Child's on the floor.

'Are they orthopaedic?' she asks.

'I beg your pardon.'

'Your shoes.' She nudges one with the toe of her flat sandal. 'Are they orthopaedic? Jason Prendergast has got orthopaedic shoes. He's got one two sizes bigger and a limp and all.'

'Who's Jason Prendergast?'

'He's in my class. He sits next to John Two. John Two is better than John One. John One once weed on the electric and had to go home.'

She has a brief urge to smile, but then a woman two sinks down sniggers and Jean feels her cheeks pinking. 'Well, he's not in your class anymore.' She turns, grabs at the greying hand towel. 'And in answer to your question, no, they're not. They're just sensible.'

'Oh.' The Child wipes her hands on the back of her dress. 'Mam says life's too short for sensible shoes.'

Jean, checking her hair, stiffens at the same time as the mirror-Child's mouth drops open and for several seconds they stare at each other, Jean willing herself not to crumple, not to reach out and clasp the Child to her, not to weep, be weak. For what does weakness get you but another pile of problems?

At that, something in her rights itself. 'If the wind changes, you'll stay like that,' she says, matter-of-fact. And, one last pat of her pleat, she straightens her skirt and walks off to wait outside.

They are more than halfway home now, trundling southward, the Child with her head hanging out of the window like a dog. She'd told her not to, then, when that fell on deaf ears and Bernard's indifference, that she'd regret it when a lorry came the other way and knocked it clean off. But the Child said she'd see it coming so not to worry.

Not to worry.

Well, she was trying. Though, honestly, the Child has less sense than her mother. But at least half as much guile, judging by the way she'd persuaded Bernard to move the wretched hamster to the back seat at the last stop, so that now she can smell the must of it, hear its scratching and scuffling whenever they run over a bump. How long do these things even live for? A matter of months, surely. Then the cage can be packed away along with the box in the boot.

She has no idea why Bernard would insist on bringing all of . . . whatever it is. Essentials, he said. Paperwork and personals. Though how he could discern 'essentials' in the mess and spread of that disordered drawer, the clogged-up top of the wardrobe, was a mystery. That house. She shivers when she thinks of it. It reminded her of a Hieronymus Bosch picture she'd seen in a magazine once – the product of a diseased mind.

Perhaps, she thinks grimly, Constance's mind *had* been

diseased, along with her heart. It was certainly as if Jean had taught her daughter nothing. Or perhaps Constance remembered everything and this was revenge. Spite. Yes, she wouldn't put it past her. Although the Child insisted most of the claptrap belonged to this Elvis person. Though what on earth he thought he was going to do with a dozen broken foot spas and several incomplete jigsaws of the Bay City Rollers was anyone's guess. And probably not even legal. Even his name was absurd – the sort of awful thing Americans go in for.

Perhaps *he* was revenge as well. And the cruellest kind – class. Because God and Constance both knew how long Jean had spent escaping it.

She smells it then, the stale air of the school dinner hall – meat and gravy and sweat – four hundred girls crammed in tabled ranks, clattering plates and clinking glasses as if they're debs in Dior and Jacques Fath, not first- to fifth-formers in box-pleated pinafores. But that's the cleverness of it, the trick – because, in here, a dinner girl, stuck in front of the custard, ladle in hand, might listen in to the clip of their vowels, the cadence of their sentences, the cut-glass tinkle of their contrived laughter. She may lack their grades and their banker daddies, but if she is a fast learner, if she practises her pronouns and politesse as assiduously as she does her nightschool typing, she might find herself elevated to the giddy heights of Islington Town Hall, assistant to the clerk, no less. The kind of girl one can rely on to file precisely, to flatter a manager, to flaunt, even, to a client.

But while the men willingly bought it – even Bernard at first, though he'd found out the truth soon enough – the women were less persuaded, still treated her as if she said 'blimey' or worse. As if her upbringing had left an indelible smear on her forehead, marking her out as common. Because they knew where she'd come from, of course. Knew her feckless father – a man who plunged in and out of work like a gull on the water – her slovenly mother, her brother Gerry with his habits.

That was the thing about class. It was wily. Conniving. It trapped you. Chose you for its team at birth and refused to relinquish you to higher leagues no matter how hard you tried or well you played. The astonishing unfairness of it once rinsed through her like salts. Still chills her if she dithers and dawdles along the path to the past. Which is precisely what she is doing now. Honestly. What is wrong with her? It's sleep, or lack thereof. She'll be better once she's rested. Better tomorrow. And with that thought tangible as the tissue gripped in her fingers, she tunes back in to the back and forth banter between Bernard and the girl.

'Why'd you stop working?'

'Because I'm old.'

'How old?'

'Sixty-five.'

'Blimey.'

'Precisely.'

'Are we nearly there yet?'

'Yes. Nearly home.'

'It's not home. It's Harlow.'

'Well, it's my home. And yours –' he pauses – '. . . for the moment.'

'Why's it called Harlow?'

'It's Old English. Ancient, really. It means hill of rocks.'

'That don't sound very nice. Anyway, if it's a new town, why didn't they pick a new name?'

'There was an Old Harlow there long before the new town was built. That's the bit we live in.'

'Still. There's got to be better names than Hill of Rocks. I bet I could think of one.'

'Go on then.'

The Child begins a roll call of ridiculous suggestions, miller's daughter to his Rumpelstiltskin.

She'll never guess it anyway. Who could, when faced with the concrete sprawl before them? But back then, Bernard was convinced and so she was too. At first it was to Italy he turned – sculptures scattered about the market and parks and water gardens as casual, as integral to the architecture as the Trevi Fountain to Rome. But then his vision had burgeoned along with Gibberd's ambition. And she sees him slip then from this sixty-five-year-old man in his slacks and Sunday shirt to one half his age and suited and already a town clerk. Sees him standing, his hands spanning the heft of his desk, his eyes wide and smile guileless. 'Listen to this, Jean,' he'd said to her. Then read: '"There will be opportunity for everyone – for the housewife and the business manager, for the factory worker and the schoolteacher – to contribute."'

She'd looked back at him blankly, which he'd taken as a nod to go on.

'"It will be large enough to support the social and

educational services, yet not so vast that the individual will be lost in the mass."' At that he'd paused, as if for applause.

'What's that then?' she'd asked eventually.

'It's the Harlow Town Plan. That place in Essex I was telling you about. Remember?'

'It sounds like communism.'

'Oh no, Jean. Not quite communism,' he'd said. 'It's Jerusalem. It's our new Jerusalem.'

And so high on it was he, as if imbibing the very ideas had left him punch drunk on possibility, that she felt giddy with it too. 'Our?' she echoed, a question.

'I'm going to head up the management committee. I start next month. In Grosvenor Square at first, but I'll move eventually, of course. When the houses are built.'

Utopia, he'd gone on to call it. Paradise just twenty miles from Plaistow.

Folly, she'd thought, or told herself – a mirage in a desert. Who'd move to Essex, anyway? The transport was notorious and the landscape flat and mostly farm.

But then he'd asked her if she'd consider it – just as his assistant, nothing more implied – and, for a minute, so glittering it seemed reflected in his eyes that she almost said yes on the spot and had to pinch herself and tell him she'd think about it.

Of course she'd turned him down, at first. Because two nights later there'd been the promise of somewhere else – Paris, no less. The great white city. And how could Harlow compete with the tree-lined Champs-Elysées? The glass-domed Galeries Lafayette? The pleasant Seine, its banks littered with picnickers? Of course Paris had been the bigger folly. The pie in the sky. Wretched French, she curses to herself now – even now – then apologizes.

But it wasn't Jerusalem. It wasn't even close. Paradise for years had been a view onto wasteland and building sites. And when it was finished, its tower block topped – the first in the country – its pastures lacked livestock, its England's valleys green were all engineered, and littered now with tin cans and cigarette ends and teenagers doing God knows what.

But still, here she is. Here they are, in fact, trundling along Mandela Avenue towards Mark Hall Moor.

'Blimey. What's that?' comes the voice from the back.

'It's a church,' says Bernard.

'It is not.'

'Oh, it is. Really.'

'It looks like a flaming spaceship.'

At this, Jean coughs, a hasty segue from a snort of laughter, astonished to find she agrees. Because she's always thought it a monstrosity. Eyed it snidely, Constance as slack-mouthed as the Child is now, as brick by glass brick it was thrown up on the grass. What must God have thought looking down on that? Same as her, she expected: a travesty. Blasphemy, almost.

Not that Bernard agreed.

'Our Lady of Fatima, it's called. Its spire had to be lifted on by helicopter. Imagine that.'

'There's a girl in my school called Fatima. Fatima Brown. She once ate a frog. Not even a dead one. It were . . . was only little, but still.'

Class, she bristles again. Fatima. Deborah. Elvis. No, the Child is better off without. Better off in Harlow. A fresh start.

But immediately she reels. Because now she's talked herself into a trap. Boxed herself into a corner, and a job besides. A colossal one.

'Are we nearly there yet?' asks the Child.

'Nearly there,' confirms Bernard. 'Nearly there.'

Sadie

It weren't the longest she'd been in a car. That were four years ago, after Wales but before Leeds, when they were bobbing between there and Manchester, depending on jobs. That summer her and her mam had gone with Honest John – with his swagger and his one-eyed dog – all the way to Southampton to catch a ferry to the Isle of Wight, which she'd been disappointed to learn weren't even a foreign country. Only there'd been a row in a Little Chef about something or other and Honest John had driven off before she'd even got her lollipop for finishing her beans on toast. He'd come back five minutes later, but that was only to chuck their bags out in the car park. They'd hitchhiked home – in an egg lorry and then a Hillman Hunter that smelled of lemons. They'd had to get out of the egg lorry somewhere near Nottingham because Sadie had thrown up her beans on toast, once in a plastic bag and once on the floor. Then out of the Hillman near Sheffield because the man put his hand on Mam's leg instead of the gearstick and she slapped him and called him a 'dirty old pervert' and he called her a 'filthy little slapper' and that was that. They'd finished the journey on the back seat of the bus, and that was when Mam said she was done with Manchester and with men. And she'd stuck to the first at least.

Sadie'd felt sick this time too and the Grandma said it was because she hadn't listened when she'd told her she shouldn't have had ice cream in that pub, and the Grandpa said, 'Do you remember Constance being sick on the way to Windermere?' But the Grandma hadn't seemed to hear him because she was scrabbling for a bag – a British Home Stores one – which she made Sadie hold in front of her 'just in case'. But the Grandpa said actually she should sing something to take her mind off it, so she did. She sang 'Son of a Preacher Man' and he joined in and all.

The Grandma didn't though. Perhaps she didn't know the words.

Sadie weren't sick in the end but she weren't allowed a packet of Spangles when they stopped at the services for a wee neither. After that it'd only been an hour and then they were there.

Here.

And here is weird.

Not bad weird. Just weird. For a start, it's mainly grass and gardens. And the houses aren't stuck together, all matching like a string of paper dolls; they're mainly in pairs, just holding hands, or out on their own, even. There's no ginnels, no snickets, no undies like bunting strung from lamp post to fence. There's no Mehta's on the corner, no Donna-Next-Door, no Deborah. There's no—

'Come along.'

Sadie, only half out of the car, starts, snaps her head back round to the Grandma, chivvying still, always.

'Come along,' she repeats.

Sadie turns to the Grandpa, unpacking the boot.

'Go on.' He nods. 'I'll be in in a minute.'

So along Sadie comes, up the path to the grey-painted, stained-glassed front door, breath held as if she's about to enter an enchanted forest, or haunted castle, or Narnia perhaps. The key clunks and the handle clicks and Sadie says 'open sesame' because that's what she's always done – what they've always done. Only this time it's silent, to herself, because she's pretty sure the Grandma already thinks she's soft in the head.

And then – abracadabra! – they're in.

Only it's not Narnia, nor Aladdin's cave. It's not even Leeds. It's the wrong side of the wardrobe. All odd and solid. Like a doctor's office or the town hall. Mam's friend from work Big Sue got wed to Fat Alan from the bookies in the town hall. Everything there were mahogany-glossed. Everything there were neat and gleaming. Everything there looked expensive and all.

Although 'everything' is too big a word. Too portly. Because truth be told it's awfully bare.

There's no knick-knacks. No porcelain dolls or floral saucers. No spoons from the seaside. Nothing taped to the fridge. There's not even any photos save one of the Grandpa and a tall man in a suit.

'Who's that?' she asks.

'Prince Philip.'

'What, the actual Prince Philip?'

'Yes, the actual Prince Philip.'

'It never is.'

The Grandma gives her a look. The sort Mr Wilkinson did when her and Deborah got caught doing their routine in the junior loos.

'It absolutely is. Why on earth would we have a picture of a . . . a fake Prince Philip?'

Sadie shrugs. She has a point. 'What's he doing with Grandpa?'

'He was opening something. The market, I think. It was years ago.'

'Did you meet him? Did the Queen come? Did you meet her and all?'

'"As well" not "and all".'

'As well,' she repeats carefully. 'So did you or didn't you?'

'I don't remember.' And that is the end of it, and of the snapshots. Though Sadie reckons there must be albums somewhere. In a row. Identical. Maybe she'll find them later. If she has time. Before Elvis fetches her, that is.

Upstairs is as strange a landscape as the kitchen and sitting room (not a 'front room', because it's not in front and we're not in the North anymore). No pictures save a sewn square of Binca saying something about God behind glass. And Sunday quiet. As if the whole house is dead or hollow somehow.

'Whose is that room?' she asks as they pass the master, door ajar, on the landing.

'Mine. And your grandfather's.'

Sadie risks a quick glance and pulls a face. What grown-ups sleep in single beds except for the Fawltys? Mam always slept in a double with Elvis. Except when he'd had too much beer, or she had, and one of them had started in on something like getting wed or not, or moving south or not, and then he slept on the sofa. And in Wales everyone had slept together in the barn, or in a tent in summer. That was all hands in faces and a tangle of legs; too many nude people and too much farting. Horrible oniony trumps. Sometimes she woke up with Eoin Heffernan directing his bare bumhole right in her face, or his stink-filled fist ready to give her a gypsy's kiss.

She don't miss Wales much. Nor London before that, with its cold and coal bunker and outside lav. Swimming with worms and patrolled by spiders, it smelled of pee and Kleeneze and worse if Desmond or one of his mates had been in before you. But the inside one had no door and no knowing who might walk past while you were getting down to business, so better risk the creatures and the heave of faeces than that.

Faeces. That were a good word. A Mam word.

'One day, we'll have a gold toilet,' she'd said. 'And someone to wash off faecal matter and wipe our backsides besides.'

'And there'll be gold taps,' she'd joined in.

'And a marble sink.'

'And beds made of marshmallow so we can eat in our sleep.'

'And our own stage with footlights and a glitterball and all the seats packed every night.'

Then they'd moved to Leeds. It weren't exactly the palace she'd imagined, the one her and Mam had gilded and tasselled and dropped an observatory on top like a cherry. But she'd had her own room for the first time. There were no farts in her face. And she could poo in peace and all.

'Here we are. It's . . . It was your mother's.'

Mam's room. When she was a girl. Well, this is it, she thinks. This is where she'll stumble upon the treasure chests and jewel boxes and photo albums and all. And she pushes through the doorway like she's been queuing for tuck, bursts in with a practical 'ta-dah!'

Then stops, disappointment solid as rock cake. 'Where is it?' she asks.

'Where's what?'

'Where's . . . my mam's stuff?'

Where's the rest of the Whimseys she'd talked about? The chequered bedspread with the cherryade spill? The pictures of Mick Jagger and Jimi Hendrix and weird Syd Barrett, the bit where their lips were worn out with kissing?

'It's . . . Well, it's a spare room now.'

'Here.' The Grandpa's appeared, like Mr Ben, as if by magic. Hands her her bag. 'Why don't you unpack, and perhaps we can find some things to brighten it?'

The Grandma does that look at him but he don't register or don't show it.

'Can we?' she asks.

'Yes,' he says, still oblivious. 'Sometime.'

'Sometime when?'

'Sometime soon.'

Then they're gone, bickering on the stairs in hissed whispers and then louder in the kitchen, all 'why on earth did you say that?' and 'why on earth shouldn't I?' and 'she's a child, for heaven's sake'. Which is weird, because the sound should be muffled like it was in the old house, like it's wrapped up in scarves, only here it seems to funnel in all crisp. Then she sees it, where it's coming from – a grille on the floor with a lever to open and close it. She lies down then and listens hard, ear pressed against the strips of metal so they dig into skin. But they've stopped, for now any road. So she gets back to her bag, to the unpacking.

She puts her Scooby-Doo nightie on the bed; her yellow dress and elasticated snake belt, red and white, over the back of the chair; two T-shirts, three skirts and six pairs of knickers in the top drawer. Then lines up on the windowsill her I-Spy books, her Whimsey goat, her pine cone, still rattling with seeds, her commemorative wedding coin she'd queued behind Deborah for and her dictaphone from Elvis, no batteries. The photo, though – of her mam – the photo needs somewhere better, needs pride of place. But there's no drawing pin and, anyway, they're bad really, Mam had said, as she'd pushed another one into the woodchip. Leave holes for things to get in.

But she has a plan, takes out the packet of Hubba Bubba Deborah gave her, sticks a pink wad in her mouth and chews determinedly for several minutes until it's ripe. Then she takes it out, pleasantly wet, and sticks the picture to the wall above her bed.

'Come along!' she hears from the hole in the floor.

And she thinks for a minute, then kisses the picture – not wetly, like her mam kissed Elvis, or like she'd kiss Bobby G if Deborah would let her. But full of love all the same.

Then she sticks her nails into her palms to stop any weird feelings from brimming – her mam taught her that and all – counts her treasure, and bobs downstairs to see what the Grandma wants.

Connie

Leeds, February 1981

She hadn't made the appointment in the morning. Truth was it had been nearly a month until she'd got round to it – there had been shifts in the way, then a gig in Wigan that she couldn't turn down, then she'd caught Sadie's cold and she didn't want to pass that on to the pensioners who lurked in the waiting room as if it was God's own. But she's here now, isn't she? Wedged between a Pakistani with a wet cough and Mrs Higgins from Number 11, who's already edging away from her, mouth pursed, as if she might be harbouring the Black Death or, worse, something venereal.

'Miss Holiday?'

Connie looks up. The receptionist, scrawny and bored, is staring at her. She stands. 'It's Ms,' she says. Then, seeing the receptionist clearly at sea with that, adds, 'Never mind,' and scuttles into the surgery, feminism shelved for convenience, for a quiet life, as it often is these days.

'So, Miss –' Dr Potter, an overweight locum approaching retirement, with the protruding bottom lip of a petulant child, peers at her notes – 'Holiday?' he finishes. 'Unusual name.'

'Like Billie,' she explains. 'Or Golightly. And it's "Ms".'

'I beg your pardon?'

Honestly, how is she supposed to smash the patriarchy when they're deaf as well as uncultured? Or just plain brazen, like Elvis. Germaine didn't have any advice for that. 'Never mind,' she says. 'It's not important.'

'Not from round these parts, then.'

She frowns.

'The accent.'

He can hear some things, then. 'No,' she replies. 'Not originally. Harlow,' she adds. 'You won't know it.'

'New town,' he counters. 'Essex. Strange place. All those housing estates and statues.'

Against her will, she bristles, though she's said it herself often enough. 'I suppose.'

'So, Miss Holiday. How can I help you?'

She takes a breath, tells him about the uncanny hammering in her chest, the strange fainting. 'It's probably nothing,' she adds at the end. 'Exhaustion, my friend thinks.' Actually, Donna'd said 'knackered', but that sounded even less technical, or treatable.

'And is your friend a medical practitioner?'

'No,' she concedes. 'Mobile hairdresser.'

'Right, well, let's have a listen, shall we?'

He gets out his stethoscope, checks her chest, checks all sorts, the majority of it not warranted she suspects.

'And you're eating properly?'

'Yes.' She is, as well. Had Steakhouse Grills the night before, and the potato wasn't even Smash.

'Drinking?'

95

'A bit. The odd glass.' Or three, or four. But nothing like New Year's Eve, despite Elvis's attempts to get her to stray, telling her to 'lighten up', to 'get one down' her, to 'have some bloody fun for once'. No, she's sticking to her resolution this time.

'And nothing as a child?'

'No— Yes. I mean, I fainted once or twice. But . . .'

But her mother had dismissed it as attention-seeking, a sign of moral weakness somehow. Her father had worried though, suggested a check-up, and so she'd been marched, red-faced and protesting, to see Dr Beston, with his too-thin nose and too-thick glasses and certificates on the wall just in case you thought he might be a fraud.

'Iron,' he'd concluded. 'She's feeble.'

'Feeble?' her mother had repeated. 'Hardly.'

But, her mother's doubt notwithstanding, she'd suffered liver for tea twice a week for a month after that, the tubes snapping elastic in grey, grainy flesh, all of it swimming in thin gravy. So when she'd fainted again a few years later – coming off the train from school – she'd kept it to herself, begged Martha not to blab, for fear of suffering another stint of offal hell.

Dr Potter doesn't think it's anything as simple as iron though, nor Donna's 'exhaustion'. 'I'll book you in for some tests,' he says. 'At the Infirmary. Though there'll be a waiting list.'

'How long?'

'A couple of months, I should think. Four, five tops.'

The band around her relaxes. 'So it's nothing urgent, then.' Can't be, or they'd be rushing her in, wouldn't they?

'Probably not.'

And 'probably not' is as good as a no, isn't it? Better than 'possibly' at any rate.

And she's singing as she walks back down Roundhay, turns left onto Adelphi Terrace, clatters through the front door.

'Where've you been?'

'Nice to see you too,' she tells Elvis as she hangs her coat on the hallway hook, curtseys in her supermarket uniform. 'At work.'

'I thought your shift finished at four?'

'I was only chatting,' she makes up quick.

'Charles and Diana are getting wed!' Sadie blurts through a mouthful of baked beans, the juice spattering the stolen salt and a bottle of brown sauce. 'Deborah said her mam said it was on the news! She'll be a princess and everything.'

'Another leech on the little people.' Elvis spoons beans onto a limp slice of white, pushes the plate into her place.

'Thanks,' she says, sits herself down. Though truth be told she doesn't fancy it. Fancies a gin. A celebration of 'probably not'. Probably she'll pop round Donna's in a bit.

'Did you hear, Mam? There'll be a royal wedding.'

'Not with your mouth full.'

'Sorry.' Sadie swallows. 'Can we watch?'

'No,' says Elvis. 'It only encourages them.'

'Christ!' She glares at him, turns to Sadie. 'Of course you can, love.'

'I thought you hated them and all?' Elvis is pointing his fork at her, accusing.

'Why would you hate them?' Sadie's genuinely perplexed. 'Have you seen her hair? Deborah's getting hers done like it. Can I?'

'No. Maybe. I don't know.' She wants to tell Sadie that her father met one of them once, shook his hand before he cut the ribbon at the Harlow market. She can't remember it herself but he'd said she was there, must have been. Though what's the point with Elvis here? He'd only mock, scoff, call her stuck-up. Besides, the less she says about him – them – the better.

'I don't hate the royals. I think it's . . . nice.'

'Nice?' Elvis scoffs, stabs a bit of sausage. 'Flaming hell. You'll be saying Thatcher's not so bad next.'

She flinches, treads on eggshells. 'Not nice then. Just . . . I don't know.'

'You said Thatcher was a breath of fresh air,' says Sadie to Elvis, her memory elephant-like, and her feet just about that size as well. No eggshells for her. Yet.

Though Sadie wasn't wrong. He'd backed her – Thatcher – when she'd stood, said she was the only one who gave two hoots about the people like him, and her as well: the little people with big dreams, the entrepreneur, the entertainer. Wasn't she only a grocer's daughter herself? And now look at her. Least she's got ambition.

But now he's embarrassed, fidgeting in his hollow on the sofa. 'Bollocks,' he says.

'Her hair's mental,' Sadie points out.

And no one can disagree with that, so for a brief moment, order is restored. But then—

'You could get married. Couldn't you?'

Connie drops her knife with a clatter. 'What?'

'Not "what", "pardon",' says Sadie. 'Mr Wilkinson told us. And I said you could get married.'

Connie glances at Elvis, sees his eyebrows raised, his smug air of expectation. 'I don't think so,' she says.

'Why not?' she asks. 'I could be your bridesmaid. And Deborah.'

'Yes,' adds Elvis, a level of threat detectable. 'Why not?'

'I . . .' She scrabbles for something, anything but the truth. 'I don't believe in it,' she manages. 'It's just a bit of paper.'

'No it in't,' says Sadie. 'It's a party with a dress and a cake and everything.'

'We can have a party any time if that's what you're worried about,' she says.

'Can we?' Sadie asks, successfully diverted. 'When?'

'I don't know. For your birthday?'

'Or for yours,' says Elvis, his smile slipping into a leer. 'Thirty. Big one, after all.'

Christ. That's all she needs. 'Thanks for reminding me,' she says, then smiles, quick, so he knows it's a joke. Then, to Sadie's 'Can we, though, Mam?' offers a 'Maybe.'

Satisfied for now, Sadie's back to her beans, and then on to *Corrie*, her perennial obsession, her and Deborah as wrapped up in the intricacies of Deirdre Langton's love life as Donna is in Betty Chiswell's from Number 15.

But Elvis isn't so easily distracted.

*

'We could get married,' he says later, in bed. Then, when she looks at him like he might as well have slapped her, adds an angry, 'Why not?'

She turns away, takes a breath, tries for humour. 'Not much of a proposal, is it.'

'Oh, so it's the ring you're wanting, is it, Miss Fucking La-di-dah? The bended knee?'

'I'm not la-di-dah,' she says. 'I don't need anything. Why would we, anyway? Not like we've got parents to please.'

'You could please me.' He pushes into her, laughs, throaty and filthy. A laugh that once sent her spinning, begging for him, but that now leaves her, not even cold but the opposite: hot with something – shame, perhaps, though if it's at him or herself she can't yet tell.

'Not now,' she says. 'I'm on.'

But he's not budging. 'You were on last week.'

'It's still here.' She flings the covers off, swings her legs out of bed.

'Where are you going now?'

She pulls on her Morrisons overall for want of something closer. 'I need a glass of water,' she tells him. 'That's all.'

But it's not water that's in the glass on the kitchen table. And it's not a shopping list in the red Silvine notebook either.

Whatever love means, she writes.

Prince Charles had said it on the telly. The reporter had asked if they were in love and Lady Diana had blushed, simpered, said, 'Of course.' But Charles had replied, 'Whatever love means.'

And she realizes as she writes it that even she doesn't know the answer. With Sadie, well, that's different, a given. Not like her own mother, who had not one jot of maternal instinct or, if she did, kept it squashed down or stoppered. But Elvis? Love? Not now. Not anymore. Perhaps it would come back if she gave it a chance. Perhaps it just needs her to pay attention. She's been occupied, after all: with turning thirty; with clutching at London – her last-chance saloon; with just the day-to-day drudge of everything that eats away hours like they're minutes, minutes like they're seconds.

Or perhaps it was never love in the first place. Perhaps it was just lust. Or not even that. Just a childish need for attention, for someone to tell her she was sexy, clever, great on stage; or for a spare parent, for someone to pay half the gas and electricity, to boil up beans when she's on shift, to fill some space.

Christ, is she that shallow?

Irritated, she flicks back to the first page, scores a triumphant line through *Doctor – make appointment*. Then lets her biro – a new blue bookie's number, replaced within a day – hover over number seven: *Elvis*.

Ten seconds later, she drops the pen, downs the dregs in the glass.

Well, one in a day isn't bad. Yes, one is enough.

For now.

Jean

Essex, August 1981

It's hellish, all the questions.

'What was she like when she was four . . . five . . . my age?'

'Did she have her hair plaited?'

'Did she drink milk?'

'Did she sit in this seat?'

'Did she have jam or Marmite?'

'Did *she* eat brown toast?'

'But *why* is white bread wrong?'

Query after query, all probing, prodding, picking, until memory lane – once a dead end, its gutters thick with dog mess, 'Here Be Dragons' slung across its bollards along with a nice red no-through-road sign – is thrown open and the memories march through fast and hard and breathing fire.

Memories of the adolescent, sullen and troubled, slinking about the house like a guilty cat, or raging at whatever was on offer that morning: the Church, the 'Man', the dying of the light. Memories of the pre-teenager, that irritating sing-song imitation of something she'd heard around Michelle Spencer's on that infernal pirate radio. Pirate radio, indeed.

She'd imagined a ship full of terrible men with rum and cutlasses and had been almost disappointed when she'd seen their photograph in *The Times*, lined up with their long hair and necklaces and ridiculous grins. Though she knew they were no less menacing for it.

Better are memories of the child, puppy fat and pitter-pattering along the corridor, following her like a dog. Obedient too, or mostly. But then regret threatens to inch its way in through the chink and so she has to slam the door, barricade herself against this snakeish danger. History, she thinks, is best confined between the pages of books or at most on television. But then the next volley comes rattling out and the defences are breached once more, this time with snapshots, perhaps, of times before Constance, before Harlow, before she was Jean, even.

'Why's that thing on the landing say "Margaret" on it?'

'What thing?'

'The Binca with the God cross-stitch.'

'I—'

'Who's Margaret? Is Margaret *your* mam?'

She stiffens, snaps. 'No!' Then, embarrassed, backtracks. 'Sorry. It was . . . someone else. And please try to say "mum". We're not in Leeds anymore.'

'Mam's Welsh, not Leeds, but sorry anyway. What was your *mum* called?'

She cannot complain. She set this up. 'Joyce.'

'Did she make you eat brown toast?'

'What?' She forces a smile. 'No.'

But in through the crack it comes, as clear as if it were

being screened in colour in front of them: her with her hair pinned and her lips crimson as the girl's on the Coty counter; her mother, face grey as ash and painted with a sneer. '"Margaret", I ask you. That was your father's idea, not mine. Got it off a novel. Should have flaming stayed there. Given you airs and graces it has, ideas above your station. You should have been a Rita or a Shirley like Betty's eldest. Nothing of the fancy-pants about her. No pie-in-the-sky inklings in her head.'

But that wasn't why she changed it. Or not only.

That was down to *him*.

'*Comme la princesse*,' he'd said to her. '*Ma princesse*. My Margaret.'

So she couldn't keep it, could she. She couldn't keep hearing *him* whenever her name was called. Hoping it was him. Hating that it wasn't. Then praying she never heard it again.

Not that 'Jean' wasn't without incident.

'I've just realized,' Bernard had said, the day after the wedding, their bed at his parents' slept in but unsullied, because she wasn't doing *that* in hearing distance of anyone. 'You'll be my very own Jean Harlow. My own painted lady.'

At that she'd smacked him. Then sobbed and said sorry, sorry, she didn't know what she was thinking. Said sorry to God as well later, begged his forgiveness, not for the first time and certainly not the last. Because she went on saying sorry every Sunday, adding Constance's shortcomings to her own.

This is why the Child can't stay long term. She may be less . . . garish than Jean imagined. Bright enough; kind, even. But hadn't Constance managed that when she wanted something? Before she descended to begging, and then to threats. She couldn't . . . wouldn't go through that again. She can't be saddled with another litany of sins. There'd already been the incident with the gum.

What had the Child been thinking? Well, she hadn't, had she. Plainly.

At least she'd put an end to that: bubble gum was banned, also chewing gum (yes, any flavour), and any sweets not bought by Bernard or her, and she had better not get any ideas about that because it would be once a week on a Saturday and depending on behaviour. And then, inspired, she'd drawn up a list of things not to be brought into the house, begged for, or preferably indulged in at all:

* gum of any kind
* crisps and biscuits
* television, unless suggested by an adult, and in any
  case no more than an hour an evening
* further to the above: no soap operas, nothing
  American and no Thames Television
* Radio 1
* Ribena
* dogs.

The Radio 1 for obvious reasons, the Ribena because it stained, the last because there'd been an incident yesterday when next-door-but-one's German Shepherd 'Nelson' (whose name she couldn't even begin to deal with) had been off its lead – why exactly was anybody's guess, because she'd suggested several times the folly of this – and the Child had lured it onto their lawn where it had proceeded to defecate merrily. In the end, Bernard had gone out with a carrier bag and a shovel, which she'd made him disinfect, twice. Though he'd then refused to take the carrier bag round to the Starlings' and instead had left it in their own dustbin, where no doubt it would begin to smell, what with the heat and it being several days off bin morning.

But not even the list, written in ink, not biro, to be typed as soon as practicable, could prevent the endless questions.

'Why's the roof come halfway down the house?'

'It was designed like that. The Canadians like it.'

'Why've some houses got garages *inside*, like under the bedroom?'

'To save space. You should really be asking Bernard . . . your grandfather about this.'

'But he's still in the bathroom. He's been ages. He probably needs to eat more prunes. That's what Deborah's dad has to do, otherwise he can be bunged up like a clogged drain, specially after he's been away and only eating junk for months.'

'That is quite—'

'Why's the heating in the floor?'

She counts to three, takes a deep breath. 'Hot-air vents.'

'But why?'

'I . . . I don't know,' she admits, realizing it only now. 'It was quite the thing in the sixties. Bernard liked it.'

So had she, back then. With Bernard so endlessly zealous

in his preaching about the appeal of this new Jerusalem, this tomorrow's world, it was hard not to be caught up in his enthusiasm and she had at least appreciated some aspects. The sheer cleanness of it all. No clanking radiators, no coal fires belching out smoke or spitting out embers that snapped and crackled and caught on the carpet, or the bottom of overalls if her father was slumped too close.

The newness of it too. Nothing here had been junk-shop bartered. Nothing hand-me-down, half-used-up or on its last legs. Everything was fresh, she'd insisted on it, brought up from London because the shops here had yet to be built. The Pyrex from Debenhams, the cutlery too, twenty-four pieces with extra for best; the shelving hand-made by his father, though she'd have preferred shop-bought of course; the toys – a plastic zoo complete with fencing, a trolley with blocks, an abacus – all from Gamages, long gone now. And everything clean, neat and efficient. Like Bernard himself.

Of course it had all proved too good to be true. Cracks had appeared in the drawing-room walls as the newly used ground shifted along with the seasons; the heating was belligerent – failing to fire up some mornings on nothing but whim; and several pieces of Pyrex had been broken or lost or, worse, taken to the garden and used to brew mud into 'magic potions' with that dreadful Michelle. And the lack of privacy was another matter. People peering over the back fence, or wandering across the front lawn because everything was so open. 'Democratic', Bernard had called it, 'encouraging discussion'. Well, she didn't want to discuss anything with Michelle's mother and told him so, but he'd shrugged and said others loved it, as if she were the aberration, the odd one out.

Even after they'd moved into the old town, the difficulties persisted. Yes, Michelle had been downgraded thanks to distance and the rigours of Constance's public school time-table, but the new house turned out to be jerry-built in places and still they'd been lumbered with these wretched grilles in the floor that meant tempering everything in case *someone* was earwigging. Of course, she'd have to start worrying about that again now, wouldn't she.

'Can't I have cereal instead of toast?'

She comes to, concentrates. 'We don't have cereal.'

'We've got muesli,' says Bernard, back from the bathroom, his red face betraying his endeavours. Really, human bodies were repellant. All the secretions and excretions and smells. It would be better if everything were just absorbed properly. Now, that would be efficient. She wonders that God hasn't managed it.

'What's muesli?'

'It's like cereal but it's got raisins and things in it. Hang on, I'll fetch it.' Bernard scuttles off before she can tell the Child to make do, is back within seconds – a jiffy, he'd have it – with the packet and a bowl, which he's filled without being bidden.

'Oh, you mean Alpen.' The Child's face falls.

'Oh dear,' says Bernard.

Oh, for heaven's sake. 'What's wrong with Alpen?'

'It's just . . . It's that—'

'What? What is it?'

Startled, the Child stares at her, spits it out. 'It's 'cause Mr Angelou, who was this man that lived above us in the flat in Manchester, he kept his wife in an Alpen box. Dead Beryl, she were called.'

'Don't be absurd.' She cannot be hearing this.

'I'm not!' the Child protests. 'The urn broke 'cause his cat knocked it off the mantel and the Alpen box was the only thing he had big enough. He'd tried a Nescafe jar but she wouldn't fit in.'

There is silence then, sticky and thick, but she will not be the one to break it. She will not concede defeat. Instead, she picks up the milk – silver top now that Bernard has to be careful – and pours it into the bowl until the muesli is swimming. Then holds out the spoon.

'I'm not that hungry anymore,' says the Child quietly.

'Nonsense. You were hungry a moment ago. And besides, it's poured now and wasting food is a sin. Think of the children in Africa.'

'Jean,' Bernard tries.

'What children in Africa?'

'The orphans. They're starving. They'd be glad of Alpen.'

The Child is louder now, defiant. 'Well, they can have it, then.'

Her nerves are taut as nylon line. 'Really!'

'Jean,' Bernard repeats, a warning now.

'What, Bernard? What is it? Do you think this talk is acceptable all of a sudden? Just because . . . Just because . . .' But she can't say it, can feel herself teetering.

Bernard sees it. 'Here,' he says, taking the bowl from the

Child. 'I'll have that. Better for the bowels,' he adds, as if anyone wants to hear it.

The Child slips him a grin, which she pretends not to see. Instead, she stands, sending her chair scraping. 'I'll see you later.'

Bernard, a spoonful of strangely grey muesli hovering mid-air, frowns. 'Where are you going?'

'Work, of course.'

'Yes, but . . . I thought Maurice had offered you a fortnight off to . . . to adjust.'

'I don't need to adjust,' she says, carefully, measured. 'And anyway, *Mr Collins* needs me. Half the staff are off on annual leave and the accounts won't file themselves.'

'Don't worry,' says the Child, clearly to Bernard. 'We'll be all right. I know how to make beans on toast and spaghetti hoops on toast and cheese on toast and most things on toast, actually.'

'Well, I look forward to that,' Bernard says, and smiling at her, then Jean, swallows his muesli.

And, just like that, they're a pair.

And she's the odd bobbin, all by herself.

Sadie

Essex, August 1981

The most astonishing thing, Sadie reckons, is that every time she wakes up, her mam is still dead.

She'll slip from a dream into neverland, that in-between place that cushions you from truth, then her eyes open and for a second, just a second, she'll expect the clatter of pans, or the tinny sing-song of Radio 1 as she peers in the mirror, or the open-throated holler of her in the makeshift shower. Instead there'd been Deborah's cheesy feet in her face, with the broken toenail and two verrucas and all, or Donna with her sniffing and cigarettes, and now the Grandma with her fidgeting and her frowning and her back-of-the-cupboard smell. And Sadie's body will slump, shrink into itself as if remembering that there's a bit missing, that there is less of her now. Less Mam. Less Sadie.

It's been a week and it hasn't lessened – the sting of it. The crisp disappointment every time she sees the Grandma beaking in at her, or yanking back the curtains and sending neverland packing. Still, least she's got the photo, sitting on the sill in the silver frame now. The Grandpa did it for her after the hoo-ha with the Hubba Bubba. She'd said she was only trying to save the wall from pinholes, but the Grandma wasn't having it, and to be fair it did take half an hour and a packet of frozen peas before the pink could be chipped off.

She weren't happy about the frame but Sadie placated her. 'It's all right,' she'd said, 'you can have it back when I'm gone.'

The Grandma'd gone odd at that and all though, disappeared off and written out her list of things Sadie weren't to do. *No crisps, no sweets, no TV* kind of thing. The crisps she can live without, just about, for the summer anyway. Soon as she's back home, there'll be a packet in her lunch box every day if Elvis has owt to do with it. The telly thing is tricky though. She's not allowed *Coronation Street* 'under any circumstances', even though Deirdre and Ken are off on honeymoon and Fred's just stormed out the Rovers. There's something about Ribena and all. Or is it fizzy pop? Maybe it's both, but anyway they're bad and banned and so are dogs and cats and any creatures that belong outside, which is all of them aside from Dave, and even he has to live in the utility room on top of the washer, not in her bedroom like before. 'It's the carpet,' the Grandma had explained. 'I don't want it ruined.' But how is he going to do that? His poos are hard as pavement – you can pick them up with your fingers without flinching, not like dog muck – and he only ever wees in one corner. He's good like that. But the Grandma had insisted and so the utility room it is.

Then, this morning, there'd been the bother with the muesli.

She'd not even asked for it, only what it was, and the next

thing there's a bowl of flaming Alpen in front of her: lumpy ashes swimming in milk. She'd said about Mr Angelou and Dead Beryl – even though those weren't the ashes that were niggling in her, making her queasy like she'd gone over a humpback bridge too quick – but the Grandma didn't get it and had told her to eat up or the black orphans would be sad.

For a moment she'd thought she'd have to do it and all. Shovel in the dust. But her throat had closed and she couldn't swallow, not even her own spit. The Grandpa though, he'd done it for her. He'd eaten the Alpen, every mouthful, even though the Grandma had gone, even though she could tell he were thinking he'd rather have something that weren't so cremated.

'Mam won't come in an Alpen box, will she?' she whispers after he's made her a slice of brown with marmalade.

'No, Sadie,' he says. 'There'll be an urn. A proper one. Unbreakable.'

She thinks for a minute. 'That's good,' she says, and, satisfied, takes a bite of her breakfast. 'Thanks for picking out the pieces of peel,' she adds, her mouth still a bit on the full side.

But he don't tell her off. He smiles and says, 'So, what shall we do today? Harlow is our oyster.'

Sadie laughs then, a blob of orange flying from her gob to the coffee pot. 'Sorry,' she says, wiping it off and licking it quick. 'Mam said that!' she tells him. 'She said, "Where'll we go today, Sadie? The world's our oyster!" Only she meant Leeds, I think, and we always went to Roundhay Park.'

'We could go to the park if you want!' He's seized on it, like it's a diamond when it's not really, only paste, and out of fashion anyway. 'There's swings near the Post Office or over at Mark Hall Moor.'

'I'm a bit big for swings,' Sadie says.

'Of course you are,' he replies, his face a blur of hurt, and she feels sad for him then, like she felt sad for Elvis when he'd brought flowers to say sorry for whatever it was, only they were garage ones, ninety-nine pence from the Texaco on the ring road, and Mam knew it and told him not to bother next time.

'I don't mind though,' she tells him then. 'If you want.'

He shakes his head. 'There's plenty of other places,' he says, then thinks of a list. 'There's the paddling pool. Though that might be a bit too young too. Or the farm?'

'I don't mind a farm,' says Sadie.

'Then the farm it is. Well, it's more of a petting zoo, really. But there's goats.'

'A goat ate my socks once. It was in Wales. A girl called Moon bet me a biscuit that he wouldn't but he did. I got the biscuit though, so that were okay.'

'Moon,' he repeats. 'Well, we'd best keep our socks out of reach then.'

'I won't be wearing any anyway,' Sadie explains. 'Not in this heat. You could fry an egg on my forehead.'

The Grandpa does wear socks. And a proper shirt and trousers and all, though he's taken his tie off this time, which is something. Sadie's not sure what the point of ties is and the Grandpa's none too enlightened either.

'You know, I've never even thought about it before.'

'I have,' Sadie says as they trundle along the path into the new town. 'And handkerchiefs. What's with them? What's wrong with tissues? Who wants snot in their pocket all day?'

'No idea,' replies the Grandpa, pleasingly baffled.

'And see-through knickers,' she adds, warming to her theme now she's got a captive audience. 'I asked Mam why she had them once and she said I'd understand one day, but I won't. Who wants to see your bum crack?'

The Grandpa doesn't have an answer for that, or any words at all, but the quiet isn't so bad, not like the Grandma's, which is tight as a tie round your neck.

'That's The Lawn,' he says eventually. 'First tower block in Britain.'

'Weird name for a skyscraper,' she replies. Though perhaps not, given the green that takes up most of the landscape – so flat and massive it is, she feels almost dizzy with it, like she's stepped off a roundabout.

'Well, it's hardly a skyscraper,' he says. 'Not anymore.'

'I wouldn't mind being up there,' she tells him, 'on the top floor. You could see for miles up there. Probably to London. Even Leeds.'

'Well, perhaps not Leeds.'

She's disappointed at that, the seed of a plan scuppered before she's even given shape to the idea. 'But London though?'

'Maybe,' he says, though she suspects it's mainly to please her. 'So, goats then?'

'Aye,' she replies. 'Goats.'

*

There are seven of them, all with names, though none as everyday as Dave or off the wall as Not Even Our Cat. She misses him then: the pleasant weight of him on her feet at night, the rumble of him when she puts her head to his stomach, the meat smell of his teeth. But the Grandma is adamant he can't come to stay, not even visit.

'Is she allergic?' she asks. 'Is that it?'

'No,' says the Grandpa. Then, smiling, 'Not to animals, anyway.'

'Right,' says Sadie, not sure what to make of that answer, though her mind instantly lists all the other possible things that might give the Grandma hives or even close her throat, like Angela Lamming who got stung by a wasp in the playground and had to be taken to the Infirmary, so red in the face and swollen was she. Perhaps it's wasps. Or crisps. Or *Coronation Street*.

'What now?' asks the Grandpa after they've stroked the goats for over an hour and got evil-eyed by a red-faced boy who's told his mam she's hogging the one called Carnation.

Sadie shrugs. 'I don't know,' she lies, eyeing the swings, not too old after all, it seems, for that flying-high feeling. But she can't say that and the Grandpa won't know it. Besides, he's got something else up his sleeve.

'I wouldn't mind something to eat?' He says it like a question. Not the 'lunchtime sit down hurry up' she's got used to.

It's a weird feeling. Like she's got a say. And she sings with it for a second, the mam in her head saying, 'Should we have chips, do you think? Or perhaps a pie. Your choice, Sadie.'

'I wouldn't mind it neither,' she replies. 'My stomach thinks my throat's been slit.'

The Grandpa laughs. 'Is that . . . Is that something your mother used to say?'

'No,' says Sadie. 'Vera Duckworth.'

'Oh.' The Grandpa frowns. 'Is that one of your neighbours?'

'No,' says Sadie. 'But I think you'd like her.'

For lunch, they go to Masons' Bakery and order baguettes as big as her forearm. They can choose anything from the plastic tubs as a filling, so she picks egg mayonnaise and Branston. The Grandpa says it might not taste right and Branston's for cheese really, but she tells him about the time Elvis Jenkins had it on his breakfast when the brown sauce was gone, and also how cheese on digestives is better than you think. But the best bit is that he gets them crisps and all – prawn cocktail for her, plain for him, which she don't see the point of really, but she don't tell him that.

'Don't tell your grandma,' he says.

'I won't,' she says, ripping open the pink packet and licking the inside. 'I know which side my bread's buttered.'

'I've never understood that,' he says then. 'Isn't it obvious from just looking?'

'Me neither,' she admits. 'But I like how it sounds.'

'Me too,' he agrees.

She rips his packet for him and offers it up to lick, but he says he'd better not, so she has his crumbs and salt and then pops both in the bin and wipes the evidence on her backside.

But that's not the only secret.

'I got you something else,' he says when she gets back. Hands her a postcard.

It's the alien church. Our Lady of Fatima.

She thanks him and nabs it, not minding the smudges of crisp grease she's leaving because she knows Deborah won't either.

'I thought you could add it to your collection,' he explains. 'The pine cone and whatnot.'

'Oh,' her voice slips along with her spirit.

'Unless you've someone to send it to?' he adds quicker than a wink.

'It's not that I don't want to keep it, just that—'

'I've an idea,' he interrupts, full as a balloon with something. 'Don't move.'

He's off again to the shops, and for a minute she hopes it's another packet of prawn cocktail, but what he comes back with is better: another postcard, matching; a pen – a blue Bic, the see-through kind she likes; and a stamp.

She writes it out in best, though it's hard given the questions and that she's got to pop the address on and all. But she manages it somehow, only one line curving round a corner and up the side like it's gone for a wander. *Can you tell me what's gone on on* Coronation Street? *Thank you. This is my address underneath. See you soon!* She pauses, then adds a *Wish you were here!* down the other side, like Elvis did that time he was in Morecambe and Mam said, 'A likely story', but smiled anyway.

They drop it off in the Post Office itself, because she

reckons it'll be quicker that way, even though the stamp is first class, which she's not seen before except the ones her mam steamed off bills when the postmark had missed. 'Do you think I'll hear by Friday?' she asks as they walk back along Mark Hall Moor and under the main road. 'I should have asked for weekly ones. Like a regular newsletter. I could check the *TV Times* I suppose, only I 'spect you don't have that because of no Thames. Why don't she like Thames? We don't have Thames, we have Yorkshire Television back at home. It's all right, you know. It's not dangerous. Well, maybe *The A-Team* is, but not *Coronation Street*. In Wales we didn't even have a telly. Can you imagine that? It's 'cause it might rot your brain, only Mam said it didn't, not really. Not like toffee does to teeth.'

'Is that why you left Wales? The television?'

'That and the lentils. And a man called Wigan Mick, I think.'

She's still chat-chat-chatting like a jackhammer when they round the corner to Fore Street, then onto The Green, turn up the drive, the gravel slipping in the sides of her sandals so she has to stop and shake it free while the Grandpa goes ahead and unlocks the door for them.

That's when she sees him – a boy, her age or thereabouts, sitting on his Grifter, his skin dark as Jimmy Mehta's and his hair better than Elvis. And most surprising of all – staring straight at her.

'If the wind changes you'll stay like that,' she tells him.

He freewheels over, leaning back like he's on a hot rod. 'Good,' says he.

'What's your name?' she asks.

'Nirmal,' he says. Then adds, practised, 'Like *normal*, only with an *i*.'

His voice is odd. The accent strange. Not Indian, but not like the Grandma either. Not normal at all.

'Sadie,' she says.

He nods. 'When'd you move in then?'

'I've not,' she snaps back. 'I'm only staying.'

'Lucky for you,' he says.

'Why lucky?'

''Cause at our school they flush your head down the toilet when you're new. It's called a bogwash.'

'They do that at ours too. Least the secondary. Didn't think it were allowed at primary.'

'I'm not at primary,' he bats back. 'Not anymore.' Then tips his head. 'You sound like Cilla Black.'

Sadie flames. 'I do not.'

'Do too.'

'She's from Liverpool,' she snaps. 'Not Leeds.'

'Same thing,' he says.

She's almost glad when the Grandma pulls up in the car. Almost.

'What on earth are you doing loitering out there?'

'I weren't,' she says. 'What's loitering?'

'Lurking,' says Nirmal.

'Wasn't,' says the Grandma.

'Wasn't,' echoes Sadie.

The Grandma turns to the boy. 'And nobody asked you, young man.'

Nirmal shrugs and slides off, legs propelling him along the pavement instead. But before he turns the corner he waves at Sadie, and before she can stop herself she waves back.

'Inside now,' chides the Grandma.

And she don't bother to argue. No, inside Sadie slips, a postcard in her pocket, contraband crisps in her belly and the wave of a boy called Nirmal in her noggin.

And though the Mam-sized gap in her is still fat as a maw, and raw and all – not aided by the telly ban or the fact she can't phone anyone, not even Deborah – the edges of it soften somehow, as if he's a salve, not a nit on a Grifter.

Not a nit on a Grifter at all.

Jean

Essex, August 1981

It is typical Bernard that he would take the Child's side; he always did want to be wanted, couldn't bear to be out of favour for even a minute. Always pandering, conceding defeat without even a parry. She should be unsurprised, then, at this gruesome muesli business. An Alpen box, of all things. What would the poor dead Beryl think? What would God think? She's not even convinced God is entirely on board with cremation anyway, despite the vicar's insistence; it seems rather hellish to her.

But God has been remarkably absent of late. She has asked His advice on a litany of Child-related issues – the hamster, the bubble gum, Elvis Jenkins. But God, she is reminded, does not supply guidance willy-nilly and not for such mundanities in any case, heaven knows, she tried enough times with Constance. No, while God remains her eternal Father, it is a mortal man who has been her guiding light, her shining example.

Maurice Collins.

Maurice will know what to do. Maurice always knows what to do.

And, satisfied, she clicks on the indicator and turns left onto Edinburgh Way.

'Covenanters.'

'Covenanters,' she repeats, as if saying it aloud will suggest its meaning. 'Is that . . . ?'

'It's the new youth group.' He leans back in the swivel chair she ordered for him, filed against income even though leather seemed excessive, wasn't necessary really. 'Terrible name, but Barbara says they're quite dynamic.'

Not the choir, she thinks. He doesn't suggest that for her. And who can blame him? He's probably wondering if theft's hereditary. Perhaps it is hereditary. She should start keeping her purse under lock and key and—

'I really am awfully sorry.'

She starts, steadies herself.

'About . . . well, everything,' he continues. 'It must be difficult.'

He is fidgeting now. Ill at ease. Dealing with feelings is so very messy, she thinks. Especially for a man like Maurice. A man's man. In charge. Feelings are a weakness, feminine. To emote too much is unseemly. Uncouth, almost. Something Bernard has learned.

'It's quite all right,' she says briskly. 'Please don't concern yourself. We're doing very well.'

'You're a friend,' he says then. 'Not just . . . well—'

'Covenanters,' she interrupts hurriedly.

He brightens. 'I'll ask Barbara to talk to you. There's a week, end of August I think. Some sort of camp.'

She nods an acknowledgement. 'I'll have these back to you by lunchtime.'

'Sorry?'

'The Butterworth accounts.'

'Right. Yes. Of course. Thank you, Jean.'

At lunch, she eats her sandwich – cheese and cucumber – on a bench beside the patch of grass behind the Pinnacle building, the malt smell thickening the already clinging air. Perhaps she should have packed the pair of them a lunch as well – the Child and Bernard. He's fine for an egg or some salad, but beyond that his skills are limited, and cheese sandwiches? Well, she's not even sure he could locate the grater. But he was the one who wanted this, she tells herself, let him fend. Let him find out how difficult it is: occupying a child, feeding it, keeping it on some sort of invisible lead.

She wonders, then, if they'll have stayed at home. She hopes so. It's all very well Maurice knowing their business – that is necessity and he can keep his own counsel. But she can do without the Shelley Pledgers of the world poking their noses and wagging their tongues. Lesley Berwick at Number 1 has probably already alerted the Women's Institute via whatever telegraph it is she pressed into service when Gloria Spurling had a lump removed and Carol Morton a prolapse. Really, it was awful knowing these women's every issue, every emission almost. What had happened to suffering in silence? There was a lot to be said for stoicism.

At least the social club doesn't open until five. Darts is the last thing that child needs exposing to, and then there's the risk of crisps. What Bernard sees in the place, she has no idea. No, that's not true, she knows what he's attempting – his great levelling of men, the town-plan promise of classes working and playing side by side. Maurice had the sense to stay away, never mingled with the masses. But Bernard was determined: the architect and his hodmen, having a pint. 'You know they despise you behind your back,' she'd said once.

He'd been hurt. Had shut himself in the shed, up to who knows what. Sometimes you have to be cruel to be kind, she remembers telling Constance.

Two days later, Bernard had taken their daughter down there to watch the wrestling on the television. Two common vulgarities and his greatest act of daring at that point.

She didn't forgive him for weeks.

Still, he's retired now, so perhaps there's no pull anymore. No need. That will be one thing she will not miss. That and the dinners she was bidden to cook: for his deputy, for his secretary, even, once, for Gibberd himself. The days she spent consulting *Good Housekeeping*, Mrs Beeton, and Barbara, besides. For how else was she to learn that boeuf bourguignon was acceptable where hotpot was not; that prawn cocktail was 'the thing'? Until it wasn't.

She misses the manor house at Terlings, of course – the corporation's old headquarters – though that's long gone, sold off like the family silver, then itself knocked down to make way for the future. Cricket on the lawn, she recalls, a garden party with Bernard in shirt sleeves and Constance in a party dress, jam-sticky. This was the world she had drummed up for herself as a child – the numerous rooms, the aproned staff – things she had read about and added to the imaginary inventory, to be ticked off, she was sure, at a later date. And she had, hadn't she? Though she couldn't confess to being that wide-eyed girl, had to pretend it was nothing she hadn't seen before. That she was to the manner born. Manner. Even that she'd got wrong, assumed it was 'manor', only to be corrected by Barbara, who'd laughed – laughed! – at her. As if *she* were a lady. She wasn't. She was from Leighton Buzzard. But she'd been to a minor boarding school and had a horse and a sister called Felicity and so she came with that stamp of approval – no need for check-lists or even aspiration, especially not once she'd got Maurice.

She'd never even worked, Barbara, at least not properly, not to put food on the table, to fill the meter. There'd been an art gallery once, for a month or so, but nothing since Martha. Of course she couldn't fathom why Jean persisted, it wasn't as if they needed the money, she told her over tea (darjeeling, from a pot).

But they did need it. At least then. Or rather, Jean did. Not for her own pocket, but to pay Maurice back for what Constance took. Though he'd never docked her pay for it as she'd suggested – begged, even. Had been affronted at the very idea. Still, penance she saw it as. Or had at first. And a public thing too – for the other mothers who'd ostracized her, whom she was sure saw her as complicit, as guilty by association, by begetting the bad egg and letting it fester; for the fathers who'd lost their deposits, had to dig deep again and spend money they'd eyed for golf clubs, for watches, for holidays; for Maurice, who'd had to change church along with her, who had lost as much as she had, if not more.

So, penance it had been back then, but now it is vital to her somehow. *She* is vital, indeed. An essential pin in the machine, a cog in the clockwork. Pinnacle Biscuits would founder without her precision and efficiency, she is convinced of it and, more than that, so is Maurice.

And, buoyed by this single certainty, she closes the lid of her lunch box, dusts crumbs from her skirt and heads back inside to set the wheels spinning once more.

She is still ticking with it, still forthright, when she turns the Vauxhall Viva onto The Green at 5.22 and finds the Child, unmonitored, on the street – the street! – and talking to a boy of Pakistani persuasion on a bicycle. Or perhaps he's Indian, she thinks, but whichever, he's not English, and not welcome. She's seen him before, trailing round Marks and Spencer (Marks, I ask you) behind his curry-smelling mother, or cruising up and down, up and down on that absurd contraption, designed to look like a deathtrap.

This is the thing – she'd been right that first time, back at Bernard's desk in Islington. It was folly, all of it. They'd wanted to build paradise but then they'd bussed in the slum dwellers, who'd brought with them not only their meagre belongings but their bad habits as well. So that the very people she'd sought to avoid had become her neighbours again.

Honestly, one has to keep up a constant vigil about these

things. Class is like dirt, or, worse, nits: it rubs off, is catching. Avoidance at all costs is advisable and the Child has already had a bad start with this Elvis Jenkins and that Donna-Next-Door and the Deborah girl with her awful cawing.

No, she will see to it that while the Child is here she will be exposed to decent people. Better people. Maurice is right: church is the only thing for it. Covenanters it will have to be – this week away will be character-building and, until then, she can at least mix with children whose parents place an importance on God (the real one) and a value on education. Yes, that friend of Maurice from the council – Bob Watkins – he has a girl. What is she called? Annabel or Isabel or Ophelia? Something ambitious, anyway. Well, Maurice will know. Maurice always knows. She will ask him in the morning. Suggest a get-together at the Collinses. A tea, perhaps.

Yes, that's it. A tea.

'Come along!' she repeats, and then slams the door behind them.

And the relief is as quick and fulfilling.

Sadie

Essex, August 1981

She don't see him for a bit – the Nirmal boy. Not to talk to, any road, though he's up and down and up and down the pavement outside, sending the Grandma into a right tizz about the Highway Code. The Grandpa says it's not as if it's Piccadilly Circus out there, and no one's hurt, are they? But the Grandma says that's not the point and the Grandpa don't reply to that because 'not the point' means it's the end of it.

Sadie says something though. 'Can I go out?' she asks.

'Out where?' asks the Grandma. 'Out to do what?'

Sadie thinks. 'To the park?'

'I thought you were too old for swings.'

She casts a glance at the Grandpa, whom she suspects of betrayal, but he's behind his paper again.

'For the fresh air,' she suggests, knowing the value of this in the Grandma's scale of priorities, along with enough fibre and clean knickers.

'We'll get plenty of fresh air later.'

That 'we' is a wet blanket, a pee on a bonfire. 'Where?'

'We're going out for tea.'

'To a cafe?' Sadie perks up at this, a Knickerbocker Glory

pinging into vision like a prize in her mind, or a rum baba from the Wimpy, sticky with syrup and whipped cream from a can.

But the Grandma frowns. 'Why on earth would you think that?' she demands, as if Sadie is slow-witted, as thick as Louise Hinkley, who still couldn't do her three times table at the age of ten and thought the moon got switched on at night.

'I don't know,' she says, her voice slipping into sulk, though it's not in her nature, not really. Least, not until now.

'Why don't you go and read for a bit?' the Grandma says then. 'In your room.'

The last bit isn't a question or even a suggestion, so Sadie traipses up the stairs, a sigh trailing behind.

It's not as if there's anything good to look at anyway: her I-Spys, *Heidi*, which she's finished twice already, and a dog-eared Oxford dictionary. And you can't read a dictionary, not really. So she counts her things, changes their order, moves the pine cone to the left of the Whimsey and the dictaphone to the far right, at the top of the line. Then, satisfied, she sits with her elbows on the sill, head in her hands, and watches Nirmal: watches him wheel in a figure of eight, graceful as a skater, then skid to a halt, a miniature CHiPs. He looks up once and she waves, but he don't seem to see her, pedals down Fore Street instead and off round the corner, out of sight.

At that she slumps back onto the bed, pulls down the dictionary, after all. Perhaps she'll learn a new word a day to impress Deborah when she gets back, set her in good stead at secondary. Though, according to Deborah, the world there turns more on the stack of your platforms and whether or not you like Madness than on knowing how to spell *minuscule*. Still, there's nowt else to do and so she opens it, sees a silverfish, velvety grey, slip across the pages from *abacus* to *abalone*, then scuttle under to bide its time. She's not scared of insects, not even spiders; caught plenty between a pint glass and a *Racing Post* while her mam stood by squealing. So this one she leaves be, flips forward instead to find something eye-catching, gets that and more. Because some words, she spies, are underlined, in faint pencil that can only be Mam's because who else in this house would highlight *bastard* and *bugger* and *bum*.

There's more and all, a whole lexicon of sex stuff and swearing: clap and fanny, tits and testicles and, best of all, vagina – a womanly word that sounds warm and kind, not at all clinical, she thinks. Deborah's going to go mental when she finds out everything's been sat there all along, all the secrets of the universe in the same book they use to look up how many 'i's in definite and what on earth an aardvark is. She makes a mental note to write to her, but inside an envelope, or maybe she'll save it for September, when she's back in her bedroom, kissing Mike Nolan or him out of Dollar and—

'What are you up to, then?'

She starts, goes scarlet. 'Nowt,' she says, slamming the book shut and sitting up smartish.

But the Grandpa isn't accusing, she sees then, just asking.

'I . . . I was learning,' she adds.

'Well, good,' he says eventually. 'Jean— Your grandma says can you please wash your hands, and perhaps your face, if it needs it.'

Sadie touches her cheek, worried that the *bastard* has stained her somehow, marked her out as wanton or weird. 'For what?' she asks.

'Tea,' he says. 'Remember? We're off to the Collinses.'

'The Collinses,' she repeats.

'They're old friends. Your mother, she knew them too. Their daughter Martha was at the same school, and Maurice . . . Well, anyway. Run along.'

So run along she does, though she's not as swift as she might have been if it was the Wimpy she were off to. But a friend of her mam's can't be all bad. And teas always have some Mr Kipling, or what's the point? And with that thought she wipes the damp flannel round her mouth, switches off the tap and trips down the stairs for fresh air and French Fancies, if she's lucky.

But the Collinses are not what she imagined. And nor for that matter is the spread.

There's cake, but it's got bits in and isn't for mains; you've to have savoury first, which is hard-boiled eggs with yellow paste like Vesta in instead of yolk, and triangles of bread spread with fish paste and meat paste and something called tongue.

'What's tongue?' she asks.

The Grandma frowns. 'It's tongue.'

'Yes, but *what* is it?'

132

'Tongue,' repeats the other woman, pink-cheeked and sheeny, with the air of a pig.

'Yes, but . . .'

She looks to the Grandpa for help. He sticks out his tongue. Wiggles it.

'Oh.' She puts that slice back, decides to stick to the meat paste; you know where you are with that 'cause it comes in glass jars. And the tea, though that's mainly milk from the look of it. But no matter, she tips herself another cup.

'Oh, Sadie!' the other woman – Mrs Collins – calls out. 'You've forgotten the strainer. There'll be leaves!'

'Oh.' Sadie sets down the pot, puts its cat-shaped hat back on. 'I don't mind. Besides, you can read it after.'

'Read it?' Mr Collins peers at her – he's been doing that all afternoon, though this is the first time he's said anything.

'Aye – I mean, yes. You can read your future in the tea leaves. Like horoscopes, only every day. Twice, if you like.'

'That's nonsense,' says the girl next to her. Not Martha – she's not even here – but another one called Olive Watkins who's eleven as well, but clearly thinks she's sixteen, so much does she know about church and the world. Though mainly church.

'It's not nonsense,' Sadie says. 'Mrs Fazackerley – she comes for a shampoo and set on a Thursday – she reads leaves. She'd do Mam's and it were always the same – a tall dark stranger. Only Mam said no thanks, she already had one of them, because of Elvis. And Donna said he were strange all right. And Mam said too right.'

She waits for the laugh, like everyone did when Donna

said it, only all she gets is looks, and black ones at that.

All except the Grandpa.

'So did she read yours?' he asks. 'Mrs Fazackerley?'

'No,' she says quietly. 'I were drinking cream of vegetable Cup-a-Soup and she said she couldn't do that.'

'Horoscopes are blasphemy,' says Olive Watkins later.

'No, they're not,' says Sadie, making a note to look that word up when she gets back.

They're playing draughts in the sitting room while the women finish clearing the table and the men sit in the velveteen chairs and talk about the news. Sadie would rather be doing either really, but the Grandma said a game would be bracing, a way to get to know each other, so a game it is.

'Any guessing like that is disrespectful to God. That means rude,' she adds, smiling. 'In case you didn't know.'

Which she did, but she don't bother saying. 'Why?' she asks instead.

'Because He's in charge of what happens. King me.'

Sadie stacks a counter on top of the other, the fifth king Olive's got to Sadie's one. 'I don't see why God would mind,' she says. 'It's only tea. He's got wars to stop.'

'God doesn't stop wars,' says Olive, knowledge running to most things, it seems.

'Then what *does* He do?'

'If you don't know, you're obviously a *heathen*.'

Sadie adds that one to the list and all.

'Don't worry.' Olive smiles again, but thin and mean. 'They'll teach you how not to be one at Sunday school.'

Sunday school. The grown-ups talked about that at tea, about how she's going tomorrow, to learn about God, even though it's the holidays. And about school school, and which one she'll go to, even though she won't be going to any of them, because she won't be here by then. She didn't say owt though, and don't say owt now or Olive's head'll get bigger. Lets her listening drift to the men's conversation.

'Terrible business,' says the Grandpa.

'Terrible,' agrees Mr Collins, hands on a stomach that bulges over his belt like the froth on a pint or the top of a fairy cake. 'The "Fox" they're calling him.'

'It's like the Ripper all over again.'

Olive's head flicks up from the board. 'Who's the Ripper?' she asks.

'Doesn't matter,' says Mrs Collins, back in the room now, on the sofa with the Grandma and some knitting patterns. 'Concentrate on the game.'

But Sadie's brimming with it, with knowing something brainbox Olive does not. She's heard of the Ripper, seen the invisible villain send her mam and Donna back to the drinks cabinet for fortification, send Donna's John mad with worry, him being too far to do owt if the Ripper showed up at the door or down the ginnel. She can't keep that to herself. 'He were a rapist,' she says, bold as brass and loud as a clang.

Olive, counter in mid-air, frowns. 'What's a rapist?'

The silence that follows is solid. Sliceable as butter. Scolding Sadie, who don't even know the answer anyway, except it can't be anything good and might be something to do with the French, because the Grandma was mithering about them earlier.

'I'm so sorry,' says the Grandma, the knife pressing down. 'She's from Leeds.'

'It's quite all right,' Mrs Collins replies, though Sadie can see it's not because she's pinker than ever – red, if she's honest.

Without looking at her, the Grandma stands. 'I think we'd better be off, after all,' she says. 'Bernard?'

The Grandpa heaves to his feet, nods at Sadie to do the same.

'Sorry,' she says on the doorstep, though she's not sure what for. And anyway, Olive's inside and the Collinses ignore it, just say they'll see her tomorrow, ten o'clock sharp. God don't like dawdlers, it seems.

Nor does the Grandma, who's stridden ahead so it's the Grandpa takes her hand to cross the road for the walk home.

'I didn't mean anything,' says Sadie as they maunder down Fore Street.

'I know,' he says, and squeezes.

It's nice that, the tightness of it. Safe. She squeezes back.

'For the record,' he says, 'I don't think Leeds has anything to do with it.'

Sadie says nowt, just keeps hold.

'Your grandma, she's just . . . It's all a lot for her to take in. Fresh air,' he adds.

'Aye,' she agrees, and breathes it in while she can, decides to eat fibre ten times a day if she has to. She already changes her knickers every morning. Everyone she knows does, except the Richards sisters, and that's only 'cause there's three of them, so it costs three times as much for new.

She goes to bed early, to be ready for God in the morning.

'You can read for ten minutes,' the Grandma tells her.

'Thank you,' says Sadie.

When the door sounds the *thock* that means it's closed as it can be, she pulls the book off the floor, turns to the 'r's, scans the page for the *rapist*.

See under rape it tells her. So she does, flicks back a page, and finds it in an instant. Because this word is underlined twice.

Connie

Leeds, April 1981

April, and she's still waiting, waiting, waiting.

Waiting for word from the hospital.

Waiting for word from London.

Waiting for herself to do something about Elvis.

She's called the London bookers, asked if they've listened to her tape, if they want to see her at the Legion – she's there most Wednesdays, Saturdays too, except the last of the month when it's bingo and a big band. They're polite enough when they answer – the secretaries – claim to remember her name, claim the tape is definitely 'on his desk', but not a one has said they listened, not a one has said they loved it, not a one has said, 'Yes, come down, we'll whack you straight on the bill'.

That's why she's not bothered with Elvis yet, she suspects. Because this is when he's at his best, the only time he's worth it: telling her she's special; telling her she's got what it takes; telling her bookers are bonkers or bastards or both. Then he's attentive, tender almost, and so she lets him do what he wants when he wants. Still with a condom, mind. She's not that soppy or stupid. But he gets it, that's the thing.

Knows what it is to be out there, under the spotlight, in front of the crowd, even if it is only in a jumped-up men's club on a backstreet in Leeds. Knows the pull of it, the kick, strong as a shot. Knows it can never be a question of 'if I make it' but 'when'. Even when it's been, what, twelve years now, thirteen, she's been panting for it.

She remembers it then, the first time: on the scuffed parquet of the school stage for her choir solo. She was supposed to sing 'Pie Jesu' but instead, inspired by her latest seven-inch single, infuriated by her mother's disgust at it, she'd struck up Dusty's 'Son of a Preacher Man' to the whoops of the upper sixth, and swift ushering off by Miss Bixby.

Her mother had been told, of course, and there'd been punishment – no pudding, possibly, or no music, and certainly no television. But she barely cared because by then she'd caught the fever; she knew what she wanted to be when she grew up and it wasn't a doctor or a teacher or nurse, nor any of the suitable careers on the vetted list at Essex Ladies. It was 'vocalist'. Or 'pop star'. Or sometimes, if she was feeling really ambitious, or mildly drunk, 'singing sensation'. And she'd had visions of herself in tall hair and short dresses and eyes ringed with more black than a panda. She'd be taking the stage at the Palais or the Lyceum or on a television special, even. Not at first, obviously, she'd have to do the rounds, serve her time, but within only a few years, so sure was she of her talent. And of just deserts.

Of course, with Sadie, the scales had fallen, at least a few of them, and she'd seen that the world didn't always work the way you wanted it. That some of those doors had been closed to her, or some she'd clunked shut herself with her questionable choices, her needling doubts, her need to just pay the rent. So that now she'd be glad of a gig anywhere with a mic and within a few miles of the Underground. But still she clung to that 'when'. 'When', not 'if'. Because as soon as you conceded that, you might as well put on three stone and your slippers and settle down in front of the telly every Saturday until kingdom flipping come.

'It's starting!'

Sadie's yell snaps her to, the sound of the Eurovision Song Contest opening credits. 'Coming,' she calls back. And, lighting herself an Embassy, topping up her water glass from the Gilbey's bottle Elvis brought back from long-haul (duty-free, so she's a duty to drink it, hasn't she?), she trails smoke and discontent from the kitchen to the front room, where she's forced to squeeze in with Elvis, the girls already claiming the sofa with their Wotsits and score-cards.

Two hours and four top-ups later, she's dancing with Deborah and Sadie, managing to yank her skirt clean off where they only pretend.

'Blimey, Mam!' Sadie protests.

'I can see your knickers,' adds Deborah, as if butter wouldn't melt, though her own mother's got a pair that don't even close underneath.

Crotchless, she called them. And Connie'd laughed and said she'd have to try some on Elvis. But she never bothered. He didn't need encouragement. And they'd be off in seconds anyway, so that would be three pounds fifty wasted.

'Come here!' he says now, grabbing her hand and pulling

her to him so she stumbles, bare-legged and breathless, into his lap. 'Should be you up there, you hear me?'

'Give over.'

'I mean it. You're yards better than them. Miles. It should be you.'

And just for a moment, she feels it again – that draw to him. What keeps him here when half the time he's clogging up the house with boxes; leaving trails of cereal across the kitchen, pants along the landing; losing his rent, his temper.

'Sing for us, Mam!' Sadie begs.

'Go on,' says Deborah. 'Do "Making Your Mind Up"!'

'Do "Don't Go Breaking My Heart"!' contests Sadie. 'You can be Kiki Dee and Elvis can be Elton John.'

'Christ. Do I have to?' he asks. 'That's a downgrade right there.'

But he's only half serious, and so Sadie hauls him up, pushes him to her mam, forcing her hand into his.

And they sing.

And sing.

And sing.

And then, hairbrush and biro microphones dropped on the floor, they kiss.

And kiss.

And kiss.

'DisGUSTing!' declares Deborah when Terry Wogan's gone home and the box has gone off but the snog's still going on half a minute later.

Connie pulls away, shocked at herself. Surprised as well, that she can conjure it up from somewhere, that feeling, that need. 'Sorry,' she says. 'God, I don't know what came over me.'

'My sheer animal magnetism,' says Elvis, and he slaps her backside, still bare but for her pink bikini briefs.

'Like Charles and Di,' says Sadie. 'I bet he does that to her. I bet he's an animal magnet.'

'I bet she don't let him,' says Deborah, decisive. 'Not yet. Not till they're married.' She gives Connie a second disapproving stare.

'They will be soon enough,' says Sadie.

'What?' Connie's insides lurch; her legs as well, giddy perhaps from the gin or the singing.

'Charles and Di.' Sadie pulls a face as if she's an idiot. 'End of July's only –' she counts in her head – 'sixteen and a bit weeks away.'

'Oh.' Connie realizes her mistake, rights herself, checks Elvis to make sure he hasn't seen.

But he's busy with a cigarette now, one hand flicking the Zippo she got him for Christmas, the other scratching his balls.

He looks up. 'Get us another can, love, will you?'

And, relief washing over her, she agrees.

And she agrees when he suggests she fixes another gin for herself, and then another, and then perhaps they start on the Polish liqueur, the plum stuff he got off Thick Jim.

And she agrees when he says Deborah's home, Sadie's in bed, they can just do it here in the living room, can't they?

But then he says the condoms are upstairs in his drawer, but it won't matter just this once. And she says no, don't, please. Just get one. I'll get it for you, even. But she's drunk and tired and he's hard already and halfway inside her and so she doesn't bother to say no again. Just lets him do what he has to, grunting, shut-eyed, shut off, so she might as well be anyone to spill into – his several exes, Donna next door, Lady flaming Diana. But then it's over. And the next day, sober, sorry, she checks her calendar, washes herself out with Coke, crosses her fingers. And that night, Elvis off on a job, she sits in the kitchen, the notebook open, pen poised. God, she has to sort this out. Has to.

But then she thinks of him, spinning her round the front room like the bare bulb's a glitterball, telling her it should be her on TV, telling Sadie he'll fetch her her own cassette player for her birthday, and the tapes to go with it. And two days later she has the hammering and blacks out again. And besides, she's nearly thirty, for God's sake. She's already getting crow's feet, her tits are an inch below where they used to fall. And he's better than many. And there's Sadie to think of and she seems not to mind him.

And, anyway, who else would have her now? Her with another man's kid as it is. Isn't that what Elvis said?

And then, carbon-paper firm, and in indelible ink, she puts a line through number seven, because it's dealt with.

She's got to stick with him.

For better or worse.

Jean

Essex, August 1981

At least it went well with Olive Watkins, the Fox matter notwithstanding. She shudders at the memory of it, the shame. Though surely Barbara can't blame her. She's not been afforded a chance to correct this sort of awfulness, corral it; there's eleven years to catch up on. Unless perhaps it's like rickets, or some kind of vitamin deficiency has affected the Child at bone level so that she will never recover, not fully. The accent, though, that will go; that kind of aberration, she knows from experience, can be flattened and her manners, at the table at least, honed. Yes, she will send her back with a raft of improvements and instructions. In years to come, holidays in Harlow can be an inspiration, a respite even. She congratulates herself at the challenge, practically salivates at the anticipation. But then . . . Holidays, she repeats to herself, as if trying to hold on to the line of a kite or catch a falling coin before it drops into a drain.

Of course the subject of school was bound to come up.

'You'll need to talk to the local authority, of course,' Barbara had told her. 'No point calling round in August.'

'No,' she'd agreed.

'All off for the summer,' said Bernard, pointlessly, she might add.

'Six weeks,' said Maurice. 'Lucky so-and-sos. Would that we could all take six weeks off to lark about.'

'You'd hate it,' said Barbara. 'What would you do? God help us when you retire.'

She saw Bernard shrink slightly, already small against this admirable slab of a man.

'So, which are you thinking?' Barbara turned to Jean again.

'I'm sorry?'

'Schools?'

'Oh, yes, well—'

'I'm going to Mark Hall,' said Olive Watkins, as if attending a state comprehensive was something to trumpet.

'Really?' Barbara seemed queasy, as well she might.

Olive nodded. 'I'm in "A" stream. We took the test.' She looked at the Child. 'You'll have to take it before you start. You might be in "B" stream but we could still walk together. It's practically over the road.'

'Is that where my mam went?' the Child had asked then.

She'd bristled at that, blustered out a 'Heavens, no!' Then had to correct herself, pull her thread in. 'I mean, no.'

Barbara touched the Child's arm. 'She went with Martha – that's my daughter, the one that's getting married? – to the day school near Stortford. They had to get the train. And they had hats! Remember, Jean?'

A sudden snapshot of the pair of them: hats and macs and matching satchels, hers all name-tagged, *Earnshaw, C.*

'Though I don't suppose they wear those anymore,' Barbara said then, a touch of lament in her tone.

'But why did she go there?' the Child had recommenced, staring at her. 'If the other school's next door? Was it just for the hats?'

'The other school's private,' said Olive, knowledgeable, but somewhat wallowing in it, which was offputting in a child, especially a girl. 'You have to pay.'

'How much?' The Child's eyes were as wide as her mouth, which Jean saw, to her utter disgust, was still partially full of masticated sandwich.

'We don't discuss money,' she'd said then, an end to it. Or so she'd hoped.

'Why not?'

'Because it's . . . it's unseemly.'

'What's unseemly?'

'Rude.' Maurice nodded at her. A discreet 'you're welcome'.

Jean smiled. A silver thimble of thanks.

Though perhaps, she thinks now, the Fox, the talk of school, wasn't the worst of it. Perhaps, after all, it was Barbara's concern, her kindness – albeit well intentioned.

'Would you help?' Barbara had asked, as she'd stood to stack the sprigged porcelain – an unexpected request; they were guests, after all.

But Barbara had ulterior motives.

'Jean, dear,' she'd begun – always a bad sign. 'How are you holding up?'

She'd not answered at first. Had had to scrabble for something to distract her, managing in the end to be on the sharp side of snappy. 'I'm quite all right. Why wouldn't I be?'

'Jean.' Barbara put a hand on her then. Her fingers liver-spotted, her forearm fat as a baby's, as if tied at each end with butcher's string.

That hand had sat there before, a shovel of comfort, countless times. That had been how they'd met. At the mother and baby group in the old church hall. Barbara with a beatific Martha dandling on her lap; her with Constance, cantankerous, even then desperate for attention. The base need of the thing appalled her, the clawing at her body, latching on and then spitting her nipple out as if it were poison. She recoils at the thought, at that word, too – nipple. Bottle feeding had been Barbara's idea, of course. Everything had been Barbara's idea. All the attempts to placate her. She'd even admitted to her once – delirious on lack of sleep – that she was struggling to love it. 'She,' Barbara had corrected. As if that were the problem.

No, the problem went far deeper than names. It went straight to inheritance. Perhaps that's why it— *she* hadn't taken to Jean either. Perhaps she knew she'd got there under false promise. Begat by accident. Though, in that case, why had she complied for Bernard? Stopped sobbing if he picked her up, let him wind her, then, when older, followed him round like a small dog, even to his office. Until she'd told her to stop, that her father had important things to do and he didn't need her getting under his feet. 'She's not,' Bernard had insisted. 'She's only crayoning.' 'It'll be on the walls

147

before you know it,' she'd snapped back. And then taken the child to the park, where she'd proceeded to scream for several minutes. Until Barbara had arrived with Martha.

'Jean?'

That hand. 'Where's Martha off on honeymoon?' she'd said then – a parry, a confetti-strewn diversion to draw her off course.

That had been another mistake. Of course it would be France. Martha had excelled at the language, after all, excelled at everything, gone on to Oxford. Though nearly thirty was late to be wed, and to an estate agent, a smarmy sort – Barbara could hardly crow about that. But France, of all places.

She knows her loathing is misplaced. He was from Perivale, for heaven's sake, never been beyond Dover, hadn't even owned a passport, she supposed now. But he'd managed the accent all right. So that now it sounded false on anyone, even Maurice, who'd once called a hat of hers 'très chic'.

Especially Maurice.

She didn't want him tainted, not when she equated anything from 'over there' with the inglorious and tawdry. All puffed-up and put-on and godless. No, it was false idolatry, being French, and Maurice was not that. Not that at all.

They'd left soon after, because of the Fox. But this morning the Child had asked again – not about the word, but about who he might be.

'Just be wary of strangers,' Bernard had replied.

'But everyone's a stranger here,' the Child pointed out. 'How am I supposed to tell?'

Bernard had seemed flummoxed by that. 'I suppose they might look a bit . . . different.'

'What sort of different? Like long hair? Like a gypsy?'

Eyes, she'd thought to herself bleakly. That's what you had to watch. The man from Perivale had had the eyes of a mesmerist. Transfixing. As if you were the only object in the room or were hewn from gold.

Not like Bernard, whose eyes, though trapped behind spectacles now, are as transparent as a dog's or a cow's. That was one thing about him. Eyes that couldn't lie.

'Just stick to people you know,' offered Bernard in the end.

'Like who?'

'Well, me and your grandma.'

'Olive Watkins,' Jean had added. 'You can talk to her at church in a moment. And Mr Collins.' He was going to be working with the church again; he'd volunteered at tea. Or rather Barbara had volunteered him. Said they needed someone for the 'sing-song' section and he was certainly qualified. 'More than qualified,' Jean had pointed out. Though she'd regretted it then, raising as it did the spectre of why he'd ever stopped. And 'sing-song' was beneath him, she knew that, but it was a sort of moving on, and for that she was thankful.

'Good man,' Bernard had said later. 'Perhaps I should try something?'

'Don't be absurd,' she'd replied.

'Olive Watkins,' she says in her head as they troop out to the car – church is a drive away now of course. She may be going to Mark Hall but she seems sensible, and her family decent at least. The father is at Gilbey's, she thinks, middle management, and a councillor too, and the mother? Well, that's of no consequence really.

'Sadie!'

She spins so quick she almost slips on the gravel, feels her insides slip as she sees the Indian boy at the gate.

'Where're you going?'

'Church,' the Child replies. 'Sunday school.'

'Bad luck,' he replies. 'Want to knock about later?'

'Sadie,' Jean demands, but her voice is reedy and thin.

'It's all right,' the Child tells her. 'It's not a stranger. It's Nirmal.' She turns back to him. 'Maybe after?'

She musters, has to. 'We'll be eating lunch.'

'After that, then?' he tries.

'That'll be fine,' Bernard says quickly.

Jean turns to him, but he is already lowering himself into the driver's seat, as if he doesn't want to hear her sudden plans for a narrowboat outing or an afternoon of Yahtzee.

'See you later,' says Nirmal.

'Aye,' says the Child.

'Yes!' she says. 'It's not "aye", it's "yes"!'

'Yes,' repeats the Child, agog at the outburst.

'Thank you.' And with that she neatens herself, sits briskly in the passenger seat and slams the door.

But this time the satisfaction does not come.

Sadie

Essex, August 1981

She's only been to church once before – a visit to Leeds cathedral in Mrs Bantam's class, hand in hand along the Headrow and up Cookridge Street hoping she didn't catch lurgy from Peter McCrea, 'cause Deborah'd gone off with Karen Batty to talk about horses. And she's a vision in her head, now, hasn't she, of stained glass and high ceilings and pillars. So many pillars. So the plastic chairs and purple curtains are disappointing, if she's honest. So are the rules. Almost as many as actual school. No fidgeting, no whispering, no kicking the chair in front – not when the man with the blue suit and the dandruff, Mr Kittering, is talking about the lady with the bent back and someone called Lazarus.

Lucky she has Olive Watkins to tell her what to do and what not. Olive tells her a lot of things:

That Mr Kittering's son, Colin, was once on *Blue Peter* and he'll show you the badge for a Twix or a Mars bar, but that's bribery, which is a sin, so she's never seen it.

That it's good of Mr Kittering to let Sadie into church, given her mum wasn't married when she had her, or ever, even.

That God spoke to her in the bath once.

Sadie sits up at this. 'Did He? What'd He say?'

'None of your beeswax.'

'How'd you know it were Him?'

'Who else would it be? I don't go round hearing weird men in my head all the time.'

Sadie pictures a weird man. One with a beard and trouble about him. 'What if it were the Fox?' she whispers.

Olive, pale and thin as skimmed milk, pinks and twitches. 'Shut up.'

'Sorry,' says Sadie.

But Olive's stomped off already and then Mr Kittering blows a whistle and a boy with taped-up glasses and a green tank top says, 'Sword drill!' and for a moment Sadie gets mildly excited at the thought of some kind of fighting. But it turns out to be Mr Kittering calling out the numbers of chapter and verse in the Bible and quickest to find it wins. Only they don't get a prize except the joy of winning, which isn't much of anything, so Sadie don't mind that she's not got a clue where Judges is, why there are two Samuels or that E-fee-shans is actually spelled with a 'p'.

'How was that?' the Grandma asks at the end, when they're let out into the big hall again with the grown-ups.

'It was fine,' she says, chuffed at suddenly remembering her *was*es.

'Fine,' the Grandma repeats. 'And did you sit with Olive?'

She nods. 'She reckons God spoke to her. In her head.'

The Grandma smiles, but odd, not proper. 'Isn't that nice for her.'

Sadie shrugs. 'I suppose. Though I think I'd rather it was Shakin' Stevens.'

Lunch is cold ham and potatoes and no she can't have salad cream, only mustard, but that makes her cough out a blob of meat, so she won't be having that again. She's not bothered though, not even when the Grandma pulls a face at the palaver, because after lunch she gets to 'knock about' with Nirmal.

Though knocking about don't seem to mean what she'd hoped, which was having a go on his Grifter or going up the park for a bit. It means sitting in the dining room with a box of Fuzzy Felt the Grandma's got from a jumble sale. Bible Stories it is, only half the pieces are missing and there's odd things in instead, like a tractor and a mermaid and a monkey with one arm missing.

She'd longed for the stuff once. Deborah had three sets: Fairy Tales, Pets, and Playmates, and she'd been allowed to use whichever Deborah hadn't bagsied, which was always Fairy Tales, because of the dresses. But they were seven then and she's eleven now and too old for it. Nirmal's not bothered though. He's slapping a camel in mid-air and the one-armed monkey in the manger.

'We could be in a gang if you want,' he says out of nowhere.

'How can it be a gang if there's only two of us?' she asks.

'*Red Hand Gang*'s got five, plus Boomer.'

'Boomer?'

'The dog! Have you not seen it?'

He tugs at the collar of his shirt – checked and a bit sweaty, if she's honest. 'We only got a telly again last year.'

'Is that 'cause of being Indian? 'Cause the Mehtas had a telly.'

'No.' He gives her a look. 'It's 'cause my brother broke our old one with a football and Radio Rentals said we had to keep paying anyway because we didn't have the insurance, so we couldn't afford a new one for ages.'

'Oh. You got a dog?' She's hopeful of this, at least.

'No, worse luck. But we could ask some others. For the gang, I mean.'

'Like who?' Her head fills with stranger danger again. It had better be someone she knows, she supposes. 'Like Olive Watkins?' she suggests.

'What? Horrible Olive?'

She nods. 'She can't be that horrible, 'cause God's talked to her. Actually right at her, out loud.'

Nirmal snorts. 'Well, she is. She once grassed on Nigel Banks for weeing on the field, but the toilets were broken and he was busting. So why would God pick her for a chat?'

'Oh.' Sadie hopes Nigel Banks won't be in any gang. 'Well, I don't know.'

Nirmal sticks a crown on the flying camel. 'My cousin reckons he saw Jesus in a slice of toast once. He was trying to get it on *Tomorrow's World* but it went mouldy.'

Sadie shimmers at this thought – that Jesus might be hiding in a slice of white Nimble and she might find him and that'd be as good as God in her head, better than, and that'd show Olive. Only she don't suppose he'd be so easy to see in seedy brown. Then she frowns as she thinks of something. 'I didn't think Indians believed in Jesus.'

'I don't. He's just a bloke with a beard.'

'So it could have been anyone in the toast,' Sadie protests. 'It could have been . . . Dave Lee Travis. Or . . . or Kenny Everett?'

'Could have been,' he admits.

She ponders. 'I wouldn't mind finding Kenny Everett in my toast though. Or anyone really.'

Nirmal nods. 'Nor me.'

They're quiet for a bit then, no more Fuzzy Felt to fit on the board and she's not sure what to say, but suddenly he blurts it.

'Sorry about your mum,' he says.

Her stomach jumps. 'How'd you know about that?'

'Everyone knows,' he says, as if it's obvious. 'I thought you'd be crying, but you're not.'

She shrugs. 'Got to look ahead,' she says, repeating the Grandma. 'I felt a bit sad yesterday. But then my grandpa, he let me watch a bit of *Pop Quiz* when my grandma were having a bath, so it weren't too bad. Paul Nicholas were on. And Gary Tibbs.'

'Who's Gary Tibbs?'

'Adam and the Ants,' she tells him, happy with knowing. 'He plays bass.'

'Oh. Why've you not been here before?' he asks then. 'To stay, I mean.'

'We were estranged.' She sounds it out, long and important.

'What's estranged?'

'It means my mam and them fell out.'

'Over what?'

But Sadie don't know. She asked once but her mam was having one of her 'moments' when she had to lie down on the sofa and eat cornflakes from the box, Frosties if they had them. 'Not now, love,' she'd said. 'You don't need to know.'

'Recipes probably,' says Nirmal then. 'My mum still isn't talking to my auntie over something to do with soup. It'll be that, or men.'

Sadie nods. 'Men, I expect. So what would we do, in this gang?'

Nirmal smiles, and, when he does, dimples sink into his cheeks like water pocks in sand. 'Solve a mystery?'

'What kind of mystery?' she asks. 'Like a murder?'

'Maybe. Only no one's been murdered. Unless your mum . . . ?'

He don't finish the sentence but she knows what he's on about. Same as Deborah was. 'She weren't murdered,' she says, grim and chippy. 'We thought it were a sausage at first but it was her heart. It just stopped working. Anyway, you can't murder someone with a sausage.'

'You'd be surprised.' Nirmal raises one eyebrow. 'My cousin reckons you could do it with a spatula if you really wanted to. Or even a spoon.' Sadie must look as weird as she feels, because he says, 'But not a sausage probably,' dead quick after that, then adds a 'sorry'.

''S'all right,' she says. Though it's not. But it's not terrible neither. Not the worst in the world. And she's to look forward, hasn't she? Focus on the positive. 'What about the Fox?' she suggests. 'Cause if they're hunting for him it's not stranger danger, is it. Not the same. They'd be like the police, and the coppers can't be worrying whether weirdos with beards are strangers or not, they have to be catching them.

'Who's the Fox?'

'A rapist. I looked it up. It means—'

'I know what it means.'

'So what d'you think?'

He concentrates, nods. 'We could do it tomorrow.'

'Aye, all right,' she says.

'Aye,' he mimics. But not meanly. In awe, almost.

Before she goes to bed, she stares at herself in the bathroom mirror – the only one in the house – tries to lift a single eyebrow or will dimples. But she only succeeds in looking oddly contorted or plain mental, Deborah would say. She sighs as she clicks off the light and tramps back to the bedroom. Perhaps she'll hear God, though. Or see Jesus in her breakfast.

Or perhaps they'll catch the Fox. That'd be something to tell Deborah next term.

Only five weeks now, she's counted. Five weeks till she's home.

And, the Whimsey tight in her hand, she kisses her mam, clicks off the lamp, and counts Fuzzy Felt monkeys till she drops off proper.

Jean

Essex, August 1981

Church has made it worse.

It's the sudden abundance of children, of course. In their shorts and skirts now, demob-happy, but, come September, in longer hems and heavier blazers, some off with Olive Watkins to Mark Hall she doesn't wonder, the others Burnt Mill or further. She says nothing, tries to file it away in a special in-tray for attention at a later, unspecified date. But Bernard isn't so efficient, has never held with this system, though he's gone along with it for her sake, she knows. Until now.

'We really need to think about school,' he tells her that evening.

The Child has been sent to bed to read and they are doing something together for once: setting the breakfast table – Pyrex bowls for cereal (she has conceded to Weetabix), second-best plates for toast – the Suzy Cooper set (Bernard's choice) kept for deserving company.

'What about school?' she asks obliquely, cleaning a knife on a napkin then resetting it unnecessarily.

'Jean.'

'All right!' she snaps. Then, feeling the heat of shame,

softens. 'All right. But let me chase the Jenkins man again. We can't do anything until we know what his plans are.'

'It's not really up to him though,' Bernard explains patiently. Pointlessly. 'He's – what? A boyfriend? And how long has he even been around? He's certainly not particularly visible at the moment.'

'He's in Skegness.'

'Yes, well. That's no excuse.'

She is nettled, nervy. 'Let me at least try. I'll call from the office tomorrow. Maurice won't mind.'

'No. I don't suppose so.'

And so the matter is settled. She will telephone Elvis Jenkins. Though not 'again'. As far as she knows, the only message he has even possibly received was from Mrs Maltby, and probably incoherent at that. Oh, she's thought about it – several times, after the Fox nonsense. But something has always stopped her. Not fear, not really. More, reluctance to engage with anyone from the chaos that was obviously Constance's life. Well, not anymore. She will phone him and demand he faces up to his responsibilities.

Yes. She will be forthright and focused. A lady not for turning.

Of course, it would be better if there were a real father. The actual father. But she's no closer to knowing who that is now than she was on Michelle Spencer's doorstep eleven years ago. And heavens knows what the Child's been told, given Constance was a habitual liar with a wild imagination – the worst possible combination. Not the truth, that's for sure. The truth's probably far messier than Elvis Jenkins.

Anyway, perhaps he's not as bad as all that. Methodists, most of them, the Welsh. God fearing; good voices.

Yes, she will call him. And she will call Olive Watkins's mother as well. First, in fact. The Child has decided to see that Nirmal boy again later, before she or Bernard could rule otherwise. Though she suspects that Bernard isn't bothered anyway, suspects him of enjoying this – his socialist dream achieved, after all. His melting pot. His wretched Jerusalem.

Or perhaps he'd just rather get back to his crossword.

No. It's not that. It's worse. He's enamoured of her, the Child, she can see it. Someone to play chess with, to teach about the intricacies of buildings, to dog him, obviously, following him round the house with her whys and whens and wheres.

She can see the same look in the Child as well: not tolerance, or even mere interest, but something bordering on adoration. As if they were thrown from the same mould, cast from the same clay.

As if they were actually kin.

Does he know?

She'd assumed so, once upon a time, given his intelligence. But, like so many things, has managed to calm that concern and shelve it as well, because he'd said nothing to anyone, least of all her, had defended her when questioned. When her mother remarked on the size of the child, when his own wondered wasn't Constance 'bonny' given she must surely have been conceived on the wedding night, he'd simply said she was a 'blessing'. Perhaps he'd hoped the worst anyone would imagine was that they were fornicating before they were officially permitted. Or perhaps he was genuinely so unaware of the intricacies and intimacies of procreation that 'bonny', a 'blessing', was the extent of it.

Whichever, he's said nothing to her and so she'd left it, at first to fester, but then, later, to be covered with dust with the rest of the baggage she'd brought with her and stored. But now, with the Child, it's as if Pandora's box might be opened any moment and the truth flume out in a horrible torrent, black as tar and sticky too. So, yes, the Jenkins man. He will absolve her, surely. Make it all go away, at least in term time. Holidays will be sufficient, a suitable duty for someone her age, for someone in her position, and Bernard's.

But the next day, when she calls from the office, the woman who answers is almost incomprehensible, not aided by the radio in the background, blaring horrible pop music.

'Can't you turn it down?'

'What's that, love? Can I what?'

'The radio. It's awfully loud.'

'Knob's stuck,' says the woman. 'It's that or nothing.'

Nothing would be preferable, but it seems too obvious to suggest, so she settles for the message. 'Elvis Jenkins,' she repeats. 'He's to call this number.'

'Shall I tell him what for?'

'His . . . Sadie. She's my . . . daughter's child. I was wondering when he might collect her.'

'So you're the mother-in-law, are you?'

Her indignation is visceral, alarming. 'I am no such thing.'

'All right, love, I was only checking. So he's to come and

fetch her, is he? I can't say when that'll be, 'cause he's on every night and he does the bingo twice an afternoon. Ladies love him, they do. But season ends in September, so—'

'Can he just call?' she pleads. 'Not in September – now. Today. Or tonight. As soon as he can get to the phone.'

'Well, I'll tell him, but, like I say, it's all go here, bad as Las Vegas. Mind you, I don't suppose it rains there so much. Lucky buggers.'

By the time Jean manages to hang up, her forehead is damp with the same patina of sweat that sees the receiver slip through her fingers and onto the desk, knocking a pot of pens that scatter in a clatter of plastic, and threaten to topple her tea, only rescued in the nick of time and, even then, the spillage is significant.

'Everything all right?' calls Maurice through the adjoining door.

'Quite,' she replies. 'Nothing broken.'

There's a pause. Then a 'Good,' that even she can hear is tinged with relief. Men like Maurice don't want to be bothered with problems, she's learned that at least. They don't deserve to be either, have more important matters at hand.

Unlike Shelley Pledger, who chooses this moment to wander in, aimless as a seven-year-old and about as subtle.

'Blimey, Jean. Out late last night, were you? Bit of a big one?'

It's a joke, and at her expense. They know she's all but teetotal, josh her to her face about it, and mock her behind her back. 'Afraid you'll be dancing on the bar with no knickers?' Lorna Hawkin had said to her once. Oh, she'd marked Lorna's card after that, docked her for being late even if it was only ten minutes and only the once. But respect is essential and Shelley Pledger is no exception.

'Those orders won't type themselves,' she tells her. 'And we're almost out of PG Tips.' She taps her watch. 'Harrington's shuts in half an hour.'

Shelley screws up her nose. 'Tea can wait, can't it?'

Jean smiles. 'It most certainly cannot. We've visitors first thing and they'll expect refreshments. We can't serve Pinnacle biscuits without a pot of tea. You know that.'

Shelley snatches the petty cash from Jean's hand, stalks out of the office. Lady Di ambitions but none of the breeding, Jean thinks. To be pitied, really. And with that thought as fortifying as any port or Dubonnet, Jean gets back to her filing.

Connie

Leeds, July 1981

It starts with the riots. Police brandishing batons and gas in their long arms of the law against black boys packing decades of rage. The first pressure cooker to boil up and burst is Brixton, then Liverpool, whose own spark catches the tinder in Manchester, and how long before that flame creeps over the desiccated Pennines and sets off something here in Leeds?

She'd lived for this as a child; had knelt in front of the television drinking in reports of acts of damage, of students taking to the streets, of sit-ins, dissidence, impending change in its wake. Until her mother had told her she'd get ideas if not square eyes and snapped the thing off, reminding her father she'd never wanted it in the first place, she'd warned about just this sort of thing.

Back then, Connie had been brimming with it herself, fit to burst with the need for something new, for anything that wasn't her parents, her small town, her school with its rules about skirt length and hair length and swearing. But now she feels a needle of fear prick-prick-pricking at her and, along with it, a familiar wash of disappointment that nothing she'd dreamt of, prayed for even, has turned out to be half of what she hoped. Not civil unrest, not singing and certainly not men. None of them white knights when it comes down to it, their armour that shines with the drink or under the glitterball tarnished in the broad light of day; none of them worth the work and the hurt and the all-too-quick wishing she'd chosen better.

'I don't blame them,' Elvis says, cracking a can and settling back on the sofa like he's watching *Grandstand*, 'the niggers, I mean.'

'Coloureds,' corrects Sadie.

'Niggers, coloureds, same thing. I'm not racialist, anyway; I'm a communist, me.'

'You can't be a communist and want to make a million,' Connie points out, then regrets it.

'Says who?' he snaps. 'When I'm rich, I'll just spread it about to everyone. Even the niggers. Just you see.'

'Like Robin Hood,' says Sadie. 'He robbed off the rich to give to the poor.'

'He's not robbing anyone,' Connie says quick.

'Maybe I should,' says Elvis. 'I could be Buster Edwards. Sitting pretty in Mexico right about now.'

'He was arrested, remember?' Connie reminds him. 'Did nine years. And he's not in Mexico, he runs a flower stall in Waterloo; it was on the news.'

'We could double up then. Bonnie and Clyde. What do you say?' He tries to 'cheers' her, sloshing his can against her glass, but only succeeds in spilling both.

Jesus. She mops herself off. 'They died,' she says.

'Who died?' asks Sadie.

'No one,' Connie mutters. 'Doesn't matter.'

'What's communism, any road?' asks Sadie.

'It's when everyone looks out for each other,' says Elvis. 'Like one big community. And no one has more money than the man next door.'

Sadie frowns. 'What if it's a woman next door?'

'Or her.'

Communism. As if Elvis was capable. Anyway, they'd tried that in Wales: a Cuban flag sagging on a washing line, arguments about Marx, the insistence on sharing everything – food, work, child-raising. But look what happened there. The petty jealousies over who got the plum jobs and who got the bogs. The hogging of contraband chocolate. The endless unwritten rules, and then, once Petra bloody Unsworth had her way, the written ones. Petra was the reason they'd left in the end. Turns out she hadn't wanted to share everything, least not Wigan Mick. Not that he was worth sharing, it transpired. Penis practically thin as a Peperami and a way of saying 'hospital' with an inexplicable 'ck' in it that made her want to shudder. Another disappointment in a heaving list.

'Pardon?' She's suddenly aware she's being addressed.

'I said what if the riots come here?' Sadie repeats, her voice half terrified, half hoping. 'Will *we* get looted?'

'No, love,' she placates. 'Not us.' Though it's no more than a sop because how can she be sure? The streets, the people here aren't that different from Moss Side or Toxteth, are they? Broke, broken and simmering with the indignity of it. And at that a vision pops into her head, needling, nudging her: the same vision that Gibberd must have had when he first mapped it out just miles from London – of generously spaced semis, of countless parks and gardens, of so many acres of sky that there was no tinder, let alone a spark, no pot waiting to brim up and boil over onto cobbles, because everyone had work, had purpose, had space to breathe.

But then she fetches the pin, pricks her own bubble. Because for all its proximity, it wasn't London, was it. Might as well have been Leeds, the number of times she got to go there. And because, for all the space, she couldn't breathe. She was stifled even in that flat atmosphere. So what is she even thinking? No, they're staying put. Never mind the riots, never mind she's as restless as a trapped cat, never mind Elvis telling her again she's to come to Skegness.

He's got a summer run, starting in a week. Headline act at Summer Paradise, with some blue comedian called Denny Helmet as support. Not exactly Las Vegas and he'll have to mind the bingo in the afternoons as well, but it pays steady and he'll have time off in the mornings to enjoy the facilities (heated outdoor pool, leisure lounge, crazy golf). Or nurse his hangover, more like.

'What's Skegness?' asks Sadie, hearing it for the first time.

'Nothing,' she replies.

'Holiday camp,' he says. 'With our own caravan.'

'A caravan!' says Sadie, as delighted as if he was touting a suite at the Ritz.

'Got a double bed for me and your mam, and a bunk for you.' He nods at Sadie. 'And an en suite and all.'

'I should hope so,' says Connie. 'I'd hardly be traipsing across a campsite at midnight for a pee.'

'So you're coming, then?'

Shit. 'I . . . It was hypothetical.'

'Hypothetical means only maybe,' says Sadie. 'Mr Wilkinson said. Like, hypothetically, Darren Banner might play for United one day, but it's not very likely.'

Connie thinks of Mr Wilkinson with his crisp brown suit and his trimmed moustache and his keenness to see her on parents' evening. Perhaps she'd be better off with a man like him. A man like her father: keen and clever and whose ambition was limited to more achievable things.

'Why only maybe?' says Elvis.

'What?' says Connie, as if he can see inside her head.

''Cause he's two left feet,' says Sadie.

'Not Darren whatsisname. And I wasn't talking to you.' He kicks a socked size ten at Connie. 'Why can't you come to Skegness? What else are you going to do? Or have you got a fancy man I don't know about?'

She inches away from his range. 'Work?' she says. 'We're not all otherwise unemployed.'

'Freelance, thank you very much.'

'Freelance,' she repeats, suddenly aware he's not smiling. 'It's just . . . I can't get more than a few shifts off at a time. Not with everyone else wanting a week around the wedding.'

The date's set now – twenty-ninth of July. Kenneth Kendall had said it on the news. There's going to be a street party here, with trestles and chairs and bunting. And all the mums are to make plates of sandwiches or savouries, or bring biscuits or crisps. There is a list, written up by Mrs Higgins, with names next to each so there's no doubling up. She's got sausages on sticks, which she doesn't mind. Bunging them in the oven is hardly a hardship. And it saved the hoo-ha with Mrs Mehta, who'd said perhaps she wasn't the best person to be in charge of chipolatas, given, you know. But Mrs Higgins hadn't known and had huffed when it had been explained to her, said, well, it was going to mess with everything and she'd have to swap Donna off vol-au-vents and she'd requested them especially. So Connie had volunteered, said Mrs Mehta could take her place on Twiglet duty. So there's that.

'So you'll come before. Kid breaks up from school ages earlier, doesn't she?'

'On the Friday,' Sadie confirms.

'I—'

'Please!' begs Sadie.

Easier to lie, she thinks. Let him – both of them – think she might. 'Maybe,' she says.

'Hypothetically?' checks Sadie.

'Hypothetically.'

But it's not. And it's nothing to do with shifts or the wedding but because the thought of six days, let alone six weeks, cramped in with him has sent her stomach clenching every time he's brought it up. It's bad enough here, with solid walls and a flushable lav. But there, in a caravan, with walls like paper and everyone to hear him at her, fucking or fighting or both.

And anyway, the date for the hospital tests is set. And

she's supposed to have told him but somehow she can't get the words out. Doesn't want to. And she doesn't entirely know why. Not even like she's that worried about them, because it's 'probably not' urgent, or anything at all. But still, something stoppers the truth up in her whenever she tries to tell him.

Perhaps because he missed Sadie's birthday because he was out cold on Thick Jim's floor and then the cassette player he'd promised her turned out to be a shitty dictaphone.

Perhaps because he's forgotten the fainting anyway, the London bookers, hasn't asked after either since.

Perhaps because twice now he's pushed himself into her without a condom on and she's not even sure the trick with the Coke's true – she'd got it from Michelle twelve years ago, after all, and look what had happened then.

So her staying here and him being in Skegness gives her a breather at least, time to work out what to do.

God, she hadn't bargained for this. Hadn't imagined, when she'd sat on the carpet in Harlow in 1969, that this is what her life would look like at almost thirty: coming off shift at a shitty supermarket to arrange sausages on paper plates; begging some bloke called Colin to come to a dive in Leeds to listen to her croon out covers that were out of date a decade ago; living with a man who said if she offered this Colin a blow-job she'd stand a better chance of getting him halfway up the A1. And yes, he'd laughed it off as a joke, but after she'd gone down on him (because it was that or an actual shag) he'd said, 'Colin'd sign you like a shot, babe. I'm only saying.'

Why's life never like it is in stories? Never gilded. Not even pretty. She'd pictured herself taking Paris by storm in pink hair and a ballgown, and, Christ, look at her: stuck in a two-up two-down with no phone and the gas about to be cut off and the rent overdue because Elvis reckoned he'd pay it and it turned out he'd spent it all on a job lot of those sodding dictaphones that no one round here but Sadie even wants, because what do they need one of those for when half of them don't have a job, still less one as a private detective or hack?

Sadie.

Her saving grace, Sadie'd not been in the story book; hadn't been planned, not even yearned for, but Sadie's the one thing that's golden, bright as a new penny and ever thankful for the smallest things. And wordlessly she snatches at that thought, and grabs the girl herself, holding her so tight she eventually yelps.

'Sorry,' she says, releasing her, but only an inch or so.

''S'all right,' says Sadie, eye level now. 'What were that for?'

'Nothing,' she says, tamping down the girl's hair, tidying it in a way that would have irritated her at that age but which Sadie, of course, bears without complaint. 'Just . . . you're a diamond, you know that? My own bobby dazzler.'

Sadie, self-effacing where she was cocksure, just shrugs. A fact that irks her, because if there's one thing she's determined to pass on as a mother it's that Sadie should believe in herself. Should be proud. Because then there'll be two of them that think it. The only two you can ever rely on.

And sometimes not even that.

'What about me?' says Elvis then. 'Aren't I a bobby dazzler and all?'

But Connie says nothing. Just holds the child as tight as she'll let her, while behind them batons clash and sirens wail and Moss Side, barely fifty miles away, burns.

Sadie

Essex, August 1981

Elvis is fetching her. She's heard it through the floor-boards.

She'd asked to watch *Ask the Family*, only 'cause it seemed the safest bet on the *Radio Times* schedule. It even had the word 'family' in it, which meant it was healthy.

'What's that?' demanded the Grandma.

Sadie picked up the magazine again. 'A game show,' she'd said. '"Sixteen families have fought and two have survived to battle for victory in the last match of the contest. Robert Robinson is in the chair and Wales meets England for the last time when the Griffiths family from Llan– Llandudno in . . ." somewhere "meets the Almond family from Tilehurst, Reading. Who will emerge victorious?"'

She'd read the last sentence with as much mystery as she could muster. But it wasn't washing.

'Game shows are for the lowest common denominator.'

Mam had said that and all. Yet she'd sat there anyway, with her bowl of crisps and her Bensons or Embassies, and every answer on the tip of her tongue. She knew all sorts, everything – the capital of Yugoslavia, the second president of America, Sonny Bono's real name. Donna had told her she should be a politician, or a teacher at least, not on the checkout and at Mrs Beasley's beck and call, the fat cow. But Mam said she could hardly be gigging here and there if she'd to be at school every morning. And what if she hit the big time? She'd have to give a term's notice and stardom didn't wait for O levels to be over or Christmas concerts to be sung.

'There's *Six Fifty-five Special* on the other side,' Sadie'd tried then. '"Comedian, mimic, raconteur are three descriptions that can be applied at any one time to sum up the multi-faceted career of Michael Bentine." Oh, I like him. Him off *Potty Time*.' The Grandma don't seem to agree, but she carries on with the printed description and a sliver of hope. '"To the public, he is best known for his zany humour, but few people, apart from his family and friends, know him to be a spirit medium. In tonight's programme, Michael Bentine talks to host Donny Mac– Mac– Macsomething about the paranormal and a book, *The Door Marked Summer*, he has written on the subject. Music comes from Kiki Dee." Kiki Dee! I like her. What d'you think? Paranormal sounds good, don't it? Maybe he's seen ghosts. Maybe he's—'

'I think you'd better go upstairs, dear,' the Grandma had interrupted. 'Do some reading.'

So she had. She'd looked up *vagina* again, and come across *clitoris* and *cunt* as well, which was weird because that meant vagina and a *contemptible person of either sex*. She'll probably not use that one in front of the Grandma, but that's two words for vagina she knows. Though there's loads more for penises. Boys always get more.

She were just pondering whether or not to investigate if she had a clitoris, in case she ever needed it for something, when she heard the mumble from the front room move into the dining room, as if someone'd turned the volume knob up or fiddled with reception. There's something about school, but she's not bothered about that, not yet. But then she'd heard Elvis's name and the Grandma saying she'd call him again and tell him to come get her. Call him tomorrow. First thing in the morning.

So now she eats her Weetabix without even grimacing, even manages a piece of marmalade peel, though she has to chew it twenty times before she can swallow it. She don't even moan when Horrible Olive shows up saying she's invited, that the Grandma rang her mum and said she needed a 'guiding light' and that Olive was that light, because of talking to God, obviously.

Nirmal squirms at that, pulls a face so she'll laugh with him, but she nudges his ankle with her toes to tell him to belt up for now and he does.

'So what shall we do?' Horrible Olive asks.

'You can see my hamster if you like,' says Sadie, remembering. 'His name's Dave.'

'Dave's a stupid name.'

'No it in't,' she says, defensive. 'What about all the other Daves? Like Dave Lee Travis and Dave Allen.'

'And Chas and Dave,' adds Nirmal. 'How's that stupid?'

Horrible Olive sighs, as if pitying their idiocy. 'For a hamster,' she explains. 'You can't call a hamster Dave.'

'Well, I did,' says Sadie. 'So there.'

'I'm not bothered,' says Olive then. 'Hamsters aren't even proper pets. They don't even do anything. Not like a dog.'

'Have you got a dog?' asks Sadie, instantly forgiving the Dave comments.

'A collie,' she says, proud as you like. 'Pedigree. He can herd sheep and everything.'

'What sheep?' asks Nirmal. 'You haven't got any sheep.'

Horrible Olive glares. 'Any sheep that need it.'

Sadie nudges Nirmal with her knee, 'cause they need a dog and if it can herd sheep perhaps it can herd the Fox and all.

But Nirmal moves his leg so she can't reach him. Leans back, cool as you like. 'You still can't be in our gang,' he tells Olive. 'Not unless you pass the test.'

'What test?' says Olive, before draining her lemon squash (non-staining and allowed once a day). 'What gang?'

'We're in a gang,' Nirmal confirms, chest puffed like a skinny pigeon. 'Me and Sadie.'

'Two isn't a gang,' Olive informs them, grabbing a garibaldi (containing raisins, so healthy enough). 'Everyone knows that. Anyway, what do you even do in your gang?'

Sadie looks at Nirmal and him back at her, and he nods, so she says it. 'We're going to catch the Fox.'

Horrible Olive stops mid-biscuit, swallows. 'The rapist?'

Nirmal nods. 'Aye.'

'"Aye"? What does that even mean?'

'It means yes,' he tells her. 'In our gang.'

Olive rolls her eyes. 'Well, your gang's stupid. Because catching rapists is dangerous and against the law.'

'No it's not,' Sadie says. 'Or how would the police do it?'

Olive folds her arms, tilts her head. 'They've got special licences,' she tells them. 'Everyone knows that. So if you try, I'm going to tell my dad. He's a councillor. He's in charge of things.'

Nirmal folds his own. 'You would not.'

'Would too. And *your* dad.' She nods at Nirmal, then smiles at Sadie, crocodile-like. 'Not yours, though.'

Sadie stiffens. Hopes Nirmal won't say owt. But no such luck.

'Why not?'

'She doesn't have one.' Olive is triumphant.

Sadie slumps.

'Yes she does,' Nirmal insists. 'Everyone has one. We did it in biology.'

'Well, Sadie doesn't,' says Olive. 'My mum said, and she never lies or God would punish her.'

'Well . . .' Nirmal is struggling, but she don't know how to help him or herself besides. 'Jesus never had a dad,' he snatches at last. 'So maybe Sadie's like Jesus.'

Horrible Olive sucks in a breath, hard and fast. 'I'm telling my mum you said that.' And Sadie thinks she might cry she's that mithered, but no, on Olive blathers. 'And anyway, Jesus did have a dad. He had two. He had Joseph AND God!'

Sadie thinks Olive is definitely contemptible, might even be a cunt, but she don't want to say so and she don't want anyone to tell anyone else's dads or mums about the Fox or Jesus, so she has to come up with something. 'I do have a dad,' she manages.

'Do you?' Nirmal asks.

'I thought you knew *everyone* had a dad,' Olive reminds him. 'So why're you asking?' She sits back, satisfied as a cat. Nirmal ignores her. 'Do you?' he repeats. 'Who is he?'

These are the facts Sadie knows about her father:

1. That in July '69 he did 'it' (the mechanics of which she is still unclear on) to her mam, and nine months later – pop! – out comes Sadie, enormous and squalling. Eight pounds seven, according to her mam; so big they had to haul her out with tongs like the ones Mrs Higgins used on her twin tub.

2. That her mam's not set eyes on him since.

And these are the fictions she's been given:

1. That he was an acrobat, a magnificent man on the flying trapeze who had swung down long enough to fall in love with her mother before a lion got him or the circus left town.

2. That he was royal, a prince from a distant kingdom, who had come incognito to experience the world and had wanted to stop with Connie but the laws wouldn't allow it, wouldn't allow him to admit he had a daughter, so they had to content themselves with knowing her blood must be blue.

3. That he was French, a poet, shut away for months in a turret, years perhaps, while he penned his masterpieces that would astonish the world, and then and only then would they be able to rescue him, Rapunzel-like, by climbing his hair.

So many and marvellous were the stories, that she'd assumed for a while that he was some kind of magical jack of all trades, a master of everything – butcher, baker, candle-stick maker – and she had marvelled at the enormity of his ambition and achievement, told everyone at school his latest adventures. Until one day – nine, now – her mother, rum-drunk and sulking, spat out the truth, or an approximation of it – that he was nothing, a nobody, and Sadie were better off without. But by then she'd told too many people about the dazzling version and to change her story would be to concede an impossible defeat. So she swallowed the truth down and stoppered it up and plonked that bottle at the back of the cupboard and instead tried to keep hold of the charlatan father, preserving his brilliance like a pickle, or a cocktail cherry perhaps, pink and glistening and not at all like the real thing, but perfect in its own artificial way.

'He were just a man my mam knew,' she admits now. 'When she lived here, a long time ago.'

'Is that it?' asks Nirmal. 'No name or nothing?'

Sadie shrugs.

Nirmal frowns, eats his digestive – won't try the squashed-fly garibaldis, even though Sadie said they were nice once you knew they were just dried fruit. 'There'll be a way,' he says eventually.

Sadie's suspicious, and a little bit sick. 'How?'

'I don't know yet,' says Nirmal. 'But there must be.'

'What if he turns out to be someone bad. Like a criminal?' suggests Olive, smug as you like. 'You'd have to visit him in prison. He'd be bald. And have a tattoo—'

'My dad's not a criminal,' Sadie says sharpish.

'Might be,' replies Olive.

'Shut up, Olive,' Nirmal snaps, then nudges Sadie, a sharp elbow, all bone, but soft somehow. 'He's not in prison,' he promises.

But Olive don't shut up. 'Anyway, you can work it out,' she says. 'You can tell by eye colour.'

'How d'you mean?' she asks.

Olive sits up straight, pauses for her audience. 'Well, my mum's eyes are brown and my dad's eyes are brown, so mine are brown. Because brown rules everything. Even if my mum had blue eyes, my eyes would be brown. It's like a law.'

'My eyes are brown,' Nirmal points out.

'Well, duh,' said Olive. 'All Indians have brown eyes.'

'Do they?' Nirmal is unconvinced.

'Mine are green,' says Sadie, widening them so that both of them can see. 'But my mam's were brown.'

'So her dad's'll be green then?' Nirmal turns to Olive. 'Right?'

Olive fidgets. 'I only know about blue and brown. But green is weirder, so probably.'

'I know what we could do!' Nirmal blurts.

'What?' says Sadie.

'In our gang,' he clarifies. 'We could find your dad!'

Sadie's gob drops as her turning world judders to a halt, everything still, everything silent for just one second until—

'I bet that's illegal too,' Olive retorts.

Nirmal's having none of it. 'I bet it's not.'

But Sadie's insides are still spinning; she's remembering what her mam said: that he was a nothing, a nobody; that she's better off without. 'I don't know that I want to find him,' she says. 'Besides, Elvis is fetching me.'

'Elvis is dead,' says Olive. 'Everyone knows that.'

Sadie stiffens. 'No he in't. Not this one. He were my mam's boyfriend. For a year and seven months.'

'When's he coming?' asks Nirmal.

'Any day now,' Sadie says, sure all of a sudden. 'Probably tomorrow.'

'Oh.' Nirmal seems to shrink in his T-shirt. 'What shall we do until then then?'

'Ludo,' says Horrible Olive. 'I always win.'

Connie

Leeds, July 1981

She goes by herself in the end, to the Infirmary. She could have asked Donna, she supposes, but Donna's back in Connie's kitchen, snipping Joyce Caldecott's greying helmet into a Diana – the second already that week – and it's got to be Connie's because the car's failed its MOT and the drains are playing up and there's nothing to be done about either until her John gets back from wherever he is. Not that she minds that much. The company's nice when she's in and, when she's not, Donna can mind Sadie, so it's working out well for both of them.

Of course, Elvis hadn't agreed, but then Elvis is gone. Away in Skegness, singing 'Heartbreak Hotel' on a nightly basis to a bunch of Brummies on their yearly jolly, so his opinion counts for just about nothing.

She'd rung him. Decided she'd give him a last chance to redeem himself after the slap the night he left, when she told him she couldn't get time off, after all. Said could he pop back for a day – didn't say what for; hoped he'd twig. But he didn't. Said if it was 'the blinking kid' that needed minding then she could just leave her to Donna or leave her full stop because she wasn't the kind to set anything alight and if it was rapists she was worrying about then the Ripper'd just been given life and was banged up in Parkhurst, so to stop being thick.

She'd told him she was sick of him then. Sick of his bitching and his hitting, and that he was dumped. Then she'd hung up. He'd called back seconds later, swearing, telling her not to talk bollocks, that she'd regret it, that he'd come back and make her regret it. She'd held the phone out from her ear and then, when he'd done, told him again it was over, then left the phone off the hook so he couldn't tell her otherwise.

And so here she is, sitting alone on the cracked plastic in the back row of the department waiting room, seventeen patients ahead, all of them with several decades on her, which should set her mind at rest because she's in better shape them them, isn't she? But something about them, about the smell of disinfectant and death about the place, has sent her potentially fragile heart skittering already, a panicked mouse.

'Oh, belt up,' she says to herself. What are the chances of it being something to worry about? Ten per cent? Five? Probably I'll be sent back with a flea in my ear for wasting NHS time. Probably it's nothing at all.

Probably.

Afterwards, a nurse asks if she wants to ring someone to fetch her. Of course, she should have brought someone anyway, to something like this, just in case. Because you never know.

Well, she knows now. She's got it. Got something anyway – with a long name and a longer list of things she's got to stop doing: no drink, no drugs, no strenuous exercise and, yes, that means getting up on stage in the sweat and smoke of a club, she's not to do that, not anymore. And she's to take potassium – bananas, he said, that'll do – and come back for more tests in a few months' time; there'll be a letter telling her when.

She could drop dead any moment, see. She 'probably' won't, he'd added, the doctor with the list and the disinterested air about him, but look where probably had got her so far.

'Any questions?' he'd asked at the end, sounding like he hoped very much there wouldn't be.

But, 'Is it hereditary?' she'd asked. 'I mean, could my daughter have caught it?'

'You can't "catch" it,' he'd said, adding patronizing to his impatient tone. 'But, yes, it can run in families. So she'll need to be monitored at some point, if there are any signs she's having trouble. Is she?'

'No.' Thank God.

But that's not the worst of it.

'Are your parents alive?'

'What?'

The doctor sighs, as if he's dealing with someone particularly stupid or difficult. 'Your parents. Are they alive?'

She nods vaguely, suddenly muddled. Because she can't be sure, can only assume, and that fact knocks her for six.

'Well, you'll want to discuss this with them, I think. They should be seen.'

'Be seen?'

'By their GP. Are they local?'

'I— No.' She shakes her head. 'They're . . . They're in Essex.'

'Well, there, then. There'll be a waiting list. But they should be seen quicker now you're diagnosed, which is something.'

'Yes,' she says, not sure what she's agreeing with, not sure of anything at the moment because her head is hot, filled with a sudden rush of blood that whistles in her ears and renders her giddy, so that she thinks it might happen now; she might keel over right here in the assessment room.

But she doesn't. The dizziness passes as swiftly as it arrived and, after a plastic cup of water, she's sent back out into somehow inappropriate sunshine to catch the bus back up Clay Pit Lane.

At the corner shop, she picks up two packets of Frazzles and a bunch of browning bananas before heading back up the street and into the kitchen.

Donna's still hovering over Joyce Caldecott, who must have been finished an hour ago but seems to be enjoying the on-tap tea and gypsy creams too much to get back to her dusting. She looks about as much like Lady Diana as she does Angela Rippon, but Connie tells her she's a picture, and Donna says it's a shame old Charlie boy hadn't clapped his eyes on Joyce first.

She pops her string bag on the counter, away from the hair.

'Crisps!' says Sadie. 'Can we have them now?'

'Go on,' she tells her, watching as she and Deborah snaffle a packet each, take them into the back yard for sucking until the flavour's dissolved and they're nothing but mush on your tongue, like she'd taught them.

'You want one?' Sadie calls in.

'No, you're all right,' she calls back, and peels herself a banana – practically black and entirely claggy – instead.

'Get them from the Mehtas, did you?' says Joyce. 'State of them.'

'Thought you were popping to Morrisons?' adds Donna. 'Isn't that where you went?'

'Yes . . . No. I ended up just walking. In the sun,' she adds, like that makes it normal.

'Soft in the head,' mocks Donna. 'Or drunk. Talking of which, must be time for a quickie.' She nods at the fridge.

'Not for me,' says Joyce, cramming the last gypsy cream in her pink-lipsticked mouth and standing at last.

'Nor me,' says Connie.

'Spoilsports. That's a tenner,' she says to Joyce, who hands over two crumpled fives, both covered in crumbs.

'I'll sweep you out,' Donna says, going for the broom.

'Leave it,' says Connie. 'I'll do it later.'

'You all right?' Donna asks.

Joyce hovers in the doorway, hoping for a last morsel of gossip to add to the platter she's likely already been handed by Donna, only to embellish and pass on again.

And once Connie would have told her, happy to blab whatever, whenever, because who cared, really? Only the stuck-up and small-minded. Only the pursed-lipped. But now the cat, or shame itself, has got her tongue and she only wants to be alone.

'I'm fine,' she says. Then, desperate, adds, 'Sunstroke. I just need a lie-down.'

Donna tilts her Silvikrinned head. 'Ah, love, you go on up. I'll give the girls their tea.'

But bed's no better. The rottenness follows her up the stairs, dogs her when she kicks off her clogs, nags at her as she yanks the flimsy curtains shut and flops onto the mattress, now mercifully empty. Not the threat to her career, which is, she sees now, effectively dead. Not that it wasn't already, because not one of the London Colins or Clives or whoever-they-weres with their shiny suits and their fat cigars and their magic wands had shown up at the Legion, ready to say abracadabra and make her a star. Not a one. So no, not that, but rather the threat to her health. Because even though she 'probably' won't, what if she does drop down dead? What'll happen to Sadie then? Donna can't have her, not with her heading for divorce as it is. So that leaves who? Elvis? Christ, even if she'd not already dropped him, the thought's impossible. He was in and out of the house like a fly, and then there was the drinking, his slap-happy hands. He'd not used them on Sadie, but then he hadn't been making packed lunches five days a week, washing socks, helping her with homework, and God knows, they're drudgery enough, and at times unbearable – or tolerable only by locking yourself in the toilet and counting to ten. No one tells you that about being a mother, do they?

No, she's not courting Elvis again just for this.

Then she remembers it: the monster the doctor had raised, the kraken awake from its slumber.

Are your parents alive?

But, assuming they are – and she has to assume – that's not the real question, is it? No, what she has to know now – Christ, it's like a vision, a singing thing, vivid in front of her – is would they take Sadie?

And, more, would she want them to?

Jean

Essex, August 1981

The postcard is propped on the hallway table. It must have come this morning, though why Bernard hasn't done something with it is beyond her. Even simple household tasks like dealing with post – filing in priority order, or binning anything political – seem to evade him at times. What does he actually do all day?

She picks it up as she passes, eyes the picture – a whimsical kitten – with bristling distaste and not a little suspicion, turns it over:

Dear Sadie, she reads. Well, that explains it. She masks a sigh, continues.

Len and Rita have fostered a boy called John AND his rabbit, only he's friends with a punk! (John not rabbit). Glenda's up to something with Brian Tilsley and Gail's about to find out coz Vera's told Ivy. Also Sherie Melhuish is pregnant and everyone reckons it's Black Darryl. Love Deborah. PS When are you coming back? PPS Not Even Our Cat ate a dead sparrow and was sick on the bathroom mat.

How very repellent.

She steels herself, strides into the sitting room where

Bernard and the Child are playing some sort of board game – new, she notices with a nick of irritation, and, worse, gaudy. With noises. 'What on earth is that?' she demands.

But Bernard holds his hand up for silence while the Child, frowning with apparent concentration, pulls a pair of tweezers out of an anatomically incorrect cartoon man in pants.

'Look!'

She looks. In them is what appears to be, inexplicably – unforgivably – the wishbone of a chicken.

'Oh, well done!' Bernard says, praise as ever entirely out of proportion with achievement. Then he looks up at Jean, face lit with unmitigated glee. 'It's called Operation,' he explains. 'It's awfully engrossing.'

It's awful, that's for sure.

The Child holds up the offending piece of plastic again. 'You've to pull out his body parts without making it go off.'

'It's terribly clever,' adds Bernard, as the Child redoubles her efforts on a butterfly. A butterfly! 'All done by batteries.'

'It doesn't look clever. That's not even a piece of a person.'

Bernard pulls his mouth into a moue. 'Oh, it's only a game,' he says, strangely playful. He's been acting very odd recently, since the arrival of the Child – increasingly secretive and perpetually shed-bound. Though, whatever he's got going on in there, it's hardly likely to be gunrunning or an illicit still. At that impossible proposition, she snaps herself out of it, is about to remind Bernard that games can be dangerous, to point out that this one is misleading at best, when the Child fumbles and a drubbing buzzer sounds again and sends her heart skittering. 'Oh, honestly!'

'Good, in't it!' exclaims the Child.

She rights herself. 'Isn't it.' She turns to the other matter at hand, no less distressing. 'So, tell me, who are these people?' She holds up the postcard. 'Your neighbours, I assume?'

The Child laughs. Laughs, I ask you! 'Don't be daft. They're off *Coronation Street*. Brian's married to Gail. She's all right. Deborah reckons she looks like a monkey, but I don't mind her.'

The relief is almost thrilling. 'Thank heavens—'

'Except Sheric Melhuish,' the Child continues. 'She got kicked out of school last year and now she works at Morrisons with Mam.' She pauses. 'Only not anymore, I suppose.'

The silence thickens like Bisto.

'Well, you'd better finish up,' she says eventually. 'Dinner will be in fifteen minutes.'

It was twenty in the end, as she'd remembered *him* – Elvis Jenkins – and had to steady herself, had thought for a moment to open the Christmas port, then told herself off for being so predictably weak. Instead, she'd stood propped by the counter until her hammering heart had slowed to steady. Then, throughout dinner – eggs hard-boiled that morning, ham, a salad of halved tomatoes and some questionable lettuce – she is tense and restless, as if she's the one pulling plastic from a cardboard man. She can't concentrate, half an ear out as it is for the telephone; can't swallow properly, a mouthful of ham, claggy and bland, stuck on her tongue for more than a minute. But she is suddenly aware that the

Child has said something and awaits a reply, something that Bernard seems unable or unwilling to answer.

'Pardon?' she asks.

'Your eyes,' the Child seems to repeat. 'Yours are green and my grandpa's are blue, but my mam's were brown, so yours or Grandpa's should be brown by rights and all.'

'As well,' she says without registering.

'As well.' The Child dips half a tomato in mayonnaise – another new addition, and uncountenanced as well, though at least it isn't salad cream, she supposes. 'But they're not.'

'Not what? I'm not sure I follow.' She looks to Bernard for explanation but he is staring resolutely at his lettuce.

'Just that brown, eyes rule everything. So if my mam's eyes are brown, then one of you two's eyes should be brown and all – as well, I mean. Like, my eyes are green and my mam's eyes are brown, so my dad's eyes've got to be green and all, or where does the green come from?'

Jean thinks she might be sick, grips the underside of her chair so hard the ridge digs into her fingers. 'Who told you that? Nirmal, I suppose.'

The Child shakes her head. 'Olive Watkins.'

The perils of over-education. 'Well, you can tell Olive Watkins that she's wrong. There are . . . aberrations.'

'What's an aberration?'

She breathes deeply, an attempt to settle the swell in her stomach. It is impossible to be sick with air in your lungs; she read it in the paper. 'An anomaly.'

The Child frowns. 'But what's an anolamy?'

'An-OM-aly.'

'An-OM-aly. So what is it?'

She snatches for a simpler description. 'A black sheep,' she says then. And Bernard looks up at last, their eyes meeting over the plate of pickled beetroot. She senses the swell again and looks away.

'Was my mam a black sheep?'

'Well, obviously,' she mutters. And it's her turn to stare at the table, back as she is in the dark parlour in the side street off Myddelton Square.

'What colour are those eyes?' her brand-new mother-in-law had asked. 'Eyes change,' she'd said quickly – something a nurse had told her, with an edge to the friendliness, as if she understood the stakes. 'Of course,' Bernard's mother had murmured. 'Of course.' But with all the willing and hoping and praying in the world, Constance's eyes had remained a stubborn mud brown.

Her own mother had been another matter.

Bernard had insisted, said they couldn't visit his parents without seeing hers. They'd only find out, after all, Islington being what it is.

She'd known he was right, known gossip was passed down the Pentonville Road quicker than dysentery in a prison camp. And so they went, one October morning, summer still clinging to Finsbury, and Myddelton Square. But further in towards Farringdon, in the damp, cramped front parlour of the two-up two-down, the light had petered out, a weak beam struggling through the filth on the window before being swallowed by the rotten rug, snagged by dust and dead woodlice and empties.

'Bit big, ain't she,' her mother had said. 'For an early one.' Not a question, a matter of fact.

Jean's stomach had stuttered, insects flapping at the walls. But Bernard had rescued her, albeit unwitting.

'That's on my side,' he'd replied. 'We were all enormous. I was ten pounds four. We don't stay big though. None of us is tall.'

'No,' her mother had agreed sourly. 'You're not. Whose hair is that then?'

Another wing beat.

'My father's,' said Bernard again. 'He was quite dark, before the grey.'

Her own father, balding and awkward, grunted, though whether it was in assent or disagreement or just post-lunch drunkenness she'd not been able to tell.

Her mother, though, was not so easily persuaded. 'Dark horse, ain't you, Margaret,' she'd slipped in when Bernard went to fetch the kettle to top up the pot. 'Got him fooled. But you can't pull the wool over my eyes. I know what you are.'

They'd left not long after, Bernard oblivious, still. Or so she'd hoped.

'Am I?'

The Child's voice is whining now and she comes to with a jump. 'Sorry?'

'An an-OM-aly. Am *I* one? Am *I* a black sheep?'

The Child's eyes – green, she sees it now – are filled with something. Worry? But why all of a sudden?

'Of course not,' Bernard steps in, cat let go of his tongue.

'Your grandfather is right,' she adds, as if her testament makes it unquestionable. 'And anyway, it hardly matters now.' She feels herself flap loose, grabs for distraction. 'And enough of the questions. We're eating.' She turns to Bernard. 'Chop chop. There's peaches for pudding.'

And that is the end of it. No more prying or probing. No more threats of revelation.

But no blessed telephone call either.

It's gone eleven when Mr Jenkins eventually telephones. When they are already in bed – Bernard immersed in some pointless spy novel, still wishing, no doubt, that he'd grown up to be Bond; her feigning sleep. But at the shrill ring she sits bolt upright. 'I'll go.'

'But you have work,' Bernard barely protests, obviously angling to finish his chapter.

So by the time she replies with a whispered, 'It's fine,' she's already hauling on a dressing gown and halfway out the door.

She treads carefully past the Child's room, then slips down the stairs, takes the telephone from the hallway stand into the dining room, its spiral wire taut round the door.

'Harlow double two three one nine.' She is aware she sounds breathless, almost desperate. 'Jean Earnshaw speaking.'

It comes in a torrent, a horrible sobbing peppered with swears. If it wasn't for the anticipation, and the accent, she'd have hung up, reported a nuisance call. But she knows who this is, needs to keep him on the line until he's intelligible.

'Slow down,' she tells him, quells the urge to demand he

'use his words', something she'd said to Constance on more than one occasion when she was in another of her flapping tantrums, prostrating herself on the hallway floor when forbidden to go to the swings or, later, when grounded, banned from the Birdcage, threatening death to herself or willing it on her mother.

There's a pause while he snorts and – oh, dear God, spits – then, 'Where's the kid?' he asks at last.

The kid? She's more measured now, steady, because she must not mess this up. 'She's here,' she says brightly. 'Asleep.'

'Can I talk to her?'

She checks the clock on the mantel – Bernard's prize for retirement, that and a photograph, the one with the Prince. 'It's half past eleven,' she says. 'That's rather late to wake a child.'

'But I've got to say . . . I've got to say sorry.' The man is blabbering.

'For what?'

There is a groan and some other indeterminate but unpleasant sounds. 'I shouldn't have done it,' he says wetly. 'I didn't mean to. I never mean to.'

She stiffens. Things are beginning to clarify. 'What did you do?'

'It wasn't even that hard. And I'd been drinking. It was only ever when I'd been drinking.'

With that, something in her sours, solidifies.

This man is not to be trusted, to be believed about anything, she realizes. Of course the Child has painted him an angel. A sheep in wolf's clothing, treating her to sweets and the cinema. Bringing in tat that she sees as treasure. But he's a fraud, like all the others. Like Jean's own father, who claimed to be out earning when he was losing *her* wages on a bet on a dog. Who claimed her own mother – sly and nimble – had walked into a door not once but three times, the last landing her in hospital.

'Can I see her?' the voice asks, plaintive now, pathetic.

'No,' she says. 'Not right now.'

'I meant on a weekend or something.'

'Like I said, not at the moment. She's . . . recovering.'

'Will you not be bringing her back to Leeds for the funeral?'

So he hasn't even bothered to ring the Donna woman. Of course he hasn't. He's been drunk or distracted for days now. Months, probably.

'There isn't one,' she tells him, matter-of-fact. Well, there isn't. Because how could they stand there, honestly, in front of God, and mourn? What good would that do anyone? And a funeral's no place for a child, anyway.

'But—'

'And Sadie will be staying here.' And there is the end to it.

The sobbing recommences, segueing into a cough so guttural and productive that she has to hold the receiver away from her ear.

'Goodbye, Mr Jenkins,' she says eventually, and hangs up the telephone, the receiver clicking into place like a full stop.

'Who was that?' asks Bernard, barely even looking up from the page.

'The boyfriend,' she says, getting into bed. 'He's not . . . able to take her.'

Bernard puts down the paperback. 'So, schools, then,' he says, with undisguised excitement.

'Not now, Bernard, please,' she says, feeling a terrible sensation, a welling of salt water, an imminent brimming. Before he can notice, she turns to the curtain and clicks the switch at the wall, plunging the pair of them into near pitch.

'Jean?'

She hears him, reaching across the twin bed breach between them.

But his hand rests for barely a second on her shoulder, then retracts, leaving her to fathom if the tears are in anger, in frustration or – almost unthinkable – sheer relief.

Sadie

Essex, August 1981

Mornings are the tricky bit. When she wakes and for a golden moment everything's soft focus and blurrily hopeful, and then she remembers: her mam is dead, she's fetched up in Essex, and now Elvis Jenkins in't even coming to rescue her.

She'd heard the phone call – had snapped awake with it, slithered out of bed and listened in with her ear pressed against the hot-air vent in the hope of catching at least snippets of it. But none of the sentences seemed to make any sense. It were all a lot of quiet and then short words hissed out so she couldn't hear right. She'd opened the door a crack more then, waited for the Grandma to get back upstairs and tell the Grandpa what time Elvis was due, maybe even in the morning, maybe she'd even have to pack right away, slip the pine cone, the I-Spys, her new Operation game into her suitcase, ready for the off.

But when she heard the words, they weren't, 'He'll be here any minute,' or, 'Nine o'clock sharp on Thursday morning,' or owt like that. They were: 'He's not able to take her.' And with those seven syllables her world tripped over for the second time in weeks. Because she knew then she was stuck: trapped with a grandma who don't even like her, not really. And the Grandpa's nice but he's old and he'll probably pop his clogs soon, and then where'll she be?

And all of a sudden she'd felt urgently queasy, as if she might be sick on the carpet, so she'd opened her suitcase, ready gaping on the chair, and held it under her mouth in case. In the end, nothing came up, and after a while she found she was shivering in her nightie and so she dropped it and got back into bed, cold and sorry.

She'd kissed the picture for a bit then, her and Mam, the Whimsey snug in her hand, but nothing fixed it and she was sweating anyway so the Whimsey slipped and got lost under the covers somewhere and she didn't have a torch and she couldn't turn the light on without the Grandma swooping in to ask if she was ill or needed a wee.

As it was, she'd been too tired to get up the next morning, said her stomach hurt and all. The Grandma put it down to sugar – Nirmal had brought round strawberry Chewits, it was true, plus they'd had all the garibaldis – told the Grandpa to make sure she had only savoury today – soup, preferably, or hot Bovril. But when she was gone, when the door had clunked shut and the car idled down the drive, he'd brought her up a mug of hot chocolate – cocoa, he called it – told her not to say anything to the Grandma.

'Is it true?' she'd said then. 'That Elvis Jenkins in't coming?'

He'd looked odd then, dropped his head, put his hand on her leg where it hid under the cover. 'I'm sorry, Sadie,' he'd said. 'But it's probably for the best.'

She'd said nowt to that, just sipped at the drink, though it tasted strange, a bit like floral gums, and she wondered if he'd washed the cup up wrong and not rinsed, 'cause men were like that, her mam always told her, so she'd put it down on the bedside table next to the picture.

'Feeling a bit under the weather, are you?'

She'd nodded.

'Best stay in bed, then. Maybe a game later.'

And so there she'd stayed for nearly two days, bar needing the loo. Reading the dictionary; playing with Dave, who got brought to her bed, though she'd to pick up his poos and flush them down the loo before the Grandma got home; listening for Nirmal, who knocked every day.

'Are you sure you don't want to see him?' the Grandpa'd asked on the third morning.

But she hadn't. Hadn't wanted to tell him that Elvis had let her down. To tell him it had all been in her head, and her mam's, just like her dad being a trapeze artist or a pirate or a prince.

But by eleven she's twitching, bored of sticking Dave down a toilet roll, bored of dirty words, bored of Operation, even, 'cause the Grandpa's not trying to win and where's the fun in that?

'Why don't you write to Deborah again?' he suggests after they've had a rich tea biscuit, a glass of milk. 'You could tell her about Harlow.'

'Tell her what?' she asks.

'I don't know. The garden. Olive Watkins.'

Horrible Olive. She's not been over since she lost at Ludo,

'cause her mam said she'd a weak constitution and couldn't be catching anything before Covenanter camp.

'You could ask about *Coronation Street* again.'

'What for?' she says, belligerent as a scolded toddler. 'I can just read the description in the paper. Not like I'm ever going to watch it again, is it.'

'I'm sorry,' he says. 'But I still think you should try to write something.'

'Fine,' she sulks. 'If I have to.'

The Grandpa don't seem to mind that she's moody, helps her with it even. There's no glossy snapshot on the postcard this time, it's just a blank one from his drawer, but she can draw a picture, he says, or something. In the end she does something: she sticks on a picture of David Essex she's snipped out of the *Radio Times*. Then, on the other side, she writes:

Dear Deborah,
    I'm not coming home, so you can keep the cat. Brian Tilsley's an idiot.
    Love Sadie

'To the point,' says the Grandpa.

She shrugs, still determined to be sullen if she can manage it, though she has to admit the snipping out pleased her somehow.

'I've an idea,' the Grandpa says then. 'Why don't you go and post it now? You could do with some fresh air.'

Fresh air again. Why were old people so obsessed with it? What with that and the brown bread, she were the healthiest she'd ever been. But then the next thing he says perks her up another touch.

'You can go by yourself.'

'To the postbox on Church Street?'

He nods.

'Past Nirmal's?'

'Why not?'

Why not? she supposes. Why not post it and call on Nirmal and all? She don't have to say owt about Elvis, just say things have changed, just for the moment. That they can be in a gang, after all. Least for the summer. They can hunt for someone. Solve a crime. Become heroes.

Then it comes to her, sudden, loud and precise, as clear as if God himself were talking: 'We could find your dad, Sadie,' it says. 'Fetch him home.'

And so brimming with it is she, shimmering and tipsy, that she thinks it probably were God that said it, and that'll show Horrible Olive what's what. Which isn't the point, but is nice, besides. Though then she remembers that it might have been Nirmal said it before. That maybe she'd muddled them. But what did it matter? The point was to do it.

'No talking to strangers,' the Grandpa says as he hands her the stamp.

'I won't,' she replies. 'I promise.'

And she'll not, because Nirmal's not a stranger.

He's her friend. He's in her gang, her detective gang, and now they've a job and it's urgent and all.

And off she bobs, out the door and into the morning.

*

And all along Church Street she thinks of him – her dad – and of what he might be like. He might be a doctor, an army medic like Hawkeye or Trapper or Klinger in *MASH*. No, not Klinger, she don't want him wearing a dress necessarily. But Hawkeye'd be fine. Or better, he could be a vet – he could be Christopher Timothy with his hand up a cow, or Tristan Farnon, who's a bit of a handful but handsome enough. Or he might be a vicar, a kind one though, and without the dandruff like Mr Kittering.

'I don't think he'll be a vicar,' says Nirmal, now they're back at the house. 'But he might be famous, like Prince Charles or Elvis,' he says. 'Not Jenkins, I mean, the real one.'

'Elvis is dead,' she tells him. 'Everyone knows that.'

Nirmal shrugs. 'My cousin reckons it's a lie and he's just living in a massive mansion somewhere or on the moon eating peanut butter and watching telly. Anyway, he wasn't dead in 1969, and that's what matters.'

She looks at him, nose screwed up. 'Duh, it's not what matters. No point finding him if he's not alive. Or where'll I go to live?'

'Oh.' Nirmal slumps somehow. 'I didn't think of that. You definitely going, then?'

'Definitely. Once we get him.'

'Right.'

'So come on then.' The need is so pressing, the want so hot, she can barely stop her legs from jiggling. 'Where do we start?'

'Birth certificate.' Snapped to, Nirmal is whirring with it. 'I saw it on *Coronation Street*.'

Her insides jink. 'You watch *Corrie*? But you're from Essex.'

'So? I'm allowed, aren't I?'

'Aye.' She smiles inside.

'So, d'you remember when . . . thingy found it, with his dad's name on? Only it wasn't who he expected.'

'Aye!' she yelps with it, forgives the 'thingy' 'cause he's only a boy after all and he must've missed loads when the telly were broke.

'So where d'you reckon it is, then?'

She thinks for a minute, goes through the places the Grandma might hide things. Then remembers that nowt's been brought in from the shed, not that she's seen, any road.

She asks the Grandpa for the key.

'What do you want to get in the shed for?'

'Gang hut.' Nirmal grins.

Sadie nods.

The Grandpa puts his hands on his hips and looks into the distance like he's thinking about history. 'Gang hut indeed. Well, as long as it's between us and you don't touch the tools or the paint, I'm sure you can use it.'

'Skill!' Nirmal whispers.

She nudges him back as the Grandpa hands over the key and a plate of six rich teas and all. 'Here,' he says. 'Don't—'

'Tell my Grandma,' she finishes. 'I won't.'

And he nods at them and watches them off, Nirmal balancing the biscuits as he runs, her with the cold metal heavy in her hot hand, ready to open sesame the door and reveal Aladdin's cave of treasure.

Only it's less splendid than she expected. There's nowt shining or gilded, no jewels to dazzle them, just jars of nails and shelves of paint tins and plastic bottles, and at the top a row of cardboard boxes – one cat food, two crackers, one something called Le Piat d'Or, which must be wine 'cause there's a bottle on it – and above it all a strange taint of creosote.

'So, what's the box look like?' Nirmal asks.

'I don't know,' she says. 'I can't remember.'

'Did she eat a lot of crackers?' Nirmal tries. 'Your mum, I mean. Or drink tons?'

'No,' snaps Sadie, defensive. 'And she didn't eat cat food, neither.' Though this is a white sort of lie, 'cause they'd tried the hard sort once, slipped the biscuits into their mouths on a bad day. They weren't as bad as all that.

'My cousin reckons he knows a man who's tried it. Says it's like Fray Bentos, only cold.'

'That's disgusting,' she musters.

'Yup!' replies Nirmal, then adds an 'aye' like he's trying it for size, smiles at her.

She smiles back. 'Hang on.' She snatches at something. 'We have got a cat, though.'

'Eureka!' he shrieks. 'That's what someone said when they found something famous. Can't remember what, though.'

Mam'd know, she thinks. But still, she feels like *The Sweeney* then. Or *Cagney and Lacey*; the fat, brown-haired one, 'cause Deborah's always the blonde.

'I'll fetch it,' he says. And before she can stop him he's climbed on the workbench and is teetering on his knees, hands grabbing the bottom of the Kitekat box and yanking it out.

'Careful!' she tells him.

'What?' He turns, box balanced like he's a washerwoman. 'It's only paper, anyway.'

'Aye, but . . . watch yourself. You don't want to –' she thinks of something – 'get a blister.'

'Blister,' he dismisses, dropping the box on the bench and shimmying down, like he's the cat in the picture. 'Here.' And he lifts it again and plops it on the floor at her feet. 'This it?'

She has to peel back packing tape before she can open it, and even then she does it slow, like she's scared what might fly out – bats or beetles or secrets, perhaps. But then she sees an envelope on top, sees her mam's name typed out neat, sees the red of the letterhead squint from inside, the words *final bill* stamped fatly. 'This is it,' she says.

'So come on then,' Nirmal says, squatting frog-like on haunches next to her. 'Let's find your dad. And if it's Prince Charles or the actual Elvis, you owe me ten pence.'

'Aye, all right,' she replies. 'Ten pence.'

She's won that one at least, 'cause there's no way it's Elvis, or Prince Charles, not with them ears.

But somewhere in here, she's convinced he'll be hiding, with his pale eyes, not brown ones, his freckles maybe, and his love for her mother, eleven years ago.

Connie

Leeds, July 1981

The box is on top of the wardrobe, pushed to the back behind a wide-brimmed sunhat that last saw light in the summer of 1976, a pair of stack-heeled stage boots in cracked silver, an old bong. She has to teeter on a chair to get to it, brush off months of dust, but here it is now, sitting on the bedspread like Pandora's own, not that she can remember who Pandora was exactly, Classics being one of many lessons she'd spent adrift in her own imagination or slack-jawed at the window instead of riveted to Miss Whoever. But she knows instinctively there was magic in it, and menace as well; bad things that, if you prised it open even an inch, might fly at you and unleash terrible memories or fates worse than death.

At that thought she glances out the window again, checking that Sadie's still walking the wall, her and Deborah in lemon-yellow mini dresses they picked out (or Deborah did) from the Littlewoods catalogue, dresses she and Donna have still got to pay off on the monthly. They were meant for best, for the wedding, but the minute the packages arrived they were itching to get in them, turning themselves into Cheryl and

Jay, wrapping towels over the top to whip off in the middle of their routine. That's what they're at now – performing for an audience of gawping small Mehtas, Billy Hepworth, and Mrs Higgins, no doubt, twitching behind her nets.

She's safe, then. Happy. For now.

Because Sadie's the thing. The point of it all. It's for Sadie she's even thinking of doing this. Because someone's got to be responsible for her, if . . . if you know what. Got to look after her, clothe her, pay for her, anyway. And she can hardly ask the father, can she? A year ago she might have begged Elvis, but things have changed. Everything's changed. And who'd want to take on someone else's kid for that kind of never-never, if they were honest? Only one person she knows. A man she hasn't seen in exactly twelve years – since the night they put the man on the moon. He'd jump at it, she thinks. But it's not him she's thinking about, not really. It's who he comes attached to.

Sometimes, she can't believe she's even considering it. Because what would that Connie have thought? That seventeen-year-old, hurt, determined version of her. But that girl's gone, or mostly, worn down from years of hard graft and high tar and low rent. Only here she is, looking for that very girl at the bottom of a Kitekat box she'd got from Morrisons when they were first moving here from the flat in Chapeltown. Two days before she got the job. A few weeks before she played the Adelphi and met the man she's sent merrily to Skegness and then packing for good because, when it came down to it, she realized they were all the flaming same.

Except one.

She steels herself then with an Embassy, lighting it with the Zippo Elvis left on the bedside. She shouldn't be smoking, and she won't, once this is settled. She'll give it up properly, along with the gin and the gigging. For Sadie's sake, if not her own. Because that's what mothers do.

Christ, she can't keep stalling. Time and tide and all that. Besides, Sadie'll be in in a bit, wanting crisps and a drink and to ask for the hundredth time why they can't go to the caravan. She stubs out the cigarette on Sadie's ashtray, grasps the cardboard in both hands and yanks it open like the gaping maw of a wound.

But the world does not stop spinning; a whirl of crows or ghosts do not soar out black-mouthed and clattering; her heart doesn't cease to beat. Instead, she hears the squeal outside as one or other of them trips off the bricks and onto the pavement, and the claps of the Mehtas as they right themselves and start the song again.

Fine, she says. I'm fine.

And then she sticks in her hand and pulls out, not a plum, but the first in a stack of identical notebooks, dog-eared and battered, but still glossy and red and all bearing not just the print of the brand name, but inked italics spelling out her own.

Constance Earnshaw. KEEP OUT!

Breath held, chest tight, she turns the page to find the date, *1 January 1969*, and her opening gambit, which is so obvious she coughs out a sort of scorn at herself. Because what else would she have written at seventeen? What else could she have scrawled out than, *I actually hate my mother*?

Perhaps she did. Perhaps she still does.

That's what she's going to try to find out. Hope that she can overcome. Because this – not London – is her last-chance saloon. She sees it now. Elvis is dead. Or sent packing at least. She's written a letter saying not to bother coming back except to fetch the rest of his clothes and the tat in the back room.

No, her future – Sadie's future – isn't with him, nor any fancy man, as Elvis would have it. Nor even, maybe, in Leeds. But perhaps, just perhaps, in the concrete walkways and water gardens, the landscaped parks and serried estates of a still-new town two hundred miles away.

And here, between these pages, is where she'll check.

And, steeling herself a second time, she begins to read.

Jean

By the morning any doubt had been dispelled, dispatched with the practised yank of the curtains, and a strong cup of tea. They would keep the Child, mind it, raise it right. And there'd been relief – brief but appreciated – that something maternal burgeoned in her, after all.

Only now, in place at Pinnacle Biscuits, she is suddenly overcome with the enormity of it: hemmed in and flailing, precarious, and yet pinned down at once.

She remembers this feeling.

The fear of being stuck with her mother, stuck with the pair of them, a fool and his fishwife, in that coop of a front room. Forced to wash their pots and fetch their slippers; being sent out for chips, for cigarettes, for gin, then coming home only to be told she'd got it wrong. A future mapped out and it's no more than two roads wide and four roads down and the rest of the landscape's not even worth eyeing.

It was as if she was crammed into a pickle jar or pressed between pages, to be shelved and forgotten. No wonder she'd fallen for him; no wonder, when that blew up so

212

spectacularly, she'd turned to Bernard. She could have shared, she supposed, found a house with a girlfriend. It wasn't a crime, after all. But at that word, she'd baulked, even back then. For who among her female colleagues could she call a friend? Not Cynthia Wigley, with her seamed stockings and staggering lack of tact. Not waxy Elsa Ray, who smelled of death. And certainly not Julia Horvath, who had made it perfectly clear she thought Margaret – not Jean, yet – was a bad penny just waiting to be shone up and scorned.

Oh, the Child's not like that, that's not what she's saying, but still she is somewhat lumbered with her. There'll be all the tedious intricacies of school to sort out, after all – which one, and where, and whether they'll even accept her with that upbringing and accent. And she's probably terms, if not years, behind in her learning. Probably never heard of Archimedes or Crete. Can she even complete her times tables, for heaven's sake? She'll have to test her, she supposes, tutor her. And for what? To have it thrown back in her face or frittered away eight years later when she falls for the first thing she sees in trousers or fancies herself a pop star.

No thank you very much.

But then she feels the spill of it, like sump oil or treacle, inky and thick and choking. Because she hasn't got the option, has she? Not anymore. Not with Mr Jenkins such a mess and a terror, and with no father to speak of. Of course, if she could work out who it was then that might be another matter, but the birth certificate was clear on that, and where else would he be hiding? Constance obviously didn't want him contacted, so heaven knows what's wrong with him. No doubt something will manifest later. It always does. A weak knee, asthma, a habit of mendacity. Look at Constance.

'Jean?'

Maurice is calling her, still hasn't mastered the internal phone.

She shakes off her reverie and picks up her pen.

Pinnacle Biscuits business, and Maurice, must come first now. School and the Child can wait. It's still summer, after all, there's Covenanter camp to come, and who knows what might happen then. Perhaps God will talk to her, guide her down the right and righteous path. Yes, she must hope He will answer her finally – His Christian soldier, marching onward despite His seemingly stubborn silence.

'Jean?' Maurice repeats.

'Coming,' she flusters. 'Coming at once.'

Sadie

Essex, August 1981

'"Unknown"?'

'Aye, "unknown",' she repeats, the certificate stiff between her thumb and forefinger, a thing she'd never thought to ask about – never even knew existed, not really. And now wishes she'd not bothered. 'If she didn't even know, what hope have I got?'

'What?' Nirmal shakes his head. 'No, you don't get it. He's not actually unknown. I reckon she just put it on there to cover it up. Because it's such a big secret. Because she doesn't want anyone else finding out, see?'

Sadie nods, she does see, but she also don't see how they can do anything now and says so.

'There'll be other stuff.'

'Like what?'

'I don't know.' Nirmal lifts his shoulders. 'Clues. Maybe a letter from him. Or a letter to you!' He's seized with it then. 'Maybe she's written, in case of emergency. My cousin's mate's mum did that when she had cancer. Wrote all his birthday cards for the next – I don't know – loads of years.'

Right then she wishes so hard, she puffs up like a balloon

with the hoping. Then sticks a pin in herself – pop! 'But my mam didn't know she were going to die.'

'Well, she must've known it'd happen one day.' He holds his hands up. 'We're all going to die, Sadie. That's what my uncle says. Only not "Sadie", 'cause that'd be weird.'

She don't know what to say to that, don't want to think about her insides shrivelling and bits of her blacking up and falling off or whatever happens when you get ancient. 'Shall we just look?' she says.

'Okay. But slowly. You know, bit by bit. We don't want to miss vital evidence.'

'Did your cousin tell you that?'

'No,' he says, serious as a teacher. 'Columbo.'

Most of it's bills, and red ones at that. Her mam owed loads, even ones Elvis reckoned he'd sorted for her. There were a letter as well, from the landlord – Mr Cavey, with his too-big forehead and his too-short trousers and his spittle at the corners of his mouth that made Sadie feel sick. Told her if she didn't pay up the three months they owed, they'd be out by September; he'd bring his own van if he had to. That one were weird 'cause she remembered her mam giving Elvis the twenties – brand-new ones from her pay, so he could take them round on his way to Jimmy King's. Thick Jimmy King, as Mam had it.

The pause is taut when Nirmal gets to that one and she can feel the fidget in him, the fear.

'I won't tell,' he says to her. ''Specially not Horrible Olive.'

She takes it, grateful.

'Is it like *Coronation Street?*' he asks then. 'You know, Leeds.'

'Don't be daft. Leeds is miles from Manchester.'

'Daft,' he repeats, the 'a' short now, like hers.

'Anyway, it's telly, in't it. Not real.'

'But the Rovers? And Bet?'

'Not even a real pub,' she says. 'Just propped-up wood with the name painted on. It's all filmed in a studio.'

'How d'you know?'

'I've seen it, in't I. Not inside, like. But driving past.' In the front of a van, maundering through Salford with only one wiper and the drizzle thick as milk.

'Lucky,' Nirmal says.

She shrugs. She don't feel it.

They get back to the stack in silence, picking off each slip, each slice of cardboard or torn-open envelope or printed receipt with a scribble on the back, but it's gas and leccy and *Friday 9th Wigan WMC*, which was a gig, she knows that.

It's useless.

'Maybe there in't owt,' she admits, her insides sinking, the flicker of diamond-bright possibility guttering and going out. 'Maybe she really didn't know who he was.'

But Nirmal's determined. 'There'll be something,' he tells her. 'I bet Columbo wouldn't give up.'

He's a bit thick, she thinks then. Kind, but not all with it. 'Columbo's not even real,' she says with a sigh. 'He's like Vera or Bet or . . . or Brian Tilsley.'

'Tell that to my mum. She'd marry him if it wasn't for

217

my dad. Columbo, I mean. Not Brian. She doesn't like his hair. Too bouffy.'

He slaps a red exercise book on the finished stack, gets back to the drabs at the bottom of the box.

But Sadie, liking the writing – 'Silvine' in swirls – snaffles it back, thinking she'll keep it to use for something – for poetry or pictures. Then she sees it, at the bottom, not printed but in black italic and fountain pen besides. *Constance Earnshaw. KEEP OUT!* But not just that, 'cause then the *Constance* bit is crossed out and *Connie Rocket* written in its place, then the *Rocket*'s gone and *Holiday*'s there instead.

'What's that?' Nirmal asks.

'I don't know,' she admits.

'Give us a see.' And he grabs it. '*Holiday*,' he reads. 'Is that your surname?'

'Aye.' But then she remembers. 'Only not hers. Hers was Earnshaw.'

'But perhaps your dad's was Holiday?'

'I don't think so. She hated him, remember?'

He squints, tips his head. 'But maybe she didn't back then.'

She watches, gape-mouthed as a fledgling then, as he opens it wide, pressing it down so the spine might snap. 'What d'you think you're doing?'

'What d'you mean? I'm reading it.'

'But it's secret. A diary's private, in't it.'

He looks at her like she's the idiot then, thick as mince. 'Exactly.'

The air crackles for a second, blistering with possibility. Then they hear it.

'Sadie?'

The pair of them flap at that, the exercise book dropped, the stack knocked over in the panic. 'Grandpa,' she says, as if he don't know. Then she sticks her head out the shed smartish. 'Coming!' she calls. Then, back to Nirmal, 'Quick.'

But Nirmal don't need telling, not even once. He's packing the paper back in the cardboard cat box, not too messy neither, so's it's not obvious what they've been at. Then they've hauled it up on the workbench, her on tiptoe on top of the lawnmower to help him slot it in place.

The red exercise book she's kept, though, stuffs it down the back of her trousers.

Nirmal pulls a face.

'What?' she demands. 'I had a wash yesterday.' She thinks. 'Or maybe the day before. But I'm clean, honest.'

'Never said you weren't.'

'Come on then.'

He grins at her and she's fat with it – their gang and her dad and her mam's words down the back of her pants.

She has to walk funny, though, a sort of bandy-legged stagger.

'What's wrong with you?' the Grandpa asks when they're at the back door.

'She needs a wee,' Nirmal says for her. 'Been busting for ages.'

Sadie reddens.

'Silly thing. You should've come in.'

'What'd you say that for?' she demands after she's been up to the lav and back, and the Grandpa's safely in the kitchen setting the table.

Nirmal taps his nose. 'Cover,' he says. 'Columbo says the best detectives are as good at lying as criminals.'

'Really?'

He shrugs. 'Don't know. But it sounds like something he'd say, don't you think? And it's only a white lie, anyway. Not like you're saying you didn't deck someone when you did.'

'Fair enough.'

'Where'd you stash it?' he says then.

'Under my mattress,' she says.

'*Cagney and Lacey*?' he asks.

'No. My mam.'

'Nice one. So I'll see you tomorrow maybe? You can report back. If there's any evidence.'

'Tomorrow,' she nods.

'See you later, alligator,' he says then, his grin as wide as a reptile, but nicer, real. 'Bye, Mr Earnshaw,' he calls out.

'Bye, Nirmal,' comes the reply.

'Bye, Columbo,' he says again. 'That's you, that is.'

Then he's off on his Grifter, wobbling down the drive 'cause gravel's no good for riding, skidding round the corner and back to his flat.

She's desperate to get to it.

At dinner she fidgets, picks at her food so the Grandma says, 'Honestly,' and the Grandpa asks if she's feeling peaky again.

'It was too soon for visitors,' the Grandma says, pith-bitter. 'You've probably caught something.'

Sadie stares at the Grandpa, panicked. 'What visitors?' she feigns, remembering Columbo.

'The gravel had bicycle tracks in it, so there's no point denying it.'

Columbo hadn't thought of that, and she sighs.

'It'll need raking later,' the Grandma adds, beady-eyed at her husband.

'He was just checking on her,' the Grandpa explains. 'And he seemed perfectly well.'

'That's not the point.'

'Perhaps I'd best get to bed,' Sadie says quickly. 'Just in case of germs and stuff. Do some reading.'

The Grandma nods, even manages a smile, so for a moment Sadie feels wicked for telling a fib, even a white one. But only for a moment, because then the smile slips. 'Well, run along then. And do your teeth!' She looks at the Grandpa. 'I know she was at the biscuits again. I counted.'

'Maybe *I* had biscuits,' he says.

'Six of them? I should hope not. You'll get diabetes.'

'Night,' says Sadie, before anything else kicks off.

'Night night,' says the Grandpa, and gives her a grin as neat as a wink.

The Grandma only nods this time, but she don't care, not anymore.

'Cause in less than eight minutes, according to her watch, she's got gleaming teeth and a flannelled face and never mind the lies, whatever colour – they'll wash off and all, once this is sorted.

So under the covers she slips, curtain open enough that a

segment of sun sends the Silvine exercise book, back from the mattress, a startling scarlet.

Taking a breath and saying a prayer to the god who told her to do this, she opens the cover.

1 January 1969, she reads, and feels a flicker. Only seven months to go before she – Sadie Marie – appears on the scene. Or in her belly, any road.

She gets back to it.

1 January 1969

I actually hate my mother.

Connie

Essex, January 1969

Her vexation has texture, is thick and viscous as syrup, which she only knows because she's been allowed it at Martha's on a Sunday after church with steamed pudding, or spooned from the Lyle's tin when her mother's on the telephone to Mrs Wentworth, who does the flowers. No wonder Martha's still so big, though, if she's pinching syrup and biscuits and who knows what else from the larder every time Mrs Collins' back's turned. Why does she even pretend to be on a diet – all those bitter grapefruit segments and endless weak tea – if she's bingeing in secret? She should just come and live at Connie's house for a week – that would slim her instantly. No biscuits except crackers, no pudding except fruit, no syrup on anything.

She thinks of her mother then, prim and thin, as if taking up too much room in the world is a sin in itself. Squeezed tight in a tweed two-piece, hair forced into a pleat. Rigid. Frigid. 'Got a right pole up her arse,' Terry had said once, and he wasn't wrong, though she flinched at the time, a spasm of embarrassment sending her cheeks flaring and her indignation sourer still.

223

Not that Terry is a model citizen. He gets in a terrible mood at times. She'd rather Mick Jagger, whose image on an LP sleeve she kisses at night before she goes to bed, whose girlfriend, Marianne Faithful, she's modelled her latest look on – all big hair and doe eyes and cigarettes, the filthier the better. Or Bobby Kennedy, even. According to Harriet Wright-Cooper, he carries a copy of Camus around in his back pocket. Round here you're lucky if it's a comb and a condom.

God, she loathes it. Loathes them – her parents. They had the world as their oyster and they chose the edge of wretched Essex. This town where nobody comes from. Because it was clean, green, new. Which to be fair it is, but all that green seems so terribly bleak to her. A waste of potential houses, potential people. God knows how anyone in the villages copes. All those trees, that space. Where every day is like Sunday because nothing ever happens. Might as well stick her in a coffin now if this is it.

All around the world – in San Francisco, Paris, London, just seventeen miles up the road (she's checked on a map) – people have been rioting, staking a claim on a different future. She's seen it on the news on television and read it in the papers – *The Times* and the *Mirror*, thankful her father is as broad-minded in his reading material as he is about her behaviour, unlike some people. And she's been waiting for a ricochet or even a mere ripple to make its way to the Harlow hinterlands but there hasn't been so much as a riffle of wind. Life plods on in its staggering mediocrity and she, less than patient, sits in this staid waiting room of a town, praying for life with a capital L to begin.

Her mother's no help.

'But what are they against?' the woman had asked, exasperated, as Connie thrilled to the pictures of students brandishing placards and barricading themselves in.

'Just the order of things, I think, Jean,' her father replied.

Her mother's lips had thinned so much she looked more pious than Miss bloody Bixby, fifty-something and still a virgin, according to half of Essex Ladies. 'Well, I don't think disorder is the answer, do you?'

Stifling a groan, but unable to do the same with her words, she'd blurted out, 'It's you.'

'I beg your pardon.'

'Not you, literally,' she'd clarified, sensing a sending to bed in the offing. 'But it's people like you they hate. You know, old people. The middle class.'

'How absurd. It's probably jealousy, then.'

'God, you really don't get it, do you? They'd rather die than be you. So would I,' she'd added, quieter, though not so quiet it wasn't caught.

Her latest affectation, her mother had called it – professing to despise the middle class.

Well, it isn't an affectation, it's the truth. She hates the pomposity of it, the hypocrisy, the horrible hierarchy that marks her and Martha out as acceptable because of the stupid blue uniforms they wear, the name of the road they live on, and marks Michelle Spencer as 'common' or 'vulgar' or somehow undeserving. 'We all fart,' she'd said once, and earned a slap for it – a flat hand across the back of her thigh – even though she'd kept the 'and fuck' under her breath. 'Well, maybe *you* don't,' she'd added then. 'Or, if you do, it probably smells like bloody Windolene.'

That one warranted grounding and no television for a week.

So, she's damned if she's going to turn out like them, or like *her*, anyway. When she's grown up – or more grown up, given she's already seventeen – she'll have a flat on a Paris backstreet off the Boulevard St-Michel, and eat nothing but bloody macaroons dripping with syrup. If she eats at all, because she's pretty sure French women exist on Gauloises and black coffee. She'll have a dog as well, something thin like a whippet, perhaps. Her mother won't have dogs. Dirty animals, she says, and cats are barely better, licking their 'area' on the sofa without an iota of shame.

Well, she'll have a sodding dog, just wait and see. She'll call it Pierre and feed it chicken in aspic and let it shit on the carpet if it wants. And she'll change her name to Colette or Brigitte or Margot with a 't'.

That will show her.

And even better that it's French.

Her mother's inexplicable fear and loathing of that country is as baffling as the rules about gypsies and patent leather and television. Other people's families go to France all the time, these days. Harriet Wright-Cooper had gone to St Malo in the last long vac and Dinard in the spring as well. Even Martha has been to France, and *her* mother thinks black people are savages, so France can't be all that bad. 'How do you even expect me to learn French if I never meet any French people?' she'd asked.

'You see Mademoiselle Picard twice a week in class. That's plenty.'

The urge to curse was unbearable; it was always unbearable. 'She's from Sible Hedingham. It's hardly the same!'

But her mother was immovable, a pillar of something. Salt, probably.

And she'd wished, not for the first time, that she was adopted, so sure was she that she couldn't share anything with this brittle stick of a woman. She is certainly destined for better – for bigger things, brasher too. A singer, if she has her way, and she's got the talent for it, even Mr Collins agrees, although he's probably thinking Wigmore Hall, not the Marquee or Astoria or Hammersmith Palais.

She sighs, and pries idly at the woodchip behind her wooden bedhead, a pleasing bald patch forming after months of diligent picking. Her mother had said it would happen with this sort of wallpaper, but her father insisted it was new, the future.

Everything is the future with him.

Except bloody London.

Connie

Leeds, July 1981

God, the precocity of her. It was practically embarrassing. Not that it wasn't without cause, of course. Heaven knows she was goaded into it, moaned at at every turn, every utterance. But still, she'd not seen herself as quite so . . . adolescent. In her head, she'd been more . . . more eloquent, witty, better bred; almost Austenesque in her observations, rather than Pooterish. Perhaps she'd deserved it. No, she had deserved it – at least some of it. What had she been thinking?

Was this normal? To see one's younger self in such stark, unforgiving light, see the flaws and the fakery and the horrible posturing? And how naive she'd been, how green, at the world and at herself – her own abilities and allure – and at men. But off she'd gone, trolling after every Bobby Kennedy, every Mick, every Terry. No wonder she—

But at that she stops herself. She's not there yet. Not even close. There's seven months of dense sentences, of breathless confession to get through before she comes to . . . that. And that's not the point of this exercise anyway. She doesn't need to rake over that messy ground, dig up that particular skeleton. She just needs to check she's not making a terrible mistake.

Because what she's considering is so fat and crackling with potential failure, so fraught with pitfalls and mantraps and snapping alligator jaws, she can't say it out loud, not even to herself. But she's written it, in the twin of this, in her 1981 version.

I'm thinking, she's written, *of taking Sadie to Pram Town.*

Pram Town with its petty grievances, its nose in your business, its choking parochialism. Or so she chose to draw it, back then. But those, she sees, are skulking everywhere, from Llandudno to Chapeltown. And now, in some sort of brisk epiphany, she has glimpsed what Gibberd envisioned, what her father saw even in its eventual rendering: the honesty of it, the attempt at something better. The gleaming precincts, the pedestrian centre, the Clock House to watch over it all. The housing in 'hatches', the wedges of mellow parkland like cake slices between them, the green belt that cinches it all in. And, scattered throughout, its statues – Hepworths and Moores – and butterfly pubs – the Essex Skipper, the Purple Emperor, the Painted Lady, where the factory girls drank.

Perhaps there is something in it, after all.

Something for her and, better, something for Sadie.

And with that possibility as bright as mica, she picks up the old notebook and picks up the thread.

Jean

Essex, August 1981

'Can't you do it on a Saturday?' she'd pleaded.

But Bernard had said no, it was inconvenient, though he conveniently failed to clarify for whom.

'Well can't you take her with you, then?' It wasn't as if the Child wasn't keen; she'd asked when she was going 'home' enough times it was riling.

'That won't be . . . appropriate. To be cooped up in the car with . . .'

. . . Her mother. He can't say it.

Though nor, it seemed, could she. 'Put . . . it in the boot,' she'd told him. It's only ashes, after all. 'Only' – she had to say that, because it was all she had now and what use were they?

'There's too much else,' he explained. 'All the . . . whatnot.'

Whatnot. The house clearance to organize. The landlord to pay off – of course, Connie hadn't been up to date with her rent, or anything, according to Bernard. No savings, save a coffee jar, and even that was mostly coppers. Heaven knows what she'd been squandering it on – she'd had a job, hadn't she? A man? Though at that, she reflects, perhaps not a good enough one. Of either.

230

'I'll have to ask Maurice. I can't guarantee he'll agree.'

Though that wasn't true and Bernard knew it. Of course she'd ask and of course Maurice would say yes, once he knew what it was for; he'd say yes even if he didn't. Though it's fair to say he's been a little odd – off – since it all happened, hasn't known how to handle her exactly. Treading on eggshells or avoiding her entirely at times. He had been so fond of Constance, far more than she was, at least when the girl was at her worst, disappearing for hours on end, then stamping about and swearing when she was at home. But isn't it always easier for those who don't live with them?

Anyway, she's glad he has the Covenanter camp; he's not sung since that summer, so that's one good thing this . . . situation has elicited.

The rest of it is hardly ideal though. Because here she is, on a work day, in charge of not one but a pair of eleven-year-olds.

Oh, not that Nirmal boy. She'd ruled that out as swiftly as it was suggested, said she wasn't equipped with the wit or where-withal to handle a boy. Wouldn't know what to do with him. And besides, she didn't know his mother. But Olive Watkins would be welcome, and was keen, too, from the brief phone call she'd had with Mrs Watkins, suggesting collection at ten.

The Child had pulled a face at that, as if there was something sour lodged in her mouth.

'What's that supposed to mean?'

'Nothing.'

'Good. We'll go to the Town Park. There's a miniature zoo, I believe.'

'Farm. And I've seen it.'

'Well we can see it again.' Honestly, what was wrong with the Child? She'd been odd last night, disappearing off like that, and since then she'd been fidgeting, as if she had ants in her pants, or a secret that needed keeping. Just like her mother— At that, she snaps to, musters. Well, fresh air and some animals will do her good, will be educational – the first of her many lessons she will bestow in her bid to ensure she measures up, and fits in.

But the miniature zoo is less impressive than Bernard had painted it (isn't everything?). Pets Corner, it's called (not even an apostrophe), and it comes with a few desultory chickens and several goats, one of which busies itself with chewing the Child's skirt.

'Stop it!' Jean shoos it with the newspaper but it snatches at that as well, swallows it.

'Why didn't you move?'

But the Child shrugs.

'If it tried to eat your arm you'd let it, I suppose?'

'Maybe.'

Well, that's a lie. Probably to impress Olive Watkins. Well it's fallen on deaf ears, what with Olive concentrating on drawing a hen, as instructed, her coloured pencils in a row on the bench, her sketch paper clipped to a board. There's a sudden rush of something then – a sort of indignant sorrow – that this is the kind of child she should have had: quiet, compliant, Christian. Instead, in Constance, she'd got herself a heathen: ignorant to the perils of sin, indifferent to displeasure, and hell-bent on doing the opposite of what Jean told her, and what God would want her to.

And with Sadie, the apple has probably fallen barely inches.

'Can we have our sarnies yet?' she says, as if to confirm it. 'I'm starving.'

And the enormity of the task ahead elicits a sigh.

After sandwiches (cheese and beetroot, which was a mistake as it's stained their fingers seemingly indelibly and there's no sink facility she can find, which is, frankly, a hazard, given the animals) and carrots, Olive Watkins asks to tour the Hepworths and the Henry Moores, and she can hardly say no, given the alleged educational value. So off they march towards town, Olive keeping step with her, the Child plodding behind like a told-off dog.

'What's it supposed to be?' the Child asks when they get to the first.

'*Upright Motive No. 2*,' replies Olive Watkins, pointing out the plaque.

'That don't mean anything. It sounds made-up.'

Though it needles Jean to admit it, that is the nub of it. Not only is there something uncomfortable about the sculptures – raw, pagan almost – the fact is she doesn't actually understand them. It's as if they're written in secret code for someone with a greater capacity for art and enlightenment. Someone who's studied at Oxford or, like Bernard (who professes to adore them, of course), with a future fetish.

'We'll be the Florence of the north,' he'd said to her, when the list was issued. 'Statues as far as the eye can see.' She'd almost scoffed at that. 'I thought this was supposed to be Jerusalem,' she'd replied. 'It can hardly be Israel and Italy too.'

Then, when the sculptures arrived, and she, weakened by another battle with Constance – over gloves, or shoes, or who knew what triviality – confessed her ignorance, he'd tried to reassure her. 'They're not asking to be understood,' he'd explained. 'They're just asking for a response.'

'Well, my response is that they're a waste of money,' she'd said, with not a little malice. 'They'll only be ignored. Or urinated on by dogs.'

She's been proved right, to her satisfaction. Several were graffitied last year. The rest are at best climbing frames – the times she'd had to call Constance down as a child. Not that she'd stopped. Once she'd seen her and that Michelle Spencer sitting in the lap of *Family Group*, eating sausage rolls. It was bad enough eating junk food in the street, but on a Henry Moore?

'Mrs Earnshaw!'

She comes to. The voice is plaintive.

'Pardon?' she asks Olive Watkins, whose face is as raw and pink as a prawn, the child obviously unused to exertion.

Olive points across the oblong pond. 'Sadie's on the statue!'

She follows the girl's rigid finger.

'Well, honestly.'

'I did say,' says Olive, pride on the wrong side of smugness.

'Yes, you did. Get down!' she calls, just short of a holler.

The Child looks up, slides down the statue, her T-shirt riding up as she does, revealing her bare belly, as if it wasn't bad enough she was behaving like a gypsy.

'I told her,' says Olive Watkins smugly. 'But she wouldn't listen. She never does.'

She forces a smile. 'Yes, thank you, Olive.'

They head down past the Harvey Centre – still half building site – Olive Watkins detailing Paul's road to Damascus, the Child gape-faced at tat in charity-shop windows.

'Can we go in? They've a stylophone and it's only a fiver.'

'Absolutely not.' She hates the places. All shrunken cashmere and coronation mugs and the smell of other people and poverty.

'But—'

'Please don't argue.'

'Anyway,' announced Olive Watkins, 'I've got to get home. Uncle Edward's coming.'

'There you are. Thank you, Olive.'

And on she marches, mildly triumphant.

'Who's he?' asks the Child, still trailing lazily.

'My mum's brother,' says Olive over her shoulder. 'He's a doctor in a hospital. He puts people to sleep. It's called anees–anees– something.'

'Anaesthetist,' she interjects, unable to bear the stutter, or the ignorance.

'Anaesthetist. That's it. What's yours?'

'What's my what?' asks the Child.

'Your uncle.'

'I've not got one.' The Child, audacious as she is matter-of-fact, tugs at the back of Jean's blouse. 'Have I?'

She shakes her off. 'It's "haven't got one". And no.'

There had only been Constance. Not that they hadn't tried. She'd done her duty in that respect.

'God's will,' she'd said, after three years of Bernard's unbearable hoping and her abject failure. But he'd not taken God's decision as final, had insisted he be tested, medically. She'd told him he didn't have to, that it was undignified. Then, when that didn't work, begged him not to. But he'd gone anyway, done his business into a bottle.

They were all dead on arrival.

'That's odd,' the medic had said. 'You already have a daughter, don't you?'

'Constance,' he'd replied. 'Yes, she's—'

'A miracle,' Jean interrupted.

Later she'd said that perhaps the birth had damaged her somehow.

'Perhaps,' he said. But he apologized anyway.

That was the worst of it all.

Bernard returns late – gone nine, by the carriage clock – the Child long in bed.

'Where did you put . . . it?' she asks when he sinks into his favoured chair – the green velvet wingback. 'The . . . you know.'

He picks up the paper, frowns at the missing front page.

'A goat ate it,' she clarifies.

He nods, seemingly unflustered. 'In the shed,' he says. 'With the rest of it.'

She nods. 'Best not to tell the Child,' she suggests.

But if he agrees he doesn't say so. 'The woman next door,' he mentions instead. 'Mrs Maltby – Donna. She asked about a memorial service.'

Her as well, she thinks, remembering Elvis Jenkins, his slurred words, his blurry indignation.

'Not yet,' she says by way of an answer.

'But sometime?'

His insistence is grit, irritating her eyes. 'Please don't pressure me, Bernard.'

'Of course. Whatever you say.'

She nods at that, dabs her eyes efficiently with a napkin. Bernard is up to something though. She's in bed by ten, but he stays up – reading, he claims; tinkering, in truth. Because she can hear it: the shuffle of slippers in the kitchen, the click of the back door and the clunk of it shut. Restless and meddling.

Well, she has work in the morning, so she's not about to chase after him to check. And on his head be it when he's in charge of the Child with only six hours' sleep. If he lets her watch extra television she'll have something to say about that as well. Honestly, why can't he just do what he's supposed to? What he's always done?

Why can't everything just be normal?

She feels herself teetering and kneels then, prays in a practised manner, clicks off her light and rolls into position, awaiting her allotted eight hours.

But fifty minutes later Bernard is still missing, the back door is still not locked properly, and the shed, shut – she'd seen from the window – is pulsing with something. With a dull thudding that will not be dampened with fingers in ears or her head under the pillow.

It's not until she slips into sleep, long gone one, that it peters out at last.

And it will be gone for good in the morning.

Of course it will.

It must.

Sadie

Essex, August 1981

She's read nigh on nine pages now, but there's still no prize, no gilded 'this is your dad' secret to take to Nirmal and work on.

But there's other details, the chipped-glass whispers that might not be diamonds but shine nicely in the right light:

The picture her mam kisses at night.

The whippet she'll keep when she's living in Paris.

The list of things she despises – Miss Bixby, the middle class, her own mother – at least two of which she never gave up, though perhaps Miss Bixby was forgiven, 'cause she'd never heard her mentioned since.

Not that Nirmal will be interested in those, 'cause it's her dad they're looking for, not her mam. But she's sure it's important, sure Sherlock would nod and say she'd done right to find them, to build up a picture so pin-sharp and big. So those she won't hand over but hoard for herself, slip them into her collection between the pine cone and the dictaphone – invisible treasure, mementoes of Mam. The Grandma can't have a cob on about those, still less confiscate them. Can't even find the exercise book, so cleverly concealed it is between the springs and the crinkly plastic mattress cover in case she pees in the night, which she won't, but the Grandma says she's not taking any chances.

Who knew all this life would be stacked up and packed into one box – one book? Maybe she should keep a diary, write down all the things she's bored of, or worse: the brown bread, the hardly any television, the no Hobnobs, no Wotsits, no pop. But the thought of the Grandma uncovering that sours her stomach. It's hard enough keeping this one hidden. So much for being Lacey, the Grandma makes Miss Marple look half-hearted. Always there, always beaking in.

But not today. Today the Grandpa's back from wherever he's been and, like Elvis Jenkins after a trip to Thick Jimmy King's, he's come with a present – a microwave oven. And best of all, this one works.

'It's the latest thing,' he'd told them earlier. 'The future.'

'How does it work?' she'd asked, agog.

'Radiation waves,' he'd replied. 'Invisible things.'

'Like nuclear war?' she'd suggested.

'No!' he'd said, quick as he could. 'Nothing like that.' Which were a relief, to be sure, because she's seen that on the telly and she don't want to get sick or have her hair fall out.

'We've got a perfectly good oven already,' the Grandma had said then.

But after she'd gone he'd plugged it in anyway – had to take the toaster out to do it – and they've microwaved all sorts to test it out. She's written a list with him, of results, like it were a proper experiment:

Soup – it said – *excellent.*

Eggs – *messy.*

They're going to microwave two biscuits with a square of chocolate in between for a snack later, for her and Nirmal.

And just like that the doorbell goes, and she almost 'pings' herself.

'Can we use the gang hut?' she asks the Grandpa, Nirmal in, and the pair of them hovering with want.

'Yes, of course,' he says, then corrects himself with a too-loud 'No!', pushes the back door to, practically trapping her fingers. 'Best use your bedroom, for now.'

She's too thrown to ask what's with the shed. So instead she checks, 'Really?'

'Really.' He nods. 'Just . . . you know.'

'I know,' she says, not having to add the 'don't tell my grandma' anymore.

And then, lickety-split, her and Nirmal are grabbing the bannisters and running upstairs as if their lives or pride depended on it.

'What's that sound?' asks Nirmal as they settle on the bed, the red exercise book between them like a crystal ball or a ouija board.

She sits still, listens, hears the Grandpa singing to himself. Something about a Wichita lineman, which is weird, but not the weirdest song she's heard, given her mam's repertoire.

'Nowt,' she says. 'Just the kitchen.'

'Can you hear everything?' he asks.

'Not everything. Just some.'

Enough. But then she has always been a brilliant listener; it comes from sitting on the kitchen counter, watching Donna at work – her and the other mams barely registered her presence and gossiped on regardless, chattering like jackdaws about work and the weekend and men. Mostly men. And she caught snippets like snips of falling hair, pocketed the treasure for the playground currency later, or just for the sweet satisfaction of knowing things.

Now, though, it's got an urgency to it, a purpose.

But none so big as this book.

Nirmal touches it like it's treasure or dangerous. Perhaps it is. 'Is he in there?' he asks. 'Did you find him?'

She shakes her head. 'Not yet.'

Then she tells him about Paris, and Mick Jagger, and singing. 'There's a boy,' she says. 'Terry. But I don't think she likes him much.'

She reads that bit out then, pleased at Nirmal's nods and, once, a gasp.

'She probably only wants him for his money,' he says then. 'My cousin says most women are like that.'

Sadie bristles but says nowt, 'cause there's a pip of truth in it, she thinks, if Donna's owt to go by; her mam and all, at times. 'He sounds like a right div, anyway,' she declares. 'And besides, she's off to London in the next bit. That's full of men.'

'Where in London?'

'The Natural History Museum.'

'Who's she going to meet there? A gorilla?'

'A museum . . . person,' she manages, and presses the pages down. 'March the tenth, nineteen sixty-nine,' she says. 'Kensington.'

*

242

She reads aloud and then he does, taking it in turns a page at a time, glad of each other's voices, not even trying to read ahead when the other stumbles. Nirmal makes his bits sound like a thriller or a police story – fat with drama and drawn-out pauses. Hers is more comedy, doing the voices – her mam not with her northern vowels now, but clipped, spiffing as a St Trinian's girl, and just as terrible too – the swearing swallowed or whispered, the description of willies skipped over, the pair of them swearing themselves this time, declaring being grown up is disgusting and weird.

For more than an hour they're absorbed in the story, in the desperate tale of a girl trapped by birth and circumstance, if not a wicked witch of the east. Then, just as Miss bloody Bixby sticks her oar in, up through the vent filters the sound of the Grandpa about to do the same – the radio clicked off, the cough, the spit in the sink. Then the trip-trap, trip-trap tread before he shouts up that it's time to ping biscuits.

Sadie, stomach jumping, shuts the book with a dramatic slap and shoves it under the covers. 'Come on,' she urges. 'Or he'll wonder what we're at.'

'I reckon it's him, after all,' hisses Nirmal, as they scuff down the stairs. 'That Terry. Don't you?'

She shrugs, not quite registering, still in the thick of the willies and Miss Bixby.

'Here. I almost forgot.'

'What's that?' she asks as he pushes something into her hand, damp and plastic.

'It's a torch,' he tells her.

'I can see that. What's it for?'

'Detective stuff. So you can look for clues. Read with the lights out and stuff. It's also got a glow-in-the-dark compass and a Jesus keyring.' He points at the attachments.

She nods in acknowledgement. 'Where'd you get it?'

'My cousin. His mate was selling them off down the market for ten pence 'cause Jesus's only got one hand.'

She checks – he's right. Best not let the Grandma see that, for all sorts of reasons.

'Thanks,' she says, and pockets it.

'Aye,' he replies. 'You're all right.'

And then they're busy with the biscuits, testing the food of the future, adding to the tally of what works and what don't. Nirmal's bent over and staring at the spinning dish as if it's television itself, the hum of it a theme tune, or the tinny tinkle of a ballerina inside a music box. And she's here, in the kitchen with him, in the now and the moment, but also stuck on a bus more than a decade away. Because, while in her pocket rattles a plastic one-handed Jesus, in her head jangles a boy called Terry who, if his eyes are the right colour, and if he's still doing 'it' in July, might, just might be her dad.

Connie

The bus to London is interminable.

The weather being unreasonably clement, she is trapped inside a tin can on wheels with seventy sweating sixth formers, several of whom have clearly never heard of antiperspirant or even a flannel. Martha being one of them. Though she supposes it's not easy with the extra flesh. She can help the moaning though. All the derogatory comments about the dirt, the dinginess of the terraces, the 'foreigners'.

'Ghastly,' she apprises. 'I pity them.'

Not Connie though. To her, this is Xanadu and Nirvana rolled into one hedonistic merry-go-round. The promised land: lean black men in trousers so tight you can see the outline of their thingies, and women in wigs – or at least she assumes so, given their precarious height and improbable colour.

She knows what her mother would say: 'Vulgar.'

But her mother's miles away, probably polishing the door-knobs or washing the floor for the umpteenth time. Or reading the bloody Bible as avidly as if it were *Peyton Place*.

And she, Connie, is here, in the rushing, pulsing, gloriously dirty heart of it all.

In London.

The museum is rather less impressive, though. All hollow corridors and reverence and the click-clack of heels on marble. The main displays are dreary to boot – gorillas in glass cases and plaster-cast whales. 'Was my great-grandfather a monkey?' she'd asked once, or something along those lines. Whatever it was it was unwarranted, apparently, as her mother had blanched, pale as whey. 'Blasphemy,' she'd managed.

But, no matter, as apes are not the point. The point is just being here and— Yes! Now that she thinks about it, listens – even inside the museum she can feel it, see it: the buzz and thrum of it; the something about to happen. The men with hair curling over their collars and women in skirts that would never pass Miss Bixby's ruler test.

They are simmering with something. Simple possibility, perhaps.

Or sex.

They're in the human biology section when she hears the first of the sniggers – Mary O'Halloran and Angela Day, peering at a model of a penis.

'What's the matter?' she asks. 'Never seen a prick before?'

Mary pauses, appalled. 'And you have, I suppose?'

She smiles, as if to say, 'Maybe I have, maybe I haven't'.

Angela stands akimbo. 'How big was it, then?'

Connie holds up her hands and lets them spread wider, wider, wider until the girls' smirks slip to incredulity.

'I'm joking,' she says then, and waggles her little finger. 'Not worth taking my knickers off.'

'You never did!' Martha is startled, and indignant, not privy to this new information.

'What if I did?'

Not one of them answers, but she can read their disgust as vividly as if it were printed in ink.

The truth is she has and it was a bitter disappointment.

She'd expected better of Terry. Had hoped he was worldly, or at least well equipped. He'd been so full of it, full of bragging and swagger and swears when she'd met him on the market that first time. He was manning his dad's meat stall, measuring out pink mince in accurate pounds, and producing eggs from behind her ear like he was some sort of magician; white coat and striped apron then, but leather jacket on him later, like James Dean, hair in a slick quiff – a fifties throwback. He was common, she knew, but he had class. More class than the jug-eared boys in duffel coats she had to suffer on the seven thirty train every morning, or at end-of-term dances. She'd rather cha-cha-cha with Bunty bloody Cummings.

'You can take me to the Birdcage if you like,' she'd told him, bold as anything, though she'd had to rehearse it several times to herself in the shoe aisle in Marks and Spencer, had had to check her affected boredom in the mirror before she'd mustered the courage to saunter up.

But he had; he'd taken her that Saturday, when she was supposedly at Martha's practising Latin. Had acted the gentleman as well, begged to see her again.

So she had. Again and again and again, until the inevitable happened.

She'd seen a willy before – Martha's cousin Hugo had got his out in the garden one afternoon when the grown-ups were playing whist or bridge or something tedious and Martha was on the toilet 'with her bowels'. A horrible thing it was – like a limp pink slug – but fascinating all the same. He'd asked to see hers and she'd said, 'I've not got one, stupid.' But his breath was hot and he'd said, 'You know what I mean.' And so in the end she'd given in for a shilling, had lifted her dress and pulled aside her knickers so he could get a glimpse of the bareness beneath.

She'd made nearly half a crown after that from the boys at the prep school. Would have made more if Mrs Gypp hadn't caught them. She'd told her mother they forced her, of course, on pain of a beating or possibly death. But her mother barely believed her, even if Mrs Gypp did, confiscated the coins she'd found in her blazer later and put them all in the church collection. Lucky Jesus. Even Jesus had a willy though.

Terry's was bigger than Hugo's at least, but no less distressing in its strangeness. And instead of lying there, flaccid as a pair of slacks, it was livid and stiff. Perhaps a rubber johnny would help, only he hadn't managed to get one, but he would, he said, for the next time.

The next time. They hadn't even done it once yet.

'You sure you want to?' he'd said, though with such an urgency a 'no' wasn't really on the cards.

'Just be careful,' she'd replied.

And he had been, she supposed. Careful and quick. Too quick, really. Over in minutes, with a sting and a sudden fullness, then a wet dribble down her thigh when she stood up to scrabble for her uniform.

'You didn't do it *in* me, did you?' she'd said.

'No, I said I'd never.'

'Well, good,' she'd replied.

That was the last thing she needed. A squalling baby to contend with. That would ruin her Paris plans.

'So was it all right?' he'd asked.

'Yes,' she'd lied. 'Lovely.'

'It'll be even better next time. You'll see.'

But she's still waiting, still doing it in the hope that she'll feel whatever it is that women in novels and films seem to find so appealing.

'Slut,' mutters someone – Mary O'Halloran, probably – as they reboard the bus.

'Frigid knickers,' she blurts back without turning.

'Constance Earnshaw, come here at once.'

Miss Bixby is calling. And, handing her bag to Martha without asking, she tramps back down the front, where she's forced to sit next to the science mistress, who smells of egg sandwiches and insists on reading bits of her guidebook out loud.

But Connie's not bothered.

Connie's in her head. In her promised land. Thinking of Parisian whippets and soft-lipped singers and women in brilliant wigs.

And willies. Loads and loads of willies.

Connie

Leeds, July 1981

'Christ, you should have seen his thing,' Donna had said to her only today, as she swept up the debris of Mrs Michael's tight perm. 'Like a flaming python.'

Not John's, but some navvy she'd once shagged in the Black Horse lavs. John's 'thing' is still out of favour; persona non grata. 'Penis non grata, more like,' Donna had said to that, added a, 'What's that mean, any road?' Connie'd shrugged, decided not to mention Elvis and his penis being out of favour as well, for good.

Connie thinks of the penises she's seen then, the men they're attached to: Elvis, Honest John, Wigan Mick, Barry Venables the bus driver, the bloke from the dole office who did her a favour, and, in London, the unnameable, unmemorable who passed through the flat.

All of them she'd let take her – worse, had pulled inside her. Hoping that each, in turn, would take her further from . . . him. Would somehow swill out the mess he'd left of her.

Not that she hadn't enjoyed some of it. The run-up, the hunt, the being so obviously wanted. But then came the main act and that was ever a let-down. Like ripping open a ribbon-tied parcel and finding the box empty or holding only an orange and some socks. Even with Terry. Especially with Terry.

What had she seen in him? An escape? A pastime?

A stick to beat her mother with?

The last, most likely.

And it had certainly worked.

Connie

Essex, March 1969

God, what is wrong with the woman?

She's on about boarding school now. Connie's heard her through the ventilation grate suggesting it, that it would be 'better for everyone', that there would be more structure, more discipline, more round-the-clock monitoring. Fewer opportunities for 'misdemeanours'.

Misdemeanours. What does that even mean? The woman can't know about the sex – Martha providing her alibi each time, albeit unwillingly – so it can only be the swearing or the snapping back at the schoolmistresses, for which she's suitably punished by them anyway; the palms of her hands endlessly red.

No wonder she's desperate for Terry. For his difference, his daring, his devotion to her no matter what words she uses or what dress she wears. He might not offer a tomorrow that rings with distinction but at least she'd be free to wear lipstick without inviting a slap.

She's seeing him at six, has told her mother she's bicycling over to Honor Bell's to collect the girl's reply slip for the choir trip – a favour for Mr Collins, because he wanted them all back last week, but Honor, conveniently docile and famously slow-witted, had forgotten hers and now she's off with scarlatina. Of course, she has the letter already – has had it since this morning when she got it off Celia Fairley who got it off Caroline Coutts who got it off Honor's sister Grace, who's in third form and has fat ankles, which is hard cheese when you have a name like Grace, really. Though perhaps her parents should have thought of that before.

It's like Constance – steady, reliable, endlessly there.

Well, she won't be. Not once she's eighteen.

And not within minutes, as she's off on her brand-new Raleigh Shopper – her Christmas gift – smug that her mother handed her the means for escape in the interests of 'fresh air'.

She'll have half an hour with him if she's lucky. Not that he'll need that long, his idea of foreplay a fumble under her Cross-Your-Heart bra, his main-stage performance amateur at best. But, squashing the last thought as if it's no more than a bothersome moth, she slips out the door and off to something – anything – that isn't this.

Jean

Essex, August 1981

That infernal Nirmal is there again, she can sense it.

He's like a bad smell, she thinks, or is it a bad penny? Always lurking. Always turning up.

They're thick as thieves, the pair of them, whispering away. Bernard was all for letting them into the bedroom, but she's put a stop to that idea and they're allowed in the dining room or sitting room, and the latter only if Bernard's not in there with his paper, and not with the television on in any circumstance.

She'd asked Olive Watkins over again as a sort of sop, rung her mother from work only minutes ago, but Mrs Watkins said not until Thursday as they were off to Saffron Walden to do some brass rubbing today and then Thaxted perhaps the next.

Well, you could have asked the Child, she wanted to point out, but decided against it and instead let it fester until afternoon tea was belatedly suggested for Thursday. The girls can talk about Covenanter camp and Sadie can borrow the kit list to make sure she's shipshape and Bristol fashion. 'And we grown-ups can chat about school?' Mrs Watkins had offered.

'I'm afraid I won't be able to make it,' she'd said, wondering suddenly if she might try for another afternoon off work.

'Of course, of course. I'd forgotten your little job.'

Little job? Little job? She puts the pin in Pinnacle, doesn't she? Any minute she'll be typing and filing and keeping everything orderly and neat and on precise time. How could she even think of taking time off? She'd been minded to tell Mrs Watkins this, but remembered her manners, and the threat of wall-to-wall Nirmal. 'But I assume Sadie may still come?'

'We'd be pleased to have her. Does she eat . . . normal things?'

She takes a measured breath, strangely defensive. She's from Leeds, not Venus, she wants to say. Though sometimes the one seems as alien as the other. 'I'd prefer if she didn't have too many crisps. I don't want her running to fat.'

The air crackles with static.

'Thursday then, at half three? Will Bernard bring her?'

'Yes, I—'

'Or I can send Olive around to fetch her. They can walk together, get used to the idea for school.'

She doesn't correct this either. For what's the point until she has an acceptance letter from . . . elsewhere. 'Yes, that would be splendid. Thursday,' she repeats. 'Half past three.'

Until then it's Nirmal, who she has now discovered is heading to Mark Hall himself, so obviously she's crossed that one off the list.

Though at least they're getting fresh air later, she supposes, instead of fiddling with that wretched microwave. Honestly, what was Bernard thinking? She doesn't trust it. There's something foreign or space-age about it. Something almost blasphemous. Tampering with the way of things. 'It's no more mysterious than the cooker,' he'd said to her. 'Yet you trust that.'

'That's different.'

'No it isn't. Can you explain why cake rises?'

'Chemistry,' she'd snapped back.

'Science, exactly. And this is science as well. Physics.'

She'd crossed her arms at that, a wall of defence, and declared she would never eat anything from it. That would show him. That would be her protest against the future, against marauding technology. Also, there were to be no more melting experiments; they were a waste of good food. So Bernard's going to take them to finish one of the I-Spy books instead. *Number Plates*, she assumes, as there are precious few sea creatures around here, bar the exotic tank at Dennings' Pets, and the garden wildlife is mostly cats and sparrows.

Of course, she'd dreamt of the green when she was trapped in Farringdon, had imagined herself quite the country wife, with a gun dog perhaps, and ducks (not chickens) for the eggs. But dogs brought dirt in, meant more endless mess and attention, and ducks were a menace, it transpired; a muscovy had bitten her one Sunday on a day trip to Audley End, snapped at her with its red beak a bloody maw almost. They'd not even managed a cat – in her limited experience of the Collinses' Persian, the things were sinister, disobedient, and she'd had enough of the latter with Constance.

257

So, apart from the Town Park – the goats and the hens – you'd have to travel back to the capital for anything interesting, to Regent's Park Zoo or the museums in Kensington. Constance had gone once, with school. Up on the bus with a packed lunch and a Kodak Brownie and strict instructions to stay with Miss Bixby in sight at all times. But she'd come back with the same bored expression she wore after grammar or Latin or maths.

'What did you see?' she'd demanded.

'Nothing. A stuffed bloody monkey.'

'Constance! How many times? It's not big or clever and I am not impressed.' She tried again. 'What about the dinosaurs?'

But Constance had shrugged at that, wandered off to stand in the bland gaze of the Electrolux, picking at cheese.

It was maddening: the affected ennui of youth. As if they'd seen it all before, whether it was a duck or a monkey or a dinosaur. It was ungrateful, that was what it was. And unconscionably rude, given what they'd paid to put her through eleven— She corrects herself: ten years of private schooling. Though now that she thinks about it, Constance had already seen a stuffed monkey – a crippled thing with a missing eye in a glass case in Stebbing. Bernard, without thinking, had explained to the then seven-year-old that man had developed from apes, had tried to apprise her of evolution. And so Constance, of course, in her wilful stupidity, had asked if her grandfather had been a monkey.

She'd had words with Bernard later, about Genesis and seven days. He'd argued back, pressed Darwin into service, had called the Bible 'no more than a story, an allegory, not to be taken literally'. Surely she knew that?

She did, of course. And wasn't even convinced it was a good one, so improbable did it all seem, so untouchable, despite trying. But the disloyalty had stung and she'd slapped him, or Constance perhaps? No, not a child, she would never have slapped a seven-year-old. Would she? No, that came later and was the least she deserved. In fact, perhaps it was the lack of smacking that let Constance wander astray. Perhaps Jean should have been tougher, should have pulled down her pants and given her three on the bare bottom like she knew Maurice did to Martha when he caught her fingers in the biscuit tin without permission.

Can you smack an eleven-year-old? she wonders now. And will she need to?

But her thoughts are drifting; she has strayed too far down that dead end of yesterday, and that will not do.

Focus, Jean!

She slips a sheet of stiff letterhead paper into the typewriter and snaps down the bail. *Final reminder*, she types, a suggestion of pleasure in the trip of her fingertips. *Your account will be closed and all future orders refused if this bill is not settled within three weeks of receipt*. She checks the desktop calendar: September the second, if she catches the post.

Carriage return.

Please ensure, she begins. But then stops, her fingers slipping and misprinting a 'p', her insides heaving as she realizes the significance.

In September – in three weeks – school will be starting.

259

In three weeks she will have had to decide what to do with the Child.

For almost a minute she sits, panicked as a rabbit captured in the glare of headlights. Then, it comes to her, not from God but from Maurice – from something he once said.

And, at least weakly confident, she picks up the Tippex, erases her mistake, and begins the sentence again.

Sadie

Essex, August 1981

It's definitely Terry: the boy off the market with the slick hair and the leather jacket and the roaring motorbike that her mam catches a croggy on and hopes she don't get caught.

And they've done 'it' and all, loads of times, round his nan's house in Passmores, 'cause she goes out to the bingo and the bed's a big one. Though Sadie's still no clearer what 'it' might consist of, 'cause all her mam wrote about that were that it were a bit disappointing and damp, and she'd to wash her own knickers when she got back and dry them in private lest the Grandma saw them and caught on.

Anyway, she'd changed her mind about 'it' later, going by ticks in the diary and the squawking with Donna – all 'He never!' and 'The size of it!' and 'I thought I'd pass out just from looking!' – her and Deborah listening beneath the window with their Mivvis or chips and grimacing at the illicit thrill of it.

But that's the secret right there: fat as a sapphire and gleaming and all. Terry is the big ta-dah and today her and Nirmal are going to find him.

*

'Terry,' she'd said, as if she were handing over a golden ticket or the World Cup. 'He was a meat man.'

'Terry,' Nirmal had repeated. 'What's his second name?'

'Malin.'

'May-lin?'

'Aye.'

'Malin's Meat!' he'd said then, a hint of the 'Bingo!' about it himself. 'It's only four stalls along from my cousin.'

She felt as if she'd pulled a rabbit from a hat, not a dad from a diary, so pleased was he, and she basked in it, being golden, at that moment.

The I-Spy idea, that was Nirmal's though. He said it were cover, like Columbo might try. So they'd look like they were doing something while they scoped out the market square for butchers with quiffs. They picked number plates because, even though there's hardly any cars in the market, there's more of them than badgers or bladderwrack. So the plan's a smasher, can't go wrong. Only the Grandpa's got it in his head that he's coming and all, says he's looking forward to it. Has been telling them about the Dagenham factory, just down the road, which is why Ford plates have got 'OO' and 'NO' in them – for Essex. Then he'd started in on the strikes – the women with placards marching on parliament, fighting for their rights to earn as much as men. 'Perhaps you'll go on a protest one day,' he tells her.

'For what?' she asks. Though she doesn't think the Grandma would approve of that sort of shouting. Or the placards. Or the marching at all.

'For whatever you believe in.'

'Vampires,' she says, then regrets it when the Grandpa pulls a face.

'Perhaps something more . . . life-changing.'

She thinks it'd be pretty life-changing if a vampire bit you, but she don't say so. 'We could go on our own,' she suggests instead. 'Me and Nirmal. To do the I-Spy, I mean. It'd be like a protest about . . . independence.'

'Well, I—'

'I can borrow his sister's bike. I'll be dead careful. I did cycling proficiency at school and I never fell off. Gary Flack did but that's 'cause he ate a whole packet of Tooty Frooties at break and the sugar went to his head, that's what Mr Wilkinson said anyway. Only I reckon—'

'Slow down!' The Grandpa holds up his hands. 'If you cycle as fast as you talk, you'll come a cropper in no time.'

'Sorry,' she says smartish. 'I were only trying—'

'Look,' he interrupts. 'I'll tell you what. Let me see you ride a bike and I'll think about it.'

'Like a test?' she says.

'Like a test.'

The bicycle's pink and metallic, a Raleigh Shopper with ribbons hanging off the handles and a plastic carrier on the back. 'For the book and the pens,' Nirmal had said. 'And biscuits.' He'd produced two Wagon Wheels at that, fat in their wrappers, as forbidden as crisps, then stowed them away, ready for later. 'It's a long ride to the market,' he'd said, 'at least fifteen minutes.'

Back round at Sadie's, the Grandpa touches the bike like

it might explode or it's magic. 'Well I never,' he says. 'Where did you get it?'

'It's my sister's,' he says. 'Before that, it was my cousin's. Not Jamal off the market, the other cousin. Who's a girl.'

The Grandpa seems fascinated. 'Was it new then?' he asks. 'When she got it?'

Nirmal pulls a face. 'I don't know. Maybe.'

'Why?' Sadie wonders aloud.

The Grandpa seems to snap out of something. 'Doesn't matter,' he says. 'Come on. Show me what you're made of.'

'Okay,' she says. Though she's not quite. Her hands are damp and her legs a bit queer, as if the bones in them are nowt but marrow just now. But she steps on all the same, pushes off the pavement and out onto Fore Street, her legs pedalling steady, her eyes on the road.

She shows him everything she's got: her left turn, her right turn, her slalom manoeuvre – like she's on *Ski Sunday*, all eyes on her.

'No tricks!' calls the Grandpa.

'Not even a wheelie?' she hears Nirmal asking.

'Definitely not that.'

She pulls up ten seconds later, the brakes squealing.

'Are you all right?' she asks the Grandpa, who's rubbing his right eye.

'Just dust,' he says. Then, better, 'Needs some oil, don't you think? A quick squirt of WD-40?' And off he wanders to fetch the can.

'So can we?' she asks, after he's oiled not just her bike but the Grifter and all, and in several places.

He stands, can in one hand, hands on his hips, thinking. 'Okay. But only for an hour or so.'

Her and Nirmal turn to each other, grins gleaming and hearts singing high as tin whistles.

'But no taking shortcuts and no talking to strangers.'

'We won't,' they promise, and it's not even a lie because Terry Malin's not a stranger, not really.

Or least he won't be by three.

They head along First Avenue, pedal past the point of Our Lady of Fatima, past park and the pool. And she feels for all the world as if she's flying, not sure if it's the speed or the fear that's sending her stomach fluttering, full of the flaps of trapped butterflies or colourless moths, perhaps, wings dusty with something.

Perhaps it's the precariousness of it. There are so many what ifs.

What if it *is* him? Terry?

What if the man on the market has the right eyes, and the right timing? What if he wants to take her home with him, there and then, to live in his house and be his long-lost daughter?

What if there's sisters? Or brothers, even? Will they look like her? Will they like her?

Then there's the next questions:

What if he is, but don't want her? Can't be mithered with a child, 'cause he's too busy with the meat or he's got too many other ones already.

Worst of all: what if he's not? What if he's just a man

who happened to knock around with her mam twelve or so years ago, but that's where it ends.

She baulks at that one, wobbles on her Shopper. No – he's not just nobody and she knows it. He's in the diary. He did 'it' and you only do 'it' with someone if you love them, least that's what Deborah reckons, and she'd agreed, though she totted up at least seven men her mam had loved in the eleven years she'd been round to count. Eight, if you added Terry Malin.

Terry.

She sounds it out in her head, to try it for size. Though she won't call him that, will she? No, she'll call him 'Dad'.

'Dad,' she says, aloud this time, but not so's you'd notice. It sits nicely, she thinks, round on her tongue, but soft and all, like a toffee bonbon.

But then she's to swallow it, sucking it down to the soup of her stomach, because they're already there under the watch of the Clock House, its blue and white timer silently tocking them on.

They lean the bikes against the wall of the pub then chain them together.

'Oh-oh-seven,' Nirmal tells her, as he sets the combination. 'Like James Bond. Good, hey?'

She nods, though she's not sure it is, to be honest. That were three boys' lock numbers at cycling proficiency and the lady in the tabard had told everyone to be sensible then, and pick something tricky, something no one could guess. Two-nine-nine, hers had been – the twenty-ninth of September; Mam's birthday. No one would guess it but her and the Grandma.

And maybe Terry.

They're in the midst of the market now, I-Spy open, pencil poised for show, though there's only dusters and buckets and boiled sweets to look at.

And meat.

Trays of it, raked on display, and garnished with green plastic parsley. And behind it a man, holding up chops to be chosen. His hair too thin to be quiffed now, but it's combed over, greased and neat, so it might just be him. And at that slim possibility, she feels a swill of the soup in her, threatening exit.

'What do you reckon?' Nirmal asks.

'I don't know,' she says. Don't know if it is, don't know what to do about it any road.

'Well we'll not find out stood here,' Nirmal says, and before she can stop him he's grabbed her arm and dragged her over, the pencil slipping from her fingers and skittering along the concrete and under Huggins' Fudge.

The man hands over the chops – wrapped and blue-and-white bagged – clatters coins into a plastic ice-cream box, wipes his hands – fat, a man's hands – on his apron.

The customer gone, Nirmal nudges her, and her mouth opens but her words are stuck, so she's left gaping like a pigeon chick, begging for food.

'Never mind,' says Nirmal. And he looks up at the man himself. 'You Terry Malin?' he asks.

The man glances at them. 'Maybe. Who's asking?'

But he smiles as he says it, so wide she spies a tooth missing and thinks she'll have to help him with his dental skills.

Nirmal nudges her again, his stick-thin elbow digging into her ribs.

'Me,' she blurts.

'And who might you be, love?' He's frowning now, taking the measure of her.

'Sadie,' she tells him. 'Sadie Holiday.'

'Sadie. Right. Not from round here, are you?'

She shakes her head. 'Leeds.' Course he won't know her name. 'My mam,' she says then. 'She—' But the words have stoppered in her gob again.

Then she feels it – an arm linked through hers, holding her up. Steadying her. Begging her to speak. 'Connie,' she manages, though it's mouse-quiet. Then, buoyed by her ability, 'My mam was called Connie.'

The Maybe-Terry frowns. 'Connie Holiday?'

She nods, then remembers. 'No; Earnshaw, actually.'

'Earnshaw?' he repeats, his forehead creased as his own mince.

'Aye,' says Nirmal, hogging the word and plopping it out for himself.

But she waits, bated, as Maybe-Terry thinks and thinks and then dredges up the stuck-in-the-mud memory with a suck.

'Connie Earnshaw!' He slaps it out like it's a fiver. 'Blimey O'Riley. That's a blast from the past. I en't seen her in, what is it – nine, ten—?'

'Eleven years. Nearly twelve.'

'Eleven years. That's right. Well, how is she?' Then he swings his head, scouts the thinning crowd. 'Christ, is she here?'

'No,' says Sadie, thrown for a moment. Then she realizes. He don't know. 'She . . . She died. In July.'

'Shit – I mean, sorry,' he says. 'Oh, crikey. I wasn't expecting that. S'pose you weren't neither. Shame. She was a lovely girl. Clever. 'Spect you're clever.'

But Sadie's staring. Has remembered something else. Something bobbins. 'Your eyes,' she says. 'They're brown.'

He nods.

'Mine are green.'

He peers over the counter, leaning so far his white coat meets offal and tinges pink. 'So they are. Not common,' he adds. 'You're a rarity. Like hen's teeth. And goals at Highbury.' He smiles. 'And yer mum. She was a rare thing.'

'Never mind,' says Nirmal softly.

She leans into him then, feels the solidity of him, skinny though he is.

'We'll find him,' he adds. 'There must've been another boyfriend.'

'Hold on.' The man's frowning again. 'Is this . . . Did you think I was . . . yer dad?'

She shakes her head, but tears blister all the same, the sting of salt sending her blinking.

'Oh, love.'

He comes out and around the stall then, drops on his haunches, so she smells the meat on him, sees his hands, fat as hams themselves and stained with red.

'Truth is, I can't have kids,' he tells her. 'Shooting blanks, ain't I. A jaffa.' He pauses, face red as his mitts now. 'Listen. But if I could, I'd want one like you.'

She's worried he'll hug her then, with his mincemeat fingers and his Not-Her-Father arms. But Nirmal tugs at her top and, before the man can do anything, she stomps off after him, head down, not listening to what Terry calls after her, instead letting the words muddle with the market calls: ten for a pound, going for a song, cheap at half the price.

'All right?' says the Grandpa as she stamps up the gravel, not even stopping to watch as he trims the box hedges.

'Fine,' she shouts over her shoulder.

'No accidents?'

'Does it look like it?'

She feels bad about that, but not bad enough to say owt. And at dinner she's still simmering.

'Can I watch *Coronation Street*?' she asks, poking a pea with the prong of her fork. Tine, she corrects, but it's prong all the same.

'You know you can't,' comes the answer.

'What if I went to Nirmal's?' she tries. '*He's* allowed to watch it.'

The Grandma looks up to the ceiling, as if at God himself. But God's not up there tonight 'cause she looks back and snaps, 'And if he was allowed to . . . to stay up until all hours ogling *Dallas*, do you think you should be too?'

'But he's not.' Well, he isn't.

'That's not the point.' The Grandma slices defiantly. 'And that is quite enough from you, young lady, anyway.'

She goes back to sawing her chop and setting the pieces in a semicircle that she knows she won't eat, will probably be served it at breakfast like that fish finger she didn't want the day before yesterday.

'Will you stop that!' the Grandma says. 'It's food, not Play-Doh.'

'Jean,' says the Grandpa, placing a hand on her arm. But she shakes it off.

Sadie sighs. 'Fine.' Puts down her knife and fork. 'What's "shooting blanks"?'

'I beg your pardon?'

'What does it mean – shooting blanks?' she says again.

'I . . . I—'

'Blank rounds,' finishes the Grandpa. 'Bullets. So you can't actually hurt anyone. They do it on film sets, I think.'

'Oh,' she says. The second disappointment of the day.

But later, chop in the fridge under cling film, her in her bed, she looks it up, finds it under 'f' for *fire. Fire blanks. To be infertile, esp. of a man.*

Esp. means 'especially', she remembers, then remembers something else and all. 'Jaffa,' he'd said to her. Like the oranges, the ones with no seeds.

But not always. There was always one pip that made it through and had to be spat out on a saucer, or on the floor if you were out.

And it only takes one pip. One pip to grow a tree.

But then there's the eyes, she thinks. One pip, and a brown-eyed one at that, is a million to one chance. Least

Elvis would say so and he knows his odds. A million million million.

And she's not that rare. Not really rare at all.

Just a girl with a gone-off dad who never even knew her. And how sad is that?

Connie

S he is tiring of Terry, to tell the truth.
  His attractive swagger has segued into brash arrogance,
his glottal stops, once charming, now nettle her, a fact she
despises, hinting as it does that she contains a touch of her
mother after all.

Not that her mother would approve of any of the specimens she has earmarked for Terry's eventual replacement: a
gypsy, a Frenchman, a swarthy foreigner. She remembers
Eusébio, the foreign footballers holed up in a hotel at Potter
Street in the summer of '66. All those black men, polished
and glossy.

'Gods,' she'd said to Martha, who'd gasped and told her
she was asking for trouble.

'Oh, for heaven's sake, are you going to have a conniption?'

'But you're only fourteen. But they're coloured. But—'

'But nothing,' she'd interrupted. Fourteen, maybe, but
decades ahead of Martha. 'I'm going to go to the practice
pitch.'

'You never are.'

273

'Just watch me.'

But she never had. She'd been dragged to a mansion instead, to look at the rooms – educational, for history. And so she'd had to read about it all in the paper, her disappointment tempered by her mother's anguish that they had been to town at all. 'What are you afraid of?' she wanted to ask. 'Their willies?'

Because she'd heard their penises were the biggest of all. Michelle Spencer had got it off Gaynor Trent, whose cousin once played for Leyton and had seen one in the baths after. 'Like a snake,' he'd said to her, or so she recalled. 'A black bloody mamba.'

She'd relayed this to Martha, who, startled, had said she felt sick. The girl really needed to toughen up or she'd end up as wet as her bloody mother. Barbara had probably only ever seen Maurice's and God knows what he had down there. She begins to think about Maurice then. About his willy. Wonders if they ever do it anymore. Wonders how disgusting it is.

'Constance Earnshaw, will you please concentrate!'

Her eyes flick up to Miss Picard, red-faced and glaring, and she reluctantly turns from Mr Collins' knob to other conjugation. Past imperfect.

'*J'avais mangé, tu avais mangé, il avait mangé.*'

Perhaps Martha is right. Perhaps there is something horribly wrong with her. Perhaps she really is a 'nympho'. Terry reckons she is – though he thinks it's a compliment, flattering, and a testament to his prowess in bed. And it's true she read Leviticus voraciously – God's porn, in the absence of anything better. If she had a brother she supposed she might find the real thing stuffed into a cupboard, but she's almost certain her own father hasn't had sex since 1951 – nine months before she was born. Though she wouldn't be surprised if that was an immaculate conception. Her mother is more frigid than the Sisters at St Olave's. In which case, she'd be God's own offspring.

Though if that were the case, He was probably as underwhelmed as her mother with the results.

'*Nous avions mangé.*'

Still, there's the Birdcage on Saturday. And Terry's not coming because of the game – an away match across the other side of London.

Perhaps there'll be a boy there. A foreigner – French! – or American would be better. Americans are almost as persona non grata as the Frogs, are up there on her mother's list with thieves and gypsies (which are one and the same, as far as her mother is concerned). Though, topping the Yanks is anyone 'oriental', which has made the Vietnam War hard to call.

She's not told her mother about the club, of course – has said she's staying at the Collinses' after choir, has bought the unutterably reluctant Martha off with a Mars bar and some help with her French.

'*Vous aviez mangé.*'

She's tried to explain that the Birdcage is safe, that it's not wall-to-wall perverts or worse (though she's not sure what 'worse' might be – murderers?). But her mother had said over her dead body, and Connie's 'I wish' had been met

275

with a second sending to her bedroom in as many days, so this time she isn't risking it, will pack her things in her schoolbag and say, 'See you in church'.

And she slips into a reverie again – the darkness, the heat, the hum of it all – so that Miss Picard has no option but to rap her knuckles with a ruler to get her attention.

'*Ils avaient mangé!*' she yelps.

'Honestly, Constance, what *is* to become of you?'

'I don't know, miss,' she tells her, as contritely as possible.

But she does.

And it's definitely not this.

Jean

She knows what 'shooting blanks' means. She's not stupid and nor is Bernard, whatever he pretends.

Heaven knows where the Child got it – the term. Nirmal, no doubt. Well, Olive Watkins is along later and there will be an end to it, as they'll have camp to talk about. Which reminds her, she must get the checklist from the girl's mother, see if they have the supplies at hand. No doubt there'll be things to purchase. A bedding roll and plastic plates and whatnot. Of course, she'd have had all of these readily, if Constance had been the Girl Guiding sort, but she'd not even made it through Brownies, had been asked to leave. Or rather, it had been 'suggested' that the rigid self-discipline required by a Sprite or a Pixie or whatever six she was in was substantially lacking; 'not her forté'.

But then, if Constance *had* been the Girl Guiding sort, they probably wouldn't be in this situation now. No, if she'd managed Brownies, imagine what else she might have achieved: A levels, a degree, even; she might have gone to Oxford, or is it 'gone up to'? Might be married now, or about to be, like Martha; might have a child on the way, a proper one, a—

Shocked at herself, she stops, brings down the shutter with a sudden thud.

Anyway, it's not that she begrudges the money as such – school will suck up their funds far more than a few days in a tent, anyway – it's that the father of the child should be the one paying.

Of course, she'd always assumed it was that dreadful Terry, with his greased hair and meat smell. Had worked out the dates and, duly satisfied, gone to the market to, well, have it out, she supposed. But she found when it came to it that her desire for propriety far outweighed her outrage and she'd left him a letter instead, instructed him to explain himself, if not to her then to Constance, assuming he knew where to find the girl.

Bernard had suggested it was unnecessary, that if Constance wanted Terry to know, she would tell him, in her own good time.

'Like she told us?' she'd snapped back, hysterical. 'We could call the police, you know. She's not a fit mother.'

'But they might confiscate the baby,' Bernard had replied, bewildered.

'If they could find her.' She'd looked away, fixed on a trinket. 'Anyway, perhaps that would be for the best.'

She remembers his words that followed as if they were lit neon-bright and hovering: 'Sometimes I wonder what's wrong with you.'

It was the only instance of criticism in eighteen years of marriage, and she'd had no answer for him, no hot retort, for of course it was true: there was something wrong with her. Obviously. But she could hardly tell him then. Not after everything.

Anyway, the Terry point was moot in the end.

He did write back, the letter landing on the mat just two days later, in thick ink and a disjointed, almost illegible hand. The gist of it was that he'd worn a thingy. A 'johnny' he called it. So it couldn't have been him. And besides, he wrote, he wasn't the only one who'd 'been there'.

She'd wanted to slap him at that, had seen herself in her mind's eye march up to Malin's Meat and take a gloved hand to his stubbled cheek. But of course she'd merely seethed, knowing that his accusation, however glib, was likely to be true. Hadn't the girl been caught before with her knickers down? In front of four boys as well, and she was barely eleven then, so by seventeen God knows what awful fornication she was indulging in. Perhaps a queue of them. Perhaps two at once, like in some awful orgiastic painting, or pornographic magazine. Oh—!

She stops. Steadies herself.

At least Bernard had never gone in for that sort of awfulness. Not like her brother, who'd shown her a dirty picture once – a pair of naked breasts attached to a vacant stare – had had an ogle at her own when he thought she wasn't looking, had once – she recoils at the recollected shame – stuck his hand up her skirt and tried to grasp her. She'd kicked him in indignation and he'd laughed – laughed! – and told their father she was a right sort. She supposed she should be grateful the old man had never tried his luck as well.

Men like that were everywhere. The Fox, for one. The

Ripper. That Elvis Jenkins, no doubt. And then there were the biscuit workers – the jeering, leering men on the line and down the social club who ogled the Shelley Pledgers, the Lorna Hawkins, the Stacey Venns. Worse, the girls seemed to appreciate it.

Thank heavens for the Maurices of the world. The Bernards, even.

Yes, he had weak shoulders and a weaker chin. Slippery, her mother had called him. But then she decried anyone who wore a suit to work. Anyone who didn't sport a pair of overalls and fill them. Or drink five pints then throw a punch to prove it. Bernard had never hurt anyone. And there was nothing false about him either. He wore his faults as a welcome badge of sorts, bore them good-humouredly: his thinness and weakness and that boundless optimism that bordered on foolish.

She feels a prick of indignation then at the injustice of it. It should have been Bernard; he should have fathered Constance, should have given her his cleverness and kindness and hope. Instead, the poor girl had been handed a dud run of deceit, of vanity, of untrammelled appetite – traits she'd been terrified would out at any minute.

Which, of course, they had, not least in the indiscriminate way she apparently attached herself to men. Honestly, Constance probably hadn't even known herself who the father was. Though, even without Terry's confession, she can see the Child has none of his inheritance. He was far too ugly and thuggish: hairy-handed, practically Neanderthal. And the almost Chinese slant in his eyes is a family mark, passed on from his father in turn. She pitied the sister, really: 'Chinky' they called her, when she wasn't at all. But that was children for you. At Essex Ladies, they'd have kept it under their breath.

At least the Child is white as well. There is that. Not that Jean is racist, of course. But the difficulties of being different – well, she wouldn't wish that on anyone. Another reason to protect her from Nirmal. Not that she was ready for . . . any of that sort of thing. At least one would hope not at her age, her mother's anomalous behaviour aside.

Anyway, this is all fuel for the school discussion. She will raise it with Bernard . . . soon.

All-girls is best, necessary even. And boarding would mean no boys at all, not even at weekends, whatever their colour. And where better to reside, when there's danger about, than behind the gates of a boarding school, where any intruder – any rapacious man – would stand out as if painted purple?

Yes, they will settle the matter soon, very soon. Perhaps visit it next week when the child is at camp. Not that Bernard needs to accompany her. She is perfectly capable.

She is the pinnacle, in fact.

And click go her fingers then, eighty words a minute, to prove it.

Connie

Leeds, July 1981

The Birdcage! God, she'd forgotten it – up on a walkway at The High. The Stone Cross Hall when she'd first known it; Small Faces had played when she was barely fourteen. She'd begged to go, of course, wailed and railed and threatened starvation, suicide even, but it was never going to be a yes, was it. And she's not sure now she'd let Sadie either, not even in three years' time, given the state of the place. Given what went on.

And who with.

Oh, the flash of the man then in her mind's eye – long hair and tight trousers and a grin on him that could fell you at twenty paces. A poor man's Marc Bolan.

Or rich girl's.

And without even clicking her heels or her fingers she's there in an instant: the Birdcage heaving; the air thick with it, dripping down the matt black walls – cologne and sweat and something else . . .

Sex.

Connie

Essex, April 1969

Sex is everywhere: in the bare legs and bra-strap glimpses, in the whites of eyes and pink, sticky lips, in the 'come on, come on' beat of the drum. Music has done this, whipped them into this frenzy. Music is the great leveller, she sees it now, feels it, even. The tech college boys, the shop girls, the lot from St Olave's – all of them moving as one many-limbed mass. The boys with their hasty shaves and shining suits, knock-off from the Saturday market; the girls with their hair sprayed, their liner licked up, as if by a cat, their eyes wide with gin and Rimmel.

'We look stupid,' declares Martha, shifting irritable in her too-tight would-be-Biba borrowed from Connie, who borrowed it from Michelle in the first place.

'No we don't. We look perfect.'

Well, Connie does anyway: her short dress, emerald and catching the light like the carapace of a beetle. She's not so sure about Martha, whose curves are barely contained in the skinny shift, threatening to spill from the edges or split seams. Perhaps she should have kept her coat on, after all.

'I want to go home,' the girl practically wails.

283

'For God's sake,' she slaps back. 'We've only just got here.'

'I don't care. It's too hot and crowded and . . . and dirty.'

A boy in glasses, silver-rimmed, barges past, sending Connie slamming into Martha, who holds out her hands as if to say 'see?'

'Sorry,' says Connie. But she's not. She thrills to the proximity, the press of flesh.

'I'll go on my own, if you won't.' Martha is adamant.

'And what am I supposed to do then? I'm staying at yours, remember?'

Martha shrugs.

'Fine,' she snaps, then scrabbles for a solution, pulls out a plum. 'Leave a key,' she tells her. 'Under the flowerpot.'

'Mummy doesn't like doing that. Because of burglars. And rapists.'

'A rapist is hardly going to rummage around in some bloody geraniums just so he can get his hands on Barbara.'

He'd have to be desperate. Though perhaps that is the definition of it.

'All right. But I shall say it was you, if they ask. I'll say you made me.'

'Fine.'

'Fine.'

She's not even sure why she bothers with Martha anymore; wouldn't if it wasn't for choir, which is the one thing that keeps her mother off her back. That and the fact that Martha is charming, polite, believable when needs be. Every mother's dream.

But so what if she's gone? Michelle will be down later, and the rest of the girls from Mark Hall Moor and the Stow, all at secretarial school now, learning shorthand and touch typing and other tedious things. Though, at least they have freedom, have interesting friends, have Saturday jobs that keep them in coffees and Campari rather than having to pinch shillings from their mother's purse or, once, the church collection, though she'd swapped it for tuppence surreptitiously, so it wasn't that bad.

Then it comes over her in a wash, a wave not unlike nausea, but pleasant somehow, pleasing: she is free. For the next few hours she can be who she likes and do what she likes, with whomever she likes. No mother, no Martha, no Terry to stay her. She can change her name if she dares, can claim fortune, or infamy, or a father who manages bands – oh, how she wishes. And with this new vision of brilliance in mind, this glittering version of her, she ploughs into the crowd, porpoise-like, bobbing her way to the front of the stage.

An hour later and her shimmering dress is practically black with damp, her hair wet against her face, but inside she is on fire, singing with it.

With him.

With her own Marc Bolan.

He's the singer – of course he is. Long-haired and long-limbed and sinewy as a cat. But not just an animal; he's clever, she senses it. Probably writes the lyrics, probably carries Camus round like a Kennedy and quotes it to lovers, plural, in his bed in the penthouse he rents in – where? – Soho!

Perhaps he is a Camus himself. For he is – she quickens as she realizes it – a walking, talking, writhing poet, and, God, how she wants him. Wants him more than she's ever wanted anything before.

And what is astonishing is that he seems to want her too. Watches her – squashed among dozens at the front of the floor – sings to her, winks at her, she's sure of it. So that once they're done, calls for an encore fashionably ignored, she doesn't hesitate for a second before she slips from the throng and positions herself at the stage door, waiting.

She's not disappointed.

Just six minutes in, the door clicks open and here he is, in his sweaty, messy glory.

He leans against the architrave, flicks a Zippo, feigning not to notice her. But she knows he has, their minds alike, attuned, so how can he not?

'Can I have one?' she asks, bold as a peacock.

He looks up from under curls so long her mother would describe him as a filthy hippy, would declare him on drugs and forbid her to go near him. Perfect.

He is perfect, for, without question, he pulls out a second Benson, lights it with the tip of his own and rests it word-lessly on the plush of her lower lip.

Jesus, the thrill of it as it sits there. It's almost as if it's his dick, she thinks, and she keeps her eyes on him as she pulls hard and long, bracing herself against the burn, hoping not to choke and betray her amateur status.

'Oi, Connie!'

She turns then and sees him – Terry, hands on hips, silhouetted against the window of Ridgeons.

Fuck. 'In a minute, Terry,' she calls down to him. Then, to her Marc, 'He's not my boyfriend. He's not my anything.'

'Not my business,' he tells her. 'Connie.'

Connie!

He said her name, so he's made it his business. He's just playing, hiding his hand, biding his time. But time is something she doesn't have.

'Can I get your number?' she blurts.

He shrugs – affected nonchalance, she is convinced of it. 'If you like.'

He rips off the top of the packet of fags, scribbles numbers in stilted ink.

'Is that for songwriting?' She nods at the pen.

He holds it out, stares at it then. 'Bookies,' he says. 'But yeah, songs I suppose.'

Then he hands over the gilded slip with her future on it, says, 'Bye, darling,' and slips into the pitch of the Birdcage again.

She lets Terry neck her anyway, but it's his tongue she feels – the singer's – his teeth that dig into her skin, hard, too hard at times, so that when she looks in her pocket mirror she sees the purpling circle of a lovebite already taking shape.

'Why'd you do that?' she asks.

Terry grins. 'To remind you whose you are.'

A month ago, she would have been pleased with this, the

cat that got the cream. Now it picks, irritates. 'I'm not anyone's,' she says.

But as Terry necks her again, she gazes up into a sky salted with stars and peppered with possibility. Because now there is something beyond the concrete shops and ordered walkways. Something messy and irrepressible and, yes, inconvenient. It is Life, with a capital L, and now, with this ticket, this number in London, it's hers for the taking.

No, she is not Terry's. Never has been.

She's his.

By the morning, the lovebite has widened, bloomed blue as a bruise or a bilberry stain. Michelle had suggested toothpaste once, but now her neck is chalk-pink with Euthymol and stinking of cinnamon, so she's forced to borrow a scarf from Martha – a blue and white thing that looks awkward and forced and doesn't even go with her church dress.

'You look weird,' confirms Martha.

'I look French,' she says, though she's not convinced of it. Don't they wear them on their hair?

Still, it's better than nothing, better than confessing.

And it works, for a while anyway. Her mother says nothing when they arrive at St Mary's, take their usual place in the pew; ignores her successfully throughout several hymns and a sermon on something to do with Jonah and the whale, which is frankly the most ridiculous of all the Bible stories, that and the parting of the Red Sea, and the feeding of the five thousand. Honestly, how stupid do vicars think people are?

But after, on the walk back to Fore Street and The Green for them, and beyond for the Collinses, she demands Martha retrieve the thing. 'I don't want her forgetting to give it back again,' her mother says. 'We all know she's prone to that.'

A dig at her acquisitive nature. Never mind that Michelle gave her the earrings, Martha the calfskin gloves. At that, something in her snaps and, unbridled, defiant, she unknots the scarf and lets it drop, lets the purple rose unfurl to the world.

Her mother's unspoken astonishment is writ as angry and loud as the words eventually serried. 'Constance Earnshaw, get home this instant.' She turns to Barbara, white as a junket. 'I'm so sorry. I really don't know what's got into her.'

'It's quite all right,' says Barbara, making it clear that it isn't, not least for Martha, who's now being hauled towards the corner as if she might catch something.

'Oh, Connie.' Her father frowns, the flicker of disappointment that seems to go with it surprisingly sobering. She feels terrible then. It's not his fault, after all. That his wife's a monster and his daughter a whore.

'Constance!' her mother says then, both a correction and an admonition.

'Coming.' She sighs, and musters herself to trudge in their wake, when she's suddenly aware of someone's eyes still lingering.

She glances up and sees Maurice watching her, one eyebrow raised.

'Bad girl,' he says.

But he doesn't mean it, she can see.
Because as he says it, he smiles.
And when she smiles back, he flicks her a wink.

Sadie

'I've worked it out,' she tells Nirmal. 'He's called Marc Bolan and he's in a band.'

They're back in the gang hut, only now it's a makeshift tent under the dining-room table because of some rules she's not sure she understands, but she don't mind the tent, anyway – it's practice for camp.

'Marc Bolan?' Nirmal frowns in the under-table fug. 'I've heard of him.'

'Really?' She's lifted in an instant, sure now they're on to it.

'Yeah.' He nods. 'I think he's a mate of my cousin. Or else he works at Ridgeons with my sister.'

She shimmers with it – the rightness. 'You're not joking?'

'I don't joke about detective work. This is serious business.'

She nods solemnly. 'Can you find out?'

'I suppose I could phone.'

'Can you?'

'But it's lunch in a minute.'

'It's only cheese and biscuits,' she points out.

'*Microwaved* cheese,' he clarifies.

291

'I'll save you some,' she offers.

'It'll have gone cold.'

'We can reheat it. That's the genius of the microwave,' she adds, echoing the Grandpa, himself echoing the instructions.

Nirmal looks anxious, as if he might be short-changed.

'There's tinned peaches for pudding,' she offers. 'You can have mine if you like.'

'With evaporated milk?'

She nods.

'Can we microwave them?'

She thinks, levels it against experiments past. 'I don't see why not.'

She watches him weigh it up.

'All right then. I'll do it.'

'Both of them,' she says, desperate, as he crawls out on his elbows, commando-style.

'Can't promise my cousin'll be in. But I'll try.'

And with that he's off out the door with a 'Back soon' at the Grandpa, while she's left with congealed cheese and damp crackers ('disappointing but edible'), and a stomach too seasick to appreciate them, anyway.

But both routes prove unfruitful.

Nirmal's sister's never heard of anyone Bolan. Though there's a Mark Sutcliffe who drives the forklift over at the Sawbridgeworth warehouse. But he's sixty if he's a day.

'What about your cousin?' she asks.

'He just laughed,' Nirmal tells her, practically baffled. 'So hard, he said he might die of it.'

Sadie shrugs. She's no idea what goes through men's heads. They find farts funny and there's no explaining that.

'We could try the phone book?' Nirmal says then.

So they do. They haul the unwieldy thing under the table and into the hut, feel the heft of it in their laps, the tingling of anticipation as she opens it, turns to the page beginning 'Bol'. Then the swift disappointment when they see there's no Bolan at all. Just a smattering of Bolds and Boltons (none 'M') and, surprisingly, a Bollard, J. But none are close enough to be mistaken, not by someone as canny as her mam.

Angry, she slams it between her hands, but there's no satisfying *crack*, just the shuffle of tissue-thin paper. 'Stupid thing.' She shoves it off, kicks it out of vision.

'We need to ask someone who knew her.'

'What?' She's cross now, not really listening.

'Like your grandpa?'

'Like my grandpa what?'

But Nirmal don't pout or flounce like Deborah might. Just repeats it clearer.

'We need to ask your grandpa if he's heard of this Bolan bloke. If he remembers any men, you know, lurking about.'

She pulls a face. 'Don't be daft. If he knew, he'd have told me.'

Nirmal shrugs. 'Maybe. Unless he's a murderer. Or a rapist.'

'Who?'

'Marc Bolan,' he says, patient, without even a 'duh'.

But she's still livid. 'He's a singer,' she dismisses. 'Weren't you listening?'

'Singers can be villains too.'

293

'Like who?'

Nirmal twitches, tolerance finally wearing thin. 'I don't know. But I bet there is one.'

She don't tell him about the man from the Liberal Club who left her mam with a black eye. Nor Elvis. 'Cause a shiner and murder are miles apart, like *Corrie* and *Songs of Praise*. 'Who else, then?' she says eventually.

'Who else is a murderer?'

'No. Duh. Who else would know Marc Bolan?'

'You tell me.'

She thinks, digs around in all the little things – the whispers that have been written, or drifted up through the floorboards when she's supposedly asleep. 'There's Martha,' she says. 'Mr Collins' daughter. Only she lives in Ealing.'

'Where's that?'

She sighs. 'Dunno. Wales, maybe. Or the Isle of Man.'

'That's a stupid name for an island.'

She nods. 'Not even just men there,' she says.

'Stupid,' he repeats.

And, like that, the chasm that yawned unbridgeable between them is snapped back like elastic.

'What about other friends? From round here, I mean.'

'There's Michelle,' she remembers then. 'Michelle Spencer.'

'Who's she?'

'She were my mam's best friend until the Grandma and Grandpa moved here.'

'Moved from where?'

'Mark Hall Moor.'

Nirmal's eyes brighten and boggle. 'Why would you move two roads over?'

'I know. Mental, isn't it.'

They nod in unison and the smile that's tickling her lips catches on his so that they're suddenly grinning.

'We could go there,' he says then. 'And interview her. With the dictaphone!'

'Aye,' she says, but tempered, because there are practicalities to be addressed: the lack of batteries, the need for permission.

But the keeper of both is asleep in the green chair, newspaper spread on his chest, milky coffee cold on the side table, its filmy top a threatening membrane.

'We could borrow the ones from the radio,' Nirmal suggests in a whisper.

'But we can't go out without saying,' she tells him, hoping she's wrong. 'Can we? What about the Fox?'

'We won't talk to strangers, except this Michelle. And she's a woman, so she's all right.'

The relief is brief but pleasing. 'Aye. That's true.'

'And we can leave a note.'

'Saying what?'

'That we've gone to do I-Spy and we'll be back by, say, five?'

She checks her watch: 10.37. That can't be right. The battery must be going on that and all. She'll get Grandpa to change it later, when she puts the others back. He'll have spares, she thinks. Better have, otherwise how will she play back the interview? She congratulates herself on detecting well done, and they're not even out the door.

'We could say Horrible Olive's coming with us,' adds Nirmal with a flourish. 'Then he definitely won't worry.'

'Brilliant,' she says. 'Only don't say "Horrible".'

'I wasn't going to,' he tells her. 'I'm not that thick.'

Not thick at all, she reckons. Least, not for a boy, and she checks the gold clock on the mantel: ten past three. That gives them nearly two hours. Plenty of time to be there and back before he even wakes up, perhaps. Definitely before the Grandma gets home.

Course they've not got an actual address. She'd not thought of that. And there are houses and houses, and some of them aren't just one but cut up into flats, meaning more and more doors to knock on.

'We'll just have to try all of them,' says Nirmal, undeterred at anything now that he's got the dictaphone. They've agreed to take it in turns, but he's already used up ten minutes saying stuff into it about the road and the weather and a dog with no lead who was peeing on an Austin Allegro.

'That'll take ages.'

'So we'll come back tomorrow if we don't manage it now.'

He's determined and she admires that, got tired of Deborah, who complained about skating and hated I-Spying, could barely last ten minutes without whingeing and saying could they not just go to the shop or sit on the wall and watch the Mehtas head a ball for a bit.

'Go on then,' she concedes. 'You knock first.'

And he does.

And again.

And again.

The first three doors no one's home and she reckons it's 'cause they're at work, that they should have waited until the weekend. But Nirmal says some people work Saturdays, and Sunday she'll be at church, probably, so it's today or never, and she can't argue with that.

Anyway, the fourth door rewards them with a coughed-out 'Coming!' and a shuffle down the hall. The woman that answers has grey hair and no teeth, least not in her mouth right now.

Nirmal sticks the dictaphone as close as he can go. 'Are you Michelle Spencer? The same Michelle Spencer who was once an acquaintance of Constance Earnshaw, also of Mark Hall Moor and latterly of Fore Street?'

Sadie gapes at the audacity of it, the 'latterly'.

The woman gapes and all, but appalled. 'No, I'm flaming not,' she says, and slams the door so it rattles in its jambs.

'Blimey,' says Nirmal, dropping his arm. Then, just for her: 'Keep your hair on.'

They swap a smile.

'She were too old, any road.'

'Yeah. Ancient.' He hands over the dictaphone. 'Your go next.'

'All right,' she says. But she slips it into her pocket, thinks she'll not show it just yet.

The next house is a man and he says he's only just moved here and he asks them their names, and they say they've got to go, because he's a stranger and a man, so he might be the Fox, only do rapists wear gold watches and crocodile shoes?

She's not sure they do. But better safe, she reckons, and Nirmal agrees.

Then the next is dead – out for the day – and the one after that.

But the seventh is a woman and this time she's got all her teeth and her hair's a better colour. Though her face is borderline orange, as if she's an Oompa-Loompa or has drunk too much Welfare Orange.

'Is Michelle Spencer here?' says Sadie, less verby than Nirmal, but clever, she reckons, in case the lady won't own up at first.

And the pip in her tingles as sweet and sparkling as sherbet when the woman don't deny it, just says, 'Who wants to know?'

'We do,' says Nirmal, when words won't come out of her own mouth.

'Well, she's not. Here, I mean.'

'But she was?' he says, taking her eagerness as his own.

'My sister.' The woman sticks a hand down her top and fishes out ciggies, a lighter, and Sadie goggles as she sparks up, shoves the stuff back into her bra. 'Lives in Leyton now. Why?'

Nirmal nudges her, dislodges some words. 'She knew my mam.'

'Not from round here, are you?' The woman narrows her eyes.

She shakes her head.

The woman watches her, fathoming something, working her out, Sadie reckons – a detective herself. 'I've got a number,' she says in the end. 'I can dig it out if you want.'

She wanders off down the hallway.

'Go on,' Nirmal nudges again, pushing her over the threshold so she's got to follow, down the corridor that smells of dog and meat and cigarettes and into the kitchen, where one of the culprits – a panting Alsatian – sits improbably on a bar stool.

'He won't bite,' says the almost-stranger. 'Soft bugger.'

But neither her nor Nirmal will touch the bugger, soft or not.

'What are you after her for, anyway?'

Sadie braces herself. 'She might have . . . might have known my . . . my dad.'

She can't believe she's said it, but there it sits, dog-like, waiting for attention.

'Oh, right,' says the woman. 'What's his name then?'

She braces again. 'Marc Bolan.'

There's a pin-thin pause, then, 'You having a laugh?'

'No.'

'It's not funny,' Nirmal confirms. 'This is serious business.'

'Never said it wasn't.' She frowns, sucks on the cigarette again. 'Marc Bolan?' she repeats. 'As in the band?'

Bingo! Sadie nods with the promise of it.

'Weird trousers? Long hair?'

'That's him!' Up it brims inside her: hope, shimmering like tinsel, and her mouth flicks into a grin.

But the woman's not smiling. 'Well, I hate to break it to you, darling, but he's dead. Been dead since seventy-seven.'

'What?' Sadie feels her face fall along with her stomach.

The woman nods. 'All over the news. Surprised you missed it.'

Nirmal presses against her, skinny arm to skinny arm, and she's grateful for it. 'How did he die?' he asks for her.

'Crashed into a tree, I think, up in town. Never knew he'd been round here.'

Nirmal nods for them.

'You want to tell the papers. Sell your story.' The woman is wittering now. Tells them she knows someone who slept with a footballer, got a good five grand for it 'cause he was married. Got a kid to show for it and all, half black. But Sadie don't care; don't say 'ta' when the woman hands her Michelle's number, says she'd be glad to hear from her; don't say owt at all, all the way back to the corner of Fore Street.

'We could call Michelle,' Nirmal suggests.

'Why bother?' she says. 'He'll still be dead.'

'But—'

'But nowt. I'm stuck here now.'

'I know, only—' But then he spies something, makes a face. 'Blimey.'

'What?'

But he only nods, and so she follows his eyes, sees it: her grandma's car, parked on the road, because on the drive is the Watkins' Morris.

'Blimey,' she repeats. 'I'd better be going.'

'I'm sorry,' he says then. 'You know, about Marc Bolan. Shall I see you tomorrow?'

But she don't answer, just turns and trudges to her judgement.

*

They're all there, at the table: Horrible Olive, brandishing a digestive like the cat who got the clotted cream and the scone and all, Mrs Watkins with a cup of tea, the Grandpa hovering.

And then the Grandma, who had been facing the wall, which was odd but preferable to now, where she's snatching Sadie's hand.

'Where have you been?' she wails. 'I was about to call the police.'

'We thought the Fox had got you,' says Horrible Olive.

'No we didn't,' says her mother.

But Olive smirks at Sadie anyway.

'I were only out with Nirmal,' she admits. 'We were . . . looking for stuff.'

'You said you'd be along Church Street, but you weren't,' says the Grandpa, holding her note. 'You said Olive was with you.'

She curses Nirmal then, for saying specifics would swing it, that all detectives told fine white lies.

'You were supposed to come for tea,' says Olive. 'I came to fetch you. But you weren't here!' she adds dramatically, and entirely unnecessarily, thinks Sadie, given her absence is established.

'That was my fault,' the Grandpa says. 'It slipped my mind.'

'Yes, well, that's beside the point,' snaps the Grandma. 'She shouldn't have gone out at all. You shouldn't have gone,' she repeats, louder and directly at Sadie, in case she was too stupid to get it the first time. 'Anything could have happened. Anything!'

'Well,' says Mrs Watkins, standing. 'We'll see you on Sunday, shall we? You've got the list now.' She hauls her daughter to her feet.

'Will she be punished?' asks Horrible Olive, having finished her biscuit.

'Olive!' Her mother nudges her.

But Olive ignores it. 'Well, will she?'

'That's a matter for us, don't you think,' says the Grandpa.

But 'us' is misleading, don't include him.

He's chivvied to his study and it's the Grandma who has at her, tells her she's selfish, and stupid besides, marches her to her room with margarined crackers and a beaker of water that's not even properly cold. Which Sadie, incensed at the injustice of everything, not least the lack of jam or even yeast extract, tells her.

'Well, you'd better get used to it. The water at camp comes from barrels.'

She slumps against the headboard. 'I don't want to go if Nirmal won't be there.'

'Well, he won't and you're going. Oh, for heaven's sake, why are you crying? Most children would be grateful to sleep in a tent. Think of the Africans,' she adds.

But Sadie won't think of the oft-mentioned Africans, isn't even sure why they've been dragged into it again. 'It's not camp,' she manages. 'It's 'cause Marc Bolan's dead.'

'Marc Bolan?' The Grandma's face pinches in. 'What on earth has that man got to do with anything?'

But this second lack is whelming. 'I want my mam,' says

Sadie, bordering on a sob. 'When's her ashes getting back?'

The Grandma clasps her forehead. 'I don't know,' she says, more irritably than ever. 'Anyway, that's beside the point.'

Beside the point. Beside the point. Everything is beside the point. Marc Bolan. Ashes. Africans.

Though perhaps ashes *are* beside the point. Ashes aren't a mam or a dad, after all. She needs flesh and the feel of her: needs her singing Dusty or Billie when she's ill; needs her skipping widdershins with her round the yard; needs her tucking her in and telling her she's the cherry on the cake, she's golden.

Instead, all she's got is a single photo in a borrowed frame. And the diary.

She rolls onto her side then, hears the comforting crackle, slips her hand in the gap to grab it. Then remembers too late she's not yet alone.

'What's that?' demands the Grandma.

She feels herself pinking. 'Nothing.'

'Nothing is always something. Show me this instant.'

And so she's got no option, has to pull it out, plum-like; has to hand it over like it's a bomb or a filched biscuit, not an old red exercise book.

But the Grandma pales like it might be worse than the first one, can't even speak. Just picks it up in the tips of her fingers, and, holding it out as if it's dead or infected, steps stiffly from the room, leaving the door strangely gaping and Sadie bereft.

Jean

Essex, August 1981

Fury consumes her, seems to bear her aloft or wear her like a dress.

'Did you know?' she demands, waving the pages at Bernard. 'Well, did you?'

Her husband has his hands up, as if to – what? Defend himself? She's hardly likely to strike him, is she. Not even at his size.

'Bernard!' she prompts again.

'No!' he blurts, cajoled, forced into action. Then caveats his claim. 'Well, not that she had it.'

She pauses, sees in all too vivid detail what he's hinting at. 'So you knew it existed?'

'I . . . They were in the box of her things, in the shed. Several of them. I was going to tell you, but I didn't think—'

'That's the trouble with you, Bernard, you never do. You give everyone benefit of the doubt. Everyone—' She stops herself, drops her hand. 'Well, what's done's done now.'

'Yes.'

She sees him cling to something then. Oh, God. He's going to try to rally her.

'Perhaps it's all for the best.' He puts a hand on her arm. 'Out in the open.'

'Oh, for heaven's sake.' She shakes him off, makes for the dining room.

'Where are you going?'

'To call Maurice. He'll be beside himself.'

It's not just Maurice she telephones, though he is top of her roll call. It's the number he gives her as well. He'd given her the same one less than twelve years ago but she'd discarded it in the end, along with school reports and letters of recommendation. No need for it, after all. But this time she's not waiting for paperwork, not pressing anyone for recommendations. This time she's decisive.

An emergency, she tells the bursar. A death in the family – an orphan, poor thing.

She's lucky he's there, he retorts, more than a little bluff, she considers, given she is the one holding the cards, or rather the chequebook. But even with that she is a beggar, she suspects, not a chooser, so, 'Of course,' she replies. 'I'm terribly grateful. We *all* are,' emphasizing an alleged unanimity. As if that might buy it.

'Very well,' he says, and she almost sings in relief. 'Tuesday at three.'

She doesn't even need to see it, to be honest, but the bursar insists no one is admitted without a family visit. No, the child doesn't have to be there – that's not uncommon, not with foreign service offspring. They have children from all over the world, didn't she know? From Africa, even. She almost baulks at that. But decides the specimens in question must be white, if they're English, the parents sequestered in embassies for the duration. That will be it.

And she hangs up with an inaudible ting of triumph. Because at last she has seen the light. She and Bernard cannot handle a child – any child – but especially not this child. She should have accepted this at once, put her foot down instead of drawing it all out, letting Bernard – herself, even – think this was some sort of second chance, a redemption.

Well, that chance is over. She is not made to be a mother, obviously. She has abjectly failed, not once but twice now, to instil any discipline, any respect. Tomorrow, the Child gets taken to camp, so the house will be blessedly empty for days, then it's barely a week before school starts, before she will be – she checks the map – twenty miles away, with only one telephone call a week. She's checked, of course. Checked too that, even in the holidays, she may stay, at the head's discretion, as so many of the 'overseas intake' do. 'Poor things,' the bursar had added. Poor nothing, she wanted to retort, but had held her tongue and thanked him again.

She stalks back to the sitting room. 'It's all sorted,' she says, sitting herself on the sofa, with the paper next to her, leaving no room for Bernard or manoeuvre.

'Sorted?' he questions. 'You mean Maurice? Tomorrow?'

'Yes. That and school.' She picks up the paper, pretends to browse. 'She'll be at Friends in September. They've a place, after all.'

'I . . . How very fortunate.'

She looks up from Domestic Affairs. 'Isn't it.'

And so she dresses for bed in a state of practical satisfaction. Or at least knowing she has done everything she can in the face of such . . . such obstinacy, such disobedience, such wilful destruction.

But three hours later she is still rigid on the pillow, Bernard snoring next to her. But his is not the only sound. For from a shelf in the shed hum ashes in plastic, a thud-thud-thud seeming to thrum across the lawn and filter in through the casement window, as real and ethereal as mumbles from the air vent. She turns her back to face the wall, willing it to leave her be. But then, over the hum, comes another noise: whispers drifting from a Silvine notebook. 'Read me,' they urge her. 'Open me up.'

She clamps her hands over her ears and then, when that fails to silence them, pushes her head beneath the pillow. And there, eventually, her head in feathers, if not the sand, she falls into a fitful sleep.

Sadie

Essex, August 1981

The notebook's gone, vanished into thin air or into the Grandma's hiding hole. She's looked in the obvious places and some not so obvious ones and all, but the Grandma accused her of lurking, which is banned, as are now several more things, including the bicycle, Nirmal, and trying to find her father.

'I thought you'd be happy,' she'd snapped, sniping to hide her tears.

'Happy about what? That you lied? That you snuck off to heaven knows where, where heaven knows what might happen to you.'

'It were only the market.'

'Was. And I told you before, the market is too far, and Terry . . . Terry is not someone to be bothering.'

She don't get a chance to say what she were going to: that she'd be gone. That's why the Grandma'd be happy. But she knows it's true now, knows she's not wanted about. The Grandpa's a different matter, but he's not in charge, don't wear the trousers, that's what Mam'd say—

Would have said.

And at that she rages again, 'cause raging's better than crying and she don't want to do that again, not in front of *her*.

By morning, she's tired, contrite.

'Sorry,' she says, feeling better for it, like the Grandpa had said she would.

But it don't make a jot of difference.

'Run and brush your teeth. He'll be here in a minute.'

'Who will?' she says, imagining a man from the boarding school, clothes black as a cormorant, hunched and punishing, coming to haul her away.

'Mr Collins,' comes the reply.

That's not so bad then, she thinks. Only, 'Why's he coming?'

'For heaven's sake. Don't you listen to anything?'

She shrugs, no point in arguing.

'Camp,' snaps the Grandma. 'Remember? You're going to camp.'

The Grandma's packed her things for her, didn't even ask what she'd like, so she has to add to the bag herself, squeeze in the dictaphone, the I-Spys, the pine cone on top of the whatnot. She pushes her hand down to see what she's got, is surprised to find the Holy Bible nestling in her knickers and on top of a loo roll, wonders that God's all right with that kind of thing, but perhaps God don't mind where He's sitting as long as He's there. Anyway, it's only the Good News one from her room, yellow and papery, not the soot-black hardback she's tried and failed to pry from the shelf down-stairs.

She hears the doorbell, the mumble of something, then her name being called, impatient.

She trudges affectedly, as if the weight of the world is on her, which half of it is, slumped in her stomach and sour like a gone-off yoghurt.

'Here she is,' announces Mr Collins. 'Sadie herself.'

She sighs, rich and deliberate. 'Who else would it be?'

'Sadie!'

'It's fine.' He bends down, close enough that she can see small holes in his nose, as if someone's pricked him with a needle. 'Someone doesn't understand that camp's supposed to be fun.'

'Not too much fun, I hope,' says the Grandma.

Mr Collins, still at Sadie's eye level, smiles. 'Just the right amount, I reckon.' And he gives her a wink.

She can't help herself then, lets the corners of her mouth twitch up.

'That's more like it. You can ride up front, if you like.'

'Oh, I don't think so.'

She eyes the Grandma, guile rising. 'Yes, please,' she says instead. 'I'd like that.'

'Olive can sit in the back,' he goes on. 'I'm sure she won't mind.'

At that name she slumps a little, had been hoping to keep Mr Collins for herself for a bit. Had hoped, even, that Horrible Olive might not want to come, after everything. But being in the back will mither her, and that'll be pleasing.

'Have a nice time,' the Grandpa says then, and holds out a hand to shake, like she's the Queen herself, or fancy, any road.

So she takes it, then into her fingers feels him slip something, hard and fat and flat. Fifty pence!

'For tuck,' he says swiftly. 'Keep it safe.'

And she does, drops it into her pocket where it clinks on the Whimsey.

The Grandma don't say owt to that, which surprises her. Just nods with her forehead creased. 'Go on then,' she tells them. 'You don't want to be late.'

Mr Collins' car – a Jaguar the colour of Caramac – smells of leather, a Feu Orange air freshener, and, when he leans across to buckle her in, something potent and soapy. 'There you go, princess,' he tells her. 'Clunk-click.'

And that is satisfying. So satisfying she wants to unbuckle herself just so he can do it and say it again, but she don't, 'cause she don't want to spoil it.

She'll leave that to Olive.

Who doesn't disappoint.

'I didn't think you were coming,' she says to Sadie, climbing into the back with an apple in one hand, a Bible in the other and a scowl on her, wide as the Nile.

Not that she's seen the Nile. Nor any river, maybe, except the Leeds–Liverpool Canal, which don't really count. But she imagines.

'Don't get that on the seat,' Mr Collins warns Olive, nodding at the apple.

'It's from our tree,' she says. 'My *dad* picked it especially.'
Cow.

'Still,' says Mr Collins. 'Not on the calfskin.'

And, along with the satisfying fact that he don't call her
'princess', that's as good as wink number two. Better, even,
'cause it shuts Horrible Olive up until past Potter Street.

'Who'll be in my room?' Olive finally pipes up. 'Will *she*?'

'*She* is the cat's mother,' says Mr Collins. Wink three. 'I
think you mean Sadie. And yes, she will. She'll be in your
tent. Not room. There're no rooms.'

'I thought it was cabins? Like the *Little House on the
Prairie*?'

Sadie swings back to stare, sees Olive gaping like a landed
trout. 'Don't be daft. Course it's tents. It's called "camp",
in't it?'

'I don't even know what that means – "in't it". Is that
even English?'

'I think that's enough,' says Mr Collins.

And she's just about to award herself another wink,
another point, when he adds 'girls' on the end, and pops her
scoffing, sends her into a dull sulk for another five miles.

But then they turn off the tarmac and onto scrub and she
spies it, strung across the entrance in stamped black on
orange: *Vacation Bible Camp 1981!* it proclaims. Then,
underneath, in quieter writing: *God is with all of us.*

'Even with you,' says Horrible Olive.

Even with Sadie.

And she remembers something Olive told her, when they
were playing, something about her own dad. 'I've got two

fathers,' she'd said then. 'Mr Watkins *and* God.' 'And you've got none,' was what should've come next, if Nirmal hadn't nudged the girl to shut up.

But what if she has got one? What if she can find God and have Him as a dad. It's better than none. And if He talks to her, well, that'll show Olive *and* Mr Collins who's better brethren.

So it's with a swagger that she slips off the sticky beige car seat and onto parched grass, grabs her bag, heavy with treasure and the Bible besides, and her bedding roll, tied up with twine.

Olive eyes it sideways. 'I've got a waterproof sleeping bag,' she says. 'And a groundsheet.'

'Why? Might you wet yourself?' asks Sadie. And turning to hide her reddening face, she awards herself ten points and marches off to follow Mr Collins.

Jean

Essex, August 1981

The school is exactly as she imagined it – her expectations tempered as they are by experience and a keen knowledge of North Essex's limitations. It is perfectly adequate, is the best that can be said. Middling successful, red brick, but, above all, clean. The pupils look brighter, in every sense, than their Mark Hall counterparts, at least in the photographs, and there is a pleasing smattering of double-barrels amongst the ranks. At that, she hears her mother's caw of amusement. 'As if that makes manners. P'raps we should change our name to Billings-Flynn. Still shit, don't we?'

Except these children would never use that word, and there lies the difference, she thinks. One point to me.

She wonders why Martha had never been sent in the end. That's how Maurice knew of it, back then. He'd looked around before the girls had started at Essex Ladies but said it wasn't quite suitable, that Barbara had doubts about the distance. But for Constance perhaps, given the . . . absconding.

God – or genetics, she is latterly led to believe – has cursed her with difficult children. Though others' adoration hasn't helped. Bernard seems to think the Child can do no wrong, is still trying to take the blame for her pilfering things that aren't hers, for her taking herself off with that Nirmal boy, for her – and this she still cannot believe, still less countenance – deciding to find her father, trailing that wretched Terry to the market. Well of course she was going to be disappointed there, she could have told her that if she'd asked. Not that she's any the wiser as to who else might bear that badge of dishonour.

Anyway, none of that matters now the Child will be in school. Sleeping in a dormitory. Singing 'Onward, Christian Soldiers'— She stops herself. Do Quakers sing hymns? Or are they the silent ones? Well, hymns aren't everything; look at Constance.

Maurice had called her a 'princess' several times, an 'angel' once. She'd told him not to, told him the girl already had ideas above her station, but he couldn't help himself, he said. Not the way she sang.

He never called her that after, though.

She shakes the memory off like a bluebottle.

'Yes, I think this will do perfectly,' she says, trying not to edge her voice with the desperation that has threatened her balance, her manners, all morning. 'Shall I write you a cheque now?'

'That won't be necessary,' replies the bursar – a blustering man whose face is the colour and texture of porridge. 'We'll need school reports before that. Just a formality, of course. But you understand, I'm sure.'

'Of course,' she seethes through her set smile. 'I'll have

them sent over directly. Or I could drop them off tomorrow—'

'That won't be necessary. It really is just a formality. And so we know where to set her.'

At the bottom, she thinks. Well, there's no point lying, is there? But the school will pull her up by her socks and drum some education into her, along with a more acceptable accent, she hopes. And she is glad, again, that she didn't bring the Child – at religious camp, she'd said, terribly committed – to show herself, them both, up.

'Well, I look forward to meeting you again in September,' the bursar says then. 'Mrs . . .' He glances at his notes. 'Holiday.'

'Earnshaw,' she corrects, then winces at her explanation. 'Holiday is the child's surname.'

'Of course.'

But then, on a whim, 'Though, we'll be changing it. For simplicity,' she adds. 'Given the circumstance.'

She suggests it to Bernard when she gets in, asks if he can fetch the birth certificate along with the school reports, reluctant as she is to spend a second more than necessary in the shed, in the presence of . . . everything.

'Are you sure?' he asks. 'Shouldn't we ask her first?'

'Why ever would we ask her? She's eleven. And it's not as if she chose the name in the first place.'

'No, but . . . there'll be procedures. Adoption issues, perhaps.'

'Adoption? I'm not adopting her. I'm just giving her a proper name. It's confusing the school.'

She can tell Bernard suspects this to be nonsense, but he treks to the shed anyway, comes back ten minutes later with the papers she asked for. Papers she's surprised to see listing 'A's for maths, for English, for needlework. Though the 'could concentrate more' under religious studies is hardly unexpected.

The birth certificate is the same as she remembers from the brief glimpse on the day they had packed up in Leeds. Bernard had asked if she wanted to see it, had held it out, and she'd snapped a 'No!' even as she'd peered to see the *unknown* stamped in smug black.

'Are you absolutely sure about this?' he asks her now. 'The school, I mean.'

'Why wouldn't I be?' She slips the reports into A4 manila that she'll address and send from work in the morning. She'll pop the eleven and a half pence in petty cash to make up. She'd do it now but she's out of stamps and the Post Office is closed.

'Jean, I . . .' He goes to tell her something but stops himself.

'What is it?' she says, impatient to be done with this business.

'Nothing. Doesn't matter.'

'Well, good—'

But it does matter after all, it seems. 'Just that I was wondering if you'd . . . read any of it. The diary. If it might be a . . . a good idea.'

Nausea sways her as if on a ship. 'Don't be absurd, Bernard. Why would I read it?'

'I just . . . It doesn't matter. Maybe another time.'

'No.'

Afraid he might see the hesitation hiding behind her arrogance, she hastens to the kitchen, opens the refrigerator as if it might inspire, as if it might hold an answer. 'No,' she repeats as she stares at a half-shredded lettuce. There will be no other time. There will be no maybe. She will not read something meant to be kept hidden. Meant to—

Oh, God.

She closes the door, presses her head to the metal for a second.

Then she turns and walks along the hall and up the stairs to their bedroom.

And there, door locked, curtains drawn, heart rabbit-quick, she opens the drawer and pulls out the red notebook.

It's dog-eared, she sees, bookmarked by the Child, no doubt. And, for a second, she senses herself as a trespasser on not one life but two. But she has a right, doesn't she? Deserves an answer to her 'why'. And so, fingers trembling, lips muttering a prayer, a plea for forgiveness, she opens the pages at the marker.

Connie

Essex, May 1969

Connie wonders, sometimes, if life might improve through narration, if she had a sort of voiceover – sonorous, articulate – detailing her movements and moods, and rendering her brooding the stuff of profundity. There is something terribly enigmatic about referring to oneself in third person, something that lends a suggestion of fame, of import. Steve McQueen might pass muster. Or, if he had to be British (for it was always a he) then Terence Stamp or Malcolm McDowell.

'She stood in the front row of the Harlow Youth Chorale,' declaims Terence, 'willing the floor to crack and a chasm to swallow her. For Constance Earnshaw—' She stops. God, what a horrible name. She can't possibly shine, be beguiling, with that monstrosity hanging, flapping albatross-like, around her.

It was incredibly unfair, now she began to think of it, how names marked you, corralled you, told you how to behave, who to be, even. They were laden with expectation, something parents should remember, perhaps, before foisting Florence or Honor or, indeed, Constance on an otherwise Jill.

She has other names though. 'Princess', Mr Collins calls her. Or sometimes his 'angel', when she's performed a note-perfect requiem. Her mother had tried to put a stop to that, of course; told him that he mustn't, because she isn't and it isn't healthy to let her think so.

She's not an angel, she's not stupid. But nor is she the devil her parents portray. No, not her parents – her father's role in all this is benign; at best he is a mildly concerned observer – but her mother, then, who seems convinced she is out of control, possessed even, or spawned by a demon. She's not a devil, but she is discontent, wishes she were somewhere else, were some*one* else.

She could be Sandie Shaw or Marianne Faithful. Jane Eyre or Juliet. Or how about Joy in *Poor Cow*? Martha was flabbergasted at that one. Asked her why she'd want to meet men whose business is thieving. 'At least Joy is free,' she had said. 'At least Joy lives in bloody London.'

But then she remembers, knows who she would be, who, in fact, she might become if she tries hard enough, buys the right clothes, finds the right name. She will be Sally Jay Gorce in *The Dud Avocado*, that derailed debutante, not giving a damn.

She'd borrowed a copy from a girl called Edith, whose mother was widely and snidely regarded as 'louche'; had been handed it in a brown paper bag that smacked of contra-band, then consumed it covertly, shut in the lavatories at lunchtime or hidden inside a textbook on the train. So that now, in this moment, though she is still in uniform and pressed against a perspiring Jane Cox on one side and

Martha, smelling perpetually of baking, on the other, she sees who she is: a Sally Jay in waiting.

Yes, that's it! She will dye her hair pink, and wear red dresses; she will be friends with coloured men as well as contessas; she will argue about art and understand jazz.

'You don't even like art,' says Martha, when she confesses (of course she confesses, how can she not?). 'You said it was pointless and boring.'

'So I'll be good in an argument, then,' she practically snaps, annoyed at Martha for dampening her ardour. Annoyed at herself for bothering with someone who couldn't possibly understand what it felt like to be stuck, trapped in aspic, in a treacle-thick life that wasn't your own. Honestly, the girl already resembled her mother, had taken her practical haircut, her sensible shoes, her interest in knitting, and assimilated them without question, without even shopping around. She wonders, again, why she bothers with her, remembers she probably wouldn't if it weren't for the alibis, and perhaps choir. Then wonders again why she still bothers with that; it's not as if she believes in the God she's singing about, and her mother would loathe her either way.

But still, there is something about it. The reason she spends every spare minute stuck in a draughty church hall that smells of medicine and death, listening to Mrs Wickens plink-plonk on the ancient piano, letting Mr Collins call her whatever he likes – it is the singing; the singing is the ticket. Her reason for being, her way out of here. Singing transports her, transforms her, so that when she closes her eyes, opens her throat, she is somewhere else entirely.

And yes, someone else too. Someone better. Someone who can bleach her hair or bob it, who can wear a skirt so short her knickers are peeping, who can pack out the Palladium and lift the crowds until they're soaring with her, and calling her name: Connie, Connie, Connie.

That will show them. Show Martha, her mother. Show Terry.

He says she's 'mental'. Not bad – 'Got some right pipes,' he'd told her – just deluded because she's got brains and all, so why'd she want to slum it round the clubs?

But why wouldn't she?

And they're not slums, she wants to tell him, not gutters. They're grandstands, palaces, places of worship. Not for false idols, for tedious Jesus who's dead anyway, and was at best a cut-price magician or hypnotist, but for the likes of latter-day gods like Jagger and Jones, Brown and Bolan.

And at that name she quickens, thinks of her own Birdcage version, coming on stage, strutting his stuff, thrusting his crotch so that she and a hundred other girls dampen their pants imagining the contortions he might perform privately, and only for them.

She thrills to him in a way she never has to Terry, has conjured him up for herself under the covers, imagined him touching her so that a strange momentum builds in her, an urgency, until she verges on something, a tense precipice from which she is desperate to drop despite the assumed void before her.

'Constance Earnshaw!'

She comes to, musters, as she always does. Her mother is

calling. And she wonders, as she does, what she has done this time to warrant such pique.

'Constance Earnshaw,' repeats Steve McQueen – yes, Steve is better – 'That damned name. Well, one day . . . one day soon, sooner than you think, she'll run away to London and leave all of it behind – school, her boyfriend, her bloody mother. And Constance Earnshaw too.' She smiles at that, smug as a cat, then lets Steve pick up the thread again. 'Gone will be Constance of old, and instead she'll be Connie—' Connie what? 'Rocket', Terry sometimes called her, in the early days, when all she wanted was to get into bed. But 'Connie Rocket' sounds childish, cheap, pier-end. So not that. She digs around in the Scrabble sack, pulls out possibilities plucked from other stars – James, Joplin, Holiday. At the last – Holiday – visions brim: hot weather, and Hepburn, too, for wasn't Holly Golightly named not for the plant but for the pleasure?

'Connie Holiday,' she says aloud. Then lets Steve repeat it. 'Connie Holiday stood with a sigh, and skulked downstairs to where her mother – her wicked stepmother – was waiting to blame her for the spilled milk, and the missing cheese.

'And the awful void of her own pitiful existence.'

Connie

Leeds, July 1981

'Holiday,' she repeats to herself. 'Connie Holiday – top of the pops!' Sees it in lights, or at least in fluorescent pink on the Roxy bill. Then remembers, with a sickening slump, the end of all that. Worse, she's that gig a week tomorrow. Should get round to cancelling, should call up Billy Rigsby – greasy squit that he is – and confess she's not up to it, not up to much anymore, might be moving anyway. That she's not the girl he thought she was, or, more important, that *she* thought she was.

That was the thing, see. You can change your name to anything – Rocket or Holiday or Henderson-Briggs – but it doesn't change who you are, where you come from. It doesn't change your inheritance.

The doctor doesn't think Sadie's at risk, but what else might she have inherited?

Dicky kidneys? Liver spots?

A tendency to floridity, to run to fat in middle age?

Well, she's got a decent voice on her, anyway. Not that Sadie bothers with it often. Though perhaps only because it'd always been easier not to, with her and Elvis hogging the limelight, even in the living room. Better now that he's out of the picture, perhaps.

Though would she want her own daughter to go through what she has? The late nights, the getting legless just to get in with the bigwigs, then the rejections anyway because you're too new or too niche or too bloody something.

But then someone says yes and you're up there in front of them, the pub's shitty spotlights as dazzling as the Palais', and someone's shouting a name – 'Come on, Connie Holiday' – and you realize it's you . . .

Jean

Essex, August 1981

She ignores the insults, focuses on facts. So that's where the name came from. Not the object, or the idea – the foreign beach with palm trees and bikinis, exotic fish, or, in their case, the lakes with cagoules and walking boots, the odd deer – but the singer. That fattish black woman with the voice of a man. The last thing Constance was, in any sense. And why? What was wrong with 'Earnshaw' anyway? She'd been relieved to take it at the wedding, seeing it as honest, solid, of a far better class than Billings. And it was literary, she'd discovered, much later, immortalized by a Brontë – she forgets which – for Cathy in *Wuthering Heights*. Another wild child who didn't know which side her bread was buttered. Perhaps it was that. Constance had read the book at school, she recalls now. Had hated it, branded Cathy 'whingeing' and Hindley 'insipid', when all the time it was Heathcliff she should have been railing against. But of course there was no telling her anything.

And now the Child has inherited it – a made-up moniker predicated on nothing but whim and fancy and the foolishness of youth. Yes, she will change it, she decides, will send off for the forms pronto. Or perhaps she can telephone them? Maurice isn't to know, after all. Not now that he's at camp. Not that he'd object, to either the telephone call or the purpose.

She thanks God for Maurice then, her heaven-sent saviour. And not for the first time. When she tots up the things he's done for her – for all of them – even in the wake of what Constance stole from him, when he should have been marching every Earnshaw to the station, or at the very least severing their friendship. But no, he had stood by Jean and by Bernard, though she is the reason, the nub of it, she knows. It's her piety he admires, she thinks. That and her refusal, like him, to be cowed in the face of misfortune, of deliberate sin.

She dials directory enquiries and then, flummoxed as to whom she wishes to speak, asks for the 'name change people'.

'Deed poll service, you mean.'

'Perhaps,' she says.

'No. That's definitely them. My cousin done it.'

'Did it,' she says without thinking.

'Pardon?'

'Nothing.'

'Right, well. This is it, in any case.'

She notes down the number on her lined pad under the heading *Holiday*. Then crosses that out and writes *Earnshaw* in instead. Start as you mean to go on. Then she dials again, asks if it's possible, who must consent. Whether it will cost and then how much. Nothing would be too much, she thinks then, to rid them of this frippery.

'Going undercover?'

Her head snaps up so quickly it almost ricochets. Lurking in the door is Shelley Pledger with a cigarette and a smirk.

'I hope that's not lit,' she says. 'You know the rule.'

'It's not, but I don't see why. My brother gets to smoke at Pritchards.'

'Well go and work there, then.'

'I'll tell Maurice you said that, shall I?'

But Shelley Pledger has picked the wrong morning to mince words with her. '"Mr Collins" to you. And I'll tell him you're five minutes short every day, shall I?'

'Five minutes? Five minutes is nothing.'

'Twenty-five a week, nearly four hours a month docked.' She smiles, polite to the end. 'I'd say that was a good ten pounds' worth, wouldn't you? More than a hundred a year. When you put it like that, it's not "nothing", is it?'

Shelley Pledger flicks her hair – and an invisible 'V' sign, she doesn't wonder – mutters something under her breath. 'Frigid bitch', probably. She never was that inventive.

And there were times when Jean would have riled at that. But today she is buoyed by something, is lifted by it. Efficiency, she thinks. That's what it is. She has sorted out a school and a name change in the space of two days. Really, it was a shame women didn't run the world. In truth, she'd been unsure about Margaret Thatcher at first, but look how she's proving herself now. Taking on the unions. And she a grocer's daughter, not that you'd have known from her clothes, her manners, her pitch-perfect vowels.

She checks her watch. Five hours forty minutes to go and

most of the invoices done by eleven. If that didn't prove it, what did? In fact, she might leave a little early herself. At four, perhaps. She will tag it onto any overtime required in the Christmas rush, when she'll be glad to be corralled inside. Yes. A little early. How frivolous it seems! But things have been . . . difficult for so long, that perhaps she should grab the fancy when it takes her, which is so very rarely, after all.

She feeds a sheet of paper onto the platen, feels the pull of duty, insistent, persistent.

Perhaps just forty minutes.

Today there is no tension when she turns into Old Harlow, no sense of trepidation along Fore Street, watching as she did before for Nirmal, expecting his malevolent presence like an Indian homunculus, small but very much there. Though it's not just his absence that affords her this release, this breathing space, it is the lack of the Child herself, a hole opening up where before there'd been 'ayes' and 'nowts' and too much television.

Now, at The Green, there is silence. Blissful quiet.

Bernard had insisted Jean would miss her, that she'd have got used to the Child without knowing and perhaps now she'd see what a mistake she was making, with this school business. But Bernard doesn't feel what she feels, or see what she sees: the mess of it, the threat of it. He walks the earth with his head always slightly uptilted as if towards the sky, or the moon – or the future. Doesn't see the dirt or the dust or the dog mess. Leaves all that to her to clean up.

But this – this is more akin to the life she'd imagined as

a child. A house kept fastidiously neat and hygienically clean, in which she would eat apples and keep a cat, a slender, well-bred thing. Of course, she'd realized the foolhardiness of that last part in ample time – seen the havoc any animal can wreak to soft furnishings at close hand at Barbara's. But the rest she'd held as ideal, had followed doggedly, even as Bernard seemed oblivious and her own daughter accused her of some sort of fakery.

'Ignore her,' Bernard had told her then. 'It's just a phase. Like yo-yos. She'll grow out of it.'

But she hadn't. If anything, she'd only got angrier with age and education. Really, it was a curse having a girl, though she can't recall ever mustering such a level of ire herself, nor the vocabulary to go with it.

And the Child has inherited it as well, this violence. This railing against something – everything. Jean, in the main. So that she must suffer double while Constance is lauded as angelic again.

The unfairness of it rattles her then, spills salt and knocks over a pot plant.

Perhaps the Child should know the truth, she thinks. Should be told what her mother has done.

But what *has* she done exactly?

She'd sworn to read no more of it. Had pushed it to the back of the cabinet after the seven pages she'd raced through last night and told herself not to touch it again.

But the thing is compelling as a car crash, or a house fire, a thing so terrible and potentially devastating that you know you mustn't look, but find instead that, however hard you try, you cannot stop staring.

But then crashes are cleared and fires burn themselves out, she tells herself. And just a few more pages might provide whatever it is she's looking for and then the wretched thing can go back to the shed, or, better, be burned itself, which is probably what Bernard should have done all along.

But as she opens the page, her own dog-ear marking her place now, she forgets her own exhortations, forgets everything she should do, forgets herself even, and is a seventeen-year-old girl, standing on the cusp of adulthood and in a dress she distinctly remembers buying.

Connie

Essex, May 1969

'My life stood, a loaded gun.'

She has copied the quote out, stuck it to her mirror with tape, tried to imagine herself Emily Dickinson, or rather Connie Holiday as Emily Dickinson. But instead she stares at her reflection with something bordering on distress. Her hair is unnaturally rigid, her dress similarly boned, her entire demeanour decidedly Earnshaw, not Holiday at all.

She doesn't even want to go, only agreed in the end because the alternative her mother offered was a prayer meeting at Elspeth Leonard's, who has a tendency to foist stale biscuits on her guests, along with an ageing cat with overactive salivary glands. She's surprised her mother wants to go, given both of these deadly sins.

'It's a school dance,' her mother had protested. 'Think yourself lucky. Would that we even had such things in my day.'

She'd resisted the temptation to reply with, 'When was that? The Dark Ages?' and had promptly awarded herself a medal for managing to do so, pinned on by Steve McQueen, who has widened his voiceover remit to more of a fairy-godfather role.

As if the woman would deign to dance, anyway. Surely it was ungodly. Though possibly not when trussed up in so much clothing, the only flesh on display her calves and lower arms. It will be a wonder if she can even waltz, let alone manage the mashed potato, the twist or the jerk. Though, she doubts Essex Ladies will have the requisite LPs for that, and the band is probably fat Miss Frank's fiancé and his lower-management colleagues from Gilbey's, whose claim to fame is once being third support to Acker Bilk. She sighs dramatically at the thought, which Steve notes, poignantly.

Still patiently narrated, she descends the stairs to find her mother scrubbing an alleged stain on the hall floor – probably a muddy scuff from a school shoe not soon enough removed. Though, she'd have cleaned even without evidence; what else was there for her to do? The Harpic Queen, her father called her once, and swiftly learned his lesson. 'Cleanliness is next to godliness,' she had retorted. As if Jesus gave two hoots about dust and dead woodlice. Not if he had any sense.

'The woman stood,' says Steve McQueen, 'determined not to admit she was dazzled by her daughter, even in a dress that went out of fashion about ten bloody seasons ago.'

'Splendid,' her mother says, eyeing the baby blue encasing. 'Now, please try to be polite, and no . . . playing silly beggars.'

'No necking on the tennis courts?'

Her mother closes her eyes, already at wits' end, apparently. 'Why do you have to be so . . . antagonistic all the time?'

'I thought the whole point of this was to meet a *suitable* boy? How will I know he's suitable if I don't check?'

'There's more to life than kissing and . . . and things.'

God, I hope so, she thinks. I hope there's singing and drinking and whippets, and flats in Paris and boys in bands and a spinning, dizzying whirligig of a life I'm meant for but yet to taste. 'I'll see you at ten,' she says. And walks to the corner, watched by her fairy godfather, who adorns her in glory, and the act with a splendour and significance far beyond Harlow's capabilities.

The dance is exactly as she had imagined at her most determinedly cynical: ugly and dull and unbearably staid. The boys in Sunday suits and the girls in department-store dresses, all set on becoming their parents whilst thinking they're oh so different for once buying a Beatles' single. How pathetic, how lacking in ambition, how unedifyingly second-rate.

The thought of turning into either her mother or father is so very depressing. The inheritance of her pursed lips or pinched demeanour or his weak features only one element of it; the greater threat that of becoming so bothered by God, so indifferent to human events and effort, so generally contained. She sometimes imagines she's adopted, a foundling abandoned on the doorstep to be raised by ordinary people, while they – her real parents – go about their brilliant lives unencumbered until they are ready to collect her.

But that dream soon washed off when she saw the birth certificate, was regaled with the mess and general dreadfulness of giving birth, as though she should apologize, or be inherently grateful for her presence in this world.

There had been a chink in this invincible evidence once. Her science class had been covering genetics, and the inherited nature of eye colour – not arbitrary at all, it seemed. And, from staring vacantly out at the caretaker mowing the croquet lawn, she had suddenly swerved her attention and done some swift calculations and realized her own mud-brown irises were not the probable result of her mother and father's pairing. Perhaps, she thought for a blissful minute, her mother had had an affair with an actor – Omar Sharif or Lee Marvin, or Steve McQueen even. Perhaps she was the result of a steamy one-night stand, and stood to inherit not a receding chin but money and status and power.

But then, in answer to a similar and rather more panicked query from Melanie Jessop, Miss Bixby had said there were exceptions to every rule. And she was forced to dismiss her mother's imagined indiscretion and accept that she, Connie, was just a black sheep.

'Constance!'

She looks up to see Martha Collins dancing with a boy with a dusting of upper-lip fuzz and the unfortunate name of Herring, who is pressed against her ample breasts as if they might be the source of life itself. Mr Collins would have a conniption fit if he caught them. Although, frankly, that's hypocritical considering he stares at Connie's own décolletage as avidly as if it were a marble Venus or perhaps a golf trophy. She wonders then if he might try anything on the choir trip, if she were going. And if she might like it.

Probably not. But as she's not going (a week on a bus

touring an irrelevant section of Germany with the God squad, no thank you) it's moot, which is preferable.

Martha plonks herself down at the end of the song (the future Mr Frank, after all, with a repertoire of basic ballroom, and some inadvisable free jazz that the headmistress put a stop to). 'Aren't you dancing?'

She shakes her head. 'The Gidney boy asked, but I said I'd rather die.'

'It's a shame they won't let us bring guests,' says Martha, sounding as if she considers it anything but. 'You could have asked Terry, then.'

'Hardly. He'd be barred within minutes.'

Anyway, it's not Terry she's missing.

It's her erstwhile Marc Bolan – his hips shimmying in snakeskin, his face glittered with silver, his lips curled in a sneer at this entire ridiculous charade. Of course, she knows now that's not his real name.

No, his real name is Steve.

She's telephoned him. Finally mustered the courage, and found a time when her parents were both out – her mother at Barbara's, her father in his wretched shed, where he seemingly spent entire days – and dialled the number in London.

He didn't know her at first, couldn't place her, but she'd reminded him of the fire escape, the lit cigarette, and he'd said, 'Green dress, right?' And her tender heart had spasmed in her chest like a salmon. Then, when he'd told her his name, she'd seen it as a sign, of course, a gift from McQueen. Fitting, somehow, that her fairy godfather was not an imagined phantom after all, but her would-be beau.

He'd given her an address then, in Brixton – Winslade Road – and said if she was ever in the area she should drop in. 'Cheers,' she'd said. 'I will.' Both with practised and painstakingly repeated nonchalance, as if the invite were nothing more than a drink down the Painted Lady with Terry and his mates. When instead it's simultaneously the holy grail and a current impossibility.

But she'll find a way, a time to meet him. Meet her very own Steve.

And, clinging to this, for the first time ever she survives a school social without disgrace and returns without tardiness. Because she's not Constance Earnshaw anymore. She's new and improved, she declares (her narrator dismissed for the night). Though even Connie Holiday needs cold cream, she decides, and sits at the mirror.

She sees it then, the taped slip of paper: *My life stood. A loaded gun.*

And now she believes it. Now she feels it: she is ripe, ready, desperate for something, anything, to happen.

And if it won't come to her in Harlow, she will – like Dick Whittington, she thinks – set off to fetch it. Set off for London, and Love, with a capital L.

And best of all, Life.

Sadie

Essex, August 1981

Sadie had thought she knew a bit about God. About Jesus and Mary and Joseph. About the Good Samaritan. She can even name at least three disciples. But Horrible Olive is an encyclopaedia of biblical figures and some non-biblical as well. The saints, it seems, are her favourite. She has a list of them, and their miracles, all stored in her head for testing.

'Go on,' she urges. 'Try me.'

Sadie sighs. 'Anne,' she manages, lacking imagination or will.

'Patron saint of sailors, cabinet-makers and miners.'

'Why do cabinet-makers even need protecting?'

'I don't know, they just do. Everything has a saint. Even cleaners. Even repentant thieves.'

'Do they have to be repentant?'

'Yes,' says Olive. 'Definitely. Now, next?'

Sadie nudges the girl next to her – Jennifer Lenton, red hair and a squint – who blurts out a 'Jennifer?' revealing even less thought than Sadie, which is something.

'There isn't one,' Olive says, head tilted in pity. 'Or Sadie, if you're asking.'

Sadie twitches in irritation. 'I weren't. Anyway, I suppose Olive's the saint of everything.'

But Olive says nothing to that.

'I thought they were for the Catholics,' says Sadie eventually, and, next to her, Jennifer Lenton nods solemnly.

'Saints are for anyone who *believes*,' says Olive. 'Besides –' she scans camp as if to see who might be earwigging – 'what if the brethren have got it wrong? What if the Catholic God is the actual God? Or even Allah? Though, I doubt it. But I don't want to miss out on heaven because I picked the wrong one.'

It all sounds like a pack-load of claptrap to Sadie, but, according to Mr Kittering, that's the point. Well, not the point so much, just that if you can believe a story that wild, then God will reward you for having faith. She'd asked what faith was then, and in turn he'd asked everyone in the tent what they thought. And a girl with red dungarees and a brown hair bobble like two Maltesers had said it was believing in something even though there wasn't evidence. There was a lot of sucked breath at that, because, like Mr Kittering said, there's evidence everywhere – in the trees that lose their leaves and grow them again in the spring, in the sun that rises every morning, even in the tent that was standing firm and keeping them safe from the weather. Sadie thought the tent was more the responsibility of Mr Nevin and Mr Bent, who did all the maintenance and ran the galley, and there weren't any weather, only sun, but she tried to believe anyway, because if she didn't, why would God even talk to her in the first place?

She's been listening out for him all hours, hoping he'll tell her something important, like with Moses and the tablets, only perhaps with paper, 'cause she don't know how to write on stone. But he's said nowt so far, not even 'Hello, Sadie' or 'Thanks for believing' or, what she's really hoping for, 'Yes, I will be your father; I'll swap you for Olive,' which really would be a miracle.

Perhaps that's it, though. Perhaps she needs a miracle or to be martyred first, like Saint Valentine (beekeeping) or Saint Florian (chimney sweeps) or Saint Anastasia (weavers and healers and, incredibly, exorcists). She quite likes the idea of that. God would definitely want her then. Even the Grandma might like her.

'How do I get to be a martyr?' she asks.

Horrible Olive regards her as if she's retarded. 'You'd have to die. Like, suffer starvation or be eaten by snakes.'

'Oh.'

'Or you could get stigmata, I suppose.'

'What's stigmata?' They sounded less menacing, not involving death.

'Holes in your hands that bleed miraculously, like Jesus on the cross.'

'Oh. Do they hurt?'

'Like mad.'

Perhaps not, then.

'Anyway, you wouldn't get them. God hasn't talked to you.'

And that was the end of that.

*

God did speak that afternoon, but not to her. To Horrible flaming Olive again.

It happened in the hollow near the lat tents, apparently. She was looking for her loo roll and He spoke and told her it was actually back on Sadie's bed, because she'd nicked it. And she went back and there it was and it was definitely hers, because hers was orange and Sadie's wasn't. And it was definitely God, because He sounded exactly the same as He did last time, which is a sort of cross between Bob Monkhouse and the man off the Persil advert.

Horrible Olive is a fast phenomenon after that. Their tent has a queue of inquisitive visitors, who want His exact words, several times over, and a piece of the orange loo roll, which has achieved sacred status all by itself.

'You'll run out,' says Sadie. 'Then you'll be sorry.'

'No I won't,' retorts Olive. 'Because God will bring me more.'

'He'll just pop down Sainsbury's, will He?'

Olive snorts. 'God doesn't need Sainsbury's. He'll just magic it with His hands.'

God is beginning to sound more like a weird version of the Great Soprendo, who at least conjures up birds and rabbits, not toilet roll, but she don't bother saying, just stomps out of the tent, where she smacks straight into Mr Collins, almost topples.

'Careful,' he says, righting her. 'You'll do yourself a mischief.'

'Sorry,' she says. 'I weren't looking.'

341

'No harm,' he says. 'So where are you off to, then? Where's Olive?'

'Handing out loo roll,' she tells him. 'And nowhere. I don't know. I . . .' Then she decides to try it, because if anyone can help her, he can. 'I were going to find someone.'

'Who?'

'God?' she says, hottening with want and embarrassment.

But Mr Collins don't scold or scoff. 'Right,' he says instead. 'God, is it?'

She nods. 'Olive's heard Him and I haven't and . . . and she's got a dad and a mam and all and it's . . . it's not fair.' It bursts out of her, lava-like and scalding and all, sending her red with shame.

But Mr Collins ponders, squats down. 'Here's the thing. You've lots of things Olive hasn't got.'

'Have I?' she asks, only half believing him. 'Like what?'

'You've got talent, for a start. Like your mother.'

She starts, feels a loose thread inside her coil and tighten. 'What d'you mean?'

'You can sing,' he says. 'I've heard you.'

She shrugs.

'No one ever tell you that?'

'Only my mam, and she don't count.'

'Tell you what. Why don't I give you a private lesson? That'd shut Olive up for a bit, wouldn't it?'

He might as well have handed her sainthood on a plate or carved stigmata into her palms then and there.

'Do I bring her?' she asks then.

He shakes his head. 'Just you. Come to my tent after supper.'

'After supper,' she says, storing it in her head, as if written.

And then off she pops, not bothering who God talks to anymore. He can tell Olive she's won the pools, or will marry a prince, or is Queen of flaming Sheba for all she cares.

Because she don't need God.

She's got Mr Collins, and he's real and near and he hasn't got a horrible beard either.

Connie

Essex, May 1969

Connie's not at the breakfast table. Not sitting in frigid silence over thin toast with her perpetually disapproving mother and conveniently absent father.

She's with *him*.

She's being spun on a dance floor, her legs endless, her back dappled by light; being sung to, lyrics written for her, about her, detailing their all-consuming, ever-lasting, convention-defying love; then being fucked – no, not fucked, made love to – in a way Terry has never yet mustered, or even understood to be possible. At that thought, she lets out an unbidden whimper.

'Oh, for crying out loud, Constance.'

'What?' She snaps to.

'You're never at home as it is. The least you can do while you're here is pay attention. And it's not "what", it's "pardon".'

Reality is a wash of cold suds. 'Is it any wonder?'

'I beg your pardon?'

'I said, is it any wonder? Dad's at work or shut up in his office, and you're . . . you're away with Jesus and all his wretched helpers.'

'How dare you. I have never—' But she breaks off, unable or unwilling to finish. 'Bernard!'

Her father steps in where she cannot bear to tread. 'What is it that you're seeing tonight? That's what your mother asked.'

Her yawn is affected and audible. '*Twelfth Night*. She knows that.'

His hurt is honest and plain to see. 'We're just making conversation. Small talk, that's all.'

Guilt pricks, but doesn't sway her. 'What's the point in that? In talking about nothing for the sake of it? Why not talk about important things?'

'About what?' her mother thwacks back. 'That Bolan person, I suppose. Or ridiculous hippies.'

'How about Dagenham?' she volleys. 'Martha says Pinnacle Biscuits pays women far less an hour than the men and Mr Collins won't budge on it.'

'The women do –' what do the women there do? – 'different things. You can't pay the same for different things. And the men may be better educated.'

'Oh, what utter hog.'

'Constance! That's quite enough.'

Her mother's ire frightens her, seems to heat her blood and ready her hands for slapping. 'God, why do you always have to stop the conversation when it isn't . . . isn't going your way?'

Her mother is unmoved. 'Finish your breakfast.'

'Point proven.' At that, she stands and snatches her satchel from the back of her chair, where she'd only hung it to annoy her mother, but now she appreciates the convenience.

'Where do you think you're going?'

'Where does it look like I'm going? To man the picket lines at Pinnacle? I'm going to school.' She stalks to the door, remembers her trump card, and turns. 'Oh, and by the way, saying "pardon" is awfully common. Just thought you should know.' And with a pitying grin, she exits stage left to thunderous, if imagined, applause.

'Have a nice time,' she hears her father call after her. Then a fervent 'Bernard!'

Oh, she will have a nice time, has it all planned. But not sitting prim in the theatre with twenty-seven schoolgirls and Miss bloody Bixby.

She bagsies the seat at the end of the row, but is pressed to beg for it when Angela Pratt tells her bagsying went out with the ark, with Bill Haley. But she's not too proud to practically genuflect; claims she's feeling queasy from the bus and might need to run to the lavatory, and better she has easy egress than be sick on someone's lap. Even Miss Bixby can't argue with that, and so, when the lights dim, when Miss Bixby is engrossed in her programme and Martha in a bag of KP, she is able to slip out of the row unnoticed, out of her uniform in the lavatory cubicle, and out of the theatre, along The Cut, and onto a bus bound for Brixton.

The house is smaller than she'd imagined, and more full of people: bodies tangle in armchairs, drape over beds, lie prone on parquet flooring, some of them male, some female, some impossible to tell. It moves too – the house – or so it seems.

The rooms shifting and tipping and threatening to up-end her.

She's taken something – a pill, she thinks, or a slip of paper; it's hard to discern through the haze of herbal cigarettes and the blur her mind has become. Steve said she should, so she did – stuck out her tongue and let him press it on, let it dissolve. He said she should try a joint as well, held it out to her mouth, a gesture so sexual she couldn't help but do as he said: pulled hard, then held it in like he told her she had to, so that for a second everything stilled and then tilted.

'You feel it?' he'd asked her.

And, unable to speak, drowned in the sound of her own heart thumping, she'd nodded, hoping he'd seize the moment to kiss her, to take her to bed, but instead he'd turned to a girl in a cowboy hat and started on about Joplin. So she'd risen, unsteadily, and is now making her way to a bed – his, she thinks, hopes. Then he might find her, and realize, and Life will begin.

She wakes with the weight of someone on top of her, for a second feels the giddy thrill of vindication, then realizes it isn't even him, just a thin man with long hair and a hard on. 'No,' she manages – 'nnnng' – and pushes him off, scrabbles her naked way – did she undress or did he undress her? – off sticking sheets and onto floorboards, realizes she might be sick – *is* going to be sick – and directs it into a corner, for want of a sink or a bin.

'Jesus Christ,' exclaims the suitor.

Jesus, *please*, she thinks.

But Jesus is busy, his blithe neglect of her in her hour of need a brief 'I told you so' moment. But her triumph carries no glory for her, no punch for her mother, just an elastic string of yellow vomit that hangs from her mouth and then catches on a hank of damp hair.

'What time is it?' she asks.

'How the fuck should I know?'

She doesn't answer, pulls on some clothes – not hers, but wearable – scans the dim-lit room for her satchel, but it seems to be missing, along with her knickers. Instead she snatches a handful of coins from an ashtray next to the record player and wordlessly exits, no applause this time, no acknowledgement at all.

It's gone four in the morning when Bernard fetches her – from a doorway opposite the telephone box on Acre Lane, where's she's kept herself as small as possible, as hidden, as un-hittable. She thanks the abandoning God, the missing Jesus, that he doesn't strike her himself, doesn't chide her, just helps her into the front seat of the Hillman Hunter, places the emergency bucket from the boot between her feet.

'We were so worried,' he says eventually.

They have dropped in and out of the sodium glow of the Rotherhithe Tunnel and are now far past the thinning rim of the city, edging into slowly greening countryside and the thin light of morning.

'I'm alive, aren't I?' she replies.

'This time.'

The surge is swift and she is sick again, twice, into black plastic, the liquid almost as luminous as it is acrid. 'I'm sorry,' she says, and what begins as a whimper veers into weeping.

'We'll empty it later,' her father replies.

'I didn't mean—'

'I know.'

He rests a hand on her leg then, warm fingers on goose-pimpled skin meant to reassure, to steady her. But all it does is elicit guilt, remind her what's been done, and what's to come when she's in front of her mother, and then Miss Bixby and the headmistress, she doesn't doubt. And instead of lessening, her self-pity swells, manifesting as sorrow, and sends her sobbing into her father's handkerchief once more.

Essex Ladies metes out its punishment swiftly, but even-handedly at least. There is no trial by peers or even superiors, no inquisition, no ritual humiliation, just a brief meeting, to which she is not invited, then a letter explaining what had already been said: that she is no longer welcome on the premises.

Her mother, of course, is less steady or circumspect.

'I don't know where you get it from,' she practically spits, two days later, and not for the first time.

But, no longer weak with lack of sleep or sickness, Connie is less repentant. 'Why? Is there something you want to tell me?' she goads.

Her mother's face pales, then blooms to puce. 'How dare you.'

But Connie is unstoppable. 'I know where I come from,'

she jeers. 'And I know where you come from as well. Poor cow.'

Any further words are slapped from her mouth with the flat of her mother's hand, rigid and stinging.

'Jean!' blurts her father.

But her mother isn't sorry. And nor is she. So, cheek livid, but head held up, she walks out of the kitchen and up to her room, where she will work out a way to make the woman pay.

And a way to be free of her – of this – for good.

Connie

Leeds, July 1981

She drops the diary, her hand travelling unbidden to her cheek, placing itself in the trace of that slap.

It had stung; still does. But she'd deserved it, hadn't she? Wouldn't she slap Sadie if she'd skived from a school trip and buggered off into the middle of Leeds, or over to Manchester, with no telling where she'd gone or for how long or, worse, who with?

Not that Sadie'd try. Least not to look at her now. Top of the class, she is, far ahead of Deborah, not that she'd rub it in. Even the teacher's sweet on her, singing her praises in English and maths. Facts, that's what matters to Sadie: lists and dictionaries and ticking things off in I-Spy, not pipe dreams and fairytales, whatever she professes about wishing she were in Bucks Fizz.

Elvis asked where her brains had come from once. She'd practically slapped him herself. Couldn't she name the capitals of Europe, the states of America, the kings and queens in absolute order? Couldn't she recite 'The Tyger', 'On His Blindness', bits of Swift? If she'd not been so bloody stubborn, so taken up with men, she'd have done all right at school. Could have got herself a degree, a job, a career, even. Could have ended up like Martha sodding Collins probably is right now—

But then she wouldn't have Sadie, would she. So, perhaps not.

She presses her palm to the flesh of her cheek, pushes herself to remember. Because she knows the blow didn't come from nothing – none of it did: the intolerance, the grim indignation, the bitterness. No, her mother had reason to needle her, to beg her to do better: because she had a secret of her own.

A secret about Connie, her provenance.

A secret too big to admit, still more to forgive.

Or is it?

Jean

Essex, August 1981

She cannot imagine it, still less fathom it. Losing time, losing oneself like that frightens her; to be prone, vulnerable, no more defences than a dust mote thrown here and there on the whim of a wind. Something nurturing, maternal – maternal! – springs in her, stiffens her hand ready to smack the man that tried to take from her defenceless daughter, and, yes, to smack her daughter for getting into such a state that he might try.

Again.

She shouldn't have done it, she knows that now – knew it then, that it was fear driving her, desperation.

But then nor should Constance.

Why? she demands repeatedly and pointlessly. Why do this?

She, of course, has never touched drugs. No nicotine to pass the time, no pethidine for her to sop the hurt of birth; even aspirin is a rare indulgence and taking it is inevitably accompanied by a fractious panic at what floodgates she might open if she appreciates the relief a little too much. A small sherry is about the size of any habit, but she learned

353

her limits swiftly and then halved them, had seen what even one too many might do to a woman, worse a man. And then what he might do to her.

No, it is best to quell these things, nip them in the bud, for they only amplify that other potential addiction: desire.

With Bernard it is functional and mercifully rare. Once a year on his birthday and when they are on holiday. Though the proximity of other guests has always distressed her. As if at breakfast they might sense she was wanton, unstoppable, when in reality it was nothing but duty that let her succumb.

But with . . . him, she wanted it.

It was there already, she remembers. A – what to call it? – lust, she supposes, for something she had hitherto only heard about from girls' whispers in the toilet cubicles, or seen in that filthy picture that her brother kept under his bed and insisted on showing her, though whether it was to appal or arouse her, she never ascertained. In any case, it achieved the former, and she'd assumed there must be something missing within her, for she'd never felt that alleged desperate pressing to even hold hands with a boy. Not any of her brother's friends, not the sea cadets who hung around the hall on a Sunday, nor even any of the film stars Rita from Number 2 swooned over. Nor even Bernard Earnshaw, who had asked her to dine with him twice and each time she'd declined; it wouldn't be honest on her part, to lead him up the garden path like that.

But then she'd met *him* – at the hat counter in Gamages of all places – and something shifted and released, like a stuck nut, and all bets were off.

He'd been buying for his sister, he'd told her: 'Seester,' he'd repeated, when she'd frowned, baffled. Then, '*Ma soeur?*' 'Ah, *vous êtes Français?*' she'd replied, and at that he'd given up a smile so gay, so grateful she'd reddened, felt pathetically faint and had thought to excuse herself. But he'd put a hand on her arm, as if to hold her steady, and asked her out, just like that. She'd said no, at first, that she couldn't. But he'd said, only for a drink, '*un petit verre*', and in the end she'd agreed; what harm could *un petit verre* do, after all?

She can still see it now: the bar where he'd taken her later. The walls once a shade of dairy, perhaps, but by then, like the ceiling, like the fingers and faces of the men who leant upon them, jaundiced with nicotine and sheened with sweat and the sheer filth of people. And yet still she perched on the stool, listened to his practised anecdotes, his charm, his wit, his lingering endearments, and *un petit verre* had turned into two, and then three, and one evening into five, all ending in frustration – his that she had to go, hers that she would have to hide her dishevelment yet again from her parents.

And then he'd said he was leaving, had to go back to Paris for a while, for business, and in her bereavement, her desperation, this time when he'd begged her, she'd said yes.

If she'd imagined Piccadilly, the Ritz, she was sorely disappointed. It was a Bayswater backstreet and a stucco-fronted terrace that had seen better days, the smell of boiled meat pervading even the bedding, whose stains she pretended were whisky or wine. The overall effect was sobering; her caution, thrown so carelessly to the wind on the back of three Dubonnets, now called back, her Dutch courage waning in

355

the face of his thing, urgent and purple and pointing at her like a threat or accusation. But then he'd turned out the light, so the peeling paper became a toile canopy, the couple next door muffled into what might be Parisian passion, not Paddington rage, and in that accent he'd called her his '*princesse*', and with the promise of tomorrow and more on his tongue, she'd succumbed.

Whether it was drink or desire, all of it appalled her now. Like an appetite for money or chocolate, it had to be curbed, contained. It needed willpower to manage it, lest she become fat, or a gambler, or . . . or a whore like a daughter—

She stops, places a hand on her chest, stunned at her sudden discovery.

Constance wasn't a whore at all. She – Jean – had gone willingly, hadn't she? If perhaps like a lamb. But Constance? She'd followed someone she'd painted as a saviour – of course Jean can see he was anything but. But then she was fifty-three and wise to the wiles of men and Connie had been seventeen and stupid and on God knows what. And instead of taking her anyway, he'd treated her worse than Jean had been treated; had left her in her messy state to the mercy of other men.

But she – Jean – hadn't known any of this. Had only seen the smeared cheeks, the tear in her dress, the set jaw that seemed to swear at her, even in her determined silence; had only smelled the acrid tang of vomit. Had sent her to bed and thence to Coventry, while she'd raged at the chances she'd discarded, the opportunities cock-a-snooked. And then, just a few weeks later, she'd lost the chance to talk to her at all, when perhaps—

Oh. God! Perhaps she might have stopped it.

The thought, uncaged now, is enormous – sabre-toothed and stalking.

She checks her watch – it's barely six. Bernard – watering the lawn, she sees, now the sun can't scorch the water off – can wait for supper at eight. No need to eat early now that the Child isn't here.

The Child.

At that thought, she feels that surge in her again, feels a need to touch her, clutch her close. In place of her mother? Or as well as? She's not sure. She's not sure of anything. Except the queasy need to read on, to get to the end.

So, steadying herself, she picks up the notebook again, and picks up the thread.

Connie

Essex, July 1969

Of all the days wasted in this place, Sundays are the worst. The relentlessness of it all – the infernal chug of lawnmowers on smug lawns, the interminable hum of men polishing smugger cars, the irritating hiss of hosepipes. And all of it topped with the turd that is church.

Her mother hates that word. Turd. So of course she said it at the breakfast table, just to see what it elicited. But her mother is trying to rise above it, it seems, and it was her father who'd come out with the inevitable, 'Constance?', to which the obvious reply was a bewildered, 'What?'

But, really, what *is* the point of it all? Not life – she's not suicidal, though she's considered feigning it for affect. But this isn't Life, is it? This is mere existence, ordered according to expectation, its happy inhabitants drones of sorts while she drifts listless, discontent, a cat unable to settle. Perhaps her paws should be buttered, she thinks, like in the story, to keep her from running, to keep her occupied so she doesn't notice the terrible pleasance of everything, the pretence.

Of course, the latest charade is that her expulsion is a Good Thing, that she wasn't suited to the school and will do better elsewhere. Her father has suggested secretarial college – there are courses at the tech, she would be back with Michelle Spencer. But where once that might have enticed, now the thought of typing 'the' endlessly is numbingly dull, and what is it for? To break you in for a lifetime of subservience? Well, no thank you. She will leave that to the Michelles of the world. Oh, she admires their swearing, their swagger, but their willingness to settle for such mundanity is horribly disappointing.

'I know it's not as exciting as university,' her father tries, 'a bit boring and ordinary, but there'd always be decent work.'

'Normal work,' her mother adds.

'But I don't want to be boring and ordinary!' she rails. 'I don't want to be normal!'

'Do you think anyone grows up dreaming of a . . . a job in a shop?' Her mother has fallen at the first hurdle. 'But if you don't apply yourself, that's where you'll end up. Selling shoes or serving – I don't know –' she snatches for something, comes back inexplicably with – 'macaroons.'

'Perhaps I'll marry a prince,' she counters. 'Or Buzz bloody Aldrin. If he ever comes back.'

Her mother scoffs. 'As if a prince would have you.'

The conversation ends on the Collinses' doorstep, where they are due for lunch, a heavy affair involving too much potato and a suet pudding swimming in treacle that her mother declines and she only eats in sly defiance, her spoon scraping china a clink of triumph. Then comes the coffee pot, the box of Black Magic in place of petits fours, for which Mrs Collins apologizes – so 'very déclassé' – which is another tick, as her mother had hitherto seen them as something of a luxury – and with it Mr Collins' infinite wisdom.

'Have you given more thought to boarding school?' he asks. 'Now . . . you know.'

Oh, God. Not that again.

'There's one I'm thinking of in particular,' he continues. 'The Quaker place. Have I mentioned it before? Up in Saffron Walden. Not far, so she could come home at weekends, if necessary.'

If necessary. She almost snorts.

'You have mentioned it, yes,' agrees her father. 'But I'm not sure. Boarding school is terribly . . . well . . .'

'Middle class?' offers Mr Collins.

'Yes, rather.' His tone is apologetic, as it always is with Mr Collins.

'And what's wrong with that? Solid values, manageable ambition.'

Manageable? She doesn't want her ambition to be managed. Or even queried. 'I'd rather die,' she blurts. 'Literally.'

'Constance!' Her mother is not even bothering to be above admonishments. 'Don't say that.'

'Why? Because of the Africans?'

'Because it's a sin. And against the law.' She turns to Mr Collins. 'The school seems ideal. Do you think they might have a place?'

'You mean, do you think they'd take me?'

They both ignore her.

'There might be scholarships, in any case,' he assures. 'In case you were worrying about money.'

'We weren't,' says her father, suddenly mustering. 'It's not the money that's the problem, it's the principle of the thing.'

'But principles aren't people,' says Mr Collins, as if it's obvious. 'And Constance is worth more than your left-wing ideals, isn't she?' He reaches into the second layer to take another orange cream – banned activity in their own home, or it would be if she were ever allowed near sweets – pops the chocolate into his mouth, sees her watching and, again, winks.

'That's not—'

But her father can't finish, or doesn't want to, is defeated by queered reason.

Of course, they're all missing the point: she won't be going, whatever they decide. And she's just worked out how, has seen it pin-sharp and gleaming, how she can win her freedom and one over on them all.

'The choir trip,' she says then.

Mr Collins, still swallowing chocolate, frowns, nods.

'Is it still on? I mean, is there a place?'

Martha, sullen until now, suddenly summons an opinion. 'But you said you didn't want to come. You said it was "stupid".'

'I never said anything of the sort,' she lies. 'How very rude.'

Her mother flusters. 'But it's far too late. Honestly, Constance, this is the problem. You—'

'I'm sure we can squeeze her in,' Mr Collins interjects. 'Money won't be an issue, I assume?' He glances at her father then with an air of barely disguised contempt.

Whether her father catches it or not is moot. 'It's not,' he replies. 'As I've already said.'

'And there are no objections on principle?'

'Please, Daddy?'

Her mother holds her hands up.

'Very well,' he concedes. 'I'll send Constance back with the money later. If you think it's a good idea.'

'It'll be the making of her,' says Mr Collins. 'The very making of her.'

She smiles at him then, aware that it verges on flirting. But so be it. Men are so predictably thick, always thinking with their willies. Even the old ones. Sad, really, but playable, and to her gain. Because the choir trip is to the continent and Germany is surely only a short train ride from Paris. And there she can finally become who she was born to be all along. Forget Steve, forget Terry, forget all the men; it's sweet Sally Jay she needs: crashing in a flat near the Pantheon, dancing on a bar on the Boulevard Raspail, singing in a swing club off the Rue de Buci.

'Thank you, Daddy,' she says. 'Thank you, Mr Collins.' And, flirt that she is, fool that she is, she kisses them both.

Jean

Essex, August 1981

Jean is both bleak and seething.

Because there it ends. The next page is blank. And the next. And all the others after that. As if the notebook had been abandoned the night Constance abandoned them. Where is it? she seems to scream. Where is the next page? This cannot, *must* not, end there. There are things Jean needs to know: where Constance went and who with. And why.

But, as much as she turns the pages, searches for words, the story ends unfinished, that night in July, Neil Armstrong and Buzz Aldrin not yet on the moon and Constance at the Collinses' kitchen table. Unless . . . Unless there's another, unless this is one in a series. Yes! She must have left this one here and then started the next in . . . well, wherever she went. That's what she came back for, that Easter. Yes, it must be.

Then she remembers: the shed. That's where Bernard has kept her things all these years, and the new ones too – disobeyed her, despite her pleading. Said one day she'd see. Well, she sees, though it pains her to admit it.

She sees.

*

'Where on earth are you going?' Bernard looks up from the ornamental border, where he's doing something to the sunflowers – hideous things, common, but the Child likes them.

'The papers,' she says by way of an answer. 'There's something I need.'

'Let me.' He stands.

But she's already passed him, is at the end of the garden, her hand on the slatted door.

The shed is men's territory; is jars of hardware, hooks for tools, the smell of soil and creosote and slow industry. She'd expected it to be danker, perhaps, but the air is dry, dust motes dancing down a shaft of evening sunlight that pools on the concrete floor and around the legs of a chair she'd marked for the tip and which Bernard had 'rescued', said it just needed some glue. Odd, for a man so fond of the future, that he held so tightly to the past, gripped it in his fingers and would not let go.

But now she is glad, because there on the shelf is the past she'd discarded. In a cat-food box, of all the inappropriate things. No matter. She stands on the edge of the chair, reaches up and, balancing it on her head, manages to manhandle it down with a thump that sends another cotillion into the air and her into the seat of the chair, where she sits for a second, sweating, dishevelled.

Then she begins.

Methodical at first, lifting out postcards and envelopes, some sealed – bills – some torn; papers in all states of disarray, no order to them, unless it's by size, but even then – what was Bernard thinking? Then, without compunction, snatching and despatching with equal effort and little measure until the box, she sees, is empty.

No.

'No!'

She stifles a sob, a great hawking thing that smacks through her with the force of a slap or a sneeze. But it's no use, she's wracked by anger, by lack, and salt stings her skin as she lets it take her.

'Jean? Jean, darling.'

She feels his hand on her shoulder and tries to shake it off, but he won't let her, not this time.

'Jean, what are you looking for?'

She shakes her head, can't say it, but he's crouching now, pleading silently. 'Constance,' she eventually says. 'The notebook. It . . . It ended and—'

'It's all right,' he placates. 'It is.'

She shakes her head again, and this time he lets go of her, but when she glimpses him through the wash, he's standing, reaching for something else – another box.

'There are more,' he says. 'Another twenty or so. Two a year, I think. Right up to this July.'

What? 'Pardon?'

He nods, places the box at her feet, where she sees, on the top, a stack of Silvines, red as cherries, to be plucked from the top of the cake. Thank heaven.

'They're not in date order,' he says, his voice awash with apology. 'But—'

'I can do it.' And she snatches them, stacks them on her

lap and begins to go through, moving them, shuffling them, slipping new ones in until she is sure she has it right.

'I'm sorry,' he says then. 'I didn't know what else . . . She was my child as well.' At that, he glances up and she sees it then – the urn, its brown plastic stubbornly dull, even in sunlight.

His child.

Their child.

Her child.

'Please leave,' she says.

'But—'

'I need to . . .' To be with her? To feel her? Yes. But she can't admit that to him. Not yet. 'I need to read, Bernard. Please leave me be.'

And he does, no touching of shoulders this time, no assurance everything will be all right.

Because he can't promise that. Not anymore.

Not now.

She opens the cardboard cover, looks at the first line.

And everything else – her job, her standing, her very self – becomes irrelevant.

This is it. This is the truth of it.

And so it begins. And ends.

Connie

Leeds, July 1981

Connie closes the notebook with a clap – satisfying, dramatic – then slides it back on the stack in the cardboard Kitekat box, and that – with some shoving – back on top of the wardrobe. Because she knows how it plays out, doesn't need to go digging around for the next instalment, for the pages she'd poured her awful story into just seven days later. Evidence, she'd told herself at the time. But she's never needed it, doesn't need it now, because that part of her life – immense though it was – was just one bleak evening, and it ended not there but nine months later, and that's all that matters to her.

All that should matter to them, as well.

Because she knows what she's going to do now, whatever Elvis reckoned. Oh, he's telephoned her at work again, said it was an emergency – a family matter – begged her to change her mind. Then, when she said no, he'd called her a bitch and a prick tease and worse besides, and within earshot of Mrs Beasley, who said she was on final warning as it was and one more 'incident' and she'd be back down the dole.

Well, just let Mrs B try to send her there.

She'll have to find her first, because tomorrow's the wedding and then she's off shift, and after that . . . puff! She'll be gone.

Connie

Essex, July 1969

She's lying on the floor, one ear pressed to the vent.
Her parents are discussing the moon and the rightness
of flying there. Flying? Is that what it's called? She's not sure,
but for once she's on her mother's side: what's the point?
Though, their reasoning is light years apart: her mother's
that there's nothing up there, that it's playing God, messing
with nature; hers that the world is so expansive, so fat with
promise, why leave it when you could try Rome or Rio or
even bloody Ruislip.

Her father, for once, refuses to concede, not when the
future is at stake. 'Why not?' he says this time, a reworking
of 'because it's there', which got shouted down because
Calcutta is 'there' but he's not rushing to discover anything
about that.

'I suppose you'd swap places, would you? With Neil
Armstrong?'

'I might,' he says.

Her mother bristles. 'You'd get car sick.'

'I don't think it works like that.'

'I suppose you know all about it.'

369

'That's not what I'm saying.'

Connie scoffs. The moon! When they barely leave Essex. But at least they're preoccupied, and with that golden nugget, she pulls herself upright and slips down the stairs.

'I'm going out,' she shouts. No 'can I?', although she's still, technically, forbidden to leave the premises unless accompanied. But now the choir trip is agreed, she reasons her parameters may have expanded. And in any case, she'll say she's going to the Collinses' to drop off the money. Which she is. Eventually.

'You'll miss the landing,' her father says, voice tinged with disappointment.

But her mother's blue mood saves her. 'It won't be for hours, Bernard,' she retorts. 'If at all. They'll probably crash. Or miss it.'

She picks up her bicycle clips, peers round the door. 'I won't be long, anyway,' she placates. 'Only an hour or so.'

Her father smiles. 'Say hello to Martha for us. And Barbara and Maurice, obviously.'

Her mother doesn't. 'You only saw them this afternoon. I hardly think—'

'I will,' she interjects, before her mother feels compelled to explain again why her father is ridiculous, before her father has to defend his very empathy. And for a brief, fleeting moment, she feels something akin to guilt, not for what she's done, but for what she will do soon: for leaving, for abandoning him to her.

But it's not enough to stop her.

*

She can almost taste it – freedom – sweet as barley sugar, strong as vodka, a rush of something that sends her legs pedalling ten to the dozen as she cycles through buttery sunshine towards Potter Street. She is almost there, in every sense.

And she won't be long, she tells herself again. Just long enough to clear the path, to pave the way for her clean break, her escape.

She owes Terry that much.

But Terry is devastated, veering from a rage so red and terrible she thinks he might strike her to a dripping sort of self-pity. 'Is it someone else?' he begs.

She shakes her head. And it's not even a lie, not anymore. 'It's no one. Just that I'm going away and I think . . . it's best.'

'Away where?'

'To school. To board.'

'So? You can come home in the holidays. I'll come up on weekends—'

'No!' It's more forceful than she wanted, but the thought of it, even as mere suggestion, even though it could never come to pass, is anathema. The thought of him showing up, showing her up.

'Come here,' he says then. Not a question.

But she doesn't want to. Can't be bothered anymore. 'I can't,' she says.

'Can't or won't?'

'Does it matter?'

'You silly little bitch,' he spits then. 'You want to know what I got you for your birthday? Here.'

He yanks open a drawer, grabs something and flings it at her. It hits her on the arm then falls among socks on the floor.

It's a jeweller's box, burgundy with gold lettering.

'Pick it up,' he tells her.

She shakes her head again.

'Do it!'

Shaking now, with anger more than anything, she bends and collects it.

'Now open it.'

She doesn't need to to know what horror it contains, but she does as she's told, sees with a sliding horror the band of gold topped with a snippet of crystal.

Jesus Christ. As if she would ever agree. To anyone, let alone him.

'Why did you buy it?' she demands.

'Because I love you, don't I? It's what . . . it's what people do.'

'Well, I'm not . . . people,' she explains, despairing. 'I'm me.'

'Well, you should have said, then.' He grabs it back from her, shoves it in a pocket. 'Before I wasted a month's wages.'

She snorts. Something that slight can't have cost more than ten bob and she says so.

'All right.' He sneers back. 'A week, then.'

The truth is a slap. 'Nice to know I'm worth so much.'

'What do you care, anyway? You don't even want to get married.'

He's right, but that's not the point and, livid, she strips

two ten-shilling notes from the packet her father gave her and throws them at him. 'Here.' They flutter to the floor, and she braces, waits.

He lifts a hand and she flinches, thinks he's going to strike her, but then he pulls out his cigarettes, lights one. 'See you, then,' he says, bravado back with a clang and a cloud of Embassy.

She breathes, in irritation and relief. 'Ta-ra.' And she reaches to collect one of the notes but he puts his foot on it, missing her fingers by barely an inch. 'Fine.' She makes herself smile, fakes her indifference. 'That's just fine.' And then she turns tail and walks out of Terry's dim bedroom and his dim life and nearly, nearly, this dim town for ever.

And it will be fine.

Mrs Collins will forgive her the missing money, will say she can make it up herself later, or call it a birthday gift – generous as she is. Or maybe Martha will lend it to her – she's watched her enough times, counting her savings like Fagin.

But when she props the pink bicycle against the pale brick wall, knocks on the door, it's Maurice Collins who answers.

'Where's Martha?' she asks.

'She's gone for drinks at the Herrings'. Their television is better apparently.'

She is momentarily thrown. 'I—'

'Nice enough boy,' he continues. 'Churchgoer. Though I doubt it will last. Martha's far too advanced for his like.'

'Is Mrs Collins in?' she tries.

'Flower committee. In the middle of the moon landing, I ask you. But she'll be back by nine and I don't suppose it will be over before then in any case.'

'Oh, it's just that—'

'Come in!' He holds the door open. 'You can watch it with me.'

'I . . .' She hesitates.

'I don't suppose your mother's bothering. She doesn't hold with it, I believe.'

And at that she sees it: this way will be easier. He's a pushover, isn't he. Got a soft spot for her, obviously. And so she barges past. 'Thanks, Mr Collins.' She smiles widely. 'That would be splendid.'

'Help yourself to lemonade,' he calls after her.

She does as she's bidden, but when she returns from the kitchen, he's not in the living room.

'Hello?' she calls.

'In here.'

She follows the prompt to the study, a room she and Martha only enter on dares, man's territory as it is – all golf trophies and Wisden and the thick stink of cigar.

'I thought we were going to watch the moon,' she says.

'Oh, it won't be on yet,' he says, seating himself at his desk, nodding to her to take the easy chair next to him. 'I thought we could talk about the trip.'

'The trip.' She sits, and her eyes flick to the cash box that sits on pristine mahogany.

As if sensing her desperation, he rests his hand on it. 'I'm glad you're coming. It's been so . . . difficult for you recently.

It's difficult anyway, isn't it? Being an adolescent. Of course I remember. But being a girl – a woman, I should say – is harder, I think.'

She smiles, unbidden, easily flattered, but she knows that's all this is. Flattery.

'Though at least you're pretty, that must make it easier.'

Touché.

'Teenage boys are like flies, though,' he continues. 'You must get tired of them.'

She remembers the ten bob under Terry's size nine, leans forward. 'Oh, I'm not interested in them, Mr Collins.'

'Maurice,' he insists. 'So, tell me, what are you interested in?'

'Singing. But not the choir kind,' she replies, oddly honest. 'Pop, that sort of thing. You know.'

He shrugs. 'Well, you've certainly got the talent.' He pats her leg then, his hand damp so that she imagines it leaving a patch on the pale denim. 'And the looks.'

She should get this over with. 'The money,' she blurts. 'It's a pound short. I lost two notes. I looked everywhere.' She makes cow eyes, musters from somewhere the beginnings of tears.

'Oh dear,' he says.

'I can . . . I can pay you back after,' she tries. 'I'll have birthday money in . . . in two months.'

'Oh, Connie,' he says, his hand back on her leg. 'Don't upset yourself.'

'I'm sorry,' she says, dabbing her eyes. 'It's just that I want to go so very much.'

'I know, I know,' he placates, patting her.

'You must think I'm terrible.'

'Not at all.' A squeeze. She is winning. 'I tell you what, why don't you sing for it? Sing for your supper,' he adds, clearly pleased with his wit, though it hardly amounts to it, given there's no food in the offing.

'Pardon?' she asks, priming him, checking herself that she hasn't misheard.

'Sing something for me. The Puccini, perhaps. Or whatever you like,' he adds hurriedly. 'It doesn't matter what.'

'Anything?' she asks. 'And you'll let me off?'

He nods. 'Scot free.'

Anything. She closes her eyes, riffles through stacks of records, pulls out something by Dusty. Then flicks through her own personas, sloughs off Constance Earnshaw like an ill-fitting skin and pulls on Connie Holiday: bright and shining and brimming with ambition.

And then she sings.

For one blissful minute she sings, her notes low, deep in her throat, then soaring up, up and into the vast blanket of sky.

Then she feels it: his breath on her neck; smells it, stale with cigar smoke against her own peppermint scent. Feels his tongue then, below her ear, pressing wetly at first, then moving, insistent, as if he's trying to bite her.

And yet she does nothing.

She does nothing as he pushes it into her mouth.

Does nothing as he pulls her onto the floor.

Does nothing as he pulls down her knickers and pushes his thing into her. Again and again and again.

And as she is pinned, rigid, to the soft coral carpet, she thinks of her mother's obsession with terrible men. How absurd it is, how dangerously mistaken.

For the real villains don't come in cackling and twirling their moustaches, nor black-and-white-striped and five-o-clock-shadowed and hunched with their swag bags. The real ones smile wide, sing, and call you 'princess'.

And then fuck you in their study while their wife's arranging daisies and their daughter is watching history being made with the town councillor's son.

When he finishes, slips limply out of her, she doesn't cry, doesn't protest, doesn't *do* anything.

'Our little secret,' he says, and winks.

She flirted, she deserved it, at least that's what her mother will say. So, no, she won't tell. But nor will she wink back, give him what he wants.

Because, for the sake of a few minutes – for twenty wretched bob – he's taken all she wanted, hasn't he? For how can she go to Germany now? How can she even go to boarding school if she has to come back here at weekends, at holidays?

She should never have ended it with Terry. At least he had money; at least he could lend her enough for the bus fare to London, for a month in a boarding house perhaps. Maybe he'll take her back. Maybe, if she begs him, lets him do anything he wants, punish her even, he'll—

And then it comes to her. A blistering vision, a God-offered miracle. Or Maurice-offered, really.

'I need a tissue,' she says, sitting up and crossing her legs, his thick semen a slow slug trail down her inner thigh. 'Or a flannel, perhaps.'

'Of course.' He stands, almost embarrassed at the flaccid glistening thing, pulls up his pants and his trousers. 'Let me.' And he heads for the stairs, then, she thinks, to the bathroom.

As soon as he's gone, she stands, grabs the cash box, thanks the God that abandoned her that the key is left in. She almost gasps when she kicks back the lid – there's so much money. Too much, in fact, for her jeans pocket now; it would be too horribly obvious in tight Levi's. So she packs it into her bra and knickers, where it crackles, then dampens like a sanitary towel.

'Thanks,' she says, when he returns. 'But I'm all right now.'

'Oh.' He dangles the flannel – orange – like a dirty rag. 'Well. Good.'

'I have to go,' she tells him. 'Daddy will wonder where I am.'

He nods.

'Our secret,' she says then.

'Our secret,' he repeats.

And this time she winks.

She walks in the door with her smile fixed as if she is an advertisement for Pepsodent.

'I think I'll go to bed,' she says. 'I'm too tired to wait up.'

Her father nods. 'Your mother's gone to read already.'

She manages a laugh, quick and stilted. 'Of course.'

'Constance,' he calls as she heads for the door.

She turns back. 'What?'

'I'm glad you're happy.'

She leaves the room before he can see the lie of it.

Then, at midnight, her bag packed, her father adrift in his green chair, sailing the static hum of the wireless, the moon landing abandoned, at least for now, she leaves the house.

Leaves Constance Earnshaw on the floor of Maurice Collins' study.

And leaves Pram Town, another girl entirely.

Jean

The epiphany is brief but efficient: purging her stomach into the pristine porcelain of the downstairs lavatory, and sweeping away any vestige of respect for men and belief in God – who, when she thinks about it, hasn't ever bothered himself with her torments – and Maurice Collins – who has.

And now she knows why.

All the time she had been beholden to him, shame making her his slave, or so she saw it – wanted to see it. When he— HE was the guilty one.

Guilt had driven him to offer her the job, to promote her. She isn't the pinnacle.

She isn't anything, anyone, to him, but the mother of a girl he took advantage of. And the grandmother of— She feels another wave threaten to take her, has to swallow it down. Does he realize Sadie is his? Does he think, despite everything, he can inveigle his way in, play some benign part in her upbringing . . . ? She snaps to, nerves singing.

Well, she will see about that.

Practicality abounds now. Without alerting Bernard – who is biding his time behind the paper again, awaiting her verdict no doubt, another outburst; well, she will deal with that later – she finds her driving shoes, fetches the car keys and lets herself out the front door with nothing more than a dull clunk.

No scream or wail or railing against anything. Instead, her rage is contained, a hard ball of pain and disappointment and determination to end this all now. All thirty years of it.

Truth, it transpires, is not a panacea, not a pill of relief, but a cold wash of horror.

And with that, she pulls out of the drive and onto Fore Street with a flash of gravel and the first tyre screech she has ever achieved, much to the apparent shock of Carol Morton, who stalls in alarm on the pavement, clutching at her carrier bag. Once, of course, even yesterday, even an hour ago, she might have waved an apology, wound the window down perhaps. But that was then and everything has changed.

She remembers herself, then, in her best coat, a small bag in her pocket in case she vomited, outside *his* house in Perivale. Not Paris at all. Not even close.

She'd got the address from the receptionist at the hotel, got a hand on her arm as well, a tip of the head in sympathy. She wasn't the first, it turned out. And she shouldn't tell her, but these men needed a lesson, didn't they? And Jean – Margaret then – had nodded and taken the slip of paper, stuffed it into the pocket of her too-thin coat and taken it home, where it had pestered her for several days until at last she'd taken it out and followed it where it led. To this broad, bland semi on a street like any other. No chic corner bars, no green steel tables and chairs, no *café crème*. Just a path that needed weeding and a peeling front door. And a neighbour in a yarmulke, who'd nodded 'morning' to her and smiled – smiled!

Oh, please don't let *him* be a Jew, she'd prayed. She didn't need that to contend with as well. But he can't be, she'd decided; she'd have noticed. They do that . . . thing to themselves. Slice off the end of their . . . but she couldn't say it to herself, even silently. Though she could see it again now, stiff with intent, springing unbidden from the forest of hair as if it were an entirely separate being with a mind and a purpose of its own.

Well, it had achieved its purpose all right; she had the missing monthly to prove it.

She remembers her wrist, limp as she lifted a finger to the bell, and the shock of the buzzer that sent her fragile heart hammering, her stomach – already unsettled – into a furious soup.

But that was nothing to the torment when that woman answered the door.

Perhaps it's the keep, she'd told herself, and hope had ballooned in her, a tangible, touchable thing. But then came the pinprick and, swift on its heels, the sluice of truth. For this woman was dressed in slacks and a mended sweater, on her finger a ring, on her hip a child, with a toy elephant and *his* dark eyes.

'Can I help you?' she'd asked, her accent Kentish, if anything, or Essex, dredged from the Thames Estuary, not sprung from the Seine.

'I . . . I think perhaps—'

Was it her hesitation that gave her away? Or her sickly demeanour? Or perhaps no more than the fact than she was female, young, and wearing lipstick and silk stockings instead of a darned cardigan.

She'd snorted. 'You're not the first.' The same words as the girl at the Majesty. But this time with the added, 'But the first to make it this far. Pregnant, are you?'

'I–I – no. I'm . . . lost,' she managed to stammer then. 'That's all. I'm looking for a—' She'd snatched for a name. 'A Mr Jennings.'

The woman had snorted again. 'Jennings, is it? Is that what he's using?'

She'd shaken her head, but it was useless, she could see that now. Could see it all.

Can see it all.

Can see Maurice is a false promise of a man. A hollow bauble.

Can see that her atavistic panic at potential rapists, at takers of women has been misplaced, focused as it has been on Terry, on any of Constance's beaus, on the Fox even, painted in her head as some horrible monster, a stalking, hunchbacked thing straight from the pages of the Brothers Grimm. When all along the real villain was, like the wolf in Grandma's clothing, happily installed in the house along the road, fattening up his prey on suet pudding.

And now he's somewhere in the depths of Epping Forest, doing what? Leading another Little Red Riding Hood astray? Oh God. The audacity of him. The brazenness. The cruelty—

She snaps to. Focuses. Epping Forest, she repeats to herself. How far can that be? She only half remembers the route – from the days out, the picnics they'd taken when Constance was small. Halcyon days, they should have been, but even those had been marred by thistles, bees and, for Constance, a horrible boredom. What she would give for a thistle now, for that awful torpor.

Of course, if she'd dropped the Child off herself . . . She should have dropped the Child off herself. Should never have let Maurice— But she swipes at the thought and sends it back whence it came.

There's no gain in mulling on the past. All she can do now is right the future, and that future is praying and singing and sweating in a tent somewhere past Theydon Bois.

It takes her only three detours, two stops to check the map and less than an hour to reach the edge of the woods, and then it's not hard to find – everyone knows where the 'God-botherers' are pitched, the 'happy clappers'. The old Jean would have taken umbrage, would have stiffened, bristled, and said something pinched and snippy. But that Jean, like Margaret before her, has been fast discarded. *Vacation Bible Camp 1981!* a plastic banner proclaims. *God is with all of us.*

'Not with me,' she says.

And, abandoning the car on a patch of what looks like, but can't possibly be, sand, she stalks off to rescue the unwitting heroine and slay the big, bad wolf.

Sadie

Essex, August 1981

She thinks up the trick at singing time, when Mr Bent is fiddling with the fat black microphone, which is still suffering a bad crackle and sometimes a hum. He's saying 'Testing, testing' into it, like he's a rock star, or a roadie, and at first she remembers Elvis and feels the faint shape of loss, a sort of odd hollow. But she sends it packing pronto. Elvis in't missing. He's just too busy for her. Too rude and stupid. Too in Skegness. Then something else slips into her vision – the dictaphone, pushed to the bottom in the pink pitch of her bag. And it's still got batteries in it from before – they never swapped them back. And, quick as an imp, whispering she needs the toilet, she slips out of the main top and across to the row of serried sleeping tents, two up and four along, to hers and Olive's.

She tries it herself first off, but she can't get her voice low enough, godly enough, so in the end she finds Mr Nevin, stout and silver-haired, standing fatly in the galley, spreading marge on sliced white.

'What do I say?' he asks.

She's worked it all out, word perfect, the sort of thing a

god might muster. 'Say, "You are the chosen one, Olive
Watkins. I have big plans for you. Await my direction, tonight at six."'

'What are you up to?'

'Nowt. Well, something. But it's a game. A sort of –' she
scrabbles for something – 'treasure hunt.'

'I don't want to be getting into any bother. You or me.'

'You won't!' she insists. 'Olive's in on it. Honest.' She feels
bad at that last word, feels a smidgen of guilt, but not enough
to stop her.

He tries it for size: 'You are the chosen one, Olive Watkins.'

'Bit deeper. Like . . . Like the Wizard of Oz.'

'P'raps you should get Mr Kittering onto it. Or Mr Collins,'
he says then. 'They've the knack for the stage. I'm more a
behind-the-scenes man.'

'They're busy,' she says quick, and it's not a lie. 'And you're
fine – good, I mean! Just, a little bit deeper.'

He sighs, tries again, and this one will do nicely, thank
you very much, and then she's off to set her trap, hidden in
a sleeping bag and primed for action: five minutes of blank
tape before it – enough time to fetch Olive for something
important and then remember she's to pop off. Just for a
minute. Then she can come back and catch her panicking.

Olive don't want to go with her at first, says she's going
to do sword drill in Jennifer Lenton's tent, because Jennifer
has a packet of gypsy creams and whoever wins each round
gets one.

'That's not very godly,' says Sadie. 'Isn't it about the joy
of winning?' Which is rich, because the joy of winning is the

worst prize of all, everyone knows that. Including Horrible Olive.

'God doesn't mind biscuits,' she says, pious as you like. 'As long as there's sharing.'

She crosses her fingers to void the fib that comes next. 'But I've got Wagon Wheels,' she says. 'If you want, you can have one.'

Olive is torn, she can see it. Between the joy of winning an average biscuit and the gift of sandwiched mallow and chocolate. But, in the end, luxury trumps.

'All right then.'

Jennifer Lenton is visibly peeved.

'Maybe I'll save you a section,' says Olive. 'And we can still do sword drill after dinner.'

And then, in an unprecedented act of unwarranted solidarity, she links arms with Sadie and marches her mallow-wards.

'Where are they, then?' demands Olive, arms dropped, solidarity slipped now they're back in the tent.

'I was sure they were here,' says Sadie. 'Or maybe . . . maybe I left them in the car. I may have. Shall I ask Mr Collins?'

Olive folds her arms. 'They'll be melted,' she snipes.

'No, they won't,' Sadie insists. 'Anyway, they're better like that. Like a pudding. We can use spoons. I'll only be a moment,' she tacks on, desperate. And in the end, Olive nods, and Sadie heaves with relief and not a little fear, as, under the premise of fetching a tissue, she clicks the dictaphone on.

She goes no further than the back of the tent, squats, watching for intruders, and waiting for the word of God.

And then it comes: muffled and rumbling and strangely mechanical, so that she worries Olive will spot it. But then there's a shuffle, and a sound a bit like crying, and she bursts back in to find Olive in a state of something close to what she once saw on *Corrie* described as a conniption fit.

'What's wrong?' she says.

'God!' blurts Olive. 'God spoke to me!'

She tips from satisfaction into a sick feeling. As if she's eaten both imaginary Wagon Wheels and half the gypsy creams besides. 'I thought . . . I thought he were always talking to you.'

Olive reddens. 'Not . . . Not this loud.'

'So what'd he say?'

'I— Nothing.'

'He must've said something.'

'I'm not telling you!'

'Keep your hair on,' she tells her, borrowing words and attitude from Deborah. Then pretends to confession. 'I couldn't find the Wagon Wheels. Must've never brought them. Anyway, it's dinner in a minute.'

But Olive's not coming. And no one, not even Jennifer Lenton and her immaculate record for reciting the books of the Bible and a packet of Peek Freans can persuade her.

'I need to stay here,' she says.

'What for?' presses Sadie.

'None of your business.'

'If they think you're ill, you'll get sent home,' says Jennifer then. 'Marcia Hughes was sick in the middle of the seven plagues and Mr Bent took her back to Stansted.

'I'm not ill. I'm just . . . fasting. It's religious.'

'Suit yourself,' says Sadie. 'But it's burgers. Not even Jesus would fast for that.'

'Blasphemer!' shrieks Olive.

And nausea and remorse dissolve in an instant, stiffen like Angel Delight whipped in milk into a kind of rightness. So that Sadie don't give a monkey's that Olive's missing dinner. That she's waiting in vain for a dictaphone God to issue instruction. That she'll be the laughing stock come six, when God's not bothered.

She don't even save her an apple at Jennifer's suggestion. 'She's fasting,' Sadie snaps back. 'I can't believe you even asked.' So that then they both brim with indignation and finish their dinner in an unspoken vow of silence.

But when she enters the tent the diffidence slips. Because Olive is sobbing, her shoulders jumping up and down like a jack-in-a-box, so fast Sadie thinks she might snap something.

'What's happened now?' she repeats. 'Did God say summat else?'

Olive looks up at her, scarlet and shining. 'No!' she spits. 'He didn't say anything.'

'Surprise, surprise.'

'What's that supposed to mean?'

'He never talked to you in the first place.'

'He did too.'

'"You are the chosen one, Olive Watkins,"' she chants. '"Await my direction."'

Olive has stopped everything now – shaking, crying, breathing, it seems – and the air in the tent practically crackles. Then—

'You absolute cow!' she snaps. Then she stands and slaps Sadie smack bang across the cheek.

The pain is tremendous. Worse than when she fell off the garden wall, aged six, and banged her head so hard she was sick in the compost. Worse than when she came a cropper on her skates, aged seven, and scraped her knee so bad a flap dangled down and she asked her mam if she were going to die. Worse than when—

'No wonder your mum died. No wonder your dad doesn't want you. No one does. My mum told me. You're going to boarding school. Or into care. And you know what happens in care.' She leaves that dangling, fat as a mallow itself.

Sadie, hand still on her cheek, tears threatening to make an entrance, shakes her head.

Olive smirks. 'They beat you up and make you shave your head and rob shops.'

'They don't,' Sadie manages.

'They do too.'

'I—'

'You'll end up in prison,' Olive adds. 'Same old story.'

'You're . . . You're . . .' But she can't say it. Because it's true, in't it. No one wants her. Not really. Not Elvis, not the Grandma, not anyone. Except . . .

*

She's early, but she decides he won't mind. Not given the winks, the points he's afforded her.

There's nothing to knock, so she says his name, lifts up the flap, and there he is, on a folding stool, the Bible – burgundy, gold-embossed; the sign of a righteous man – on his lap.

'Sadie,' he says, and smiles so his teeth – big and yellow – show. 'Come in.'

She does, sits on the groundsheet, brown plastic, sniffs up the fust of it, and her own snot and all.

'Is . . . everything all right?'

She shrugs, head down.

'Girls, is it?'

She shrugs again.

'It must be hard. Without your mum to chat to.'

This time she nods, gratitude so fat at his understanding she's worried she'll be off into sobbing again.

'I knew her well,' he says then. 'Did you know that?'

She shakes her head, manages now to look up, sees the hair of his chest tuft over his shirt.

'She was a lovely girl,' he says. 'Lovely. Voice of an angel. But then you know that.'

Something in her lifts, hearing things about her, being allowed to say them. 'She still sang,' she says then. 'At clubs and the like.'

'Did she?'

She nods. '"The North's Premier Dusty Impersonator",' she repeats from a poster. 'She come second in the Manchester Talent Show. She were going to go on *Opportunity Knocks*, but she couldn't get time off Morrisons.'

'That's . . . a shame.'

'It were. Better than Lena Zavaroni, Elvis reckoned.'

There's a pause then, and she's worried it'll be over too soon, and back to God talk or Olive and what's wrong with her, so she just blurts it out, lets it take shape in the fetid tent air. 'He's not my dad,' she says. 'Elvis, I mean. I don't . . . I don't have a dad.'

'I know,' he says. 'And that's a shame too.'

And then she can't stop it, the sobs are too strong, and she's shaking there on the floor of the tent.

'Here,' he says then, and he gestures to her, beckons her over.

And, without even questioning, she settles on his lap, leans into the soap of his skin and soft flannel of his shirt and lets him wrap his man arms around her.

And that's where she's sat when the Grandma marches in.

'Sadie Holiday!'

She lifts her head, still clinging, open-mouthed as a fledgling or a cat burglar caught in the act. But the Grandma's eyes aren't on her at all.

'What are you doing to her?'

'Nothing,' replies Mr Collins. 'Jean, I—'

'Don't "Jean" me. Pin, I ask you. Pin! Well, that's enough. Enough!' She turns her gaze back to Sadie. 'Get up. You're coming with me.'

And Sadie, scared, but biddable as a dog, stands and lets the raging lady snatch her hand and drag her out of the tent.

'What about my things?' she asks.

'We can fetch them later. Tomorrow.'

'Is it about Olive?' She can hardly breathe with fear.

'Olive? No. It's – it's an emergency.'

'Is it Grandpa?'

'No. He's perfectly fine.'

'Then what?'

'I just . . . I just don't think he's all he's cracked up to be.'

'Who? Grandpa?'

'Don't be ridiculous.'

She thinks quick. 'Mr Collins?'

The Grandma staggers to a halt, Sadie wrenched still beside her. 'Him,' she agrees. 'Yes, him. And God besides.'

Connie

Leeds, July 1981

Here she sits, inspects herself in the mirror: hair teased into a beehive, face pale and powdered, lips sixties pink.

'Do I look all right?' she says. 'Will I do?'

Truth is, she tried to cancel, but Billy bloody Rigsby said who else could he get the night before the royal wedding? As it was they'd be lucky to get forty through the door and less than twenty staying on for the show. She'd argued it was a holiday tomorrow, that everyone'd want to be out drinking and singing along. So he'd said, 'Well, you'd better show up then, an't you.' And there wasn't much comeback for that.

Besides, it'll be nice to have one last hurrah. And she won't push it. Won't try to hit the high notes, or the low ones, won't stay on for an encore. Won't sit and drink with Billy Rigsby and Thick Jimmy King and the skinny barmaid he's shagging after closing. Not that Thick Jimmy's probably talking to her anyway.

'You look like a star,' comes the answer at last – the answer she's looking for.

She looks up, meets Sadie's eyes in the sticky mirror, blows her a kiss.

'You'll be all right, won't you?' she checks. 'Bed by ten?'

'Aye,' says Sadie.

'And if you're hungry, there's cocktail sausages in the fridge, but only a couple, mind. The rest are for tomorrow or Mrs Higgins'll have my guts for garters.'

'What are garters?'

'Keep your stockings up.'

'Mrs Higgins don't wear stockings. She wears tights; thick ones and all. I've seen them on the line on Tuesdays.'

'Well, heaven knows what she'll do with them, then.' And at that she stands, kisses the top of her daughter's head, fusty as that Dave's cage, and clatters downstairs on silver stack heels and into the kitchen. 'See you in the morning,' she calls up behind her, knowing Sadie's fiddling with the lipstick.

She's grabbing her bag when she sees the letter, leant against the toaster like a loaded gun or something primed that might ignite – will ignite – not with the flick of a Zippo, but by being slipped in the slot of the postbox at the end of Engleby Street.

But she hasn't got a stamp, will have to do it in the morning, if she can beg one from Donna. Or perhaps the Mehtas'll be open – the Mehtas are always open, who's she kidding?

Yes, she'll do it then. In the morning.

In the morning.

But right now she's a job to do – her last.

And she hears it already: the hum of the backing tape,

the crackle of static as the audience shifts in their seats, whispers they can't wait for what's coming, the clop, clop of her boots as she walks out into blackness and then the snap! as the follow spot clicks on and she's bathed from head to glittering toe in a shaft of dazzling light.

'And here she is,' comes Billy Rigby himself. 'For one night only . . . her last ever public performance . . . it's your favourite, my favourite . . . the North's Premier Dusty Impersonator . . . the one, the only . . .

'Connie Holiday!'

And the crowd rises as one, raises their arms, and goes wild.

Jean

Essex, August 1981

She'd gone to him once before. The day after Perivale.
Had edged on confession.

'I've done something foolish,' she'd told him.

'Whatever it is, it doesn't matter.'

'Anything?'

'Anything.'

She'd expected him to demand specifics, to be given a
name at least. But this was Bernard. *Is* Bernard. He won't
ask unless prompted, and she could keep both secrets – hers
and Connie's – take them to the grave. But the weight of
one was only just bearable – and look how that worked
out. And two? Two will cripple her. Now that God is gone,
cannot share her burden, cannot mend it, or her.

She wonders, now that He is lost, if she ever had Him in
the first place, or was she as desperate as Sadie, as Olive
Watkins? The latter perhaps. Because, for all those years, all
those prayers, He had not once spoken to her; He had not
rescued her. She had turned to Him red-eyed and desperate.
Pleaded with Him to absolve her – it was an act of atavism
surely, like father like daughter – but still she accepted the

blame, promised Him allegiance, obedience. Said she would be good, godly, beg His mercy endlessly, offer Him up a child who will not make her mistakes because it will be guided carefully, tirelessly by her, given everything she was not.

And so she had served her penance and patiently awaited the day her punishment would end and reward would be revealed, the curtains drawn back. Yet that day had never come and here she'd been, suffering still, and taking Bernard, Constance and now Sadie with her.

But not anymore.

No, God is gone. But Bernard is here and she sees now that it is Bernard she has always believed in. Bernard who himself believed – still believes – in the promise of tomorrow, in mankind triumphing over disease, disorder, disappointment. That unbridled optimism that she had once written off as naive, as childish, she sees now for the necessity it is against the terrible mess of the world, the mistakes.

And so she tells him. Everything. Starting with conception.

She spares him the worst of it: the sordid Porchester Terrace hotel, his string of women, her complicity. But the lies, the wife, the child he raised as if she were his own – that she sets out on a platter for him, ready for his judgement.

'I'll understand,' she ends, 'if you can't forgive me. It must be . . . I can't imagine. Knowing she wasn't yours.'

He's silent for an elastic minute, the soft tock of his carriage clock now funereal. Then, 'But she *was*—' he says. Corrects himself. '*Is*.'

She cannot stand it. 'But—'

'No.' He holds a hand up. 'There's really no need. I knew,

you see. I've always known. And it made no difference. Not a jot.'

He takes her hands then, holds her fingers, thin and frigid, encloses them in his own.

She casts her eyes down. 'When?' she asks. 'When did you realize?'

'At the wedding,' he tells her. 'You were sick before the ceremony. I knew then that's what you'd tried to tell me.'

She nods. 'Just nerves,' Mrs Evans had said. 'I was the same.' Later, when she was sick in the bin, her mother-in-law had blamed it on cake and that second sherry. 'I knew we should have stuck to lemonade.' She dared not say she'd not had as much as a sliver, a sniff.

'I thought you understood,' he says, 'what I was doing.'

She feels his hands gently press, feels the first prick of tears as gratitude takes her. 'There's something else,' she tells him then. 'Something worse.'

This time, she spares him nothing. Tells him all she knows – which is thankfully only the facts – then lets him read it in Constance's own words.

He puts the book down and she sees then his hands are clenched, and for the first time, without hesitation, she is the one to go to him, to offer him comfort as he sobs, a grown man, crying like a child. The sound, the sight of it is terrible, unbearable. 'I'm so sorry,' she says.

He steadies himself. Presses the palms of his hands into his eyes like cotton pads, mopping. 'You've nothing to be sorry for,' he tells her. 'It's him who . . .'

'We should go to the police,' she says then, helping him.

But the words are sour in her mouth, frightening, for then everyone will know their business, know Sadie's heritage, and the blame will be on Constance, of course. If she'd not wanted him to do it, she would have reported it herself, wouldn't she? That's what people will say. But if they don't go . . . 'The police,' she repeats. 'Should we?'

'Did you tell him you knew?' he asks. 'When you fetched Sadie, I mean?'

She shakes her head. 'I'm not sure *he* even knows.'

'Oh, he knows,' Bernard says, with a laugh that isn't: a sound she hasn't heard from him before. 'That – that bloody man *must* know.'

'So . . . what do we do?'

'We— I will talk to him. I will tell him he's to stay away or . . . or then we'll take it further.'

'Do you –' oh, God, the thought of it – 'do you think he'll claim her?'

'Claim who?'

'The Child.'

Bernard takes her hands again. 'Never,' he says.

And faith whelms her again.

'I need to talk to her,' she says. 'I need to talk to Sadie.'

Sadie is still awake, despite the time, fetching things from her pocket, setting them out on the mantel: the pine cone, the Whimsey goat, a fifty-pence piece. She wonders at their significance, or if it's the act itself, the memorizing, that matters.

She pauses at the door, hesitant now in her own house. 'Perhaps we can chat?' she suggests. Chat? She's never chatted in her life. And this isn't a 'chatting' sort of subject. She must sound a fool. But—

'If you like.' Sadie sits then, her back to the windowsill, her eyes on the bedspread, fingers picking at a thread that will surely unravel if she doesn't—

'There's something I need to tell you.'

'I know.' Pick, pick, pick at the cotton. 'It's about care, in't it.'

'Care?'

'That I'm going into care.' Sadie looks up, sullen. 'You know. A home.'

Honest astonishment slaps her; she reddens. 'Who on earth told you that?'

'Olive.'

That wretched child. 'Well, Olive is wrong. You're not going into care. You never were. I would –' she pauses, struck by the sudden truth of it – 'I would never let that happen.'

'Boarding school, then.'

A fresh flush heats her cheeks, and she sits, just inches between them. 'The thing is,' she says, 'I think we got off to an odd start. A bad one.'

Sadie says nothing.

She tries again. 'I wasn't myself. Or rather, I was. But I'm different now.'

'I think I'm the same though,' Sadie replies. 'Will you still mind?'

'No.' She almost chokes. 'I won't mind at all.'

Sadie abandons the bedspread, looks up at her, those green eyes pleading. 'Not even if I say "aye" sometimes.'

'Not even that. Things . . . things will be different. I promise.'

'If you say so.' Sadie crosses her legs, sits on her hands – a sudden snapshot of her mother on the same bed before her.

'Can I watch *Corrie?*'

What began as a sob ends in a laugh. 'Don't push your luck too far, young lady.'

'Mam said everything were always worth a try.'

'Your mum –' she corrects herself – 'your mam was right.'

Sadie

Essex, September 1981

They scatter half the ashes at Mark Hall Moor, because that's where her mam was happiest, Grandma says, when she were small. The rest they're saving for Leeds.

They'll go up in the morning, see Donna and Deborah for lunch at the hotel – with pudding and petits fours and everything. Then they're all going to the bandstand in Roundhay Park, which was where Mam practised on a Saturday, singing to anyone who'd listen and them that wouldn't and all. She'd got told off more than once, told she were trespassing, but she said it were community service and in the end they let her, as long as she left before the brass started setting up.

'Wasn't she scared?' Nirmal asks her, circling her, drawing a ring with his Grifter, and she the centre of it all.

She thinks. 'Mam weren't scared of anything,' she says.

'Not even your grandma?' He eyes her, smiling.

'Not even her. Anyway, Grandma's better now.'

And not even Nirmal can disagree with that, given he's here, in her back garden, tyres on the lawn and all.

'Will you call for me on Monday?' she says.

'Monday?'

'School, duh. Or are you not going?'

He squeals to a stop, kicking a divot into the pristine green. 'I am, I just . . . You are coming back, then?'

She shrugs. 'For now,' she answers.

'For now,' he repeats, as if saying it might harden it into fact.

But now is better than nothing. Now is all anyone's got, in't it?

And Sadie's now stretches into the lemon light of a September evening, with cheese and pickle in sliced white, and a packet of Golden Wonder between them.

And the hole in her closes, just a fraction, but closes all the same.

Jean

Essex, November 1981

The front door slams in a manner that once sent her nerves swerving. But she has learned to accept the minor threat to the paintwork, as she has so many things, and instead finds herself quite enlivened.

'Hello,' she calls down the corridor. 'Sadie?'

'Who else would it be?' comes the answer, clattering into the kitchen. 'Cleopatra?'

She smiles, a conspiracy between them. 'Then you'd best be going again.'

'Maybe later. When I've had tea.' She hands her her bag – Adidas, not a satchel; it was important, apparently. 'I got a B in history. You can look if you like.'

'I shall.'

'"Sold" sign's gone up at the Collinses'.'

She bristles, but briefly. 'Has it now?'

'Where d'you think they're going?'

'I wouldn't know.' And that is the absolute truth.

'Have you had an argument? Me and Nirmal had an argument this morning. It were over Mr T, and I won, but he said I hadn't. Is it like that?'

She smiles. 'Not exactly.'

'We're all right now, anyway. He swapped me my banana for a Mars bar.'

'Did he, indeed. Well, perhaps you can have some of it later. Half, even.'

'Too late. I ate it at last break. Where's the cat?'

She sighs. 'In disgrace. He's been sick twice. Once on the carpet.'

'He's not used to Felix. You should get him the cheap stuff like I said.'

But she knows she won't.

'We should give him a name,' she says then.

'Who?'

'The cat. Who did you think I meant?'

'I don't know. Nirmal says we should call him Michael, as in Jackson.'

She frowns. 'But he's not even black.'

'He meant because he's always howling. Anyway, I don't much like it. 'Cause of Michael Dubbs.'

'Who's Michael Dubbs?'

'He's in our class. He can burp the national anthem, but last time he did it a bit of sick came up.'

Heaven preserve her. 'Quite like the cat, then.'

'I s'pose.' She takes a biscuit from the plate on the table. 'How about Alf?'

'Alf? As in Duckworth, I presume.' She is learning – slowly, but learning.

'Aye.'

She pretends to ponder. 'All right.'

'You mean it?'

She considers, for a sliver of a second, saying 'aye', but swiftly realizes that, however changed, however benevolent she has become, she cannot manage that. 'Yes,' she says. 'Alf it is.'

'Thanks.'

She thinks Sadie might hug her then, and stiffens. Then finds herself sinking with disappointment when she sits instead. 'At Christmas, there'll be a special,' she offers.

'Of what?'

'*Coronation Street*,' she explains. 'It said in the paper.'

'Oh, aye.'

'I was thinking you could invite Nirmal over for it. If you haven't fallen out again.'

Sadie tilts her head. 'I don't think he does Christmas.'

'But he does *Coronation Street*, doesn't he?'

'Aye,' she says quietly, then falls into brief silence. 'So . . . we'll still be here then? I'll still be here, I mean?'

At that, her heart pains her. 'Sadie, you have to stop asking. Yes, you'll still be here. We'll still be here. We're not going anywhere, Sadie. Nowhere at all.'

And they're not. Though Bernard had said the world – or at least East Anglia – was her oyster.

But this town, this town is something. And the absurdity is she only sees it now, now that it is cracked and peeling a little, splitting at its seams.

'Pioneers' he had called them back then, before. As if they were lighting out for the new frontier. And she had believed him, had had to believe him. Because the alternative was that dank front parlour and her mother's knowing and poking and sneering at her very existence.

'We should be going,' Jean had said, desperate to escape that last time. 'I'd like to get her back before tea or we'll run out of bottles.'

'Bottles?' Her mother's scorn had turned into a long, wet cough, which she'd spat out in the grate. 'Hark at you, Margaret.'

'It's Jean, now,' she'd snapped, then turned to her husband. 'Come along, Bernard.' And Bernard, obedient, did as he was told, and within minutes they were in the car and on their way back east, and she could breathe.

'Can we not do that again?' she'd pleaded.

'Of course,' he'd replied. 'Whatever you want.'

The road to Essex that afternoon was soaked golden, buttery, by the sun's late afternoon efforts; the horizon wide, two arms stretched across arable landscape, expansive and grand.

It will be fine, she'd told herself. Then, ever the pedant: no, better than.

But, swift as they'd fled Farringdon, shame had dogged them – dogged her – across Cambridge Fields and Hackney Marshes and out into the edges of Essex.

But, she thinks, seizing on it now, Maurice is gone, or soon to be, and shame could follow them anywhere, couldn't it? And, besides, Harlow is home. She had dreams, ambitions, of course. But really, what bigger dream could there be than to be part of a new Jerusalem, to play some small part in its foundation and future. Even without God.

'Are you ready?' Bernard says to her later.

She nods, and though it's taken an effort to get here – to this point, this place – it's not a lie.

'Come along, then.' And he takes her hand and leads her down the garden path, to the door of the shed – now painted a pale sage – Sadie's idea, and a good one. 'After you.'

Hand flat against the handle, she pushes, letting a trickle of winter sun into the wood and metal must of it. She glances up, where the urn – where her daughter – once sat sentinel, but of course she's gone now, replaced by a pair of roller skates and a helmet, the latter with its price label still on. Still, she tried.

'Shall I stay?' he asks then. 'I'd like to.'

But she shakes her head. 'Sadie'll be home in a moment. And I'll be fine. I'll come in if I need to.'

'You could come in now. I'll bring the box for you.'

'After,' she says. 'I need . . . I need to read it – them – here. I can't explain it.'

'You don't need to.'

And swiftly he retreats, into the calm of the garden.

And she is alone.

Except she isn't, is she. Not really. Because here in her lap is a stack of Silvine notebooks containing every thought her daughter had, from the day she left to the day – almost the day – Sadie came to them.

She pats her pocket, feels the oblong outline of a wodge of Kleenex, then picks up the toppermost notebook: 1981.

Steeling herself, she lifts it up, flaps open the cover and then lets out a soft gasp as something – an envelope – falls into her lap. She picks it up, twists it over, checks the address – 3, The Green. And before she's even run a finger under the flap, she feels the tears brim up and over, because the names are both strange and theirs, or almost: *Mum and Dad* it reads, in vivid ink.

And that ink? That handwriting?

It can only be Connie's.

She lets out a sob, a great raft of a thing that bears her atop it and threatens to take her drifting out to sea.

No, she tells it. Stop it, now!

And then, eyes wiped dry, nose blown, she sits in a shed, with a box full of her daughter, tears open the letter, swift and efficient . . .

And begins.

Connie

Leeds, July 1981

The letter's where she left it fourteen hours ago or more: leant against the toaster, a lick of ketchup congealing on the steel. Sadie's obviously not touched it, not sly enough to slip it back in this position. Not like *she* would have done at that age. How had she got lucky like that? Or perhaps it wasn't luck, wasn't nature after all, but something she'd done, and her mother hadn't.

No, not hadn't, couldn't, she corrects herself, even in this state.

The thing is, she's five double gins to the wind – five too many by her and the hospital's reckoning, but she deserved them, didn't she? After the show she's given, and the final one at that? 'Good as Judy,' Billy Rigsby had told her after she'd soared to the top notes of 'Over the Rainbow' (well, she'd had to, hadn't she? They'd called for it, begged for it). And he'd know, had seen her once in '69, just months before she'd died.

Nineteen sixty-nine. That was the last time she'd seen them. Twelve years and not a word she'd sent, not an 'I'm fine' or 'Hope you're okay' and certainly no 'Wish you were

411

here'. And she thinks about it, then. Does she even need to send the letter? They could just go, couldn't they? She could tell Sadie in the morning, soon as she's up. Get packed straight away and get the first bus they can, once Di's said 'I do'. She's not going to make Sadie miss that, whatever her feelings about men.

Bloody men. She thinks then of Elvis, of the swagger of him, the audacity. The promises – you'll be a star, we'll make a fortune, I'll fetch a condom – that all turned out to be a barrel of lies, and black ones at that.

They say you always look for a man like your father – someone had told her that in school. Harriet or Honor or Martha perhaps. God, the irony. She'd dismissed it, said she'd rather die than marry a drip like Bernard Earnshaw, though she hated herself even as she said it.

Now she wishes she could meet someone even a smidge like him. But she'll be thirty in a couple of months. Getting a bit late for her – all the good ones are gone. But Sadie needs to know these men exist. Or just that one does. That's why she's doing this, isn't it? For Sadie's sake.

The room tilts as she thinks it, threatens to spin. Food, she thinks. She needs to eat. She pulls open the fridge door, letting herself bathe in it for a minute: the cool air, the savoury taint. Sausages, she senses, remembers she's made a plate of them for the street party – the street party – they'd better make that as well or Sadie'll have a cob on. She laughs at herself then, thinking in Leeds, wondering when it slipped in. Her mother'll be the one with the cob on if either of them says that in front of her.

God, the thought of it! The look on her face when she knocks on the door. And, grabbing the plate, she rips off the cling film, pops a sausage in her mouth and shuts the fridge with her shoulder, sending the kitchen back into dim shadow, the only glow from a single bulb out on the ginnel.

'Fuck!' she exclaims as she stubs her toe on the table leg, then shushes herself, scared she'll wake Sadie.

Maybe she'd be better off in bed.

And with that she slides the envelope into the red notebook, so it rests next to her resolutions, all ticked off now, then takes herself clomping up the stairs.

Yes, she'll get into bed, then crash for a few hours – five or six – and wake at eight, wedding ready and more besides.

Ready to go back.

Back to her mother.

Back to him.

Back to Pram Town.

A Note on the Real Pram Town

They told us they were building this town for Jack and his master. Well, who wants to live on the boss's doorstep, I ask you?

> Laurence Clarke, Harlow joiner, *Daily Mirror*,
> 7 January 1955

We don't like it. The children are so noisy, rollerskating up and down the street all day. Then there's the washing hanging out behind the Standard One houses. It isn't a very nice sight, particularly when some of the washing isn't even really clean.

> Harlow manager's wife, *Daily Mirror*,
> 7 January 1955

Born from the rubble of the Second World War, Harlow New Town was conceived in the late 1940s by visionary architect Frederick Gibberd, who seized at the opportunity to ease London overcrowding and create his own socialist utopia in rural Essex: managers and workers living side by side, albeit in two classes of house, Standard One and Standard Two. Front gardens would be outlawed, and kitchens would instead overlook communal pathways, ensuring a sense of community and encouraging conversation. It would be, the architects declared, a 'New Jerusalem'.

By 1951, the first citizens – almost all young couples – were being bussed in from north-east London to their brand-new homes in Mark Hall and, later, The Lawn, and the place was quickly dubbed 'Pram Town' by the press, for the burgeoning number of mothers – a symbol in itself of hope, of the future. But, by 1955, the daring experiment seemed to be failing when, under the headline 'Snobland', the same paper – the *Daily Mirror* – ran an article revealing that neither workers nor managers appreciated their proximity, while Len White from the Harlow Development Corporation admitted they'd 'realized just in time it doesn't work' and declared that, from then on, they would be adopting a 'segregation policy'.

But jump forward thirty years and, for this teenager in the mid-1980s, Harlow was a fat, enticing slice of air-dropped America: expansive avenues with numbers instead of names; brash and dank nightclubs on elevated walkways; and everywhere glamour, glamour, glamour. It seemed to me to be everything my Saxon market town was not: modern, multicultural, and with a music venue that hosted actual bands, as well as boasting fellow Essex boy and then cub *NME* reporter Steve Lamacq among its Saturday-night crowd. So, while Jean may have been one of those doubting young mothers, and Connie desperate to run to London, I was as goggle-eyed as Sadie, and am thankful for my two very happy years spent there.

Acknowledgements

My enormous thanks to my agent, Judith Murray, and her colleagues at Greene & Heaton, for singing about me and these three brilliant women; to my editor Sam Humphreys at Macmillan, for taking a punt on an Essex girl again; to my father, a former Gilbey's Gin manager, who drove me to Harlow with him at seven in the morning for my sixth-form years, me enduring Radio 4, and him, The Smiths; and above all to my Essex friends, who made the town shine so delightful: Ryan Gilbey, Cathy James, Lizzie Mattaka, Helen Stringfellow, Stuart Edge, Roger Willmott, Julia Bazley, Delia Perkins, Bernie Wilfred, Pete Allwood, Daisy Graham, Roz Bishop, Ruth Cook, Jo Cassidy, Alan Goldsmith, and the ones with whom I was only ever on first-name terms: Shelley, Tom, Al, Zach, Paul, Monica, Mark, Medina and Glenn.

Book Club Questions

1. Imagine you were a child growing up with Jean and Bernard as your parents. What do you think the best thing about your upbringing would have been? What do you think would have been the worst?

2. Why do you think the author chose to have Connie's death happen at the same time as the wedding of Prince Charles and Diana? What effect did this have on you as a reader?

3. How did knowing Connie was going to die affect your engagement with her storyline?

4. What do you think was the most tragic aspect of Connie's life? Conversely, what do you think was the most uplifting and successful element?

5. Do you see yourself in any of the female characters? If so, who do you share personality traits with?

6. Who do you think was most at fault for the difficulties in their relationship: Connie or Jean?

7. Which of the characters in the book do you feel the most sympathy for? Why? Who do you have the least sympathy for?

8. What do you think Bernard saw in Jean, and was he right to stay with her?

9. Do you think Bernard and Jean should have reported Maurice to the police? Why do you think they didn't?

10. If you could time-travel to either the 1970s or the 1980s, which decade would you be most excited to go back to?

11. Do you think Sadie was a happy teenager, and where do you think she would be now?

12. Do you think it's necessary to have lived through the 1980s to understand the novel and characters?